MURDER IN VENICE

A POSIE PARKER MYSTERY #6

L. B. HATHAWAY

WHITEHAVEN

WHITEHAVEN MAN PRESS
London

First published in Great Britain in 2018
by Whitehaven Man Press, London

(http://www.lbhathaway.com, email: permissions@lbhathaway.com)

A CIP catalogue record for this book is available from the British Library.

ISBN (e-book:) 978-0-9955694-4-7
ISBN (paperback:) 978-0-9955694-5-4

Jacket illustration by Red Gate Arts.
Formatting and design by J.D. Smith.

For Sidonia

Also by L.B. Hathaway

The Posie Parker Mystery Series

1. *Murder Offstage*

2. *The Tomb of the Honey Bee*

3. *Murder at Maypole Manor*

4. *The Vanishing of Dr Winter*

5. *Murder of a Movie Star*

The stand-alone novella, *A Christmas Case*

6. *Murder in Venice*

PROLOGUE

He was a man you'd leave everything for. Ice-blonde, with chiselled features, mysterious as the night.

'My gosh!' Posie Parker, Private Detective, narrowed her eyes, gripping at her table. 'Can it be him? After all this time?'

She'd felt immediately drawn to him the first and only time they'd met, almost two years before. And here he was again, pulling her like iron filaments to a magnet. *Was it even possible?*

Posie had been staring out through the window of the first-class Orient Express lounge at Victoria Station when she'd spotted him. Commuters hadn't been able to get in to London because of the snow, and the place was like a ghost town. Below the soaring glass ceiling, home to thousands of pigeons, and across the empty sets of tracks Posie could see into a platform café directly opposite.

It looked inviting, the lamps glowing warmly through the gloom, like some sort of early Christmas beacon. A woman was mopping the floor, a blue rag around her head. A bald, fat man, the owner perhaps, was counting change behind the roll-top counter, and their single customer was sipping tea or coffee at the one table in the window, his head bowed, hidden behind his newspaper.

There had been a sudden flash of bright blonde hair in the yellow light and the man had looked over in Posie's direction. Their eyes had met in a searing moment of raw disbelief.

'It *is* you!'

She stood up now, involuntarily grabbing at her carpet bag, pulling on her brand-new scarlet woollen coat, about to leave the first-class lounge and run across to join him. It would take but a matter of seconds.

There was a sudden tap on her shoulder. 'Miss Parker?'

Posie turned, caught by surprise. 'Oh!'

Blowing out her cheeks, she abandoned thoughts of running anywhere. 'Oh, it's only *you*, Miss Babner.'

'Is everything quite all right, Miss Parker? You look like you've just seen a ghost.'

The train company had allocated Heather Babner – an excitable, buxom young woman with all the subtlety of Captain Hook's ticking crocodile – as Posie's travel companion in the shared sleeper on the way to Venice, where Miss Babner was going to take up the role of Governess to a rich English family. She was standing at their table now, her plain black dress shiny with age under the bright overhead lights, her three chins quivering, looking concerned. She had just returned from getting refreshments.

Posie looked across the tracks again. 'No. No ghosts. Far from it. It's just…'

The table in the café was now empty, and the man had vanished.

'I think my mind must be playing tricks on me.' Posie smiled, slightly rattled, and sat down. A sense of sickly unease washed over her.

Nothing had gone to plan so far.

England was in the grip of freezing fogs, and snowdrifts covered train lines out of London. Everything had come to a standstill, even the Orient Express. And now this lounge, a shiny-smart blur of a place, mirrors everywhere, was crowded with angry people clutching monogrammed vanity bags, brandishing train timetables which didn't apply anymore. The train should have left at three o'clock. It was now almost two hours late. It was all very unhelpful. Especially if you were off to get married and needed things to run on time.

Posie's wedding to Alaric Boynton-Dale, the famous explorer and aviator, was supposed to be taking place three days hence, on Thursday, in Venice. Alaric would be arriving in the romantic Italian city of water tonight, and the plan had been that they would be reunited tomorrow, when Posie's train arrived at Venice's main station, Santa Lucia, after two whole months apart. Eight weeks which had felt like forever.

Posie was brought back to earth as Heather Babner set down a plate of iced buns with a bang. She was also bearing a stack of penny magazines under one capable arm.

'French fancy? Chocolate eclair?'

Posie was partial to a cake or two, or four. 'I shouldn't. But thank you.'

'*I* would if I was you, Miss Parker. When our train finally does get running, there's no Pullman attached, so we won't get a hot dinner until we're on the boat, past Dover. Go on!'

Posie bit into a delicious cake, not enjoying it for a second: the wedding outfit which was in her small valise had already been on the snug side when she had last tried it on a couple of days ago; the cream wool of the coat-dress fitting beautifully, but only *just.* Straining at the silver seams, more like.

Heather was chattering away. 'They say we should be on the move in about thirty minutes, Miss Parker. Seems they've cleared the worst of the snow. And we'll be able to link up to the French Orient Express at the Gare de Lyon in Paris about eleven o'clock tonight. It's going to wait for us.'

'How splendid.'

Heather grinned with excitement. She had never been to Italy before, still less travelled first-class. Their route would carry them through some of the most stunning scenery and romantic towns of Europe, albeit a lot of it would be lost to darkness: Paris, Zurich, Innsbruck, the Brenner Pass, the Dolomites…all of these would be rolling pictures outside their curtained windows.

'We'll be in Venice this time tomorrow, Miss Parker. Or just slightly earlier. About four o'clock, they say.'

'Thank goodness. This whole arrangement was cutting it a bit fine for my liking. What have you got there?'

Heather had sat down at the table and was spreading copies of *The Bystander* magazine about, the brightly-coloured covers on display. 'I grabbed these to pass the time. Do you want one, Miss Parker?'

'No thank you, I've got my book with me.' Posie indicated her copy of the very recent bestselling novel, *Whose Body?* by Dorothy L. Sayers, which was sitting on the table, unread and immaculate. Posie went back to thinking about the blonde man, and the strangeness of seeing him here. She had glanced only briefly at the magazines, but suddenly a horrible image lodged itself in her mind.

'Hang on a minute…*that* magazine!'

One copy of *The Bystander* had the heading 'CAPERS IN CONSTANTINOPLE'; its title picked out in lurid splashes of red and yellow. Heart pounding, Posie picked up the journal and shook it out in full. She stared at the picture on the cover.

'My gosh!'

Capers in Constantinople…

Indeed.

Alaric had been planning on going to India before their wedding in Venice, but he had changed his plans at the last minute, back in August, travelling instead to Constantinople in Turkey where the University there had begged him to act as an honorary temporary lecturer, promising him a fat fee. He had accepted the job, explaining to the University he would leave in late November, when he had been invited to stay as a house guest at a Venetian Palace, the home of the Count Romagnoli. And where, incidentally, he would be getting married to Posie. It had all been arranged very neatly.

Alaric had been out in Constantinople for two months now, with the occasional postcard sent, and the odd telephone call put through to Posie's Detective Agency on Grape Street to alleviate the distance.

Posie felt a cold mist close around her heart.

The red and yellow magazine cover in question was all taken up with a very blonde girl in sunglasses and a wide straw hat. A Valkyrie of a girl. A famous girl, too. In fact, she had been Posie's last high-profile client. It was the movie star, Silvia Hanro.

Silvia was standing laughing in the foreground, lipstick fresh, and there, just behind her, in front of a splendid domed mosque, was Alaric.

He was laughing alongside Silvia, smouldering almost, and they were perfectly matched: he seemed like a movie star himself, with his lean good looks and his shimmering white linen clothes, a cigarette held nonchalantly in his hand and a silken travel scarf fluttering in the breeze.

Had they known they were being photographed for the magazine? It looked like a private moment, the two of them caught unawares, mid-joke. But Silvia Hanro was a woman with no doubts as to her beauty, or her power, and Posie was well aware that she seldom did anything by accident.

Posie felt sick to the pit of her stomach. She twisted her Cartier engagement ring and it almost tore into her flesh. She checked the date and saw the magazine was six weeks old. Very much the past, now.

Why hadn't Alaric said anything? Told her Silvia was

with him six weeks previously? She had spoken to him several times since then. She tore the cover from the magazine and stuffed it in her dress pocket.

It didn't look good. Should Posie turn around now and head for home and forgo her dreams of marrying Alaric? Was she being played for a fool? But Alaric was *hers*: she loved him, didn't she? And she would fight for him, movie star or no movie star. Tears came unbidden to her eyes and she blinked them away.

'Is everything quite okay, Miss Parker?'

'Absolutely.' Posie smiled tightly. 'It's all going to be just fine, Miss Babner.'

But was it? Was it really? That sense of unease came over her yet again. Posie had a horrible feeling that it had all been arranged very neatly.

Too neatly.

* * * *

PART ONE

VENICE

(Tuesday 20th November, 1923)

One

What hit you first was the noise. The calls of porters, the whistles of the guards and the hopeful shouting of guides and picture-postcard sellers. The smell, too: burnt chocolate and ground coffee mixed together, masking something altogether more unpleasant; a seeping, rotting damp.

The train had spilled its passengers and they now jostled up the narrow Orient Express platform of the imposing Santa Lucia Station, through the train's dying puffs of steam and smoke.

Improbably, a welcoming string quartet had been placed on the narrow platform, forcing the tired passengers and their porters into single file. The quartet had just struck up a rendition of 'The Blue Danube'.

And quite suddenly, out of all this strangeness, Posie found herself staring across at probably the most frightening man she had ever clapped eyes on.

'Golly,' she whispered to herself, almost stopping. 'What an ogre.'

The ogre was middle-aged, standing with crossed, beefy arms just past the barrier, by a central meeting-point, where a small crowd of people in smart winter coats were waiting for their loved ones off the continental train. The man was absolutely huge in every direction, and wearing a fancy black uniform, its gold braids and buttons glittering in the bright electric strips of light overhead. The silver of his pistol gleamed threateningly at his belt. Two men in less showy uniforms stood on either side of him, flanking him, their arms crossed in the same menacing manner.

'Fascist police,' Posie muttered under her breath in disgust. 'Of course. How utterly sickening.'

Posie noticed how the waiting crowd were giving the man and his officers a wide berth, shifting uneasily from foot to foot. The station was frantically busy, but everyone in the place seemed aware of the trio. Even two chestnut sellers who had been fighting over the same lucrative pitch were casting nervous glances at the policemen. It seemed that fear was contagious.

Posie continued striding forwards, looking around for someone considerably easier on the eye, and normally less worrisome. But Alaric was nowhere to be seen.

She came to an abrupt halt, forgetting that Heather Babner was just behind her, causing their shared porter to drop their bags. Other passengers, like a herd of stampeding elephants behind, were also forced into stopping way back down the line. Shouting began in earnest. Posie didn't give two hoots.

'Okay, okay,' she huffed, more to herself than anyone in particular. 'Hold your horses.'

She looked left and right again, controlling her panic. And then came a sharp flash of anger. *Where on earth was he?*

'Miss Parker?' Suddenly the huge ogre of a policeman stepped forwards. Up close you could see he was only about forty, and it was simply his enormous size which made him look much older.

'Yes?' Posie snapped her head around in the policeman's direction.

'Step this way please, madam. It's urgent.'

She frowned, caught off guard, both by the man himself

and also, bizarrely, by his impeccable English. She was aware that a gruesomely expectant hush had fallen over the whole station, a sort of heavy, thankful relief mixed with a ghoulish relish at witnessing someone else's misfortune. For Posie now realised that was exactly what she had stepped into.

But what had she done wrong? She fought to contain her fright.

Scanning the station, she saw that even the string quartet had ceased to play, and the musicians had turned in their seats, goggling quite openly. The Orient Express train guards and ticket collectors in their smart blue-and-gold were also staring, open-mouthed. It took but a second for Posie to realise that, in fact, *hundreds* of pairs of eyes were watching her: women just off the train clutching at their jewellery boxes; waiters holding their order pads mid-air in the busy station cafés; customers at the little bookstalls dotted around the place. All waiting for *something* to happen.

She had the certain notion that Heather Babner was stepping backwards, keen to put a definite distance between herself and her former travel companion. Posie sensed, rather than heard, Heather's relief at spotting someone from the family who were employing her, and the Governess predictably melted away into the crowd without saying goodbye.

'Over here, please.'

Posie was led to a dark, empty archway which held nothing but a series of large left-luggage lockers, most of which were unused, their heart-shaped keys hanging mournfully on long maroon ribbons, and two modern vending machines: one selling bars of milk chocolate and the other selling cigarettes, with a large gaudy sign in English proclaiming that this was the 'ONLY PLACE IN VENICE TO PURCHASE MUGHAL CIGARETTES! GET YOURS HERE!'

The porter followed at a snail's pace, carrying Posie's one small valise in a dejected manner.

Was she under arrest? And if so, what for? In her brief glance around Santa Lucia Station she had noted that men in black shirts with gold buttons and braids were dotted all over the place: the supporting rank-and-file of Mussolini's new police force. There were two standing nearby, near the chocolate machine, firm of jaw and resolute of stance. Were they here for her too? Posie recovered her nerve and pulled up the mink collar of her red coat.

'Who are you exactly? And what do you want with me? *What's* so urgent? Am I in trouble?'

The huge man fumbled in his inside jacket pocket.

Posie was suddenly and ridiculously glad she had piled on all of her wedding jewellery when getting off the train. Posie's usual string of pearls and her engagement ring had been joined by a pair of the most exquisite drop earrings from Bond Street: huge teardrops of Indian night-sky sapphires dotted about with tiny clusters of diamonds. These comprised both the 'something blue' and the 'something new' for her big day; a ridiculously generous wedding present from her good friends Rufus and Dolly, the Earl and Countess of Cardigeon. She was aware she was flashing like a lit-up Christmas tree but at least she was making an impression on the ogre: she was a woman of importance, of means. Posie touched a sapphire drop as if for reassurance.

In the silence the man brought out his identity card.

'I am the Chief of Police for Venice, Commissario Salvo Salvarocca. At your service, madam.'

The man slowly put away his card. There was no sign of that nasty-looking gun being used, and no evidence of any handcuffs making an appearance. His juniors were still loitering a way away.

'What do you mean? You're "*at my service*"?'

The Chief of Police stepped closer. For a second Posie

thought he was about to take her arm in sympathy. His dark-skinned hands were enormous. Beneath the peaked gold-trimmed hat the Commissario had surprisingly kind hazel eyes. There was a deep sense of melancholy about the man, and up close sadness reeked off him like a strong perfume.

He spoke very softly: 'I can assure you my bark is worse than my bite, Miss Parker. You have nothing to fear on my account. Pay no notice to this uniform: the times we are living in, my dear lady. *The times*. One must learn to sink, or swim. And in a city made of water, like Venice, one chooses to swim. *Capisci?* You understand me?'

One glance around was enough for Posie to see everyone in the station was still watching them. It was important to remain calm. 'I understand.'

In a split-second, the Commissario had ordered his men to come over, issuing a stream of commands in Italian, too quick for Posie to make any sense of. The men looped around and brought up the rear, behind the porter.

'What's happening?'

'We will travel in our *motoscafo*, our police motor boat. It's waiting just outside, on the Grand Canal.'

'But what's *really* happening? I'm here to get married for goodness' sake. Where's my fiancé?'

This time the Commissario really did take Posie's arm. He started to lead her through the hordes of people, the crowds splitting apart in panic. A multitude of pigeons, fluttering up as one, swept overhead. 'I'm here simply to escort you. There's been a fire.'

Posie jerked the man's grip away. '*What?* A fire?'

'Yes. At the Palace of the Romagnoli family.'

The bitterness and anger which had built up over the last twenty-four hours towards Alaric, ever since seeing that magazine cover, melted away in an instant, to be replaced by a terrible dread. Posie whispered slowly: 'And what of Alaric?'

'He's fine. You'll meet him later. Everyone staying at the Palace is fine. But the place itself is a ruin already. It went up like a box of fireworks.'

* * * *

Two

Posie surged along. She held onto her carpet bag with one hand and tucked her other red-gloved hand firmly in her pocket, having successfully shaken off the arm of the Chief of Police.

He led the way down some stone steps onto a packed terrace outside, leading out onto a crowded jetty with boats and gondolas tethered up next to it as far as the eye could see.

The terrace was heaving in the dim half-light, as if for some sort of market, but it was presumably just normal Venetians going about their early evening business. Immaculate black-clad ladies and smart businessmen mixed together with more humdrum types: rough-looking men with conical baskets on their backs darting this way and that, bearing that day's unsold wares away from the markets, the strong smells of fish and fruit rising unpleasantly in the air; tiny dirty boys, urchins really, holding fishing nets, gazing wide-eyed at their small procession, splitting apart to let them through.

'Riff-raff!' muttered Salvarocca. 'These lads are water scavengers, Miss Parker. Watch your jewels.'

Within seconds they were standing on a bobbing island of a boat stop, under a sign marked 'FERROVIA'.

A church with a green dome soared away on the left, but what really took the eye were the tall, thin, stone palaces lining the wide canal, one after another, each one fronted by candy-coloured striped mooring posts, topped with burning lanterns. A sharp stinging breath of sea hit them as a wind got up.

'Welcome to Venice,' Salvarocca said, smiling with only one corner of his mouth. 'The Serenissima, the golden city. Get used to the cold wind.'

Posie gawped. Boats were everywhere on the teeming waterway. Gondolas of course, but more: flimsy canoes bearing young men on urgent assignations; low-sunk barges carrying loads of coal and wood; an impressive big white boat powered by a waterwheel carrying what looked like simply hundreds of people. The Commissario followed the direction of Posie's gaze.

'Ah! Our famous vaporetto.' He smiled. 'Our city's version of a taxi, or bus. No doubt you will use it yourself. Motor boats are very few and far between here. Only the police and the fire brigade have them at present.'

Salvarocca indicated somewhere to his right and the *motoscafo* pulled in alongside them. Its dark wood glinted with polish in the half-light, and its white cover and little flags gleamed. It was marked 'POLIZIE'. No wonder the Commissario was proud of it.

Ignoring the proffered hand, Posie clutched at her carpet bag and stepped down into the *motoscafo*, taking her chances. The Chief of Police himself took her valise, packing it into the hold of the boat. Posie was about to give their porter a large tip when one of the junior policemen gave the man a cuff round the ear and sent him away empty-handed. But before Posie could protest they were off.

Seething with anger at the junior policeman's conduct, Posie stood just behind the police driver at the prow of the boat, the others squeezed in behind her. The boat rocked violently from side to side on the canal and started to pick up speed.

Posie looked straight ahead into the blackness of the canal. Everything so far was a complete mess. She had desperately wanted to appreciate the beauty of Venice when she'd first got off the train; she'd wanted to embrace the romance the city was so famous for, and preferably with Alaric. Alone.

Instead, there had been shock, and confusion, and a very public encounter with the fascists.

Posie had known about the fascists, of course. For as long as she could remember now, since the Great War certainly, there had been small columns about them in the British newspapers every few days; stories about the violent Mr Mussolini and his formerly humorous-sounding party of blackshirts. But most journalists and English politicians had written the fascists off as being a loony party on the fringes of politics: moths to the flickering flame of power. They were thugs, the newspapers declared, bully boys: that was all. They'd never get into power.

How wrong everyone had been.

Everything had changed the previous year. In the October of 1922 Mr Mussolini had seized his moment and marched on the capital, Rome. The King, scared, had appointed him Prime Minister. And since then Mr Mussolini, or '*Il Duce*', as many Italians called him, had seized political power by every means possible, violence being the most usual way. He had reorganised the institutions of Italy in his own image: the police, the army, the schools. The blackshirt movement had grown massively, and while most Italians weren't fascists, Europe was watching in a slow, dazed horror at what might play out.

Certainly Posie had hoped to avoid meeting any of Mr Mussolini's supporters during her stay here. She had hoped the beauty and other-worldliness of Venice would not have been affected by the sheer nastiness of the politics which was infecting Italy.

But it was obviously not the case.

Sensing a movement behind her she turned to see the bulk of the Chief of Police squeezed right alongside her. A heavy drizzle had started up.

'You didn't ask where we're going to, Miss Parker.'

She shrugged. 'I assumed I had no choice but to accompany you wherever you saw fit.'

'Ah. Well, I'll act as your guide, then. This is the Grand Canal, the main and biggest waterway through the city, two miles long, always busy. The most splendid of the Venetian palaces are situated here. Two hundred of them. All of them beautiful, all of them mysterious, all of them decaying from within, from underneath. Can you smell the stink of rotting stone? This is a place built on impossible dreams.'

Posie turned, mouth open in surprise but the Commissario continued, matter-of-factly:

'St Mark's Square and Cathedral is at the far end. Up here you will see the Rialto Bridge, a drawbridge actually, one of only three bridges over the canal; the Rialto is the oldest part of the city. There are some lovely shops and squares here. But please, promise me not to take those jewels out with you again, Miss Parker. This is a pickpocket's heaven, and without me, I fear you would be easy prey. You will give me sleepless nights, madam.'

Posie was taking in the masses of people swarming over the Rialto Bridge, the colourful awnings of restaurants and the early diners fluttering into them. She touched her earlobes, feeling a bit silly now, feeling defensive.

'So tell me: where are we off to?'

'As you know, your fiancé *was* staying at the Count's residence, the Palace Romagnoli, on the Grand Canal, a block past the Accademia Bridge, opposite the Campo San Vio. Unfortunately, as I explained, the Palace Romagnoli has been evacuated and most of its occupants, the Count and Countess included, have now been taken across the canal, a distance of only a few metres, to the English Guesthouse. It is virtually opposite the Count's now-ruined home. The proximity was felt to be most suitable.'

'The *English* Guesthouse?' Posie repeated incredulously. She wondered if she had heard the man quite correctly.

'Yes. It's Mrs Persimmon's place. It's next door to St George's, the English church. It seemed the best thing to do, given the circumstances. Mrs Persimmon had space, naturally, it being out of season. And after all, the Countess is English. I gather most of her English family live with her. The brother of the Countess is a friend of your fiancé, isn't he? Dickie Alladice?'

'That's correct.'

Posie had actually never met Mr Alladice but had heard Alaric mention him on several occasions. In fact, Dickie Alladice was bankrolling a few of Alaric's wilder projects just now, and it had actually been *his* invitation to stay at the Palace in Venice, rather than the Count's, which had led Alaric and Posie out here.

Salvo Salvarocca was looking out of the boat, his large brown eyes reflecting the orange glow of torches on water.

'I'm sure Mrs Persimmon will make them all very comfortable. It will be a home from home. Although, perhaps, not on such a grand scale as the Palace was.'

Posie nodded her head in acquiescence, not wanting to express her thanks out loud to a man who was essentially a fascist thug, for all he had said about necessity.

'But why couldn't Alaric come to fetch me? If he's not been hurt what's he doing?'

'The last I saw of Mr Boynton-Dale he was covered in soot and stinking of petrol. He was helping the firefighters and my own men at the Palace. Dickie Alladice had left an important item up in his room, apparently, and your fiancé gave him his word he would retrieve it; said he was used to danger and tough conditions. I didn't want to worry you before.'

Posie rolled her eyes in exasperation. How typically like Alaric that would be. Tough conditions indeed!

'Mr Boynton-Dale asked me to come and get you. *Personally*. So I came.'

Posie was cross and fearful for Alaric's safety, of course, but her brain, in all the chaos – annoyingly as it sometimes did – had focused in on a strange detail which nagged at her.

'*Petrol?* But why would Alaric smell of petrol, of all things?'

The Commissario leant in closer and whispered:

'The reason the place is crawling with my men as well as firefighters is that there has been foul play.'

'With petrol? You mean *arson*?'

'It's looking that way, yes. But please keep that detail to yourself.'

'Good grief!' Posie bit her lip, frowning, wondering what sort of hell-hole she had arrived at. A wall of noise, mainly shouting, rose to greet them from somewhere up in front, along with a thick curtain of choking smoke. Posie fished out a handkerchief and held it to her face, warily.

They only just managed to pass under a huge, ugly, flat iron bridge, lit up by torches in the darkness. The boat was juddering along more slowly now, and the driver suddenly cut the engine.

'That was the Accademia Bridge, just behind us now, otherwise known as the "Porte Inglese", and ahead of us you can see the dome of the Salute Church, and then the sweep of the Grand Canal opening out to the lagoon. Perfect, is it not, Miss Parker? Some would say that right here is the best view in all of Venice.'

'It is certainly unforgettable in these circumstances, yes.'

Posie looked back at the Accademia Bridge. There was a crowd of at least fifty people gathered on it, swarming and pushing like a mountain of ants, all trying, unsuccessfully, to get a glimpse of the spectacle beyond. Many were holding candle-lit lamps of an old-fashioned variety.

'The usual ghouls,' continued the Chief of Police as the boat coasted another block and then docked into a mooring spot on the right-hand side of the canal. 'Here we are then.' He indicated over to his left, on the opposite side of the canal. 'The Palace of the Romagnoli family. Or what's left of it, anyway.'

Posie stared, sickened.

The Palace was the focus of frenzied activity. Many red boats were tethered up outside its mooring lot and the building itself was lit up by blue-coloured beacons in the now smothering smoky darkness. Flames and smoke were still belching out from the very top floor and the sky arching above it was a brilliant orange. Flakes of burning material were falling all around them into the sooty canal like gruesome confetti.

'My gosh! A fire on water. But how is it possible?'

'Oh, I can assure you, Miss Parker, we have many fires in Venice. It's a fairly regular occurrence, actually. Our Fire Brigade are often called out.'

Teams of men on ladders were dragging out heavy coils of hoses and crawling all over the façade.

Beneath this snakes-and-ladders game-board of activity, glimpses of the stone Palace revealed it to be an obviously grand building, a pale-blue colour, six storeys high at least, and impossibly ornate. Its typically long Venetian windows, and the matching balconies on every floor, resplendent with flags, were all now burnt irreparably. The dark diamond-leaded windows, where the glass remained, glittered menacingly. But there was something about the blue Palace which stopped it from being beautiful, or enticing. Even without the fire, Posie was beginning to wonder whether the Romagnoli Palace would have been a welcoming sort of a place to stay in.

Posie was questioning how on earth the man at her side could have allowed Alaric to go into that burning mess of a house at all, and she was about to give him a piece of her mind, when the Commissario seemed to guess what she was thinking:

'The Countess had rooms on the second floor, at the front, above the main *piano nobile*. As did all the guests.'

'I see. And her brother's rooms were on the same floor?'

'Yes. But his rooms were at the back, in a part of the house unaffected by the fire, and can be accessed by a metal ladder network behind the building. Otherwise I would not have allowed Mr Boynton-Dale to enter, it goes without saying. Can I help you disembark?'

Posie realised suddenly that she was the only person remaining in the motor boat, alongside the driver.

'Of course not.' She wobbled out of the boat and stood warily on the little jetty belonging to a dark, narrow, cobbled square. The two junior policemen were standing gawking at the fire opposite.

'This is the Campo San Vio. See the English church just there?'

Salvarocca pointed at a small, white, marble building, tucked in tight alongside its less celestial neighbours on one side of the square. It was neat-looking but unremarkable, its only real feature being a small bench outside the heavy front door, which had become home to a family of stray black cats. In fact, there were cats everywhere.

There were a few scrubby trees in the Campo, and an iron-capped stone well at its centre.

'Mrs Persimmon's is on the left. Just here.'

Posie saw a tall narrow house, one side facing right onto the canal. Lights were glowing behind dark shutters. A group of men scampered by, all dressed in grotesque huge-nosed masks and matching cloaks of some bright shimmery material.

'Tourists!' groaned Salvarocca. 'Off to some Casino, I

shouldn't wonder. But you'd better get used to a crush of noisy tourists and city-dwellers passing by here. Tomorrow is the Festival of the Salute, or the *Festa della Salute*, when the Venetians celebrate deliverance from an ancient plague. The city provides a temporary bridge over the water, giving direct access. But the pilgrims will still traipse along here, day and night, for twenty-four hours, in order to get to the Salute Church, further up.'

'I see. Thank you for the warning.'

Posie couldn't stand to stay in the narrow square any longer, and she gathered herself together, clutching at her carpet bag and the small valise, desperate to restore some sort of order on things.

'I can manage now. I will make my own way to the guesthouse.'

Effectively dismissed, Salvarocca nodded uncertainly, and made a mock bow. 'Let me at least get the door for you.'

He belted across from the jetty, fast for such a big man, rang a huge bronze bell, and stepped back. The door opened just as Posie reached it, a cosy amber light spilling out over the cobblestones, a uniformed manservant revealing himself there by way of welcome.

The Commissario stepped back, into the darkness, but as he did so Posie heard him mutter: 'He was right. God, but you're beautiful, aren't you?'

Posie turned, confused: '*Who* was right? What the blazes are you talking about?'

But the man in his fascist high-ranking uniform had vanished into the smoky night.

****

Three

Having secured a small, dark room at the very back of the guesthouse from Mrs Persimmon, a bright cockney sparrow of a woman, Posie stood downstairs in the main part of the house, the *piano nobile*. The Butler was bobbing about.

'Is there any news of Mr Boynton-Dale yet, Jones?'

Her hands were visibly shaking, so she stuffed them into the big pockets of the crushed blue velvet dress she had thrown on in a tearing hurry – the same gown she had been wearing yesterday – and she felt a rustle of cheap paper.

'Afraid not, modom. But the rest of your party are in the main salon. Shall I announce you?'

'No, no. Please don't bother. That's absolutely the last thing I'm sure anyone wants right now, after the shock of a fire. I'll just slip in and see to things myself. Thanks awfully, though.'

'Very good, modom.'

There was a small bench in the dim corridor, and it was all Posie could do to stop herself from sinking down upon it in tiredness, and never getting up again. A heavy door creaked on its hinges somewhere far off, needing oil.

The guesthouse was fine, as far as these things went, but

it had obviously done more of a trade twenty years ago. The whole place was coloured green inside, like an underwater lair, and a strange white mould crept up the papered walls. There were china bowls of rose-scented potpourri simply everywhere, which didn't quite mask the lagoon's ancient dampness, permeating the place with its sickly scent. Posie told herself to stop being such a snob and to be grateful for small mercies, or at least a roof over her head for the time being.

She pushed open the door of the salon, and blinked in total surprise.

'Gracious!'

While the corridors and bedrooms of Mrs Persimmon's guesthouse were all uniformly dark and gloomy, lit with dusty glass oil-lamps, this room was a match for the Mirror Hall at the Strand Corner House, and lit up accordingly.

Huge, black-spotted, floor-length mirrors plated the walls, one after another, like a ballroom. A painted ceiling and two gigantic chandeliers lent the place an old-world grandeur. Rattan chairs and side-tables were dotted about, but the room appeared to be empty.

At first Posie felt wildly disorientated, and saw only herself repeated many times over: her anxious face, pale beneath the dark cap of her shingled brown hair; her large blue eyes staring out in total astonishment.

She gulped.

But then she saw on the left, along three long, elegant windows, six people were ranged. Totally absorbed in the view from the windows, they all had their backs to her. It was here that the guesthouse overlooked the Grand Canal and the burning palace opposite. Someone had thrown back the old shutters, and flickers of red fiery light danced in the diamond-leaded glass.

They hadn't heard Posie enter the room. All except one.

A tall, dark, kitten-ish girl, almost exactly Posie's age and height, had turned and was looking directly at her. She wore an old-fashioned purple silk dress which was of a cut and design from years ago, from before the war, rather like the suffragettes had got themselves up in, although it had obviously been quite the best of its kind at the time.

The girl was lovely, with an exquisite figure. Quite the most beautiful woman Posie had seen in a long time, and that was saying something: she had been mingling with movie stars and models for longer than she cared to remember. No longer in the first bloom of youth, the girl bloomed nonetheless. And looking into those dark, doe-eyes under thick, expressive brows, there was an aching sense of familiarity. Posie had met this girl before. But where? For now she couldn't place the memory.

The girl crossed the expansive floor, smiling, extending her hand. This couldn't, *surely*, be the Countess?

'You must be Miss Parker. We've been expecting you. Please follow me over. I'm Lucy Christie, by the way, the Countess's companion.'

So that was it: a paid companion.

'A real-life detective! How exciting. Just like a character from those books by Agatha Christie and Dorothy L. Sayers!'

'Oh, hardly! Those books blow things out of all proportion. People expect too much…'

'Well, your real-life cases sound very exciting. We've heard so much about you from your fiancé.'

'Ah, well, I hope it wasn't all bad, then.'

'On the contrary,' said Lucy with an easy grace.

As they reached the windows Posie noticed a slim man in a worn grey flannel suit and a battered soft felt hat who remained glued to the window, his back to the room, following the action outside. He was sitting in a window-seat with a small, dark, frail-looking man wearing bright blue. There was something about the first man's grey-suited back which seemed familiar, but there was no time to ponder this further, for someone else pressed in quickly:

'Miss Parker? Richard Alladice, at your service.'

Dickie Alladice was in his early forties: tall, broad, attractive, with lovely dark grey eyes and abundant red hair. He breathed success and comfort, and his easy smile promised hospitality: the sort of man for whom finding a woman – as a wife or for something more casual – had never posed a problem. Odd then, thought Posie, almost frowning, that Alaric had never mentioned Dickie with a wife or girlfriend in tow.

'Delighted, Mr Alladice.'

'Oh, do call me Dickie. Everyone else does.'

Dickie spoke carefully, his rich, friendly northern English accent brushed beneath a smart, newly-acquired London voice which owed nothing to class and everything to money. He wore spats over his highly-polished black shoes, and full black tie. He smelt of smoke and there was something strong – whisky perhaps? – on his breath.

'By Gad, I *must* apologise. What a frankly dreadful muddle you've found us in tonight.'

He was jittery as hell, his grey eyes glittering with the promise of full-on drunkenness. But Posie remembered that Dickie had apparently lost something important in the fire and she presumed his thoughts were straying in that direction. She didn't blame him for his nerves, but she *did* blame him for Alaric's absence.

'I gather Alaric is looking for something of yours?' Posie nodded in the direction of the fire, her crispness containing her anger. 'It must be *very* important if he went back in there for it. It seems quite some inferno…'

Was it Posie's imagination or was the man unable to meet her gaze? Dickie gave a thick, nervous chuckle.

'The object *is* important, but I thought it would be easy to locate and to extract. In fact, *I* was on the verge of going in there myself to search it out, when Alaric volunteered. He practically wrestled me to the ground in his haste to get inside.'

Posie frowned. It fitted that Alaric liked danger but it seemed odd he would put himself in any sort of danger unless a life were at stake. Just what was this precious, unnamed object?

Dickie Alladice was checking a very expensive-looking gold fob watch. He seemed nervous as a cat.

'Dash it all, it's almost six o'clock! I can't think what's kept him so long. It's been more than an hour and a half now.'

'Tell me about it,' muttered Posie to herself, feeling another twist of fear in her stomach. But there was no use holding a grudge. She remembered her manners, almost too late. 'Thank you for our invitation to stay here in Venice, Dickie.'

Dickie smiled. 'Don't thank me, Miss Parker. The invitation was merely mine to *extend*. It's Bella, my sister, the Countess, who does all the inviting around here. Don't you, darling?'

A woman turned from the window where she had been half-hidden by an olive-coloured velvet curtain and Posie tried not to gasp aloud in shock.

Bella Alladice was simply huge, a blubbering sea-lion of a woman. She wallowed in her fat, her every move causing her multiple chins and forearms to quiver violently, like a mottled pink blancmange. She was far, far bigger than her brother, their only shared genetics being the red hair and unusual grey eyes. The Countess wore her hair cut brutally short and greased back into a wet red bob, topped by a glittering tiara. But what really caught the eye, above all else, was a huge red ruby; big as a quail's egg and fiendishly ugly, worn in a ring.

The stone seemed to capture all the light in the room and throw it out again in dangerous, dark rays. Posie had never liked rubies, and now she felt a ridiculous sense of conviction in her irrationality. The thing was truly dreadful.

'So *you're* the lady detective?' Bella Alladice chewed at her scarlet-lip-sticked mouth doubtfully.

'I am, Your Grace.'

But Posie didn't curtsey. She remembered that Bella Alladice was the daughter of a northern confectionery tycoon, a millionaire, and that Bella had, according to gossip, been courted by a Venetian Duke for her money alone. Courtesy and diplomacy were demanded here, of course, but not too much.

'I hope you didn't expect more in the way of a visual treat, Your Grace? These new detective books have a lot to answer for. I was just saying to Miss Christie here...'

But Posie was cut off with a wave of a fat bejewelled hand, dazzling with its outrageous ruby.

'Blow Miss Christie and her drab conversation: *I* should know, I have to listen to it every day. I don't pay her for her wise words, otherwise I'd be getting a pretty poor return on my money.'

Posie stared, not liking to meet Lucy Christie's gaze. The Countess was absolutely ghastly.

But the woman was rolling on: 'And you don't need to thank me for your stay. *Anyone* who is a friend of Alaric Boynton-Dale's has to be invited along, it seems. Tell me, Miss Parker. Aren't you worried sick about Alaric right now?'

At Posie's confused silence the Countess beamed like a search-light, showing small, even, white teeth, like a child's. 'It's one thing to lose a man to another woman, isn't it? Careless of you, some would say. But it's quite another to lose a man in a fire. *Tragic*, more like.'

'Oh!'

Somebody gasped over by the window and there was a horrible silence.

'I say, Bella!' Dickie Alladice was touching Posie's arm gently, and clutching at an empty bottle of whisky. 'That's not quite the ticket. Play fair, Bella, old thing!'

It occurred to Posie that the Countess might be quite drunk herself. But everyone knows that truth is often spoken when drink is involved. What did she mean?

What other woman?

****

Four

Posie was aware that the whole group were looking at her expectantly, waiting for an answer. *What other woman?*

Was it common knowledge that Alaric had accompanied Silvia Hanro around Constantinople? Was everyone else in the know? Or was it only this nasty fat frump done up as a pretend royal who had happened to see the same magazine cover she had?

Or was something else going on entirely?

Dolly Cardigeon, Posie's best friend, had forewarned her that Bella was famously rude, and prone to making things difficult for people. For creating 'situations' out of nothing. Dolly should know: she had met Bella Alladice back in London a couple of years previously, when their respective wealth and social standing had led to their sitting on a charitable board of governors together, an experience which Bella had apparently made atrocious for everyone. Posie had taken Dolly's character assassination of the girl with a pinch of salt, assuming a simple personality clash, but now she was tempted to give Dolly the benefit of the doubt.

Posie smiled into the hostile atmosphere.

'I really couldn't comment on Alaric's actions, Your Grace. Other than to say we trust each other absolutely. And

I haven't lost him to the fire. I'm sure, when he's finished being an errand-boy, that he'll get back here just fine.'

The two women stared at each other, and then the Countess seemed to make up her mind. She nodded, as if in some strange approval.

'Whatever you say, Miss Parker. I'm sure you're right. Or what you *think* is right…'

And then she stalked back to the window furthest along, quite alone, and peered out, sulking, having gathered up a huge silver bowl of pink Jordan almonds from a console table. Posie watched, revolted, as the Countess took a fistful of sweets and rolled them around in her palm, like a dice player sure of his game, before scoffing the lot.

Lucy Christie was at Posie's side, pressing a large glass of what looked like gin and tonic into her hands, whispering softly, 'Please don't take any notice of her, Miss Parker. She's just scared about the fire. And the future. Ignore it.'

And then Miss Christie was introducing the other members of the party.

A small, wiry, dark man in his very late twenties who was holding several notebooks under his arm was introduced as Roger Valentine, Personal Secretary to the Countess and to Dickie Alladice.

'Roger was an Oxford blue, you know. He's very clever: keeps us all on our toes.'

Roger Valentine laughed as if Lucy Christie had just told a good joke.

'A pleasure to meet you, Miss Parker. And welcome. It's not often one arrives to find one's promised abode burnt to a crisp, is it? I do hope you'll find that things improve. And things may not be as bad as they seem. Venice is all about mirages, after all; it's like skating on a dark fathomless mirror. It just got a bit more dangerous today, that's all.'

'Mnnn.'

Posie found herself deeply intrigued. This man was like a dark fathomless mirror himself: handsome in a vaguely mocking way, with one thick, curved eyebrow constantly raised, he gave the impression of not taking the Alladice family or their current set-up too seriously. And while he was polite enough to Posie, his eager, capable eyes never left Lucy's face for a second, greedily observing her all the while.

And Posie wondered what sort of fat salary Roger Valentine was being paid, or what sort of demons he had fled from, back in England, to make such an accomplished, clever man work for a monster like Bella Alladice.

'And this is Aunt Minnie…'

A delicate-looking woman in her late forties, also a red-head but of a paler, less dazzling variety, stepped forwards eagerly. She flapped and fluttered near to Posie like a trapped butterfly, trailing pastel-coloured chiffon scarves, wafting a strong scent of artificial lavender as she moved.

'Goodness.' The woman smiled, speaking in a thick northern accent, untamed by elocution. 'What an honour to meet *yet another* famous person out here in just a matter of a day! You've come along like the proverbial London buses: none for an age, then all at once! Normally I don't get to meet the *really* interesting guests, but, well, I suppose we're all rather thrown into one place tonight with the unfortunate events across the way, aren't we?'

Aunt Minnie was chattering away, seemingly unstoppable: 'Naturally, I follow all of your cases in the English newspapers, Miss Parker, *when* I can get my hands on one. You know they're simply *frightfully* expensive out here, not to mention abysmally late! And when you are more settled in I simply *must* ask you about that book by Dorothy L. Sayers which everyone is reading. People are saying it is quite *the thing*, especially at the English Ladies Club of Venice which I belong to…' And here Minnie turned almost red with the pleasure at being able to count herself a member of such an exalted group. 'But I can't get my hands on a copy for love nor money.'

Minnie Alladice invited sympathy: she was apparently in permanent residence at the Romagnoli Palace not out of choice, and seemed kept woefully short of both cash and interesting company, clinging on to the last remnants of home with her pathetic little ladies clubs.

Trying to end the conversation, Posie gladly volunteered her unread copy of the novel and promised to fetch it shortly. She was pulled away quickly by Lucy and led over to where the two men were still sitting at the window-seat, looking out. Lucy coughed politely:

'Giancarlo? This is our lady detective, Miss Posie Parker.'

A dark, sick-looking boy in a blue silk lounge-suit, barely out of his mid-twenties, turned from the window. He had artificially waved thick black hair. He was as beautiful as a girl and had obviously never in his life been interested in any girl. When he turned from Lucy to face Posie he gave a sad, defeated smile. He didn't bother to get up.

'This is the Count,' Lucy announced. 'His Grace, Comte Giancarlo Romagnoli.'

The Count? Could it be? A man who was so obviously not interested in women at all, tied to that fat blob? Posie had been told that the Romagnoli marriage was a marriage for money, but she hadn't appreciated quite how mismatched the Count and Countess actually were.

The boy nodded and spoke in a high, reedy voice: '*Piacere di conoscerla*, Miss Parker. It is a great pleasure to meet you.'

'Indeed. Likewise. *Piacere*, Your Grace.'

'Please excuse my lack of humour, Miss Parker. It is a sad night for me.'

'I offer my sincerest condolences.'

Giancarlo turned and went back to watching his family home burn down before his eyes. He hunkered in closely to the familiar-looking man, who still hadn't moved or turned about.

'Don't mind Giancarlo, poor boy,' hissed Lucy, stepping

back and drawing Posie with her. 'It must be quite something to watch six hundred years of your family's history disappear in a few hours. The rumour mill has found a suspect for the crime, too.'

'Who?'

'The Corsettis. They're a sort of gang in Venice. An old noble family, actually, but long disgraced and relegated to obscurity, forced to make their way as petty criminals. They have an old feud running with the Romagnolis.'

'Sounds a bit far-fetched to me.' Posie frowned. She took a sip of her drink and the gin almost burnt her throat. 'Much too much like *Romeo and Juliet*. Is it about love?'

Lucy laughed. 'No! I expect it all comes down to money. Usually does, doesn't it? Some debt not paid by Giancarlo, or something.'

'But I thought the Count was doing fine for money. He married Bella for it, didn't he?'

'A fortune, yes,' agreed Lucy, biting at her lip. 'But word is that he's blued it already. He lives very fast, does our young Count. Venice is a party playground for him and no mistake. Between you and me,' and Lucy tapped her nose confidentially, 'I think that half the treasures of the Romagnoli family didn't actually burn over there today. Most of their paintings, jewels and precious artefacts have been pawned by Giancarlo and are sitting right now in the safe at the Palazzo Corner, the city's official pawn shop. He snorted the monies he got for the treasures a long time ago...'

'Gracious!'

'Not that I know *anything*, of course. I'm just a humble companion. A servant really.'

'Come! Don't sell yourself short! It must be difficult working for such a woman as Bella Alladice?'

'Perhaps. I've had six years to get used to her, though...' Lucy shrugged, refusing to be drawn.

Posie decided to blow caution to the wind, putting her

trust in the girl. 'Can I ask if you know what the Countess meant when she said I had lost Alaric to "another woman" earlier?'

Lucy shook her head in embarrassment. 'No, I'm sorry. Bella's probably jealous of you. You're about to make a happy marriage, aren't you?' She gestured towards the Palace, and Posie had the feeling she was changing the subject on purpose. 'Bella's not in an enviable situation here at all. For all the shock involved, I expect she isn't actually that upset to see the Palace burn down, and neither am I. I've lived there for over a year, since Bella's wedding last June, and I hate it with a passion.'

'Why?'

'I can't tell you *why* exactly, save to say it always gave me the creeps, from the moment I entered it. When you imagine living in a Venetian palace you conjure up a dream. At least *I* did. But my dream was about as far from the truth as could be. Everything was wrong.'

'*What* was wrong exactly?'

'Many things. The dampness, the smell of the latrines, the stinking waters outside. There were worries about floods, and rising waters. And the dreadful rats, and the traps for rats everywhere, and the incessant dripping noises at night. All the money in the world couldn't seem to fix the place. Bella realised quite quickly it was going to be a losing battle to restore the Palace to its former glory, although she tried. She *and* her brother. But there is a darkness over there you can't hide, or paper over.'

'A darkness? You mean ghosts?' Posie demanded.

'No,' Lucy replied in a slow, measured tone. 'That's not quite what I mean, although I'm sure you could look for such things if you were that way inclined. The Palace has a chequered history, of course: sieges, attacks, murders. What building wouldn't in nearly six hundred years of history?'

'Quite.'

'What I mean is that the place is unfriendly. It hides

things. It never felt comfortable, or cosy. It has secrets and it won't yield them up.'

'That's how the whole of Venice felt to me tonight.'

'Have you heard the legend of the Mistletoe Bride?'

Posie thought for a moment, frowning. 'You mean that awful old poem by Thomas Haynes Bayly, popular in our great-grandmothers' time?'

Lucy nodded. 'Yes. About how a tragedy takes place at a Christmas wedding when the bride, in a game of hide-and-seek, accidentally locks herself in a cupboard and is never discovered. The corpse is discovered years later.'

'How horrible! And ridiculous. But what's that got to do with the Romagnoli Palace? That story was set in Yorkshire, wasn't it? It has nothing to do with Venice?'

'True, but it's a similar story, actually. As part of its chequered past, the Palace was used as a Casino in the eighteenth century. A series of multiple tunnels and hiding places were incorporated by the Romagnoli family at the time, as a way of making sure they would always be able to catch any absconders from the Casino who hadn't paid their bills, and as a way of hiding themselves if trouble ever broke out. There is a story of how, years later, when the earlier Casino-building generation had died out and the Palace was a simple house once again, one of the Romagnoli daughters hid herself one night in an old secret chamber when her father asked her to come down and meet a rich but odious potential suitor. Everyone looked for the girl but they never found her. No-one was left who knew exactly how the hiding places worked, or where they were located and the family almost knocked the place down to find her.'

'But they never did?'

'Nope.'

'I don't believe in that old rubbish. The poor girl must have got away by gondola, surely?'

'That's the nice way of looking at it. It's a horrible thing to think about when you have to live there. I know Aunt

Minnie worries about it: it plays on her nerves. She's always harping on about it.'

In the absorbing tale of the Venetian Mistletoe Bride, Posie suddenly realised that the man who had seemed familiar had disappeared from the window-seat, leaving the Count all alone. She asked Lucy about him.

'I can't tell you much, I'm afraid. He only appeared here an hour or so before you did. I think he's a commercial traveller. Mr Löhri? Löhrson? Swiss, I think. You'd be as well to ask Mrs Persimmon; he's one of her normal paying guests. Nothing to do with the Romagnoli party. Although it seems Giancarlo was quite taken with him…'

Posie scowled. The man wasn't who she had thought, then. *But she had been sure, almost certain…*

'I'll go up and grab that detective book I promised.' She excused herself, happy to escape the oppressive atmosphere in the salon. But before she had got far across that strange hall of mirrors, the door barged open, and there was Alaric, black and sooty and clutching at a curiously clean and shiny portable silver safe, the size of a wicker cat-basket.

Alaric…

Posie gasped, trying to bring her eyes to rest on the real-life figure of her fiancé, amid all the swimming reflections of him. He was safe! Everyone stared at him, particularly Bella Alladice, whose gaze seemed peculiarly scornful and accusing. Posie felt a huge wash of relief seeping through her every fibre. In her nervousness Posie instinctively tugged at whatever was in her pocket, and the rustling paper from before crackled between her hands.

'Dickie! I found it! Thank heavens Sargent and Greenleaf make such robust devices! This little number here is as sound as when you left it!'

And then he took in Posie, whose heart was inconveniently skipping several beats.

'My darling!'

He started to beam and come across to her but then, like in a bad dream, he glanced down at her hands and frowned in incomprehension. And then Posie looked down too and realised she was still holding onto the wretched red and yellow magazine cover which she had ripped off and thrust into her dress pocket yesterday at Victoria. Alaric's face fell immediately: 'You found *that* bally thing?'

'Well…'

Her head was spinning. So he *knew* about the magazine cover, after all.

Two months it had been. Two months of Alaric's absence: of going to work each day at the Detective Agency on Grape Street and going through the motions; of returning home to Museum Chambers at night to eat a scratch meal for one in her neat pale-green living room, or else meeting a friend to share a hurried London supper with. All that time with nothing but a fancy ring to remind her of him. And every day wondering how it would be when they met again in a joyous, funny, tender, romantic reunion. *Not like this.*

She hadn't as much as looked at another man in all the time she had known Alaric, and certainly not since their engagement the previous December, despite opportunities. Had she been some kind of doormat?

Alaric was angry now. 'I say, what rotten timing. Of all the things to be toting about, you have *this* along for the ride?'

But before Posie could reply properly, albeit in front of everyone, a massive, heavy shadow loomed behind Alaric, filling the doorway. It was Salvarocca.

The Commissario stepped ponderously into the salon. 'Ladies and gentlemen.' He looked around. 'Your Graces.' He nodded at the Count and Countess. 'Good evening.'

He indicated with a quick but authoritative sweep of the hand that no-one was going anywhere.

'Sit down. I have bad news.'

****

Five

'I can confirm that somebody *meant* to set fire to the Palace today.' The Chief of Police shrugged his statement into the room breezily. 'Or worse, to kill one of you. The fire was started at about two o'clock.'

Posie and Alaric sat in rattan chairs side by side, but not very close.

'Two o'clock?' Bella Alladice demanded. She snatched off her headdress, dragging the tiara's comb-attachment across her plump cheek, making angry red track-lines on the puffy skin. 'This was arson?'

'It *was*, Countess. And it was started in your own suite of rooms. A can of petrol has been recovered from that exact location.'

Alaric was leaning forwards, his singed eyebrows pulled together, puzzled. 'By Gad, it seems the devil of a thing to set fire to such an old place, with such a shocking disregard for human life. We all could have died.'

He turned towards his host in Venice: 'I say! What a mercy you'd organised that last-minute gondola trip, Dickie, hey?'

But his friend was sitting drunkenly slumped in a chair, wild-eyed, his arms tightly clamped around the small safe. So instead Alaric turned to the Countess: 'And what a relief that you decided to come with us, Bella!'

The Countess sat very still, almost frozen. 'It's as if somebody knew that I usually have my nap at two o'clock. I always take a sleeping draught with a dash of my favourite liqueur and I'm out like a light in a second.'

'So why didn't you nap today?' cut in Posie, urgently.

The Countess scowled. 'I thought I'd be a good hostess for your fiancé, Miss Parker; show him the sights on his first full day here. I'd have done the same for you. Dickie told me about the boat ride he had booked just in time and I put down my flask and my pill and came out with the whole group instead.'

The Commissario coughed importantly.

'Well, the good news is that we have our suspect already. We are holding Pietro Corsetti in custody. He was arrested not half an hour ago in a bar in the Campo Rialto Nuovo, just past the Rialto Bridge, a known stomping-ground for dissolute youths, particularly of the poker-playing variety. He was blind drunk and stinking of petrol and was in receipt of a good deal of cash. He was in the process of getting through it all as quickly as he could.'

The Count had emitted a strange kind of groan, tearing at his beautifully waved hair in distress, and Posie looked over at him with frank interest. Giancarlo burbled something in a snarl of quick Italian, but the only word which Posie understood was 'fascists'.

Her irritation must have shown plainly on her face, for Lucy Christie, who was on Posie's other side, breathed in a low whisper:

'The Count says that Pietro had nothing to do with the fire. He says the big man is barking up the wrong tree! And he has warned the Commissario not to use "fascist ways" to get the truth out of Pietro.'

'I see. I wonder which tree the Commissario *should* be barking up?'

Salvo Salvarocca was checking through a large black leather notepad. He looked around, his sad brown eyes resting on each person in turn.

'It goes without saying that the Palace is completely inaccessible: it's a lot worse than we thought. Most rooms and staircases may collapse at any moment, so please, no going back there.'

The Commissario moved towards the door, replacing his cap. He turned, and said in a slow, measured tone, probably the same voice he used in Court when convicting criminals:

'Please take this seriously. One of you was meant to die in that blaze. If any of you have any information, please do not hesitate to contact me. If any of you believe yourself to be in personal danger, I can try and ensure your safety. I will take all of your statements entirely seriously, and by the way,' he threw a mortified look towards the Count, 'I never, *ever* use "fascist" methods.'

As soon as the policeman had departed, the smart snap of Jones' step entered the room. Which was just as well, as no-one quite knew what to say, and the atmosphere was as treacly on the lungs as the smoke wafting in the streets outside.

'Your Graces, ladies and gentlemen, dinner will be served in the dining-room, next door, in half an hour,' Jones announced. He threw an anxious glance over towards Alaric: 'Which should give certain parties sufficient time to, ahem, refresh themselves…'

People were leaving to dress, but the mere thought of dinner made Posie feel sick. She wanted to be alone with Alaric. So many things seemed not quite right here. How could she *eat*? She'd pretend to. Maybe there would be a plate of nice biscuits to be had later on. Amarettis, perhaps?

'My room? Shall we?'

Alaric turned, raising an eyebrow, throwing Posie a challenge to enter a socially unacceptable situation, and publicly, too. But Posie couldn't give a hang what other people thought, so she started to follow Alaric.

However, upon reaching the top of the staircase and

coming out into a wide corridor of the guesthouse's very best rooms, Posie felt a quick tap on her shoulder. Lucy Christie cast an apologetic look at Alaric, and then back at Posie.

'I'm sorry to intrude,' she murmured, her brown eyes genuinely troubled, 'but the Countess would like to have a word in private with Miss Parker. In her room. Now. *Before* dinner.'

For a second Posie was distracted. She had seen something glitter at the girl's neck in the darkness. It was an old-style diamond ring hanging from a thin chain. It must have been obscured before by Lucy's purple dress with its high neckline. Posie felt a stab of real surprise: for all its old-fashioned setting, the solitaire at the centre of the ring was huge, and obviously very valuable. Lucy Christie had obviously got a love story of her own to keep close to her chest, hidden from prying eyes. But why was that so surprising? With a face like that…

Alaric frowned. 'Can't it wait, Miss Christie?'

'I'm afraid not, Mr Boynton-Dale. The Countess says, and I rather believe she is speaking the truth, that she needs to see Miss Parker as a matter of some urgency.'

Posie touched Alaric's dirty sleeve. 'Darling, I'm sorry.'

Alaric shrugged Posie's hand away and walked off irritably. Posie sighed, watching his retreating back. 'Show me the way then, Lucy.'

****

The Countess's room was a candy-coloured wreck. Whispers of gossamer-fine silk trailed from paper carrier-bags, and discarded slippers and opened packages of candied fruit were thrown around in a blaze of abandon.

It was hard to believe that Bella Alladice had only been *in situ* at Mrs Persimmon's since late afternoon.

Posie stared hard through all the chaos.

And then her eyes came to rest on the bed, where Bella Alladice was propped up, sipping at a pink drink through a glass straw. A huge smoke-grey Persian cat sat heavily on Bella's lap. It stared at Posie menacingly and its orange eyes glimmered across the room. Normally Posie loved cats – she had a very old Siamese cat called Mr Minks who resided in some splendour back at the Detective Agency in London – but this one sent a chill down her spine. The Persian cat looked like a puff-ball full of menace, just like its owner. The two were perfectly suited.

Posie hadn't brought her carpet bag up with her, but she dug in her pocket for the small silver notepad and matching pencil she always carried.

Bella Alladice stroked the cat in deft, measured moves. 'Petrucci here survived the fire, lucky boy. He must be onto his ninth life by now, I reckon. A fireman found him sitting on my balcony as the flames rose higher in the room behind him; not a whisker out of place.'

'How fortuitous, Your Grace.'

'Do quit calling me "Your Grace". I don't think either of us can stomach it for a minute more. Call me Bella. And I'll call you what I like.'

Posie sat down on a nearby slipper chair, staying quiet, and it was not until a couple of minutes had passed that she saw Bella Alladice was quivering all over. It was hot as Hades in the bedroom so it wasn't the seeping Venetian cold which was making the girl shiver.

Posie relented a little. 'I suppose I *am* here in a professional capacity?'

The meltingly dark grey eyes flashed. 'Of course. I need you to cover my back. I read about how you were hired to protect Silvia Hanro, that wet-weekend of a movie star. And *she's* still alive, isn't she? So you must be good at your job. I'll pay you well.'

'I'm a Private Detective, Bella, not a bodyguard. And I think the Venetian Chief of Police is sufficiently worried to make sure that none of us are exposed to further danger. Tell me, what is it you're so afraid of?'

'Off you go, Petrucci, my love.' The Countess released the huge cat and he hissed at Posie, stalking into a corner. Bella had edged herself off the bed, grunt by grunt, until she was right next to Posie. The smell of almonds on the girl's breath was overpowering.

'It's like this. I'm being watched.'

'Watched?'

'*Watched.* For about two months now. Sometimes when I go out – I have my own gondola, of course – I'm aware of a white boat, a skiff really, following us around. I go out often: I play Bridge with other English women at the Café Florian in St Mark's Square, or else I go shopping, or to the English Ladies Club. I'm a patron of a number of charities here, too. Whenever I see this white boat I tell my Gondolier to pull in at random spots, at a jetty where I'd normally have no business, for example. And sure enough, it always slows down before racing off again. It happens at least three or four times a week. I find it very menacing.'

'I should imagine so. Have you seen who is inside the white boat?'

'Oh yes. Usually the same couple of men, but I've never got close enough to speak to them.'

'What do they look like?'

'Oh, Italian, for sure, dark and good-looking. They're both young-ish, too, in their twenties, wearing caps and black shirts.'

Posie frowned. 'Real blackshirts? Fascists, you mean?'

The Countess waved the suggestion away airily: 'Who *isn't*, these days? If a man isn't a fascist, he's dressed up as a fascist in case he gets picked up by the real deal. A terrible state of affairs. A dreadful time to live here, actually.'

'I quite agree. But who do you think these men are? Are you being followed on land when you walk about?'

'I'm not sure. I've occasionally had the sense that a man is on my tail, when I'm in a shop or a restaurant, or with Lucy, or out meeting friends.' Bella Alladice's many chins quivered, and her voice rose, the northern accent becoming more pronounced with every fearful word.

'But the worst thing is that several times I've happened to look out of my bedroom window and I've been met with a flash of binoculars trained on my very room. The watcher has been sitting on the opposite jetty; from somewhere over *here*, on the Campo San Vio. It's as if I'm under constant surveillance. But I don't know why. What do you make of that?'

Posie realised the girl was approaching some sort of hysteria. She said, gently, reassuringly: 'Are you sure it wasn't just some passing tourist you saw, keen to appreciate the beauty of the Palace? Or a photographer hoping to get a postcard-shot? You are – or *were* – in the very centre of the tourist trail of Venice.'

'I'm sure of it. Besides, there's been something else.'

'Oh?'

'I got *this* a couple of weeks back. It was left lying around, with no envelope, on my dressing-table, among my make-up and perfume…'

Posie was handed a much-scrunched piece of thick, Italian notepaper, a red-and-gold marbled edge running grandly around its scalloped sides. There were four short lines of spidery writing, in Italian.

'I'm sorry, but my Italian is very basic, and I can't read this at all.'

'Turn it over. Lucy translated it for me. The English is on the back.'

Posie flipped the note around and read:

You've heard those rumours
about this house?

About the secret room where the romagnoli
girl hid long ago and never came out?

You'll be joining her there soon. Just you
and an old corpse for company.

What a way to go! It serves you right.
You and your insensitive ways...

Posie felt a shiver go down her spine. The note was ghastly, filled with hate. Quite one of the worst things she had read in her professional career. She thought about Lucy Christie and her recounting of the same Venetian Mistletoe Bride tale earlier. But, as usual, a random detail grabbed her.

'How does Lucy speak such good Italian, anyhow? She's only been here the same length of time as you, surely?'

'Indeed. But her parents were Italian. She's fluent, despite having grown up in England. She's dreadfully annoying but she makes herself useful. I'll give her that.'

'I see.' Posie looked at the note again before handing it back. 'This certainly casts a new light on things. Did you tell the police?'

Bella shook her head. 'I wanted to, but Dickie and Giancarlo thought it best to deal with it ourselves. I gathered they didn't want Salvarocca's fascist mob crawling all over poor Giancarlo's crumbling old Palace.'

'So who has seen this note?'

'Well, everyone living at the Palace. I showed it around. I asked people if they'd seen anyone creeping about, entering my apartment and delivering it.'

'And?'

'No-one knew anything. They were all horrified. Dickie went berserk: insisted we all search the house for this secret room, but of course we didn't find anything. He kept screaming at Giancarlo, saying *he* must know about it as it was his family's Palace, but poor Giancarlo hadn't got a clue. Actually, I think Dickie was suspicious about my husband's involvement in the note; it *was* written in Italian after all. And there *was* something about the note which completely freaked Giancarlo out. His reaction to it was strange.'

'How so?'

The Countess shook her head. 'He seemed more than just frightened. Shocked, more like. Completely flabbergasted. I'd even go as far as saying he was disappointed by it. Or saddened...'

'How peculiar. Was it Giancarlo's writing?'

'No. I told Dickie to stop being a fool. He gets carried away sometimes.'

'Do *you* think the secret room exists, Bella?'

Bella laughed bitterly. 'I've looked for it before. When I got here last year I'd spend hours searching, but the romance and interest soon wore off as I found more lively things to do about town, and the Palace was huge – it could have been anywhere. It's a horrid little story, anyhow. Unhealthy to dwell on it.'

Posie was frantically scribbling. 'What a can of worms! So now you're scared because you think the fire today was meant for you?'

'It looks that way, doesn't it? Either to kill me or give me a bally good warning.'

'A warning about what?'

The Countess shrugged. 'The note mentions "insensitivity", doesn't it? I rub people up the wrong way,

I always have. That was one of the reasons I was happy enough to come to Venice when my father suggested the idea, and I thought I could begin over again. I'd rubbed people up the wrong way in Leeds, and then again in London. I thought this would be a fresh start.'

'But?' Posie demanded.

'I've got on the wrong side of several people here already. The English Ladies Club of Venice is a particularly sensitive issue; several women detest me there. They hate having to address me as "Countess", which I insist upon. They feel I have no right...'

Bella prattled on about the back-stabbing nature of genteel English ladies who lived abroad in Venice. How her Aunt Minnie loved all that, how Minnie would happily spend each and every day at the clubhouse. How it was completely ridiculous...

But Posie was miles away, thinking about earlier, about the briefing from the policeman. About the man being held right now as a suspect for arson. *Corsetti.*

Pietro Corsetti. The feuding family.

'Hang the English Ladies Club, Bella. We're wasting time on that. This is all about love, or if not, it's about money. It always is. Not social jealousy, or noses put out of joint.'

She bit the pencil-end. 'Have you got on the wrong side of the Corsettis? This Pietro character? Is the Commissario right about that? Are *they* at the bottom of this? Following you about, and the note, and the fire? Or is there anyone else who would wish you dead?'

The Countess's face took on a look of weary acceptance. 'I don't know who else would wish me dead, although I'd be here a long time if I was to list everyone who hates me, my nearest and dearest included. And no, I don't think the Commissario is right about the Corsetti family. Between you and me, for all the old animosity, Pietro Corsetti is a great friend of my husband. Perhaps even more than that...'

She shrugged. 'In fact, I'm certain there is a real love between them, and the feud is a convenient smokescreen. But don't breathe a word of this to anyone: their relationship is illegal in the eyes of the state and the church, and I must trust in your discretion. Such knowledge would bring my husband down: land him in jail certainly, perhaps result in his death.'

Posie didn't like Bella Alladice one bit, but she found herself feeling a twinge of sympathy for the girl.

'Don't you *mind*?'

Bella Alladice had found a bowl of Jordan almonds, mauve, this time. She started to crunch away on them. 'I don't mind. We live separate lives. It's the best I can hope for.'

'But you must have been a wonderful prospect?'

'Financially, you mean?' Bella's face hardened, and she laughed mirthlessly. 'Yes, look at me! Can you believe it, I was thin once, and quite beautiful. I was in love with a man who was going to marry me. But he looked elsewhere. And my heart froze and I swore I could never love another man. I never wanted to. They're dangerous.'

Bella Alladice looked directly at Posie and her steely gaze was unstinting. 'Men always want *something else*. You have to be careful. So this arrangement suits me fine. It's safe.'

Posie swallowed. Bella Alladice's statement had contained a show of bravado, but was it a personal warning for Posie, too? What did she know about Alaric which Posie didn't? She remembered Bella's contemptuous gaze at Alaric when he had burst through the door of the salon earlier. A sort of disgust on her face…

Posie pursued another tack:

'Forgive me, but bearing in mind what you've just told me, you don't think it possible your husband might be in league with Pietro Corsetti? Would Giancarlo gain financially from your death?'

Bella's eyes opened very wide in that great ham of a face.

'Giancarlo would never do such a thing,' she insisted. 'And he'd be a fool to want me dead. He might not love me, but he'd be cutting off the hand which feeds. He gets a yearly "stipend" set up by my father as a condition of our marriage. It ends on my death, and Giancarlo then has no further claim on my money, or the Alladice money. He has precious little cash of his own, only the great Romagnoli name, for what it's worth. But it *was* worth something to my father: made the old man content on his death bed last year. He was happy to have a Countess for a daughter, after our humble roots.'

Posie was thinking rapidly. 'And where *does* your money go on your death?' She was writing very fast. 'You have a Will?'

Bella nodded. 'Yes. I made it a couple of months back. My Personal Secretary, Roger, dealt with it all. He told me I ought to make it with a proper English solicitor – not the little notary we use for company matters out here, who Roger said he didn't like too much – and he arranged it. The solicitor Roger got to come out here was from a firm called Pring and Proudfoot. Do you know them?'

'Of course.' The firm was an old-fashioned but highly reputable firm on Bedford Row in London, quite near her own office. Very expensive, very competent. Roger Valentine had chosen well, and he was obviously a man not to do things by halves. Posie found him rising somewhat in her estimation.

'He was very thorough, this Mr Proudfoot. He did a good job. He took my Will with him for safety back to England and he stressed I shouldn't divulge the contents of it to anyone, and that in the event of my death he would make the necessary arrangements to come back to Venice, bringing the Will with him. He said he would make sure it was read aloud exactly a week after my death: no sooner, no later. My money, of which there is plenty, is safely in Hoare's bank in London. It all goes to the British League for Neglected Cats.'

Posie just about stopped herself from rolling her eyes in exasperation, especially as she had caught sight of the Persian cat staring at her again, with a look of something like triumph in its amber eyes. But her gaze was caught again by that blood-red stone.

'And your jewels? That ruby for example?'

'They are to be sold and added to my money in the bank. To go to the cats' home, too.'

'Nothing for your companion, Lucy? Or for your family?'

The Countess pursed her lips unattractively. 'Absolutely not! Lucy has received more than enough... But you should know that I *do* have other money, family money. Serious amounts of it. It's in Alladice Holdings, a big company centred around our confectionary factories, all set up by my grandfather. Since the sale of our factories, the company is rather inactive; it only owns cash and property. But I own half of it. You wouldn't know this, but Dickie and I had another brother, our eldest brother, John – everyone called him Johnny – he died in 1917, in the war. On the Messines Ridge.'

'I'm very sorry for your loss. Did Dickie fight, too?'

'No. He stayed at home to look after the business. It was very active then: the factories were still going full-pelt, supplying the soldiers with sweet foodstuffs, and supplying the shops, of course. But Johnny's death changed the course of our lives. He died without marrying, and as I was his adored little sister, he left me all of his shares in Alladice Holdings.'

'Was that allowed?'

'Yes. The articles are drawn up so that you can leave your share to anyone as long as they are related by blood, or by marriage. They must bear the surname "Alladice". If you don't nominate anyone, they go to the current shareholders of the company, automatically. I think Johnny felt Dickie needed his wings clipped a bit, and that I would do the clipping by receiving more shares. For a while, until our father died last year, I was the majority shareholder.'

'What was Johnny's problem with Dickie?'

'Oh, nothing more than a brotherly spat, I think. Johnny always felt Dickie was getting in above his neck in things, that Dickie was too wild. Dickie has good ideas though; he's taken the company from strength to strength since our father died, the turnover has almost doubled! Johnny was very conservative, he always wanted to maintain the good name of the company; it meant a lot to him. He was wonderful.'

Posie looked up from her paper. 'And where does your share in Alladice Holdings go on your death?'

'It *should* go to my children. But there will be none. So I have nominated it to go to my Aunt Minnie Alladice; she's the sister of my late father. Dickie got my father's shares when he died, so Dickie and I have been equal owners since last year. I can't stand Aunt Minnie, she's a dreadfully annoying bore, but my father did her a great wrong and I'd like to think I'm evening things up for her at last. Doing the right thing by her.'

Posie thought about Minnie and her not-quite-one-of-the-family position.

'Tell me,' she demanded. 'What exactly is Aunt Minnie doing out here, anyway? If no-one likes the woman?'

Bella puffed out her cheeks. 'The truth is that we need her. She's a walking signature. She has a tiny shareholding in Alladice Holdings. Only about two per cent, but she needs to sign the company documents, nonetheless. We pay her a small salary to keep her here. So it's always me, Dickie and Aunt Minnie on the paperwork. Roger is Company Secretary, as well as my Personal Secretary, so he organises all the company paperwork and signs too. He's quite indispensable. He took a short holiday in London three weeks ago and I didn't know what to do without him. I was counting the hours until he returned.'

'How long has he been your Personal Secretary?'

'About eighteen months. He joined me just before we came out here in June last year. He seemed happy enough to leave England.'

Bella looked at her watch, and Posie felt herself dismissed. 'Is there anything else I need to know, Bella? Anything suspicious? Anything which may seem obvious to you, but which might provide me with crucial information? Useful background about your house-party guests, for example?'

'No. I think you have the essentials.'

Posie stared at the pages she had written on. There was a good deal of information contained within them, layers and layers. But there was missing information too, things Bella Alladice had left out, either by design or accident. And if Posie was to get to the bottom of this puzzle she would need to fill in the gaps.

This is an inside job, thought Posie to herself with a feeling of dread.

Someone who can leave a letter without going noticed. Someone with easy access to Bella's private quarters. Just like today, when someone planted petrol up in her bedroom.

A relative…a companion…

Bella's words echoed in her head, over and over: "'*I'd be here a long time if I was to list everyone who hates me, my nearest and dearest included.*'" But was there a real danger lurking, or was it all just an elaborate show? And could Posie really protect Bella Alladice, a woman she didn't like, when she was simply here to get married and enjoy herself?

'So, will you help me?'

And to her surprise, Posie found herself nodding gravely. 'I'll put my thinking cap on. But I really think you should tell the police. I have my own reservations about the Commissario, but I think that as a policeman you should trust him.'

'I think I trust you more.'

And that, thought Posie, was praise indeed. She avoided the cat, who hissed at her again, and went to the door. Downstairs a gong was ringing for dinner.

'Tell me,' she asked, looking back at the Countess, unable to let the question which had been plaguing her for the last few minutes pass by unanswered, unafraid to walk on uncomfortable territory. 'Why is it you hate Lucy Christie so much? You speak of doing the right thing by your aunt, but what is it about Lucy which means you can't treat her properly? Should I be looking to her as a suspect?'

Bella Alladice was jamming her tiara back on her head, adding a violent coral-pink lipstick. She stared at herself in the small mirror above the washstand, not meeting Posie's eye. And she shrugged and spoke very low:

'I hate her because she has a habit of stealing hearts. Hearts which are not hers to take.'

* * * *

Six

Apart from a frosty force-field gathering ominously between Alaric and Posie, dinner at the guesthouse was notable for two things. The first was the appalling food: Mrs Persimmon obviously employed an English cook who stuck to plain 'nursery' food such as mashed potato and colourless milk 'shapes' for dessert, and Posie found herself bitterly disappointed to learn that in the wake of the fire, all of the Count's servants, including his highly-rated Italian Chef, had been given a week's holiday. The second was the marked absence of the commercial traveller from earlier.

Conversation revolved naturally around the fire at the Palace, but as soon as she could, Posie managed to get Mrs Persimmon's attention.

'I say.' She smiled, crumbling up some very out-of-date Scottish oatcakes and adding a rubbery sort of cheese on top. 'What's happened to your commercial traveller? Won't he mind missing his dinner? I hope to goodness he didn't feel forced out by our little party.'

Mrs Persimmon trilled like a budgerigar in her East-End accent: 'Oh, Miss Parker, you do say some funny things, dearie!'

The owner of the guesthouse gestured around the table, as if amidst the Royal Family themselves:

'Mr Löhri, you mean? I couldn't ask such a man to eat dinner with the likes of *yourselves*, could I?' She tugged at very large and glittery paste earrings, all of a fluster at negotiating this strange situation in the right way. 'Now, don't get me wrong, Mr Löhri is an impeccable guest, from what I've seen so far. A Swiss watch-seller, in the middling price-range, so he told me, supplying the department stores, and his papers bear him out. And he's mighty busy, too: he's been on that hall telephone most of the early evening, to *Zürich*, apparently.'

The mention of Zürich was uttered in low, conspiratorial tones. Posie nodded her head dutifully.

'And fair's fair: he's got his supper all laid out good and proper in the kitchen downstairs. It don't do to encourage people to get above themselves, does it? They need to know their station in life, otherwise where will we all be? No; I couldn't have the likes of a man like that *mingling* here. At dinner.'

Was it Posie's imagination or had the guesthouse owner run a disapproving glance down the other side of the dinner table, to the very end of it, where Lucy Christie and Roger Valentine were sitting? It seemed they were only just qualified in Mrs Persimmon's book to eat in such exalted company. Mrs Persimmon obviously held dear to the idea of those who 'sat below the salt'.

And afterwards in the dark vestibule of an entrance hall, while Alaric was chatting with Jones about the weather and flicking at an unreliable barometer, Posie spent a while over by the coat-stand, shaking her red coat about her shoulders but surreptitiously scanning the large cream ledger which sat alongside the telephone apparatus.

A handwritten cream card read:

Telephone for guests only.
International calls must be
recorded and paid for in full.

There were only three entries for that day. In a scrawling, cramped hand, barely legible, was written:

Mr Stefan Löhri

1. Call to the International Operator in Rome, then an Exchange call from Rome to Zürich. (3 minutes' duration, Six o'clock)

2. Same as above (4 minutes' duration, Seven o'clock)

3. Same as above (2 minutes' duration, Eight o'clock)

It seemed that Mr Löhri was calling someone – the boss of his company, perhaps? – in Zürich, every hour. It seemed dashed odd, but the man no doubt had his reasons. And he was, to go by this telephone ledger, obviously connected to Switzerland. Nothing to do with the man she had first thought he was.

But she had been sure, almost certain.

The grandfather clock by the door was striking out nine. Posie looked automatically towards the stairs, to see if the Swiss man would be tripping down them, about to place his next hourly call. But all was eerily quiet.

'Darling.' Alaric's voice was strained. 'Shall we walk out?'

She turned to see Jones nodding triumphantly at the barometer. 'Now she's working and the glass is going back, sir. There'll be more rain tonight. And quite possibly a storm. Are you sure you want to go out, sir? It's mighty cruel here, when the rain lashes off the lagoon.'

Posie saw that Alaric was standing impatiently with his hand on the door knob, staring at her strangely. 'We'll be fine, Jones,' he insisted. 'But thanks. Nothing like a nice bit of air to blow away those cobwebs. Posie, Jones here has got us an umbrella…'

Alaric was wearing a singed leather-and-sheepskin flying jacket over a borrowed flannel suit and as soon as he opened the door he hunkered down into the large collar of the jacket, pulling the buckles and fur up around half his face. It was bitterly cold and the light rain from earlier had indeed turned into the stinging slaps of a torrential downpour.

Alaric got the umbrella up and they huddled beside each other, without linking arms or properly touching. The wind was high and they turned away from the Grand Canal, parallel to it, walking down a tiny rain-drenched cobbled street which offered a bit more protection.

'Thank goodness we're out of that awful place,' muttered Alaric into his coat collar. 'It's driving me crazy.'

'Mrs Persimmon is only doing her best,' retorted Posie obstinately, 'in quite difficult and obviously reduced circumstances. I think she's nervous. She's only got Jones, and one cook, and one maid-of-all-work and suddenly she's got a great aristocratic house-party foisted on her.'

'Oh, I know. But it's claustrophobic as hell, and it seems everyone is listening in at every corner. I haven't even had the chance to speak with you alone.'

'I didn't think that bothered you too much.'

Alaric turned and stared at her, his green-copper eyes narrowing in the reflected light from a street-lamp, their beautiful intensity almost unbearable.

'I didn't think you were bothered much, either,' he replied, coolly, balancing the umbrella in the wind. 'What the devil was all that nonsense about the Swiss fella, anyhow? I heard you drilling into old Ma Persimmon tonight, and you were obviously ferreting about in that telephone ledger for a reason.' He laughed but there was nothing joyful about it. 'Got a penchant for blonde chaps all of a sudden, have you? Or is this another of your little fact-finding missions?'

Posie gave him one of her looks, although it was

somewhat lost in all the rain and wind and general darkness. Her boots were slipping about on the wet cobbles, and she wondered how sensible it had been to accept Alaric's proposal of an after-dinner walk. But Alaric had spoken the truth: the guesthouse *was* claustrophobic, and it was good to get out. She breathed in great gulps of salty air.

'Almost there now. Where we're heading is the best place in all of Venice, the very tip of the island. See this great dome? It's the Church of the Salute. It's the first thing you see, or the last thing you see, when you arrive or leave Venice by water on this side.'

They had come out into a square, open on one side with steps leading down to the canal, and bordered on the other by steps leading up to the Salute. They walked across the square in silence, still not touching, past the Salute with its magnificent statues. Men in thick waterproofs were assembling metal poles and timbers into temporary gates outside the church, their breath hanging mistily in the night air. Posie remembered that a temporary bridge would be made ready for the pilgrims for the following day, and she supposed the men would be hard at work all night. Barges and small boats, lit up by torches, were ranged across the canal to aid the construction of the bridge, and the sounds of hammering and shouting from the carpenters out on the water rose through the wind and wet air like snatches of a song.

They walked along a passageway right next to the canal, in the shelter of what seemed to be a long, grey stone warehouse, and Posie concentrated all the way on not slipping on the stones. With a sigh of relief she saw they had reached a large, raised, triangular stone platform at the very end, bordered by a small jetty and open to the most magnificent wide views across the water. It was indeed the tip of the island, and the place was very exposed. Posie could just make out the dark, low shapes of boats and barges as they passed to and fro. An emerald-green beacon in the distance flickered on and off, throwing a ghostly light over the water and on the tall, dark buildings it sat among. The sound of the wind and roaring waves was colossal.

There was shelter provided by the very end of the warehouse, and above them were three huge porticos, the middle one of which boasted a flickering pink lantern, swinging in a frenzy, groaning on its chain. An enormous wave crashed up over the stone platform, and Posie hastily stepped backwards into the shelter of the pink-lit warehouse. Some fishermen were over on the right, drenched through and packing up. Other than that they were completely alone.

'Let's sit, shall we?'

Alaric gestured at a bench. It was mercifully dry and nicely protected, as Posie appreciated when she sat down: she could almost hear herself think again. Alaric threw down the umbrella and then played with a packet of cigarettes and his matches, putting them away again with a resigned sigh.

'I'm not even going to bother lighting up on such a wretchedly filthy night. By the way, this is the Customs House, the Dogana da Mar. And that over there is the Doge's Palace and the Campanile, lit up with the green beacon, and the back of St Mark's Square which you'll see tomorrow in the light. This is quite the best view in Venice.'

'Mnnn.'

'Look, I'm sorry I wasn't there to meet you earlier, and I'm sorry about the fire and us having to stay at this odd guesthouse and for the horrible weather and for everything not being quite perfect. But I'm not having a pleasant time, either: I'm sitting here in a rented suit a size too small because everything else got burned, including my wedding clothes, which I'm going to have to replace in a hurry. Luckily I was carrying my trusty rucksack with me when I left the Palace, so my documents are still all in order, but I'm missing most of my things. But that's life, isn't it? It's not perfect: so much of it is difficult and you simply have to make do. I'll try my best to make this trip nice for you.'

Posie stared at the man she was about to marry, at the man she had been away from for so long, whom she had travelled across several countries to meet. The man she would have crossed the world to meet.

She pulled her coat tighter to her. 'You don't need to make this "nice" for me, Alaric,' she said, coldly. 'None of those things you mentioned are your fault. And don't worry about things not being perfect: you know that most of my life hasn't been perfect. Distinctly imperfect, actually.'

'Well, even so…'

His voice trailed off. They watched a flicker of lightning catch the sky ablaze and rip it in half.

'We've been apart, Alaric. This was always bound to be difficult. It feels like we're strangers. I can't imagine what we were thinking, planning a wedding like this.'

Sudden and unwelcome thoughts of Silvia Hanro crowded to the forefront of her mind. *Better get this over with.* The words came out in a rush:

'I don't care how many scores of women you've had in the past, Al.' She flashed a sideways look at Alaric, who was devilishly handsome, and everyone knew it; it was common knowledge that umpteen women had found heaven in Alaric's arms, and in his bed. He was looking a tad uncomfortable now, bundling himself up in the collar of his jacket.

Posie carried on grimly. 'But what is important to me is now. *Now.*'

'What do you mean?'

'You know exactly what I mean. You can joke all you like about me liking blonde men, but what on earth has been happening with Silvia Hanro? I *saw* it, Alaric. I saw the magazine cover. You *know* I did.'

Alaric looked directly at Posie and held her stare. But he remained silent.

Posie ploughed on regardless. 'It was your bad luck that

I saw it in London. Only yesterday! That magazine came out a good month ago now, and it was simple chance that I hadn't seen it on a news-stall back then. Otherwise I think I would have come straight out to Constantinople.'

'Goodness. Why on earth would you have done that?'

Posie stood up, aware that tears were streaming down her face, mingling with the rain and sea-spray, and she rubbed at her eyes, black Maybelline mascara and kohl pencil running everywhere.

'Did you invite her out to Constantinople, Alaric? Have you made love to her? What sort of thing am I looking at here? And why couldn't you tell me that you wanted to be with her? At least told me before I made a complete fool of myself by coming out here to marry a man who has quite obviously gone off me? I don't even know you anymore…'

Alaric had sprung to his feet, and at last he took Posie in his arms, but she pulled away. He faced her, the light from the pink beacon falling in strange stripes over both their faces.

'Don't you realise, Posie? I was damned if I told you and damned if I didn't,' Alaric argued. 'All I could hope for was that if I didn't say anything you wouldn't find out.'

'Brilliant!' she spat sarcastically. 'This just gets better and better. You didn't count on being snapped by the press, did you?'

'No,' he admitted guiltily. 'I didn't think that would happen.'

Alaric continued, insistently: 'Silvia was virtually on her own in Constantinople: alone and unprotected, and famous. She's so damned beautiful, too: a target for all sorts of strange admirers.'

'So you volunteered your services as a tour guide?'

'It would have been ungentlemanly not to. I confess I was with her a good deal.'

'Lucky her. That's more than I've had tonight.'

'I've said sorry for how everything was when you arrived. You know I love you.'

Posie stepped away, looking across the dark water towards the unknown landmarks of Venice. Several things were bothering her. The rain soaking her to the skin was the least of her worries. Turning, she saw Alaric leaning against the huge stone pillar of the shelter. He wore a half-smile, crooked across that handsome face. More than anything Posie wished she could simply run into his arms, to fix everything, to tell him she loved him *too*.

Instead, she held her nerve.

'What are we doing here, Alaric? *Exactly*, I mean. Why does Dickie Alladice want you out here? You two seem unlikely friends: he's some sort of businessman, after all, isn't he? And not a very exciting one at that, in my opinion. Something about properties? Not quite up to your usual dangerous taste in friends. Or friends who are movie stars, for that matter…'

Alaric's face took on an obstinate look. 'You won't let that rest, will you, darling? And you haven't seen Dickie at his best. He's a first-class fellow. I met him out in Tangiers and he was very amiable, very professional. Today has totally knocked the stuffing out of the poor chap. This business with the fire, and, well, he's quite worried about his sister too. She's been receiving odd little notes and the like. It's unnerved him no end.'

'She told me. That was why she wanted to speak to me earlier. Quite the horror-story.'

'Well, you know the whole beastly thing then. Everyone's on edge but Dickie seems to have taken it badly.' Alaric grimaced. 'I don't know why Dickie's so het-up. It sounds like a mare's nest to me.'

'But it's coincidental about the fire starting in her rooms, isn't it? Following on from the note and the spying. And I don't like coincidences one bit. She's asked me to look into it.'

'A busman's holiday, darling? Just leave it well alone.'

'Let me decide that. But why were *you* invited out here in the first place? What on earth is this all about?'

'If you must know, I owe Dickie. He's been pouring money into a couple of expeditions I've got planned for early next year, including a big trip to the Himalayas. I couldn't have got much interest from the Royal Geographical Society in Kensington without his financial backing.' Alaric frowned, looking out to sea.

'But there's more, isn't there, Al? There's no such thing as a free meal ticket, that much I do know. What do you have to do in return? What is it?'

Alaric chuckled. 'You can read me like a book, darling girl. There *is* more; you're right. Dickie is starting some new venture out here. Exporting goods. Venetian glass: top-notch stuff. He's got a good deal going with an old family-run glass factory out on Murano, the little glass-production island way over yonder.' He gestured somewhere into the darkness. 'Dickie wants to supply all the exclusive department stores in England with the glassware. He wants me in on the thing, a partner in the business.'

'But you're an explorer! You don't know anything about glass.'

Alaric shrugged. 'You're right. But I can represent the company at home, drum up business. I can ensure adverts in all the newspapers and magazines, and hopefully make the stuff sell like billy-o! I'm famous, and I can use it to our advantage. I'll be a sort of ambassador for the glassware. So I've just got to sign the paperwork, there's some pressing need to get it wrapped up this week, on Thursday apparently. I've just got to check on a couple of matters first.'

Posie frowned. 'So he wants to use your name? Your fame?'

'That's about the gist of it. It seems a fair deal.'

Posie had never heard anything more unbelievable. She was about to open her mouth to give voice to these sentiments when she felt a pin-prickly sensation she always got when someone was watching her. A creeping sensation stole over her neck, combining horribly with the wetness of her coat collar and the back of her soaked felt hat. She scanned the stone platform and the jetty but the fishermen had long gone. She spun around.

'Hello?' she called.

'There's no-one there, darling. What on earth would they be doing out on a filthy night such as this?'

Strange.

Posie looked up at Alaric's face, and he looked almost like he was enjoying himself. She swallowed down her rage and her fear. '*If* you know what you are doing, and are certain of it, it is not my place to interfere.'

This is madness. 'But are you sure?'

Alaric shrugged. 'Why not? I agree some parts of it seem rather hazy, but as I say I'll check the details before signing anything. Besides, I can't keep wandering the earth forever, can I? The Himalayas may be my last big trip. Maybe I need something more stable to rely on, *safer*...'

'Why?'

'Well, despite the fact that I have no wedding clothes, I had hoped to get married out here. And that comes with commitments. Maybe I'll want to stay at home more? We might even have some children? I don't want to miss out on all that by being halfway up a mountainside somewhere. Or worse still, leave them fatherless.'

Posie swallowed. At this moment she hated Alaric. But she loved him too, and she felt that familiar desperate longing for him. 'So you *do* still want to marry me?'

'Very much so.'

'On Thursday?'

'At St George's Church. There'll be a couple of nice surprises along the way, but it will be a quiet little affair, as we agreed.'

It was beginning to sound fairly concrete. Posie smiled gingerly for perhaps the first time that evening.

'Come here, you gorgeous girl! You always look utterly magnificent when you get angry.' Alaric laughed. 'I wanted you all through dinner, you know. I was longing for you. I say, how I've missed you! And hang that bally magazine cover!'

And then she succumbed to his embrace, yielding up her lips to a kiss more spine-tingling than any she remembered, her body and soul his for the taking. They broke apart at last, reluctantly. Alaric's green gaze sought her out.

'I'm glad we cleared that up.'

'Mnnn. Me too.'

'Look, darling, this wretched thing about Silvia…'

'Yes?'

Was there more?

'There's something else I've got to tell you.'

Posie nodded, keeping hold of calm, trying not to snap. 'What is it?'

'Well…'

But just as his hesitation set off another warning bell in her head, a sharp step on the wet stones of the path behind them could be heard, as someone hiding nearby had decided they had seen and heard quite enough.

'Who's that?' Alaric reeled around, shouting into the darkness, uselessly.

But Posie thought she knew.

****

Seven

'About Silvia. You were saying?'

'Nothing. It really doesn't matter.'

On the way back they took a moment to stand in silence on the small jetty off the Campo San Vio and watch the smouldering Romagnoli Palace across the canal, breathing its last fiery melodrama into the wet night.

The fire crews had given up and the Palace had surrendered to its fate. The fire was out now, but a smoky heat could still be felt through the rain. The black windows and doors gaped open, a house of ghosts.

Posie squeezed Alaric's hand, which seemed to be trembling. His face was unusually grim.

'Don't look so glum, sweetheart. At least no-one was hurt, and you *did* manage to get Dickie's safe back for him, didn't you?'

He seemed to come to his senses at last. 'Of course. How foolish of me. It's only a bally building. And I'm sure old Salvarocca has got the thing worked out. He seems a sensible sort of chap. You know he knows Lovelace, don't you? Quite well, apparently. Some police case they worked on once involving Rome. Small world, isn't it?'

Posie raised an eyebrow in the silence.

'Indeed? I'd have thought Richard Lovelace would have

been more discerning when it comes to those he stays in touch with.'

They started to walk back to the guesthouse, arm-in-arm, both soaking. Up ahead someone was going into Mrs Persimmon's. Posie saw a long, hooded black silhouette crossing the threshold, illuminated briefly against the amber house light.

Alaric suddenly pulled up short: 'Look, darling, something rotten I'm afraid. Tomorrow you're going to have to play the tourist without me.'

It was a tense moment, breaking the fragile harmony. '*Sorry?*'

'I've got to search out something. It's very important. Precious.'

Posie thought of Alaric's things which had gone missing in the fire. It seemed entirely logical, if you weren't emotional about it, that those things would need to be replaced or re-ordered and it would take a little time.

'I suppose it can't be helped,' she replied levelly. 'I'm sure I can buy a Baedeker's guide and play the tourist well enough alone.'

Taking the key from her coat pocket she opened the front door. She noticed Alaric hung back in the rain.

'Are you coming up with me?'

Alaric shook his head uncomfortably. 'No can do, darling. I've got to get on right now.'

There was a pause. Posie's mind was racing. What on earth was there for him to do out on a cold, stormy night in Venice? What arrangements or replacements could Alaric possibly be organising *now*? All the shops would have closed hours ago.

Posie had given him the benefit of the doubt regarding his absence tomorrow, but this was entirely different. 'I see.'

But she didn't see at all. Any hopes of a romantic reunion were disappearing fast, despite that kiss just a few minutes before.

I won't beg, she thought, almost shivering uncontrollably.

'Darling Posie, you're cold. It's unforgivable of me to have kept you out here so long. Why don't you cut along to bed now and I'll join you later. You're up on the crummy side of the house, aren't you? What number room are you?'

No, Posie thought stubbornly. *I have my own honour to consider here.* Rage exploded inside her, pent up and with nowhere to go.

'Unless you have a dashed good explanation for where you are going right now, don't even try and come into my room, crummy or not.'

Alaric looked at her askance.

'No? Nothing to say?' she retorted. She grabbed at the wet umbrella almost savagely. 'Then I definitely don't want to see you later. Maybe not even tomorrow, or thereafter. Got it?'

And stumbling over the threshold, Posie pulled the heavy door behind her, leaving her fiancé out in the dreadful night. She stood on the doormat, almost panting, bent-double and breathless, as if she had run a huge race.

'Confound the man,' she muttered under her breath, shaking off the umbrella and twisting it into the communal stand.

In the shadows of the hall, lamps turned down for the night, Posie realised without much surprise that she wasn't the only one amidst the wet-weather gear. She looked up to see Lucy Christie peering at her hesitantly, almost hidden behind some bulky item of clothing which was glistening with rain. Lucy was extracting something from one of its voluminous pockets – what looked like a small dark-coloured bottle with a stopper.

'I was out, too.' The Countess's companion pointed at a black rubber cape. 'You would have fared better if you'd taken one of these big storm capes, Posie. They're for the guests' use, as well as all this carnival paraphernalia up here. I'm bone dry and I was out for a good hour, running to a late-night apothecary as Bella has one of her "heads" again. She needed something stronger than a Beechams Powder. Oh, my! Look at your lovely red coat! It looks like it's ruined. And you, you're blue with cold. Venice can be treacherous in winter: the wind is blowing as if it's the end of the world. Can I help you?'

Posie shook her head and peeled off her wet layers. 'It really is a dreadful night,' she agreed. 'I'll get a hot bath and then I'll feel better, I'm sure.'

'Fat chance! It's almost eleven now and there's only hot water in this place until seven. Talk about shabby gentility! I could go down and wake Jones for you, if you like? Say it's an emergency and get him to put a kettle on?'

'Please don't bother him. I'll manage.'

'Take this.' Lucy fished under her cardigan and brought out a small silver hip-flask. 'It's not particularly good stuff, but it's all I can get hold of. It might help you warm up. Or help you sleep?'

Posie took the bottle with thanks and watched as Lucy stood by the telephone table, fingers dancing over the cream paper ledger. From over by the hatstand in the very far corner there was a slight movement, something fluid in the darkness, and for a second Posie thought someone else, a third party, might be hiding there. That pin-prickly sensation came over her again. But the wind seemed to penetrate even here and she told herself it must have been a sudden draft.

Despite all the awful nonsense with Alaric just now, hurtful though it was, Posie focused on something entirely different which had nagged and nagged at her. It was nagging her again now.

'I say, Lucy. You speak Italian. Can you place a call for me? This needs good Italian, not just asking for a simple connection.'

The girl nodded. Posie went over to the telephone ledger and scanned it. It was exactly as she had left it: no further entries had been made. She gave Lucy her instructions and waited, arms crossed, as the girl placed a call straight to the Operator in Rome and fired off a volley of questions in a quick Italian which Posie couldn't follow.

A few minutes later Lucy replaced the receiver of the apparatus. She looked puzzled. 'There *have* been three calls made this evening from here,' she explained. 'All to the International Operator. But they definitely weren't connected on to Switzerland.'

'Tell me.'

'London. Whitehall. I asked several times but the Operator wouldn't give me the exact line.'

'Never mind.' Posie nodded thoughtfully and wrote her name in the ledger, for payment on the morrow. 'That's incredibly helpful. Thank you.'

Back in her room, on the crummy corridor where Lucy and Roger Valentine had also been billeted, Posie shed her wet garments and climbed into her flannel pyjamas. Having kicked her wedding outfit with some force under the bed, she towelled her hair dry as best she could and slavered on Pond's cold cream. She kept on all of her jewellery, just in case, and sat on the slightly damp counterpane of her bed, wishing there was a view to dawdle in front of, rather than this back alleyway filled with the sound of overflowing drainpipes and rain and mewling cats and occasional shouting. She wasn't ready for sleep. How could she possibly sleep? She took a swig from Lucy's silver hip-flask.

The liqueur tasted strange but she couldn't put her finger on why. Nice, but strange. Christmassy, even. She lay back on the pillows and traced an engraving on the side of the bottle. A fancy, leafy, old-fashioned composition which could be discerned as '*AA*'.

Thoughts of people she had met today were filling Posie's sleepy head, playing out like the start of a movie. Vivid characters swum in front of her eyes...

Bella Alladice, rich and grotesque but probably lying awake now with only her headache and a healthy dose of fear for company. Who would want to be in Bella's shoes, the recipient of horrible notes which spoke of dreadful things?

And a blonde man in a soft felt hat who had lied about who he was, and where exactly his orders were coming from. But *whose* orders in London was he following? And what was he doing here exactly? Surely he wasn't the simple commercial traveller he claimed to be?

And then Lucy Christie, and Dickie Alladice, and the maiden aunt and Roger Valentine, the efficient secretary... Something was off with all of them, that was for sure. None of them were quite what they seemed. Nor to be trusted. They formed an uneasy sea of uncertainties.

And Alaric, and that magazine cover. *He* was a sea of uncertainty, all by himself. Her eyes were closing. And then, just as a wave of sleep engulfed her like a warm, welcome blanket, a double knock sounded at Posie's door.

'Go away, Alaric,' she hissed. 'I told you I didn't want to see you again. I hope you got whatever it was done out there. Now goodnight.'

'This isn't your fiancé,' came a low, serious voice with a slight accent.

The voice was known to her.

She got up immediately and padded to the door and a pair of strong hands dragged her forcibly out.

****

Eight

The hands were icy cold and the sleeve-edges were damp, but the face was familiar.

Last time Posie had met the blonde man in front of her he had been dressed as a priest. Almost exactly two years ago. Then, she had been struck by how extraordinarily handsome he was, and now was no different. She felt a curious stab of something like excitement jolt through her whole being.

'You! I *knew* it was you!'

'Come with me,' whispered the man, putting a finger to his lips. 'I've been loitering around here until the coast was clear.'

'What, like you were loitering around earlier down by the Customs House, spying on me and Alaric, you mean?'

The man shrugged unapologetically. 'We can't talk here. The walls are paper thin. In fact, I think they *are* made of paper. Come to my room. You'll see why in a minute.'

It was fine, Posie breathed to herself. Bizarrely, she trusted the man, despite the subterfuge. After all, she had trusted his actions and his instincts in the past.

Posie let herself be led down the corridor, which was dark except for one flickering lamp, and then they turned off right, and right again down a tiny service corridor which was completely dark. They went up a small staircase. There was a strong scent of soap-powder lingering in the air, mingling with the smell of damp.

'In here.'

They ducked through a tiny, low doorway and the man closed the door gently behind them. He lit a match and then a candle. Posie looked around.

'Is this a cupboard?' She laughed. 'Does your Swiss watch company really pay you so little that you have to ferret yourself away up here?'

They were in a long laundry room, and the flickering light revealed wooden shelves ranged up the walls, filled with neat stacks of fraying towels and bedding. A small truckle bed had been made up on the floor, next to which was a wooden stool holding a black book, some pencils and a pair of glasses. A large battered suitcase, such as commercial travellers use, was the only other evidence that anyone was in occupation.

'Comfortable,' Posie announced, sarcastically.

The blonde man smiled for the first time. 'And sound-proof. No-one can hear us up here. I told Mrs Persimmon I was asthmatic, that I needed a very dry spot and I assumed she had an attic drying-room. She was happy to take a few shillings for it.'

'I'll bet.'

'But *this* is the real reason I wanted the room.' The man raised the candle and strode forward, casting light on a huge pair of ancient glass-doors, leading onto a balcony or roof garden. A step-ladder near the glass-doors and a pair of binoculars resting on top indicated what the man had been up to.

'The deck out there is the *altana*, where in the good old days fashionable Venetian ladies would sit to lighten their hair in the sunshine of an afternoon. Now it's just a balcony of rotting planks, and I won't risk your life by taking you out there with me. But the important thing is that it's the very front of the building.' He nodded. 'With a bird's-eye view out over the Grand Canal, and the Palace.'

'I see. Well, actually, I don't see.'

'Do sit.' The man pulled out the milking-stool for her, tipping its contents carelessly onto the floor. He sat cross-legged on the edge of his bed. Gingerly, Posie sat down. There were just a couple of inches between them and Posie realised the man was shivering. Up close his very short hair was damp, and his skin was still glistening with rain. He gestured to the hip-flask, which Posie realised was still clutched in her hand.

'*Ach*, can I have some? *Mein Gott*! What a miserable night!'

She passed it across meekly, feeling foolish. Too late she realised her bizarre appearance; no make-up, a towel around her shoulders, the thickly slavered-on cold cream, the dressing gown, the jewels, the hip-flask…

She pulled her dressing gown closed as tightly as she could, while the man took several pulls at the flask. He drew his hand across his mouth in disgust.

'That was dreadful! Almonds? Almond liqueur? Amaretti? It tastes like marzipan. Where did you get this from? That fat Countess who loves almonds so much?'

So that was it! That was why it had tasted of Christmas. Probably Lucy had filched some from her employer; she had said it was all she could get.

'You didn't *have* to drink it. It wasn't mine, as it happens. It belongs to Lucy Christie, the companion.'

'It was filthy, but at least I'm feeling warm again. It was freezing out on that Customs House jetty, and the hallway downstairs is pretty chilly too.'

'So you *were* hiding there, too? Listening to Lucy on the telephone?'

The two stared at each other for a full minute or so without speaking. The yellow light of the candle glimmered off his cream-coloured hair, unnaturally bright even in this dimness. He was still startlingly handsome, but he was older now, of course. And up close he seemed *much* older: late thirties, but looking ten years more than that. Posie noted how definite lines were etching themselves into the tanned skin around his deep-set, very blue eyes. The lines hadn't been there last time she had seen him, but who knew what he had been through since then? And she hadn't exactly got any younger, or any thinner, herself.

They had last met in strange and risky circumstances on New Year's Eve, 1921.

Posie and Inspector Lovelace had been working together on an undercover assignation, and Posie now found herself hurtling backwards through time, to that very dangerous night. To that unlucky party at Maypole Manor.

Atop a clifftop in Kent, overlooking the English Channel, an exclusive party had been in glitteringly full roar, when the guests had been joined very late in the evening by an uninvited thirteenth man; *this* man, this blonde man, who had been dressed as a priest, out on his bicycle late at night, seeking sanctuary during a snowstorm.

He had called himself Father Moriarty back then. But it had struck an incongruous note, as he had spoken with a marked German accent, as now. Posie hadn't believed him for a second: not about his identity, nor his real reason for arriving at that New Year's party. And as the night had worn on, when it had become evident that a murderer was in their midst, the blonde man opposite her had revealed that he was, in fact, a German medical doctor, a Dr Matthias Brenner, trained in the use and development of poisons, who had taken on a new identity and profession in England after the Great War.

And when Posie had watched him in action that night – his expert diagnosis of the cause of death of the murder victim, and his equal expertise at trying to assist the living – she had been convinced of his medical qualifications. Later, when Inspector Lovelace had had time to check out the man's identity before the Inquest which followed that case, it had all added up. The Inspector had professed himself happy with Dr Matthias Brenner and his documents, such as they were. Many Germans had sought sanctuary abroad after the war, and Lovelace was of the mind that 'Father Moriarty' should be left in peace.

'Posie Parker.' The blonde man nodded. 'I knew you were coming out here, of course. I was briefed on it. But I had no idea we would all be staying in the same guesthouse. That fire has changed many things, unfortunately.'

He indicated his spying apparatus. 'I had thought I might catch a glimpse of you across the way in that Palace, but you, of course, would never have been aware of me, stuck high up in the attic of this third-rate hostel.'

'Bad luck. I thought I saw you at Victoria Station yesterday. In that greasy spoon of a café? But I wasn't sure.'

'Yes, that was me. You gave me the shock of my life peering at me like that.'

Posie laughed. 'You made it here before me?'

He nodded. 'Only just. I travelled third-class, of course, but on the same train. I made sure to stick to my cabin so we didn't run into each other on either the boat or the train. I have no luggage except what you see here, so I got off the train well ahead of your first-class lot. I skipped across Venice as quickly as I could and got here a full hour before you. Enough time to see which way the smoky wind was blowing, and that I'd have to be very careful with you nosing around.'

'I thought it was you again downstairs in that salon of mirrors, earlier, but you wouldn't turn around and face me, would you? Or take your wretched hat off?'

'I was trapped in there; that young Count wouldn't stop talking to me. I swear I felt your eyes on my back. I managed to escape but I thought you might be suspicious of me. So I listened at the doorway when you were having dinner and I was immediately put on my guard when I heard you asking Mrs Persimmon about me. I didn't know whether to hope you'd drop the subject or whether to speak to you directly.'

'So you followed me?'

'Yes. I hoped to get a quiet moment with you, which didn't happen. And then I waited in the hallway here for you, but I didn't count on you chatting to that paid companion, or on both of you intercepting the telephone exchange. It was then that I knew the game was up and we had to talk before you blew my cover. Before you revealed who I was.'

Posie laughed. Everything was simply too strange.

'But that's the funny thing! I don't know who you are, do I?'

She looked at the man quizzically. '*Are* you Father Moriarty, with a parish near Dover, in Kent, like you told that doomed house-party two years ago? Or are you Doctor Matthias Brenner, as admitted to me over a poisoned corpse lying out in a snowstorm?'

Posie splayed her hands. 'You see, I can't reveal the name of someone I don't know. It turns out I never did know you, did I? And neither did Inspector Lovelace. You pulled the wool nicely over his eyes, too, didn't you? The Inspector even told me you had a little son in Dover, that you had a convincing photograph; the icing on the cake to prove you were really *real*. Or was that all a lot of nonsense too? Was any of it real?'

The man sighed. 'I'm sorry. If it's any consolation, it wasn't *me* doing the wool-pulling, as you say. I had orders, and orchestration, and evidence, including fake photographs of sons, all supplied from above. But you're right, I wasn't either of those people I told you about: I was there like you were, for work. For a higher authority, for those higher than the police.'

Posie swallowed, remembering the Whitehall telephone number which couldn't be given out by the Operator. She didn't know why she was surprised, or even why she cared.

'Very nice. So you're a spy? All that guff about being a doctor seeking a change after the war was a lot of old flimflam?'

The man frowned. 'I've never told anyone this before. But, you know, you're somehow the sort of woman I feel I can trust with my life.' He dropped his voice even lower. 'I may have to.'

Posie waited. She was used to the spilling of confidences, and for sudden revelations. But it needed time, and no sudden, hurrying movements or impatient promptings to halt proceedings. *Go on*, she thought, but did not say it aloud. She sat very still, waiting.

'My name is Max. I can't tell you my surname. It's almost forgotten, even to me.' The man swallowed, dredging up memories with an effort.

'I *was* a doctor, I couldn't have faked that. I trained and worked in Berlin, and then in the war I was put to work, with others in my department, developing poison gas. It was dreadful, like becoming a murderer. I almost had a breakdown, but I requested a transfer and got sent as a punishment to be an Army Medical Doctor on the front-line. I was expected to be killed. It was horrendous work also, but I kept going. You know all about that, though, don't you? You were an ambulance driver out there, among all that carnage.'

'For a while.' Posie chewed at her lip, impressed at his homework.

'Then there was a terrible offensive, with mines and everything. At the Messines Ridge. A terrible waste of life. It was June 1917.'

'*Messines?*'

Max frowned. 'That's right. Have I touched a raw nerve?'

'Not at all.' Posie waved the question away. But this was the second time this very evening she had been told about Messines. Johnny Alladice had died out there, changing the family hierarchy and fortunes forever.

'An Englishman was brought into my tent at the Clearing Station. He was obviously an officer, very senior. He was terribly injured, and I thought he would only last a couple of hours. It was late at night. Most of the staff were kept busy with our boys. I did what I could for the English fellow, nursing him almost single-handedly through the night, speaking to him in English, telling him I would get him home. I prayed for him. I realised he was a Catholic as he had a crucifix and a St Christopher on his person. I must have told him about myself too, in snippets, without realising it: how unhappy I had been in Berlin developing poison gas, how desperate I was to escape from the front-line. How I would get us both out of that hell-hole at Messines.'

Max rubbed at his eyes. He was lost in his memories of a dreadful war which had taken place six years before, but which would stay with him forever. As it would with Posie. She sat in the bleak silence, waiting for the link.

She prompted gently. 'The Englishman survived?'

'Yes, he recovered.' The German smiled, still proud of his efforts.

'And then, a week or so later, he just disappeared. Normally he would have been consigned as a prisoner-of-war, but he went missing. We couldn't search him out though, as our Clearing Station was being moved in a frantic hurry; we were retreating back over the Ridge. We had hundreds of other things to do. Two weeks later, when we had our new hospital up and running, I got a summons from the Quartermaster General, the real big chief, Erich von Ludendorff. It was the full works: ribbons and seals on the message and all the trimmings. All of my medical team were wondering what I had done wrong, what it was all about. Two men in military regalia were waiting for me on big black horses, right outside my tent. They had one spare horse for me, and they pretty much frogmarched me off. The other doctors and nurses watched me leave, open-mouthed. I didn't even have time to grab my medical bag or my identity papers.'

'How remarkably well-timed. Let me guess, that was the last day you were Max the doctor?'

The German gave a wry smile. 'That's right. The three of us rode in silence for a good couple of hours, up the coast. We were somewhere near Nieuport. They had a boat waiting there. Then they got me off my horse, and held a gun to my head. They spoke in British accents, said they were special agents and that I had been recommended to them. They asked if it was true that I wanted to get out of the German Army and would I be able to cut all ties in my former life?'

'You had no ties?'

'None to speak of. They asked me if I would join them as a special agent in Britain. In London at first, and then to be sent all over the place. And all the while they were holding a gun to my head. They were very firm that they would shoot me if I didn't agree to go with them; I might have blabbed, you see.'

'That gun must have been a real deal-clincher. Die or join MI5 or MI6 as a spy…'

Max scoffed. 'It's not MI5. Or MI6. But it's a similar set-up, and we are all aware of each other, but what I joined is in a league all of its own. We operate from the same buildings in London, with a cross-over of some staff, but it's largely stand-alone. We mainly deal with smuggling, and international arms-dealing.'

'Goodness. So all that guff about being a priest down on the south coast was a piece of elaborate staging because you were watching the smuggling around Maypole Manor?'

Max nodded. 'There were several routes and gangs I was watching, yes. It was a position I had occupied for almost a year. Normally the jobs are much shorter.'

'Isn't it awfully dangerous work?'

He shrugged. 'Yes. You must realise that your government is madly suspicious of foreign spies right now, and of German spies in particular.'

'Inspector Lovelace told me so, so he must be right. He's very nice, you know.'

A smile, and the crinkling of the deep worry-lines. 'He *is* nice. But he's easy to fool. *You* would have made a better Chief Inspector.'

Posie flushed under the cold cream.

Max laughed mirthlessly. 'I'm a gift for the British Government, and for my team. I'm a sort of double-bluff, you see: a tame German who works for the British to do their dirty work, who can suss out other potential German spies. I can never leave. I'll do this job until I die. If I went home I would be shot as a traitor.'

'And you can never tell anyone what happened, can you? It's too unbelievable.'

'You are the first, in fact the *only* person who knows this story.'

'And I believe you. You have my word that I won't tell a soul. Tell me, did you ever meet the man you saved at Messines? The Catholic with the St Christopher? The man who changed your destiny?'

Max shook his head. 'Never actively. But once, one hot summer evening, walking down a dim wood-panelled corridor at Whitehall, I thought I recognised him, walking past me. A tall, loping figure, fantastically well turned-out in an expensive suit. Of course, by the time I'd thought it might be him, and turned around, he was halfway down the corridor into the shadows. He had turned though, too, and had been staring at me in a similar fashion. I startled him and he hurried off, but not before I'd got a glimpse of a familiar face, cross-hatched with scars and shrapnel damage. I never saw him again. And I never asked after him, either.'

'Extraordinary.'

They stared at each other. At last Posie cut the silence with a whisper. 'So what are you doing *here*?'

'I can't tell you that. It's a short mission, though. It needs attention this week. Absolutely nothing to do with *you*, I can assure you.'

'Is it something to do with the fire, or the Corsetti gang?'

At his silence she continued. 'Is it anything to do with the threats being made against the Countess? I'm guessing you know about that?'

'Of course. I think it would be surprising if anyone *didn't* know. That little party are all running scared: the chatty little Count told me everything. And then I heard it all again when you and Alaric were talking on the jetty.'

He rose. 'I really can't tell you why I'm here. But what I can tell you is that I'm nobody's avenging angel. Or guardian angel, for that matter. *You* will have to step into that role for the Countess yourself, if you so wish. I am a mere mercenary, sent where I'm told. I'm a good man, but I'm not the good guy here, I'm sorry to say. I don't save people anymore. I obey orders, that's all.'

Posie felt she was being dismissed. She stood up. Max was now standing quite motionless on the top step of his ladder.

'Goodnight then.'

But Max, binoculars trained on his quarry, motioned to her with a crooked finger. 'Come here. There's room for two. Just.'

Posie frowned. But she did as she was told. She stood right next to Max, and she could smell his sweaty, woody scent beneath the dry overpowering soap-powder of the small space.

'Look.'

When she looked out through the glass she saw black night, and nothing else. Then came a faint glimmer of the red smouldering light of the Romagnoli Palace opposite. But that was it.

'Sorry, I forgot. Take these.' Max handed her the binoculars and Posie adjusted them slightly. From here there was a clear view of almost the entire Palace, all of its fire-beaten floors. She roved up and down, once and then twice. She waited. Nothing.

'What am I looking for?'

'Keep looking. There it is again.'

Hurriedly Posie trained the view-finder back, just in time to see what looked like a flashlight waver in and out, somewhere on about the third floor of the Palace. It disappeared. She kept watching and suddenly another flashlight, this time smaller, came from up near the top floors.

She looked at the German quizzically: 'So? That's probably just the Commissario's men doing a late-night check. He's probably got watchmen stationed over there.'

'The Palace is not fit to go inside. He told you all earlier. I listened in. And there are no instructions for his own men to risk life and limb in such a dangerous place.'

'So who is it?'

There was a dreadful pause. Turning, and looking down at Posie for an instant before gently taking the binoculars back, Max said in a low, hollow voice: 'What did Alaric say he was doing tonight? I heard him. He told you to go to bed alone because he had to *get on with something*. That, over there, is the "something".'

Posie found her mouth opening and shutting. 'But there are *two* lights.'

'Clever girl. He may have asked someone along to help him out. I just thought I would mention where Alaric was, and what he was doing.'

Rather than being with me.

'What is Alaric looking for?'

Max remained glued to his viewer. 'I have my own suspicions but you'll have to ask him yourself. Didn't he say he was after something precious?'

Posie stood down and moved to the door, crazy thoughts flooding her brain. Silhouetted against the window, with his back to her, Max spoke again, and Posie struggled to catch his words.

'Be careful, Posie. There is evil in this guesthouse. Even I, hardened as I am, can feel it. But it's not as bad as the evil which is being done against *you*.'

Posie widened her eyes in fright. 'I'm sorry?'

'That man. *That* man across there. Alaric. *Ach*, he doesn't deserve you. You're a clever girl in everything else. Can't you just wise up to the fact that he's a thoroughly bad lot? I don't think he means to be, but he just can't make decisions, or *good* decisions anyway. He's all over the place, he hardly knows you're here, does he?'

Anger flooded through Posie. She had been thinking the same thing not half an hour before, but she was damned if she would hear it from someone else. Someone she hardly knew, unasked for. She flushed an angry red.

'Watch yourself, sir. I'm jolly well marrying that man on Thursday.'

Max turned and stared at Posie full-on this time, and there was an uncomfortable crackle of something like electricity, or anger, or a connection of some sort flowing between them.

'Oh, but *are* you? Why don't you go around to that little English church and check? Go tomorrow. I think you'll find the wedding isn't going ahead but Alaric can't bring himself to tell you. He just pretends everything is okay...'

'Alaric's just out of sorts,' interrupted Posie wildly. 'That's all. The fire hasn't helped.'

Max tutted. 'That's what you think. Actually it's helped him a lot. You can hide things in a fire, or make excuses for things which were never supposed to be there. But I've done my duty. I've told you now. It's up to you what you do with this information.'

But Posie had heard quite enough. She stumbled

through the door, down the stairs and along the crummy corridor, back to where her room was located.

As she dashed along, she stopped suddenly as she saw a slim figure of a girl shimmy through the door into Roger Valentine's room. It was Lucy Christie, on some late-night assignation.

Reaching her own room, and closing the door as quickly as she could behind her, she found cold beads of sweat clinging to her skin beneath the remnants of her face-mask. She locked the door behind her.

It had been a long, long day.

****

PART TWO

VENICE

(Wednesday 21st November, 1923)

Festa della Madonna della Salute

Nine

Posie awoke early, pulled on a dark red tweed suit and presented herself downstairs for breakfast by eight o'clock sharp with an icy efficiency which she recognised as purely an instinct for survival. She put on all of her wedding sapphires again in a spirit of defiance and added a shockingly red lipstick for good measure. She was going to be a tourist for the morning, and she'd make sure she looked fabulous.

She had resolved not to think a jot more about Alaric, or of the strange German spy she had re-encountered last night. It helped that neither of them were breakfasting. The small dining-room was empty but for Jones, loitering at the long buffet table which boasted an impressive array of hastily-bought local pastries and sweets.

As she ate a slice of slightly damp toast and drank her morning Assam, Posie concentrated on Bella Alladice's plea for help the evening before, and she made mental notes of all the things she needed to investigate with a cool brusqueness which surprised even herself.

She rose when Bella Alladice entered the room, accompanied by her companion. Lucy took a tray and started to load it up and Posie went to tackle the Countess, who had sat down heavily in a far corner, looking puffy and tired in an enormous tweed day suit the colour of fresh candy-floss. A black leather folio stuffed with thick documents sat at the Countess's side, together with a sleek fountain pen. Posie explained about her touristy morning, and asked if she could borrow Lucy.

'It's for the language, really.' This was a lie, as Posie just fancied some company, but didn't like to admit as much.

In an undertone she whispered, 'I've had several thoughts, actually, about your, er, your *situation*. I'm going to investigate a bit while I'm out this morning, make some calls and so on. I'll try and give you some sort of report by the end of the day.'

The Countess nodded in satisfaction. 'You're welcome to Lucy: in fact, you'll be doing me a favour taking her out. I need to get through some business matters this morning.' She glanced at the black leather folder, frowning. 'It's Roger's half-day off, and he's left me with all of this to look at. I need to be alone to concentrate fully. And I need to make some calls of my own from here. I look forward to your report later on.'

And so they left at eight-thirty, and by ten o'clock Lucy and Posie had industriously trailed around the dark but impressive St Mark's Cathedral; its stolen saints and secrets glittering squatly in a sparse candlelight. They had stopped for Posie to buy small touristy presents in the square, at G. Pagan's, a smart little establishment selling sunglasses and leather bags. Posie had bought presents for Dolly and for her secretary Prudence, and even for Chief Inspector Lovelace's small daughter, Phyllis, for whom she stood godmother. They had then queued for tickets for the Doge's Palace, but had found themselves too late for a morning-slot, so they had purchased afternoon passes instead.

They both stood shivering now on the jetty outside the Doge's Palace, at the end of the small square beside St Mark's Cathedral. Posie looked up at the twin columns which marked the entrance to the city, one column topped by the prowling dark lion of St Mark, the other, more obscurely, by a pale St Theodore, looking calmly down from his somewhat perilous position atop a forlorn-looking stone crocodile.

Why St Theodore? And why a crocodile?

Posie had asked both these questions of their tour guide in the Cathedral, who hadn't seemed to know exactly why this unique combination greeted visitors to the city. It seemed likely that, as so much with Venice, St Theodore and the crocodile had been stolen on some long-ago pilfering expedition when Venice was first born and in need of some authenticity, when *any* authenticity would do. The body and the legend of St Mark too, had been stolen in just such a way. Posie looked at the place afresh: it was an odd city, for sure, a vast beauty built on absolutely nothing. The women looked out over the wide sweep of St Mark's Basin, a busy mix of barges and paddle-steamers bravely cresting the swell. They watched the empty gondolas and sandolis moored together, rocking backwards and forwards, as a vaporetto churned through the water, packed with rows and rows of tourists.

'I've been here over a year now, and I still think this is the most beautiful place in the world,' said Lucy at last, watching a fishing flotilla as it headed out to the open sea. 'It has the best light I've ever seen. I like to paint watercolours of the changing colours, of the fusion between sky and water, whenever Bella can spare me. But it's also a dangerous place. All this beauty, with no foundations. It could all collapse in a minute. It *will* collapse one day.'

Lucy gestured up at the huge red-brick Campanile rising above them. 'Like that. The Bell Tower of St Mark's. Ten centuries of being the most important monument in the city, then it collapsed in on itself twenty-two years ago. This here is only a recent remake. But you wouldn't think it, would you? It's been done so well. Nothing here is quite as it seems.'

Posie eyed Lucy keenly, more certain than ever that she knew the girl from somewhere, but still unable to place her.

She's right, Posie thought to herself. *This is a dangerous place, a place where nothing is quite what it seems. Some of us might not be able to survive it.*

Although the storm of the day before had blown itself out, grey clouds scudded through the skies in an angry fashion, sweeping across the watery mass, and the promise of more rain was not far off. You could taste the sulphur in the air. Posie tried to avoid looking out over the basin towards the jetty on the opposite side of the water where she had been with Alaric the night before. She attempted to blot out the image of his face, the memory of those two flashing lights in the Palace, searching…

'Coffee, Lucy?' she said abruptly, shivering into her still-damp coat. 'And I need a telephone, too. Any ideas where we can find both?'

'Well, there's the Café Florian, of course,' replied the girl hesitantly, indicating backwards, towards the main square. 'You know, the oldest café in the world, with windows onto the square. Some people sit there for hours, watching the world go by.'

'Casanova's hunting-ground?' Posie smiled. 'It's famous, isn't it?'

'Yes.' Lucy nodded. 'They say he met a good many of his conquests there as it was pretty much the only place in Venice where women of good repute could be seen out in public. But it's dashed expensive, for all it's still the hottest spot in town. Otherwise we could just head back to the guesthouse?'

Waving the cost aside, Posie insisted on finding a table at a window in the Café Florian, which turned out to be an art-encrusted jewel of a coffeehouse, reminding Posie with a sharp pang of the Rivoli Bar at the Ritz in London.

Leaving Lucy to order coffee and cakes, Posie walked to the back of the establishment, down a black-and-white tiled corridor, and found a baize-covered cubicle housing the public telephone apparatus. Posie sighed with relief that the corridor was quiet and that no-one seemed to be hanging around. She managed to get the International Operator in Rome to put her call through to London fairly easily, and then she asked for Scotland Yard.

At the connection she asked for Chief Inspector Lovelace.

Posie thought of London and all that was familiar, including Richard Lovelace. She pictured him now, standing in his office, loitering at the window with its view of the grey London skyline and the Embankment, a mug of tea in hand.

How reliable he was. How comforting.

'No can do, madam.' The receptionist at Scotland Yard sighed down the phone. 'The Chief Inspector is not here. Is there anyone else you wish to speak to?'

'Er...' Posie had been about to ask for the reliable and ever-efficient Sergeant Binny, but with a shock which still surprised her she remembered he was dead: killed in the line of duty just this summer, while they had all been working on a case together.

'Sergeant Rainbird?'

Rainbird was a good second-best, the Chief Inspector's right-hand man now that Binny, a favourite, and tipped to become an Inspector himself just before his death, was gone. It must have been uncomfortable for Rainbird to be filling the dead man's shoes, and Posie found herself feeling particularly unenvious of his lot.

Rainbird came on the line sharpish. After the cursory greeting and niceties, Posie asked where Lovelace was.

'Out on a case, Miss. A week long, he said, and very confidential. Can't even tell you *where* he's gone, not even if I wanted to. He didn't share it with me.' There was a sniff of something like regret down the line, but it could have been a cold. 'Can *I* help you with anything, Miss?'

Posie didn't go into the details of the Alladice case. But she pulled out her small silver notebook and pencil.

'I need information on a few people,' she said in a low voice. 'Anything you can get your hands on: police records, war records, involvement in anything suspicious, any declared or undeclared business interests these people have. Anything *unusual*...'

She heard the Sergeant swallow. He was obviously busy. But he knew the ways into the Chief Inspector's good books, and one of these was by helping Posie, whenever possible. *Not* to do so might have adverse effects for his future: the future that had been Binny's, which was now being handed to him on a plate. A plate he merely had to keep spinning, not letting it fall.

'Right you are then, Miss. Let's have the names.'

He took them down carefully, asking for a couple of repetitions of spelling. 'When did you want this for?'

'In about an hour, Sergeant.'

She heard a sharp intake of breath down the line, and some muffled shouting in the background. 'I'm here at this jolly nice café just now.' She checked the number on the telephone apparatus. 'It's 0078 on the Italian Exchange. Café Florian, if they ask. Or if I'm gone, or its much later than an hour, try Mrs Persimmon's guesthouse. It's 0065 on the Exchange. Do you think that's possible, Sergeant?'

'Anything is *possible*, Miss. But is it likely?' Another intake of breath. 'I'll see what I can do. One hour, you say? Blimey!'

The line went dead, and Posie stood holding the receiver, hearing the pips go. The London Operator cut in: 'Is that all, modom? Can I make another connection for you? You have three minutes left on this line.'

'Er, righty-ho. No, thanks. Oh! Wait a second!' An idea, perfectly formed and clear as a bell, came to her. 'Connect me through to Holborn, 1267.'

'Very good, modom.'

As she waited, Posie checked her watch and thought longingly of her small detective agency up on the second floor of a corner building on shabby Grape Street, just off Shaftesbury Avenue. How she loved it.

At this time of the morning there would normally be coffee being made, not very well, admittedly, by Prudence. And Len, her partner in the firm, would be settling down in the clients' waiting room, handing around a bag of Lyons' cakes. The lights would all be blazing as the office caught no natural light at all until the early afternoon, and on a November day such as today the chances of even afternoon light were very slim. Would any new cases have come in? Posie swallowed: she missed the office awfully. And she missed London. She would never give either of those things up.

'Connecting you now.'

After a good many rings, a breathless adolescent voice answered the telephone, in purest cockney. 'Mornin'! Grape Street Bureau 'ere! 'Ow can we 'elp you?'

'*Sidney?*' she asked, trying not to sound too shocked. 'Is that you? Where on earth is Prudence? Or Len, for that matter? It's not part of your job description to be answering the telephone.'

'Oh, but I don't mind, Miss,' replied Sidney, the office-boy, with some pride. Sidney had only been taken on since the summer and had proved himself remarkably useful in that time. Even Len, who had been doubtful about the arrangement, seemed to be coming around to the idea of Sidney becoming a permanent member of staff.

'And how are yer doin' Miss? Havin' a luvverly time, I hope? You married yet, Miss? Are congratulations in order just yet?'

'No, Sidney, I am not married yet, and so congratulations are not in order.'

'Oh!' She could hear Sidney blowing out his breath, slightly lost for words.

'Where are the others?'

He piped up cheerily again, on firmer ground. 'Miss Prudence 'as had to go home on account of her poor old mum. She's 'ad a funny turn, or something. And Mr Len, he's just nipped out for a spot of milk and a few treats from the pub downstairs.'

'Mnnn. While the cat's away…'

'What, Miss?'

'Nothing.'

'So it's just me 'ere, mannin' the fort!'

'I can see that. Any clients?'

'None. Place is quiet as the grave. Bit of luck, innit?'

'I see. Well, yes; let's be grateful for small mercies. As luck would have it, it was *you* I was after, Sidney. I need you to go out and get something for me, sharpish. Got some paper to note this down?'

'Yes. Course I 'ave, Miss.' The boy was as eager as a terrier and Posie almost smiled.

'Head down to Somerset House on the Strand, will you? The Wills Department. Cut along on the tram. It's a public record office, and so you can look at the Will I want, provided you pay for the pleasure. Take a shilling from petty cash. I trust you – the key is taped under Prudence's seat.'

'Right-ho! Whose Will do you want me to collect?'

'You won't be able to collect anything, or make notes. You might just have to memorise what you can, they're usually pretty strict in these places. The Will I want is a chap named John Alladice. His Will is stored by date of death and that will be… Hang on.' Posie desperately tried to remember Max's story about the Messines Ridge the night before. She nodded. 'His death was sometime in the second week of June, 1917. A war death. I can't be more specific.'

'What am I lookin' for exactly, Miss? Wills are pretty complicated, ain't they?'

'Cut through all the legal jargon and get to the end. That's the only important bit in a Will. Where the fella says who he wants his things to go to. I want to see how John Alladice divided his money up.'

Posie remembered Bella's comment about Johnny leaving her his business shareholdings, and how he had cut out his brother on purpose. 'See if he makes any interesting remarks about anyone in particular.'

'Got it, Miss. I'm on to it now. Where can I reach you?'

Posie gave the same numbers and returned to the table, where, much to her irritation, she found their lovely window seat had been taken over. Aunt Minnie was now perched there, but it was Dickie Alladice, dressed casually in an expensive pinstriped suit which perfectly matched his pearl-grey eyes, who was holding court, having ordered liqueur coffees for the whole table.

Dickie beamed at Posie, and she was suddenly struck by how handsome he really was, something she hadn't appreciated when he had been a nervous wreck the night before. Posie saw for the first time the man Dickie Alladice really was: putting people at their ease, luminous with a ready smile. Alaric had been right.

'Posie, what-ho! I was just saying what a coincidence it is to meet like this! We never normally come in here, do we, Auntie Minnie? But we were on our way back from the notary and we saw Lucy adorning the window, and we couldn't resist. We hope you don't mind us gate-crashing like this?'

'Not at all. It's lovely to see you both. We're quite the party now, aren't we?'

Dickie had evidently been talking about moving the Romagnoli party *en masse* over to the Hotel Metropole, one of the top hotels in town, at his own expense. He looked at Posie, as if for her approval.

'I think we may be altogether more comfortable at the Metropole. Mrs Persimmon has done her very best but it must be an awful strain on her having us all to stay. The Count is over at the Palace now with the insurance men and that big polie inspector – a dreadful job, it will take all day – and I'm sure they'll say there is no hope of anyone moving back in there for several months. If *ever*, in fact. And we can't stay on at that guesthouse. It's beyond all reasonable expectations.'

But Posie was miles away, thinking of petite little Giancarlo, the Count, tasked with such a day's sombre work; staggering through the ashes of his family's heritage. She didn't envy him, that was for sure.

Dickie Alladice was addressing Posie directly now. 'Shall I have the pleasure of adding you and Alaric to my tab at the Metropole Hotel, or will you be going on somewhere else for your honeymoon, do you know?'

All eyes turned to look at her. Posie was just taking a swig of the very alcoholic coffee and she coughed a good deal by way of convenient response.

A honeymoon?

Lucy cut in. 'Dickie, you horror! You might not know it, but it is a gentleman's prerogative to take his bride away to a surprise location for their honeymoon. And if Mr Boynton-Dale *has* shared that surprise with Miss Parker, it is likewise her prerogative not to reveal it to anyone else.'

Posie smiled determinedly, anger boiling up inside her at looking a complete fool, and thankful to Lucy for papering over a huge omission. She and Alaric hadn't even discussed a honeymoon. What else didn't she know about her upcoming nuptials or the man she was about to marry?

She didn't even know *where* Alaric was right now, or what he was doing. It seemed she knew precious, precious little. She cursed herself silently for having put all her trust and reliance in his plans. When she should have organised things herself. Like usual.

She turned the full force of her lovely blue gaze on Dickie. 'It's so kind of you, Dickie. But it's as Lucy says, I think it's all going to be a lovely surprise.'

A lovely surprise! What rot! She was certain there was no honeymoon planned. What was it that Max had said up in the attic last night? That Alaric was 'a thoroughly bad lot' and unable to make decisions. And that Posie should have wised up to that fact by now.

Dickie Alladice slapped his wrist playfully. 'Of course. Posie, how silly of me. Forgive me, won't you? Next I will be demanding details of your wedding outfit, and then where will we all be?'

He lit up an Abdullah and offered the tin of Turkish cigarettes all around. Everyone accepted except Posie and she watched how Lucy was quite comfortable in Dickie's presence, sitting next to him, blowing smoke rings, laughing at his jokes, putting an occasional hand on his knee, but somehow remaining dignified and apart; very at odds with Aunt Minnie, who was awkward with her smoke and on her way to getting blindingly drunk.

Posie wondered idly about Lucy.

Was Dickie Alladice and all of his wealth her ultimate goal? Was Lucy playing a long game, keen to escape the poverty she had ended up in by marrying this rich, showy man? But then Posie recollected the previous night: how she had seen Lucy flitting through the shadows of the dark corridor into Roger Valentine's room.

What exactly *was* her game? Was it a dangerous one? And how did that concealed diamond ring she wore fit in? Who had given her that? One of the two men out here? Or someone else entirely?

Posie stared out of the window, looking into the main square, where rain had begun to lash down, sending the tourists running in umbrella-huddled masses to the very edges of the square, along with the pigeons. A lone cellist was battling on, playing without music or shelter, right in the centre of the big grey space. The Café Florian was well glazed, and she couldn't hear the tune, but Posie thought suddenly and painfully of Richard, her elder brother, who had been musical, and had played the cello as a boy. How she missed him. He had also died in 1917.

What would he have said to see her now? What advice would he have given? Would Richard have told her to get up, right this minute, and leave this toxic city where nothing seemed or felt right? Where even the man she had waited for for two months seemed completely different.

Two months.

She must have looked lost inside her daydream, and indeed, her mind was following a new and suddenly arresting train of thought.

It had been two months since Bella Alladice had made a Will. And two months since the spying and threats had started up. But was it a coincidence too far? Posie's thoughts were suddenly interrupted: from somewhere nearby she heard something whispered very low, something extremely surprising. And her ears pricked up.

'Don't worry, darling, it will be all right now, you'll see. Not long to go. Hold your nerve.'

Posie turned just in time to see Dickie patting Lucy's leg under the table, a gesture of reassurance. But reassurance of *what* exactly? She looked swiftly away. What had she just witnessed? Posie bit at her lip, absorbed, and then she heard a shout go up from their own table.

'What the blazes?'

Dickie Alladice was rising to his feet, looking into the main square.

Out in the rain, a middle-aged man in a bedraggled wet black suit, all of a fluster, was running among the covered arches, coming in their direction. He was red in the face, and peering helplessly into the windows of each and every café and shop he passed by.

'It's Jones!' Lucy declared, standing up. 'He looks like he's about to pass out. What on earth is wrong?'

Dickie rapped on the window sharply and Jones looked up. Relief washed over his troubled face. He paused in the downpour, bent-double, hands on knees, out of breath, before straightening up and making for the gilded doors of the Florian.

Posie suddenly felt ill. She tore through the passage to the front door, almost hauling Jones over the fancy tiled threshold. The gold grandmother clock in the Florian's entrance hall was just striking eleven o'clock.

'What's happened?' Posie demanded in as controlled a voice as she could manage. But she *knew*, and she knew that her investigation and the report which she was carefully compiling was too late. That it was all futile. It had been futile from the start.

'It's the Countess, isn't it?' she hissed at Jones, as the others came crowding out into the passage.

'Aye, Miss. Mrs Persimmon sent me to look for you all.'

He had got his breath back. Posie felt a sense of dread at the inevitability of it all. The black-and-white floor was rolling up at her in uneasy waves. Or was it just the whisky coffee?

'Come on, man.' Dickie Alladice was upon them. 'So what is it?'

'It's your sister, sir.' Jones collapsed in a wheezy ball.

'What about Bella?' Dickie's voice had gone very high. It was barely a whisper.

'Dickie.' Posie touched his arm gently. 'I'm very much afraid that she's dead.'

* * * *

Ten

On entering the guesthouse, they were met by Mrs Persimmon, flowery overall immaculate, but sick with fear; a self-appointed sentry to her own dining-room, holding the key high above her head as if she thought it might drop into a swirling flood. When she saw Posie and Dickie and Lucy and Aunt Minnie and Jones she almost collapsed with relief, her face telling its own horror-story.

'Oh, thank goodness! I didn't know what to do! I locked the room as soon as we discovered the Countess, me and Mr Jones that is. No-one has been in, and I've telephoned for that fancy fat fascist policeman who was here last night. But of course that may take time, everything here does! I hope I did right. Oh, the poor Countess! God rest her soul.' She crossed herself dramatically. 'And imagine! The poor young Count, he doesn't even know as yet! I don't know where to find him.'

Posie found she had notepad and pencil in hand. Automatically she was taking charge. She reached for the dining-room key and nodded grimly as it was entrusted to her.

'You did very well, Mrs Persimmon. You and Jones found the body together, you say?'

'That's right. We had gone in together to take away the coffee things. The Countess insisted on having a cup at nine-thirty sharp. We entered later, about ten-thirty, and found her like that. Terrible.'

'Quite. But Commissario Salvarocca and the Count are just over the way, at the Romagnoli Palace. Perhaps Jones here would be so good as to fetch them? If he can bear to.'

Jones nodded and disappeared in a flash, keen to escape.

Posie looked over at Aunt Minnie who had collapsed on the bench in the hallway, gasping and gaping like some sort of dying moth. She would be no use at all here. Posie rounded up Lucy and Dickie in a business-like fashion.

'I need you both to enter the room with me. I must warn you, it won't be very nice. Don't touch anything: the police will be checking for fingerprints later, but someone with some experience must have a look at Bella now. Every second which passes is crucial: evidence is literally ebbing away.'

Dickie looked gobsmacked: '*Evidence?* By Gad, of what exactly?'

Posie inserted the key without answering and opened the door. The green dining-room looked much as it had that morning at breakfast, but it was now cleared of all food and drink. On further inspection, a chair and table had toppled over and Bella was lying on the floor.

They walked over, Posie leading, the other two bobbing behind reluctantly. Mrs Persimmon stood guarding the open doorway, anxious not to miss the drama.

Accustomed to death as she was, Posie could never quite get used to it. She felt a horrid distaste at the job in hand. She wished that the Commissario could get along quickly.

Posie dropped to her knees, aware of the others looming behind her, and the awful expectant stillness pressing down on them all. There were some urgent voices of new arrivals now whispering in the corridor outside, men, most probably, but Mrs Persimmon's excited chatter was surging and rising above them all.

Posie focused.

Bella Alladice was lying on her side, one enormously fat hand above her head, clutching at the tablecloth, her ruby ring dazzling savagely even in here, a room with a bad light and no windows. The other hand was holding a silver hip-flask. Up close, Posie could see there was a carved inscription of '*AA*' on the flask, and she frowned: the flask looked identical to the one Posie had borrowed from Lucy the night before, and which she had left outside Lucy's door very early this morning by way of return.

A pen and ink were scattered around the place haphazardly, together with a cup of coffee, empty of most of its contents. A bowl of pink Jordan almonds were dropped everywhere across the lurid swirls of the green carpet. It was obvious that Bella Alladice had had some sort of a seizure before dying. Her face was obscured by the black leather folio, lying open.

On the floor behind Bella lay the Persian cat, Petrucci, curled up tightly and rigidly in death, but somehow looking a lot more peaceful than his mistress. Obviously his luck had run out and his ninth life had been his very last.

Dickie dropped to his knees beside the body, carefully trying to avoid the pools of coffee and vomit about the place, panting with concentration. He was removing the folio from his sister's face and taking off his exquisite pinstriped jacket at the same time, looking very much like he was about to cover his sister up with it, as if she had been dragged from the sea and was feeling the cold.

'Dickie!' cried Posie in alarm. 'Please don't touch the body, whatever you do.'

'I'm sorry, but she looks so dreadful. Bella would have hated to be seen like this! Shall I put the folio back?'

'No. You'd better leave it as it is now.'

Posie looked at the dead girl's face which was now exposed and she shuddered. Bella Alladice, never pale at the best of times, had gone to meet her maker the colour of a ripe tomato. Her eyes were bloodshot orbs and her mouth was frozen into a surprised 'o' of indignation. Vomit was splashed around liberally. Posie walked around the body carefully, at pains not to move anything, but trying to take in all the detail.

Lucy made a sobbing noise. 'Oh, my! Her drops!'

Posie frowned. 'Drops?'

The girl wrung her hands bitterly: 'Her heart drops! I wasn't here to give them to her! This is my fault! They were for an emergency such as this, for a heart attack. I was in charge of Bella's medicines, buying them and administering them. She had the drops with her, of course, in her jacket pocket, but she was useless at taking them herself.'

Dickie Alladice's normal high colour was now completely washed from his face. He had sat down on a nearby dining chair.

'It wasn't your fault, Lucy,' he whispered softly. 'Don't tear yourself up about it. Maybe Bella didn't have enough time to reach for them? It looks as if it was very quick, which is something.'

Turning to Posie he shrugged and explained: 'My sister had a weak heart. She was enormously fat, *hideously* fat. Knew she had to do something about it but kept guzzling anyway. She'd been prescribed medicine accordingly. Oh, Bella! You little fool. How I hate you! I *hate* you!'

Posie stared at the man. Grief took people over in funny ways. He saw her unwavering gaze. 'Oh, I know I sound foul. But I *do* hate her. I hate Bella for leaving me. She was all I really had in the world. My baby sister! She brought it on herself! For all her worries about stalkers! She killed herself…'

Fortunately Posie saw the Commissario appear at the doorway and beckoned him over. He marched across the room with a quiet authority, dragging along Count Giancarlo, who seemed completely stunned.

Posie offered her condolences to the Count, who had

ignored the awful splashes of liquid and immediately sunk to his knees by the body, as if he were about to take his wife up in an embrace. He had to be dragged to his feet by Salvarocca.

'Bella?' the Count whispered in such a low voice that Posie could hardly hear him. 'My Bella! Dead? *Non capisco.* I don't understand.' He wrung his hands. 'How well we understood each other! Never will I find another like her.'

'You mean you'll never find another woman as *rich*?' spat Dickie Alladice accusingly, who had sprung to his feet, riven by a sudden, intense, wholly-unexpected anger. He faced the Count head-on. 'A woman who will overlook your *wandering* ways, you mean? You can rot in hell for all I care! And don't think you'll get another penny from her!'

The Count raised an eyebrow and held his head high and imperious. Posie found herself liking the man the better for his show of sudden integrity. 'How can you talk of money at such a time, Dickie? Of course I'll get nothing. That was never the idea. I *know* that.'

But Dickie was losing control, pushing up his shirtsleeves like a man possessed, like a man about to enter the boxing-ring.

'You've got a great deal to answer for, Giancarlo,' Dickie Alladice snarled. 'Bella might have died a natural death here, but I'll never forgive you for making the last few weeks a nightmare. Bella was miserable. What was going on? And that dreadful note about the hidden room! You sure as blazes reacted strangely over that. I hold you entirely responsible.'

Posie looked from one to another of the men: she remembered Bella telling her that her husband Giancarlo had acted oddly when the hate mail had arrived.

The Count was shaking his head vehemently, his hands up in denial: 'My good man, you know you're just upset. None of the awful things which happened recently have been anything to do with me. I loved Bella, in my way.'

Dickie Alladice lunged. 'In "*your way*"?' Dickie spun out of control but hit his aim: 'Take that!'

The Count crumpled, nursing a bloody nose. The Commissario bent to help the nobleman, and Lucy was pulling at Dickie, ineffectively. Dickie resisted, for all the world looking as if he would spring another punch.

'Enough!' Posie announced from her position down by the corpse.

But then she saw that a slight commotion had started over near the door, and among all the chaos of what looked like a great many uniformed policemen, the shapes of two men in civvies, both still wearing wet hats and raincoats, were hurrying into the room, taking form. As the men pushed further in, she realised it was Alaric and the secretary, Roger Valentine. Alaric was white-faced, ashen. She looked up at him, but he had sought out Dickie first, not her.

'I say, old boy. Posie's right,' he said coolly. 'That's enough.'

Alaric had grabbed Dickie by both arms, getting him into a sort of body lock.

'I heard the stuff you were saying just now. It was all complete rot! I know you're upset. This is a tragedy. But you can't go around accusing people of things. Or attacking them. Not your brother-in-law, anyhow. You need to give it up, Dickie, old chap. See sense.'

Posie watched, detached, as if in a dream, as Alaric brought out a gaudy-coloured, unfamiliar-looking packet of cigarettes – Mughals – and broke the seal of the new packet with his teeth. But the big police chief shook his head vigorously:

'Please, Mr Boynton-Dale, don't smoke. I don't want any other substance or smells in the room. I have called for our Police Surgeon and we're waiting on him now. I want him to view the body as it is. That's why we haven't covered the girl up, although it would be more dignified – I agree – to do so. In fact, it would be best if you all got out of here. Moved out, *now*.'

'As you think best, sir.'

But no-one seemed capable of moving. Like blurry images in a child's kaleidoscope suddenly coming into focus, Posie looked around the room. She took in Alaric's defeated shrug, and Dickie's despair; she observed Roger Valentine and Lucy standing together, both very pale, talking in low undertones. The secretary kept throwing sickened, frightened looks over at Bella Alladice, as if his employer might get up off the floor at any minute and chide him for being late back from his morning out. Commissario Salvarocca was looking distinctly uneasy.

'Come now,' he was repeating firmly. 'Everybody out.' The group were slowly moving into the corridor.

But that comment of his just now, about *smells in the room*, had started off a train of thought for Posie. Among the mess of the room her sense of smell was strangely heightened. It was very odd, but the awful death-scents surrounding the Countess seemed to shrink back, to peel away, and only one scent pervaded.

Almonds. Bitter almonds.

Posie glanced around. There were sugared almonds lying about everywhere, it was true. But when she leant in closely, there was no real scent coming off them. There was that wretched hip-flask, clutched tightly in Bella's hand, probably containing the very same almond-scented liqueur which Lucy had offered the night before. But on closer inspection, Posie saw that the flask was closed, the screw-lid capped tight. There was not a drop spilled.

The scent of almonds was getting stronger. Stinking, in fact. How was that possible? Was it due to the added number of people in the room, forcing the temperature up, and accelerating the decomposition processes of the corpse?

Posie frowned. She forced herself to get nearer to the body, right next to the mouth. She thought she might be sick, but she took a good lean in.

The dead could only speak through the clues they left behind, and the scent of bitter almonds was overpowering here, strongest of all, reeking up through the skin and mouth and nose of the dead girl.

'Ugh!'

Posie's sense of unease was growing by the second. A scent as strong as that, even for someone who liked almonds, or almond-flavour in everything, was unusual. Unnatural.

A quick sniff of the repulsive cat and Posie realised that it too was giving off the same almond-smell. It was reeking of it.

She thought quickly of another case she had worked on. An author, a famous one, who had died on a hot English summer's day, in a great stately home built of warm Oxfordshire yellow stone. A case very different to this. But there had been a smell of almonds there too.

A poisoning.

Posie was transported back to that time, two and a half years previously, to listen to another policeman, her favourite one of all, Inspector Lovelace, tell her about the scent of bitter almonds. The scent accompanied a certain type of drug used in poisoning cases, cyanides. In a flash Posie was certain of it. She looked down at the body again, and sure enough, a blue tinge, rich as delftware, was beginning to colour the dead girl's face, flushing the lips a deep indigo, working its way upwards over her face. Post-mortem blue flushing was usually a sign of cyanide having been used.

So Bella Alladice had been murdered, in cold blood. Under their very noses. It was dreadful.

And if, as seemed likely now, there was a killer in their midst, the most that could be hoped for was a successful murder investigation. The worst thing would be that the killer would strike again. Or escape. Posie had lost a prime suspect before, only that summer, in fact. It haunted her even now.

Brought back to the present with a horrible jolt, she went up to Salvarocca, a ball of fear lodged in her throat. 'Sir, listen to me. You need to get all of the people in this guesthouse together. Lock them up.'

The big man stared at Posie, a flicker of misplaced humour playing across his face. 'I'd be delighted to, Miss Parker, but can you tell me why?'

Posie came right up to the man's ear and hissed: 'Foul play, sir. Again. This death is *not* natural. It's murder. Get everyone to one central room while we make doubly sure. No-one should be allowed to leave.'

Any humour disappeared fast from Salvarocca's face.

'But it can't be! I've got young Pietro Corsetti locked up for causing the blaze at the Romagnoli Palace: he admitted it voluntarily last night! He's been at my station ever since, and he can have had no part in *this*. The Countess only died this morning, and she was alone here, surely? Corsetti was in his cell then. How can anyone else have been involved? It's a natural death, or at worst, a suicide…'

Posie stuck to her guns. 'It's murder, sir, and the guilt rests within this house. I don't know about this Corsetti chappie, but even if he *is* connected I believe he's a red herring.'

'A what?'

'A false friend. Now will you do as I recommend or not?'

The policeman gave Posie a long, hard stare. Then he seemed to make up his mind and he shrugged. 'I was told to go along with whatever you wanted, that to deny you anything was futile. Does that command include locking up the Landlady and her staff, Miss Parker?'

'Yes.'

'And your fiancé, Miss Parker?'

'Yes. Him too.'

'I see.' Salvarocca checked his watch. 'Well, fine. I'll get everyone into a room with some lunchtime refreshments, but I myself need to get away in a few minutes, and I'm taking the Count with me. We were interrupted by news of this tragedy. We've left something unfinished over there at the Romagnoli Palace. Something urgent.'

Posie was thrown. 'An insurance viewing? *That* can't wait? How is that urgent? The Count's wife has just died!'

'It's important, believe me. I trust you to stay with the body until the Police Surgeon gets here. He'll be at least half an hour. He's over at the Municipal Hospital, San Zanipolo, a good way away. He'll be able to tell us if there has been foul play. Do you need anything else in the meantime?'

Posie paused, thinking quickly. Half an hour was a long time to wait in a case such as this, she knew that with certainty. Evidence was decaying by the minute.

An image came quickly but forcibly to Posie's mind: a shadow of a highly-qualified man who had sold his soul in another life. A man who would know what to do right *now*.

'Hold on, sir. There's a man upstairs, sir. He's staying in the laundry room. If you get him down here, *he'll* be able to tell you if my suspicions about murder are correct within just a minute or so, rather than waiting for the Surgeon. And then you can get away, over to the Palace, knowing what you're dealing with. Only, don't let anyone see this man. Promise me? There's a lot at stake here. I can't really explain it all. You'll just have to trust me.'

Nothing seemed to surprise Salvarocca anymore. Within seconds he was issuing bullying commands, getting his policemen to walk the various guests and the staff of the guesthouse to the mirrored salon next door with the promise of a lunch, leaving no room for protests. The salon door was then locked and several policemen stood sentry outside it.

Posie retreated into a corner of the dining-room. There were no windows here at all, only an old-fashioned line-up of maps of the different districts of Venice, and the vast lagoon. Left quite alone, Posie tried not to look at the body on the floor, and focused instead on a map of nearby St Mark's, but really she was thinking about Bella Alladice and her short, poisonous life. And her painful, poisonous death. No-one deserved to die like that.

And then Posie was aware of someone standing behind her.

'Oh! It's you!'

It was Alaric with a very young police officer at his side. Alaric was throwing a disappointed look in her direction.

'What's this all about, Posie? No-one understands. Locking us all up like common little thieves on the pretence of having some lunch? As if we're hungry at a time like this! You're the only one missing and everyone is kicking up a ruckus! They asked me to come and find out what the devil is going on. A spokesperson, if you like. What is the meaning of it all?'

'It's only briefly, Alaric. It's containment.'

'Good grief! Do *I* need to be contained?'

'It would look odd if you were treated differently, wouldn't it?'

Alaric looked exhausted. 'You haven't spoken to me since I entered the room earlier, Posie.'

'I was sitting next to a dead body. It hardly induces conversation, does it? Besides, you were the one who left me all alone today so you could look for something precious. We're getting married tomorrow, for goodness' sake! This is the first I've seen of you. Where have you been all morning?'

Alaric shrugged, his face flushed with anger. 'I was just out and about.'

'No. You were at Santa Lucia train station,' she said, matter-of-factly.

'How the blazes…? I say! Have you been following me about? That's a cheap trick!'

But she didn't answer, and Alaric left, marched off by

the policeman. Posie whispered, but just to herself, 'I know where you were because of the Mughal cigarettes. The train station is apparently the only place which sells them, from that single vending machine by the locker-room. And something or *someone* drew you to that machine. You who have never smoked Mughals in your life before…'

But Alaric and his cigarettes seemed to pale into insignificance and Posie found herself staring again and again down at the shattered wreck that had been Bella Alladice. This – this murder – was more important than anything else.

They got at you, Bella, Posie thought to herself bitterly. *Two months of wretchedness and they got you anyway.*

But who had got her?

And why now?

****

Eleven

Salvarocca was back within only a couple of minutes. He threw the dining-room door wider, revealing Max right behind him. Max was carrying his large commercial traveller's suitcase, his felt hat held respectfully against his chest. There was no surprise showing on his face, its features arranged blandly, as if he had, for all the world, come to sell medium-range Swiss watches to a serious purchaser. But the clear blue eyes took in all the carnage before him.

The Commissario looked from Posie to the blonde German. 'I don't feel comfortable having so many people held in custody on what may just be a whim, Miss Parker. And who is this mysterious man you wanted brought along?'

'We can't reveal much, but this is Max: he's a fully trained doctor and he knows all about poisons. In fact, Chief Inspector Lovelace is acquainted with him, too. We worked on a case together, two years ago. It's our good luck he happens to be staying here. It's as simple as that. And this isn't a whim. Max will confirm it.'

Relief flooded the Commissario's face. 'Please proceed then. You know what to do, Mr Max? I'll stand and wait here for your conclusions. Quick as you can, please.'

'I understand. I'll do my very best for you.'

'And go gently,' muttered Salvarocca. 'I don't want you leaving your prints over everything.'

Max nodded, not affronted. 'Believe me, it would be more than my life is worth to leave fingerprints.'

Max strode across the room, and was now down on the floor at Bella Alladice's side. He had opened his case and pulled on rubber gloves, fishing out several small articles including a metal spoon and a few glass jars, and some strips of brown sugar paper. Posie stood beside the Commissario and they watched Max at work.

He sprang easily into action, shifting back through the gears into the role he had trained so hard for, all those years before. Max moved around the body without touching anything, examining the face and hands at close range. He focused on the patches of vomit and coffee. He scraped and prodded and stuck bits of paper into samples in glass jars, before setting his watch and timing his tests.

After what seemed like ages, but was probably no more than a couple of minutes, Max consulted his strips of paper and stood up.

'This is my medical opinion,' he stated calmly. 'The Countess has been dead about an hour and a half; I'd say she died between ten o'clock and ten-thirty this morning. She has died from a seizure resulting in heart failure, caused by a massive overdose of prussic acid.'

'Prussic acid?' asked Posie impatiently. 'That's a poison, isn't it?'

'Certainly is. I thought as such when I first saw her, but my litmus tests confirm it. The stuff is dreadful. It's used commercially, often as a rat poison. It smells strongly of almonds. It's a cyanide, and you can see the blue effect in the face, becoming more and more apparent as time ticks on. Maybe your murderer didn't realise that the eventual blue tinge to the skin and lips would give the game away?'

'So this *is* murder?' countered Salvarocca, his arms still

crossed. Posie felt an odd combination of triumph and despair, laced through with the knowledge that this initial report changed *everything*.

Max shrugged. 'Don't let me tell you your job, sir. But I'd wager my life on it being murder. *Ach*! It's certainly not suicide: no-one would choose to die like that. Death would have been staggeringly painful, lasting several minutes, and she would have been conscious until the very end, but unable to speak or cry out, poor woman.'

Posie had come to stand closer. 'Where was it contained, Max? The poison?'

'I thought at first it must have been in the coffee, and it *did* end up there. But I tested the open coffee-pot and the milk jug for traces of the prussic acid, and both were clear. I'd say it was in the liqueur in that silver hip-flask over there, only I can't test it because the top is screwed on tight and I promised not to leave fingerprints. I imagine the Countess added the liqueur to her poured-out coffee as a pick-me-up. It's that almond liqueur she liked, isn't it? I saw her drinking it in the salon yesterday. The stuff would have masked the scent of the poison all right, the woman wouldn't have had a clue!'

'Thank you.' The Chief of Police sighed deeply, checking his large showy timepiece. 'To be honest I'd hoped to hear that Miss Parker was wrong. I expect my Police Surgeon will merely confirm your findings when he arrives. Will you meet with him, Mr Max?'

The German shook his head regretfully. 'As I said, sir, I'm not really here. I can't afford to be a witness on any sort of paperwork.'

Salvarocca nodded and departed for the Romagnoli Palace, collecting the Count as he went, and Posie and Max were left alone with the body.

'I tried to tell you last night,' Max whispered eventually. His voice was low, a warning. 'But this murder makes it clearer. This is a dangerous place. It was dangerous for

Bella Alladice, and it's dangerous for you. This death is just the tip of the iceberg. We're dealing with lethal folk here. Folk who don't think anything of slipping a little poison in someone's morning tipple. I like you, Posie: I have since I met you. You didn't survive working in the trenches to end up dead on a floor like this, did you? Take my advice and get out now. This is a police matter. Just go home.'

Posie was unnerved. She had no idea what the next couple of days held, but she hadn't expected to flee Venice as a result of a warning. 'You're quite serious?'

'I am. The things I've seen here lead me to believe that powerful criminals are at work. This isn't just a game, you know.'

That piercing blue gaze. He continued, remorselessly: 'Is it the promise of the wedding keeping you here? Only, I thought you might have changed your mind on that score.'

At her silence he pressed on. 'Because I think you should know that your fiancé, although he is undoubtedly a man of exceptionally vivid personality and women seem to melt before him, is a liar. I'll tell it how it is: *there is no service booked at that church*.'

How dare the man! But evidence mattered, and Max was, above all things, a man who was an expert in evidence.

'How do you know?' Posie hissed.

'I checked, unlike you. And because right now, while he's locked in that salon with everyone else, Alaric is anxiously checking his watch every two minutes. He's frustrated that his plans for today have gone awry.'

'Plans?' The word was a small squeak.

A nod. 'Alaric's leaving here. He wants to leave now. I don't know where he's going, or why: that will have to remain a mystery only you can unpick. He came back to the guesthouse this morning to collect his bag and clear out. It's still sitting upstairs. You can imagine, this death has thwarted his hopes of a speedy exit.'

'How do you have this knowledge?'

'I told you. I'm a ghost. No more, no less. It's my job to know about *everyone* here. People's rooms tell me a good deal.'

He extracted a slim piece of wire from a pocket. It was dull in colour, and about the size of a man's thumb, looped back on itself in a couple of careful places.

A skeleton key.

'Clever,' Posie muttered sarcastically.

'You don't believe me?' Max looked at his watch and grabbed Posie's arm. 'We have another fifteen minutes or so before that Police Surgeon arrives. Or Salvarocca returns. And everyone else is conveniently out of the way. There's a junior uniformed policeman standing watch at the door, so Bella's body is safe. You can't help her any further now. Come on. I'll show you.'

And Posie simply followed, putting up no resistance.

****

Twelve

Upstairs, on the wide corridor which was housing the more prestigious of the Romagnoli party, Max stopped outside a door halfway along.

'Here we are.' He fiddled with the lock.

It struck Posie as faintly ludicrous that she hadn't as yet managed to enter her fiancé's room at all, and now here she was, entering it with another man, surreptitiously, uninvited.

They stepped in.

The large, heavily-furnished room was very neat. Posie surveyed the space, and found it didn't actually surprise her in the slightest that Alaric's leather rucksack bearing a recent travel docket emblazoned with the word 'CONSTANTINOPLE' was packed and ready next to the bed. A British travel pass and an identity card sat atop it. But Posie didn't even go over to check the details, nor did she race to the cupboards and desk to check for personal items. She knew there would be none.

'Thank you,' she said quietly.

Back in the corridor she stood a little taller, held herself a little more firmly. They lingered at the top of the stairs in an uncomfortable silence. Posie gnawed at her lip. The man was thorough, she'd give him that. And Max had mentioned he was keeping everyone under surveillance. She might as well ask…

'Just quickly, what else did you find out? About the others?'

The spy cocked his head to one side. 'I told you to leave this well alone.'

At her raised eyebrow and crossed arms he relented. '*Ach*, nothing as telling as *that*, I'm afraid. Don't forget, these people came with very little; just what they grabbed from the fire, or had with them when they were out. It may not be representative, but I can get a fair idea of what's going on.'

'So?'

The German pointed to another room further along, past Alaric's. 'Dickie Alladice is a private, careful man, for all that he drinks. He keeps things locked up.' Max wiggled his skeleton key ruefully. 'This isn't much use at cracking his smart little safe, unfortunately.'

He indicated further down the landing. 'The other corridor is more interesting. Lucy Christie, for example.'

'Go on.'

'Well, she lives frugally, as you'd expect. But she's obviously been used to better times. Nothing of note, except a charred hat-box stuffed full of old letters and sentimental keepsakes, and stubs from monthly money orders. She's been sending her pittance of a salary back to England, to a nursing home in the north.'

'Jolly nice girl. An aged relative, I suppose. Who else have you snooped on?'

'That secretary, now, he's an interesting chap. Has a top-range tiny photographic camera, a Leica. It must be his pride and joy, and must have cost him a pretty penny. It's not just for taking holiday snaps, believe me. I think he takes pictures of subjects he finds interesting, or profitable. *I* find it suspicious. And he *collects* photographs, too: there were a couple of fairly non-descript old press photographs he'd stuffed into a green folder containing some telling personal stuff. Did you know he's leaving his job here?'

'That's good timing.'

'I thought that would interest you. There are several cut-out advertisements from British newspapers for vacant posts, all much the same as this; secretaries, personal assistants, help needed with company accounts. He's been applying in earnest too, many letters on the go over the last couple of weeks. And his references are strange, too. All made up. That fellow is decidedly clever, but there's no way any of his past positions or employers check out. It's all a load of make-believe. I'm surprised Bella Alladice swallowed it.'

'Goodness! Are you sure?'

'*Ja*, of course I'm sure. I make my living out of make-believe and lies and I can tell a fraud.'

'He's not one of yours, I suppose?'

Max shook his head. 'No. The fellow's a rotten apple. You can spot it a mile off. He's not cautious enough, somehow.'

'I see. Well, perhaps Bella found out? I wonder if he's been asked to leave or if it's his choice to go?'

'I couldn't say. Oh, and another thing, at the back of the same green folder are money orders, all for the same small amounts. All from Lucy Christie.'

Posie started. '*What?* That makes no sense at all.'

'They date back to last year, to last June. There are payments once a month.'

Posie frowned. 'June was when they all came out here, to Venice. But I thought Lucy and Roger might be close. Might be...'

'I know. *Très chère amies?* Lovers?'

'Something like that.'

'Perhaps. Perhaps not. They're small amounts but enough to cut into Lucy's miniscule monthly salary. Maybe he buys silk stockings for her, or cigarettes? Maybe she pays him back in this way?'

Posie grimaced. Roger Valentine was getting more and more complicated by the second. 'Let's just admit it. It sounds as if he's blackmailing her. Small amounts, the same every time?'

Max shrugged. 'He hasn't cashed them, though. He doesn't need to. He has a nice little nest-egg of his own, from looking at his bank statement. Especially since he was paid a big lump-sum just a couple of weeks ago. The equivalent to about five years of his current salary, I'd say.'

'A couple of weeks ago? The same time he's been applying for other jobs? Who paid him?'

'I couldn't tell you. It came from within Venice, from a private account.'

'That could have come from anyone, then. And quickly, what do you know of Aunt Minnie?'

Max exhaled, as if in sheer disbelief. 'Is that her name? That sweet, dithery woman? "*Butter wouldn't melt*" – you English say that, don't you?'

'Not so sweet after all?'

'I'd say those soft scarves conceal a very dark soul. I read her diary. It's her only personal possession.'

'That's a bit much, don't you think?'

Max shrugged. 'My job knows no boundaries, and I can't afford to have scruples or regrets. What I found out was interesting: Aunt Minnie hates all of the Alladices, Bella especially. She blames them for her poverty. She blames Bella for ruffling feathers at an English Club for ladies in Venice, which she obviously adores. She spends most of the diary moaning about how she's been tarred with the same brush as her niece, how the respectable ladies at the club give her a wide berth and how unfair it all is. But she doesn't have a good word to say about the smart secretary or about Miss Christie, either. There was malice on every page. Evil stuff, really. It shocked me, and that takes some doing.'

'Evil thoughts leading to evil deeds?' muttered Posie darkly. 'Or just a way of letting off steam?'

'Again, I don't know, and it's not your lookout either, is it?' added Max maddeningly. 'Mention your suspicions to that big burly policeman, but leave it at that.'

Posie nodded, thoughts tripping over themselves. 'Thank you. I asked Scotland Yard for some information about this little crew, but I bet what they find isn't half as interesting as this. You're obviously jolly good at your job.' She made as if to proceed down the stairs. But Max came very close to Posie, barring her way.

'Hang on a minute.' He took her hand. If she was surprised she didn't show it and she let his hand linger.

'Don't forget what I said about getting out. And please, take those priceless jewels off.'

Posie raised an eyebrow. Quick as a flash she made a decision. Wordlessly she took off the sapphire earrings. She shook off Max's hand and opened his palm like a flower. She pushed the jewels into it.

'Take them. I'd like you to have these now. I don't need them. In your game you never know when you might need ready cash, or something to barter with, I suppose. If I ever see you again perhaps you can give them back to me, if you still have them. If not, don't worry.'

Max didn't try and argue with her, or insist on Posie keeping the stones. He shoved them instead into some section of his large briefcase known only to himself. There was the expectancy of a promise being made.

'Allow me to give you something back, Posie. I bought this for you early this morning in the Rialto market, near the Post Office. I thought it looked cheery. More usable than real jewels, anyhow. If you never see me again, which you might not, remember me when you wear it.'

He produced a string of blush-pink Murano glass beads, cheap as seaside chips, with little gold squiggles all over them. Their fastening was a fake gold screw. Posie grinned for probably the first time all day.

'Thanks,' she muttered, flushing red. 'I must go. That Police Surgeon...'

Two steps down, he called her back. He looked worried. 'One thing, Posie. We both saw that silver flask with the carved initials last night. You gave it to me to drink from.'

'It wasn't mine!' hissed Posie.

'I know that. You told me it was Lucy's. But that one flask seems to have passed through many hands. And someone put poison in it for Bella Alladice to drink today. You need to mention seeing it last night to the police.'

He turned and walked away. Posie stared at his retreating back.

She had been thinking along the same lines. That flask, the one Lucy had given her last night, which she'd returned very early this morning, had borne the legend '*AA*', presumably for Annabella Alladice, in curvy Edwardian script. Lucy had obviously 'borrowed' it from her employer and then lent it to Posie. But had she tampered with the flask before giving it back to her employer this morning at breakfast?

It hardly seemed credible. Lucy was so nice.

But there were odd things about her too, it was true. She had apparently been in charge of Bella's medicines. What *exactly* had Lucy got from the apothecary late last night? Had that dark-coloured bottle contained the prussic acid? What was going on with Lucy and the various men here? What had Dickie told her to 'hold her nerve' about? A planned murder?

But there were odd things about everyone here, and that didn't make them all murderers.

Posie suddenly became aware that the telephone was ringing insistently in the entrance vestibule downstairs, and it had probably been ringing for several minutes. Bounding downwards, and realising there was quite simply no-one to answer it, everyone being locked in the mirrored salon, or acting sentry on the door, she snatched up the black-and-gold receiver.

A babble of Italian followed, and all Posie could say was '*Si, per favore*. Put the connection through.'

Please let this be helpful, Posie thought to herself.

The welcome voice of the International Operator clicked through after a small pause.

'London calling. Scotland Yard wants Miss Parker. Will you wait?'

****

Thirteen

The front door to the Campo stood ajar, and a few flashlights were going off outside. Posie assumed that the Venetian press must somehow have got wind of the death and were swarming hungrily for news. It was the same here as in Fleet Street, of course: everyone with their crust of bread to earn.

Through the front door Posie could also see that a bevy of excitable uniformed policemen were crowding on the steps down to the jetty of the Campo San Vio. Behind them a large police barge was tethered, and what looked like forensics experts were loading out cardboard boxes and glass plates. But she watched in some surprise as, rather than come up to the guesthouse, they were pointing elsewhere, over the canal towards the Palace, seeming to argue about where to go first.

Very peculiar.

Posie's thoughts were interrupted by a voice, almost irritable, repeating her name down the telephone.

'Is that you, Sergeant Rainbird?'

It was. 'I've got what you wanted, Miss Parker. Information .. out your Venice crowd.'

Posie took down rapid notes, parrot-fashion, avoiding repeating or voicing names aloud. But the first two reports were distinctly disappointing.

1. *Countess Bella Romagnoli. Nothing exciting to note. Up to date with taxes paid to the Revenue authorities in England. Listed as a Director and Shareholder of Alladice Holdings.*

2. *Dickie Alladice. No war record (he didn't serve) and nothing on the police record. Always late with his own income tax but the Revenue authorities seem to turn a bit of a blind eye. Big charitable donations made on a yearly basis, particularly to hospitals and workhouses in the north of England. Listed as a Director and Shareholder of Alladice Holdings.*

3. *Millicent (Minnie) Alladice. No police records, no tax records of any kind, despite being listed as a minor Shareholder in Alladice Holdings. Receives a few shillings a week (as a widow) from a war pension following the death of her husband on active service…*

Posie did a double take. It didn't fit. 'Sorry? A husband?'

Sergeant Rainbird was clearing his throat. 'That's correct, Miss. She married a Henry Walters, a Post-Master and shopkeeper, just outside of Burnley, in 1913. I have the certificate right here, from Somerset House.'

'I didn't know she'd been married. I just *assumed* she was a spinster.' Posie frowned and cursed herself for her slackness. She normally didn't assume anything; that way danger led.

Rainbird was making tut-tutting noises down the line.

'It's not the most salubrious story, Miss Parker, if you want to know. Frankly I'm not surprised the lady doesn't talk about it. Seems she married this fella in her late thirties, and married beneath herself socially, too. He seems to have been a bit of a cad: declared bankrupt within a year of the marriage. I have all the bankruptcy papers here from the Court. Seems the lady had her own money, plenty actually, from the Alladice family, at the time of the marriage but he sunk it all. Huge debts were owed by 1914 to creditors of the Post Office and the shop which he ran, but also to various bookmakers. Horses. Big sums for the time.'

Posie whistled. The shame of the Bankruptcy Court was about equal to the Divorce Court, but the consequences were infinitely worse. You could marry again, for sure, but the decree of bankruptcy and the taint which came with it never really left you.

'Was *she* declared bankrupt? Minnie?'

'No. Not that I can see. The Bankruptcy Court gave Mr Walters an ultimatum: a year in the debtors' jail or serve the country in war-torn France. He was old to serve – over forty – but he went anyhow, in early 1915.'

'I say! He chose badly.'

'Quite. Died the same year and left his missus in a dreadful pickle.'

Posie shook her head, conjuring up an image of Millie Alladice a decade earlier: pathetically grateful to be shown any attention, even if it was from a man of a different social class, and even if there were suspicions that he might just have been after Minnie's money. Maybe the unfortunate Henry Walters had been easy on the eye? Or funny, or kind? An adeptness with finances and a gambling habit weren't the first things one noticed about a man, anyhow.

Rainbird was continuing, somewhat sanctimoniously: 'I'd say Minnie Alladice wouldn't marry Walters if she had her time again.'

'Oh, I don't know,' Posie muttered darkly. 'People do stupid things for some men. But what do you mean, he left her in a "dreadful pickle"?'

'Well, the sale of the shop didn't cover half the debt. Minnie Alladice took the debt on herself after her husband's death, as she was obliged to do, but she seems to have had some sort of nervous breakdown later in 1915. The Alladice family stepped in quickly and paid it off.'

'*Who* paid it, exactly?'

'It doesn't say here on the Court papers. It just says

Minnie was in a nursing home and unable to work. Alladice Holdings paid the debt.'

'Mnnn. I see.' Mr Alladice Senior had been alive back then, and he had probably managed the whole mess, cancelling out his sister's debt, using the family company's finances to do so. Obviously not the 'great wrong' Bella had said her father had inflicted on Minnie.

Actually, Posie couldn't find much that was controversial in Minnie Alladice's background, or her position back in 1915, although it had obviously been most unfortunate.

Posie's thoughts were instead returning again and again to Lucy, the companion, with her medicine bottles and her borrowed hip-flask and borrowed liqueur. She asked Rainbird for his information about the girl, and she stood with her pencil poised.

'There's nothing on your Miss Christie, I'm afraid.'

'What? Nothing at all?'

'That's right, Miss. No birth certificate, no work record, no war record, no listing with the Revenue authorities. I'd say your Miss Christie doesn't exist. And if she does, she's not who she says she is.'

Posie was stumped. She'd come across people assuming other people's names and identities before. But why would Lucy do so?

At her silence the Sergeant moved on. 'I have nothing on your young Count, either. He's not known over here, full-stop. But what *is* juicy is this Roger Valentine fellow you asked me to investigate.'

'Go on.'

4. *Roger Valentine. Went to Oxford University, studied Chemistry. Excelled. Won medals for various sports, including gymnastics. Taken on by the government straight out of Oxford in 1914. Working on highly confidential chemical war-work, often in Whitehall. All classified.*

Posie dropped her voice as low as it would go and cast an anxious look around the dark empty entrance. 'I say! Are we talking about developing poison gasses, and such like, Sergeant?'

'I'd imagine so, Miss.'

Posie was reminded for a brief second of Max, working in a similar fashion in Germany. Men everywhere, first-class brains, trained at top universities, plotting and scheming to find ways of wiping out men just like themselves. It was ludicrous. Heart-breaking, actually.

'How do you know about this, Sergeant? If it was top-secret?'

'Because Roger Valentine messed up. Big-time. It seems that whenever a team he was working in were getting close to making some hard-hitting chemical breakthrough, there'd be an accident, or an explosion, or a fire. Or plans would go missing. The first couple of incidents were put down to carelessness, but the carelessness continued.'

'Deliberate sabotage?'

'Aye, Miss. They never found out who he was in pay to exactly, but of course it was the Germans, wasn't it? He was had up for treason. It's in the official papers.'

Posie gasped. Treason still carried the death-sentence. 'But he got off?'

'Lack of evidence. So he was put in prison for the duration of the war on a trumped-up charge of dereliction of duty. When he got out he was unemployable. He was banned from ever working as a chemist again. Or working for the government, for that matter.'

'So what has he done?'

'Bit of this, bit of that. Mainly work as a secretary. I suppose he just glossed over his prison past, and his chemical "mistakes". The Revenue authorities have him listed in several jobs, all ending very suddenly, all with the payment of large amounts of money at their conclusions.'

'Interesting.'

'Isn't it just? Indicates your Mr Valentine was probably trying to blackmail his employers, making the employment situations he was in untenable, hence the large payments to see the back of the fellow. He sounds a right nasty piece of work.'

Posie's brain was working overtime. *Chemistry. An expert in poisons. A blackmailer.*

At her silence the Sergeant carried on: 'I hope it was helpful? I've got a new lad, Constable Fox, to train up. He's a bright fellow, and he helped me out no end.'

'Jolly good. Oh, Sergeant! What about the company itself? Alladice Holdings.'

A deep sigh came down the line, as if all of Fox's good work had been undone in a second. 'No can do, Miss. We spoke to Companies House, where Alladice Holdings are obliged to keep their records. Apparently the paperwork is being updated or something. It won't be ready for another week or so. There's a big note saying "OUT FOR REVIEW" in the place in the bookshelf where it should be.'

Posie frowned. 'Is that usual?'

'My lad Fox asked much the same question, Miss. It seems it's not *unusual.* Could be just Companies House checking things. Coincidental, like?'

'Mnnn.'

Thanking the Sergeant and his eager new police recruit, Posie hung up.

But there was no time to think on Rainbird's findings, for the telephone was ringing again, and she snatched up the receiver. It was Sidney. For just a second she couldn't remember quite why anyone at Grape Street might be calling her.

'Miss? Ain't I half-glad I got you! I been tryin' that café place and I been tryin' again here for at least the last half hour!'

'Sorry Sidney. Is this about the Somerset House Will?'

'Sure is, Miss! I wanted to tell you before I forgot the details. You were right: I couldn't copy anythin' down. Lucky for you I've got a first-class memory.'

'Lucky me. Carry on.'

'It was very short, this Will. I think the fella hand-wrote it before leavin' for France. Your dead chap, this John Alladice, he starts off by sayin' that while he supposes people think he might be rich, he doesn't own that much really, as all of his wealth is in the family company.'

'That makes sense.'

'He only had one treasure, a diamond solitaire, which had belonged to his mother. He says there's a girl who he loves, but he can't get up the nerve to ask her to marry him for fear she'll turn 'im down. Says he'll ask her when he returns from the war. Poor lad. Imagine!'

'And?'

'He says he's sent the ring to the girl in question already, and that folks should know and appreciate it was what he wanted. There's to be no argument.'

'I see. Is that all?'

'No, not on your nelly! He then says he owns company shares, a lot of them. He says he can only leave them to an "Alladice" and that he doesn't want to do that, that it almost breaks his heart because it's very difficult to choose between his siblings on account of no love lost between them all. Says he'll leave them to his sister Bella but only on the condition that she'll look after the girl he loves; keep the girl protected and living in the style to which she has grown accustomed. Very nicely, I suppose.'

'Gosh.' Posie frowned. 'Bella didn't mention any of this to me when we spoke yesterday. I wonder who this girl was?'

There was an exited chirrup down the line from Bloomsbury. 'You want her name, Miss?' Sidney sounded proud. 'I made sure to remember it.'

'I'm all ears.'

Posie had got out her notepad again. But she nearly dropped it in shock when she heard Sidney's answer.

'It were Lucy Christie, Miss.'

****

Fourteen

For a few minutes Posie sat, hidden from view. In her rush she had knocked down two carnival masks, the long-nosed plague doctor's mask of Scaramuccia, and the comic-sad face of Tartaglia, which must have been stuffed up on the top shelf among a load of junk.

Both masks had at some point been roughly painted black, which lent them a horribly funereal aspect. Posie hated masks and puppets and that kind of ghoulish make-believe at the best of times, and she put them down carelessly at her feet, thoughts reeling.

This recent news from Sidney was just too much.

In an instant Lucy had been transformed from being Bella's underpaid and ill-treated companion to being all of that and *more*. A wronged woman; the woman Johnny Alladice had loved, whose care and financial security he had entrusted to his sister Bella in the event of his death. And Bella had taken the company shares but not taken on the responsibility; she had 'kept' Lucy as an underpaid companion in some dreadful mimicry of what her brother had really wanted.

Why had Bella acted as she had? And why on earth had Lucy stayed on in such conditions?

Posie sighed. It was easy enough to answer the first

question about Bella's bad behaviour; that old ogre, jealousy, had been at the root of all of this. Johnny, the adored elder brother, had probably been smitten with the beautiful Lucy, and had most likely ignored his younger sister as a consequence, although not on purpose. Bella had taken umbrage at Lucy. Flashes of Bella's words, spoken last night before dinner, tumbled through Posie's mind: '*She has a habit of stealing hearts. Hearts which are not hers to take.*'

Posie frowned. *Hearts?* More than just Johnny Alladice's?

And in answer to the second question, why Lucy had stayed on in such humiliating circumstances, Posie simply had no answer.

None of it made sense.

It was a tangled web. Too many suspects, with too much history between them. The shadow of the war again, making tracks and imprints in people's lives even now, five years after it had all ended; a hopeless lurching shadow which couldn't be escaped from.

And with a stab of regret Posie realised it was her duty to report these findings on to Commissario Salvarocca. For Bella had requested Posie to help her, and Posie had failed spectacularly. She could serve the Countess to the best of her abilities now and help the police get to the bottom of it all.

On the evidence received from Sidney, things were looking pretty black for Lucy Christie. Lucy seemed to have eclipsed the others as the person who had lost out most, and very personally, through Bella's direct actions. Had Bella's treatment of Lucy finally made her snap? Led the girl to lace a flask with a poison guaranteed to cause death? But why *now*? Lucy had been the companion to the Countess for six years. It would be horrible to have to recount all of this: Posie liked the girl, after all, and now she felt sorry for her, too. But, as Max had said, the Commissario could take it forwards.

For some reason Posie kept conjuring up Inspector Lovelace's face, familiar, comforting, reliable. How she wished he was here. She heard his words, clear as a bell:

'This is a mare's nest, Posie.'

A mare's nest.

It probably was. But she went upstairs to the dining-room anyway. Count Giancarlo was sitting outside the scene of crime, smoking as if his life depended on it, shivering almost, flanked by two policemen. Giancarlo looked absolutely dreadful, far worse than earlier, sea-sick almost, his usually groomed hair spiralling wildly into his eyes. Posie presumed that the news of Bella's death together with the exertions of whatever was so important over at the insurance valuation had led to his current fragile state.

Inside the dining-room, confronted with the hostile scene-of-crime officers who were bundling Bella Alladice's body up into some sort of canvas bag, Posie sought out Salvarocca, who was in close conference with the newly-arrived Police Surgeon, a small ferrety-looking slip of a man.

Posie marched over. Behind her the door opened again but she ignored it. Probably just another forensics assistant, no doubt. Salvarocca and the Surgeon didn't look up: they were paying close attention to the black folio.

Posie stared at it. 'I say! Wasn't that Bella's?'

'We assume so, Miss Parker.'

'Where are the papers?'

'Exactly. There were no papers here. That's the odd thing.'

Posie frowned. Last time she had seen Bella Alladice, at breakfast, the thing had been stuffed full with thick, fat-looking sheets, and the Countess had indicated it would take her a good while to get through the work.

'Why not ask her secretary, Roger, what the folio contained? He put the papers together for Bella early this morning.'

'I will do.' Salvarocca indicated the Police Surgeon. 'By the way, Doctor Alessandro here confirms the findings from earlier. Murder, by prussic acid. Both the Countess and her cat: the creature obviously ingested some of the poison splashed around the place. That, or he licked at the Countess's mouth.' Posie shuddered and felt sick.

'Yes. It was careful, clever work, and not a fingerprint to be found anywhere so far, more's the pity. But Doctor Alessandro thinks we might be able to get a print off this folio.'

'You'll get several, actually,' explained Posie grimly. 'The thing was almost covering Bella's face when we found her, and many people have touched it since.'

At their defeated faces, Posie hurried on: 'By the way, there's a good deal of hot stuff I've found out. It's all dashed complicated.'

And then she blurted out a potted, amalgamated version of the information she had obtained on all of the Romagnoli house guests since she had seen the Commissario last. When it came to the engraved silver hip-flask of Bella's, and the late-night medicine, and seeing both items the night before in Lucy's hands, Posie didn't hold back.

Salvo Salvarocca stared at her. There was a curious mix of humour, dismay and disbelief written all over his face. 'That was fast work, Miss Parker. You seem to have done my job for me.'

There was a sharp laugh from the doorway. 'I'll say she has! I *did* warn you, Salvo, my old friend. What is this? Posie? It looks horribly like a dead body. Thank goodness it's not on my watch! You're supposed to be getting married. Talk about a busman's holiday!'

Posie gasped.

For in the doorway was Chief Inspector Lovelace, in a smart navy pinstriped suit which she had never seen before, holding a slim attaché case in his hands and also, as if it couldn't get any odder, holding the strange black carnival masks.

Incongruous, unexpected, and totally out of place.
But so very, very welcome.
'Sir!' yelped Posie, and ran to him with open arms.

* * * *

Fifteen

Commissario Salvarocca bounded across the room and was now crushing Chief Inspector Lovelace in an altogether bearlike and very un-English embrace.

'Richard! My good friend! I had no idea you were coming out here. But why? No, tell me later. No time now. I need to get next door where a room full of suspects awaits. It seems we may have a murderer among us.'

As they entered the salon, everyone looked up expectantly. Posie registered that Alaric, Dickie, Aunt Minnie, Lucy and Roger had been joined by the Count, and Mrs Persimmon was there together with her workers; Jones the Butler, the middle-aged English cook and the nervy-looking maid. The household staff looked ill-at-ease and miserable.

Everyone except Dickie Alladice had sat themselves down in a rough ring of chairs, and a table took up the middle of the room with what looked like the remains of sandwiches and coffee on it. Posie had forgotten that this room contained the well-stocked drinks trolley, and she saw that Dickie Alladice was stationed beside it, while most people in the room seemed to have a glass of brandy in their hands. Aunt Minnie in particular looked frightful, flushed and sweating.

'What's going on?' Dickie asked abruptly. He checked his watch. 'It's twelve-thirty. We've been in here over an hour.' He looked in confusion from Salvarocca to Posie and then on to Inspector Lovelace, who hung back with becoming humility.

'I say! Who's this fresh lad?'

Inspector Lovelace stepped forwards. His former glibness had been replaced by the usual professional calm which Posie knew so well: his eyes taking in everyone and everything in the room, matching people with the snippets of Posie's conversation he must have overheard; his boyish, gingery good-looks and gentle manner belying the core of steel and ambition which had propelled him right to the top echelons of the British Police Force. He did look a little odd, however. He was still holding the two masks.

'Scotland Yard, Mr Alladice.'

Dickie Alladice frowned. 'Heaven help us! It must be serious.'

'Please accept my commiserations on the death of your sister.' He nodded at the Count, who was now sunk with his head in his hands in an armchair. 'And I extend them to you, too, Your Grace.'

Posie noticed how Alaric had sprung up from his own chair, and was looking over at Inspector Lovelace, with not a smidgen of surprise on his face but with – what was it? – relief? A sense of expectancy?

The Commissario took over. 'I am afraid we are now dealing with a murder investigation,' he said matter-of-factly.

A collective gasp ran around the room, and people started whispering all at once, but the big man put his hand up, as if stopping the busy London traffic on the Kingsway. At his gesture an immediate silence fell.

'I have it on the advice of medical experts that Countess Bella Romagnoli was poisoned sometime this morning between ten and ten-thirty. She was last seen alive by Mrs

Persimmon and Mr Jones at nine-thirty, and then her body was discovered by them just over an hour later. To the best of their knowledge the Countess was alone during this time, writing or reading in the dining-room next door. Does anyone want to tell me anything different?'

Everyone was still, open-mouthed.

'No?' The Commissario continued on briskly. 'Well then, does anyone have anything to say about *this*?' He waved Bella's empty leather work folio in the air.

Posie watched Roger Valentine swallow and then stand up. 'It belonged to my employer, the late Countess.'

'Full marks to you, Mr Valentine. When did you last see it? And did it look like this?'

A flicker of a scowl twitched across the handsome dark face, to be replaced by puzzlement. 'I saw it very early this morning. When the Countess asked for it. And in answer to your second question: no; it did not look like that. It was full of paperwork. About thirty or more pages, I'd say.'

'Pages about what?'

The Private Secretary gestured dismissively towards Mrs Persimmon and her staff. 'Do you *really* expect me to reveal matters of a private nature in front of servants?' His tone was contemptuous, and Posie found herself hating him for it.

Roger drew himself up as much as his fairly short stature would allow. 'Besides, I was the Countess's *Private* Secretary. Even though she's dead I owe my employer a duty of confidentiality. And I also owe her a duty right now to contact her personal solicitor in London regarding her Will. I would like to be excused to use the telephone.'

'Her solicitor in *London*?' said Dickie, looking puzzled. 'Who's that? Bella never mentioned it to me. I thought her affairs had been taken care of by our lawyer chappie here, Mr Ennario? That's what she led me to understand.'

Roger Valentine shook his head petulantly: 'No, sir. Mr Proudfoot of Pring and Proudfoot in London drew up

Bella's Will and he will now need to make the necessary arrangements to come out here and read it. It's to be a week from her death. That's what my employer wanted.'

'I heard she was about to be your *ex*-employer,' muttered Posie, loud enough to be heard, and she was rewarded by Roger's sullen scowl.

The Commissario put the folder away, smiled pleasantly around the room, as if in a perfectly normal meeting, and got out his own notebook which had an important-looking gold foil badge on its front.

'You can use the telephone in just a minute, Mr Valentine. First, I want all of you to give me a description of where you were from breakfast until ten-thirty today. Posie Parker has already given me an account, and His Grace Giancarlo Romagnoli has no need to explain anything: he was with me during the entire time period concerned. But everyone else here needs to account for themselves.'

'Hang on a minute, old chap.' Dickie Alladice was frowning. 'You mean *we* are the suspects?'

'That's right, sir.'

But before Dickie could answer, Posie was surprised to see Aunt Minnie rising, anguish all over her face. And she spoke up, fairly boldly, Posie thought. 'But you're holding a fellow, aren't you? You told us so yesterday! I can't remember the exact name, some low-life. Corsessi? Corselli? So why bother to ask *us* for alibis?'

Count Giancarlo broke into a reedy peal of laughter, the scorn barely concealed. It was the first noise he had made. He still looked terrible, the greenish sea-sick hue not having disappeared. Salvarocca ignored him and smiled at Aunt Minnie benignly.

'You are quite correct, madam. I am holding a fellow for his part in the fire last night. Pietro Corsetti. But at present the two events seem completely unrelated. In fact, I intend to let Mr Corsetti go as soon as I get back to the Questura, my police station.'

'But how's that, sir?' said Aunt Minnie insistently. 'Surely my niece was the undisputed target of both dreadful events? How can you let this man go?'

'Because your niece died while Mr Corsetti was safely locked up in a cell,' Salvarocca replied icily. 'So he's not a suspect in today's murder. But *you all are*. We will reconvene here for a progress report tonight at six o'clock. Between now and then you will all stay in your rooms and a police guard will stand at each of your doors. That is an order.'

Alaric had sprung up, outraged. 'House arrest? How long will this take? You can't do that! I'm nothing to do with this whole rummy shin-dig! I barely know these people! I wish to goodness I had never come here!'

Posie thought grimly of Alaric's packed rucksack upstairs.

The Chief of Police was continuing: 'That's as maybe, Mr Boynton-Dale. But I need to treat you all the same, don't I? Maybe you'd care to start us off by telling us what you did this morning?'

Alaric shrugged moodily and said he had been nowhere near the guesthouse that morning, nor had he seen the Countess. He had walked to Santa Lucia train station very early, and had a sloppy breakfast in one of the cafés in the station, the 'Fiorenza', he thought it had been called: the waiter there would probably remember him. He had then walked all the way back, stopping to collect a new off-the-peg suit in one of the fashionable men's shops in the Campo Rialto Nuovo. He had a receipt to prove it. He had arrived back to find the police already on the doorstep of Mrs Persimmon's, the body in the dining-room…

Salvarocca nodded. He turned to Lucy, who gave her movements as being identical to Posie's.

'Thank you.' Salvarocca looked at Aunt Minnie. Grasping at the butterfly-patterned chiffon of her blouse and biting at her lip, Minnie reported that she had breakfasted later than usual, alone in her room: just toast and tea. She had met Dickie in the entrance hall at nine o'clock when they took the public vaporetto to the Rialto Bridge, and then walked the short distance to the Calle del Galiazzo, in the legal district. They had had a business meeting with a notary there, a Mr Ennario. The notary had been very busy and had kept them waiting but they had left shortly after a quarter past ten. They had walked back, coming through St Mark's Square, and had had the good fortune to meet up with the other ladies of the party.

The Commissario seemed satisfied, and requested Dickie's alibi. With much pulling of his hair and general breathlessness Dickie Alladice confirmed he had taken no breakfast, which was usual for him, relying only on a cup of coffee in his bedroom which Jones had brought him at about eight-thirty. He had dressed hurriedly and then met his aunt at nine, and the rest of his story matched hers. He couldn't bring himself to explain the foretaste of disaster when he had seen Jones come running outside the Café Florian, or the dreadful return to the guesthouse and the gruesome discovery of his sister's body. His voice tailed off, tears obviously not far away.

'Thank you, sir,' the big policeman said gently, and moved on to Roger. There was a long pause.

'I can't really give you an alibi,' the Private Secretary said at last. Everyone stared.

'Try.'

Roger shrugged reproachfully. 'I left here early. Around seven-thirty. I walked around town. I had nowhere to go and no-one to see. I just walked. Mainly around here, around the Dorsoduro.'

'For more than three and a half hours? In the Dorsoduro? There's not much to see here, is there? Once you've seen the Salute Church, I mean…'

'That's as maybe, but that's what I did.'

'Can anyone confirm this?'

'Not really. It was my morning off. Precious. I needed to clear my head and think a good bit.'

'I see. I'll let you think this over and come back to me with a clearer explanation by six o'clock this evening. Otherwise you'll come down to the station with me. Understand, sir?'

At the ensuing silence the Commissario checked and double-checked the movements of Mrs Persimmon, Jones and the household staff, none of whom had new or interesting information to add.

'Has anyone anything they wish to say before you go back to your rooms?'

After a brief pause, Mrs Persimmon stood up. 'Begging your pardon, sir.' She addressed this to Inspector Lovelace. 'But why are you carrying those masks? If I'm not much mistaken they're the property of my guesthouse: they belong in a sort of communal dressing-up box downstairs. My guests sometimes like to borrow them for a special dinner or whatnot. I just wondered, sir, why have you painted them that dreadful black? They were truly luvverly – all gold and silver and red and blue – something special. Now they look like something out of one of them horror movies you hear of at the Pictures!'

Inspector Lovelace raised an eyebrow and strode across the room, giving the Scaramuccia and the Tartaglia masks back to their rightful owner.

'Jolly sorry, madam.' He smiled. 'I simply came across them in the hallway. I have no idea why they're painted black, but if you look you'll see that it's been done very hastily: almost with carbon, like a lump of coal dipped in water. I'd bet your clever maid here will be able to get that black muck off in a jiffy with a bit of elbow grease. No harm done, eh?'

Mrs Persimmon looked less than convinced – as if Inspector Lovelace himself had been hard at work with his lump of coal – but she nodded uneasily. It obviously didn't do to argue with Scotland Yard. Not yet, anyhow.

Posie noted that the maid was casting nervous glances

over at the Inspector, and looking miserable at the thought of the task she had been saddled with.

Inspector Lovelace smiled around winningly. 'I think my friend Commissario Salvarocca will be very busy this afternoon, and if for some reason anyone has forgotten something, or some little snippet of information suddenly occurs to you which you think might be helpful for the police, please do not hesitate to come and tell me. Or find Miss Parker here, she's quite experienced at taking confidential statements, and she's very sympathetic. We will both be here all afternoon, in our respective rooms. Just like everyone else.'

People were waiting, nervous eyes flashing around. And then Salvarocca pulled the white rabbit from his hat. 'Oh! I quite forgot!'

He took from his pocket the silver flask from the crime scene and waved it in the air. The '*AA*' inscription shone in the greenish light of the room, as if it wanted to spell out the truth for everyone. But *what* truth?

He rounded on Lucy Christie. 'I believe, Miss, that you were in possession of this very flask last night? A flask which belonged to your employer?'

Lucy's dark eyes were round with fear and something else – betrayal? – and she looked for a second at Posie, who felt like a prize rat. A rat who has told the truth, but a rat all the same.

Lucy flicked her eyes back at the policeman and held his gaze, defiantly. She didn't answer.

Salvo continued: 'We are almost one hundred per cent certain that the poison – prussic acid – was in this receptacle. What do you have to say about it, Miss Christie? Do you deny that you had this bottle with you late last night? You were seen with it. It is a highly unusual specimen, with this engraving. Do you deny it belonged to the Countess? They *are* her initials, after all.'

Lucy said nothing. She looked down at the floor.

Dickie was livid, dancing from foot to foot, right up next to the Chief of Police: 'What are you implying, sir? Be jolly careful. Of course Lucy didn't have Bella's flask with her last night. Why would she? Nor did she have anything to do with the poisoning.'

But then, for a fraction of a second, it was as if time stood still. Posie felt a flicker of something pass between Dickie and Lucy, and it buzzed in the air. An understanding? A reproach?

'Hang on, sir. Did you say *prussic acid*? Good grief! I must be mistaken!'

And then, like an echo, Roger Valentine was whispering, but just under his breath, and Posie wondered if she had heard him correctly: 'Prussic acid? *Again?*'

What was the fascination with the means of poisoning? Why was the type of poison so significant?

Dickie quickly drew himself up. Shaking his head, throwing doubts to the wind.

'Well, I'm sure you're wrong. Miss Christie was, it is true, in charge of all of my sister's medication, and I know she went out to the apothecary last night, but she was never in charge of Bella's liqueur. Bella kept that flask with her constantly: it was given to her by someone she felt very strongly about, once, a long time ago. There's no way she would have lent it out.'

The Commissario turned to Lucy. 'For the last time: do you deny, Miss, that you had this flask with you last night? You'd better speak, otherwise I'm arresting you on suspicion of the murder of your employer and I'll take you back with me to the Questura.'

But Lucy remained silent.

Salvarocca went to the door, called someone's name, and a tall, uniformed policeman entered, his blue, Slavic-looking eyes full of interest. He pulled out a pair of glimmering handcuffs and clipped them around Lucy's slim wrists. Before anyone could protest, or Lucy could say anything to anyone, she had been whisked from the room.

'I say!' breathed Dickie Alladice, steadying himself against the drinks trolley. He appealed to Salvarocca. 'You've got this wrong, sir. There's no way…'

Dickie's voice tailed off, and the Commissario was now matching each of the room's occupants with one of his police force. He smiled brightly all around.

'Until six o'clock then! Off you go!'

* * * *

Sixteen

'I need to speak to the Chief Inspector.'

Alaric, the last of the group to leave, flashed anxious eyes at Inspector Lovelace. 'I say, have you got it, Inspector?'

Richard Lovelace nodded, and unzipped his attaché case. From it he drew a thick brown manila envelope, roughly the size of a business folio. It was marked 'HIGHLY CONFIDENTIAL – LEGAL DOCUMENTS'.

'Here you go.'

Posie was thrown. What on earth did Alaric want of the Inspector? It was almost as if he had asked the Inspector to bring him something especially, all the way out to Venice. But that was preposterous! And what legal documents did that brown envelope contain?

Alaric turned to leave, tugging at his caramel-coloured hair, clutching at the envelope almost angrily, when Posie cut in. She *had* to ask:

'Are you leaving me, Al? Leaving *here*? Why are you packed up ready to go?'

Alaric almost dropped his papers. An angry scowl settled itself on his gorgeous features. The Commissario cast interested eyes upon Posie's betrothed, watching his every move. When Alaric spoke, at last, he let the words fall carefully.

'No. I'm not leaving you, but I was planning to leave *here*. I had started to think there was some nasty snoop around. Late last night I found someone had gone through my things, despite the fact I'd locked my door. So I did the "hair test". I packed all my gear together this morning into my rucksack and placed one of my own hairs across the zip. I haven't been up yet to check on it but it sounds as if I shouldn't bother. The hair will have fallen away as you've obviously picked my lock and had a good old rootle around! By Gad! I never thought it was *you*! These are new depths, Posie. Don't you trust me or something?'

'Not really, no.' She hardly felt bothered to mention that the nasty snoop hadn't, in fact, been her. Let him believe it, if he must…

Alaric glared at Posie and she felt her heart hardening towards him, unable and unwilling to reach a peace. They were both proud, that was their trouble, and neither felt able to back down. And she *didn't* trust him: that was what it essentially boiled down to.

'Children! Children!' Inspector Lovelace looked embarrassed as Alaric turned on his heel and left sharply with his allocated policeman.

Salvo Salvarocca, looking thoughtful, crossed his arms and addressed Posie and Lovelace.

'What a welcome to Venice, eh, Richard? You both must be starving?'

As if on cue Posie's stomach rumbled audibly and both Police Inspectors laughed.

'Cross the Accademia Bridge and get away from these festival crowds. Turn left and then go straight on. There's an excellent trattoria on the Campo San Maurizio. Their speciality is boiled seagull. Tell Enzo, the owner, that I sent you. Be gone an hour, no more, and then come back and make a pretence of staying in your rooms. I trust you both to make sure nothing untoward happens here while I am away. Oh, and for goodness' sake, don't eat the trattoria's home-grown oysters, or the mussels: I've already got one dead body on my hands. The water in these canals where they're grown is pure filth. You'd be better off in an open sewer, not that there's much difference, really.'

The Commissario smiled ruefully. 'My recommendation is the spaghetti vongole. The vongole are straight out of a tin, all the way from Sicily. Much the safest thing.'

'Thank you, sir.' Posie nodded. She was warming ever so slightly to Salvarocca now. The tiniest sliver of a thawing, mind, not an all-out melt. 'Can I just ask? The Corsetti boy – the one you arrested yesterday. Why *are* you letting him go when you are convinced he started the fire at the Palace?'

The Commissario shrugged. 'I need his "help". It seems Pietro Corsetti only started the fire for money. Of course, eventually I'll get him in as an accessory to a serious crime. But if I let him go free now, chances are he'll lead us to whoever it was who paid him for starting that fire. Gamblers usually go back for more when they have located a good source of income.'

'Good plan,' assented Lovelace.

After the Venetian Chief of Police had left, Posie and Inspector Lovelace fastened their hats and coats on in the hallway, ready to brave the cold Venice air.

'So you're staying here at Mrs Persimmon's too? Lucky you.'

'I am. Can I expect you to be picking my lock and spying on me?'

'Very funny, sir. It's a long story, and not a good one.'

'You'd better tell me about it. But can I just say one thing?'

'Go on.'

'It's a mare's nest, Posie. Everything I've seen so far.'

And she quite agreed.

****

It was nice to get out. Lovelace and Posie stood for a minute in front of the Romagnoli Palace.

'Was that Salvo going in there?' muttered Lovelace, shading his eyes in the smoky light. Although it was only lunchtime, it could well have been evening.

'No, I must have been wrong. What would he be messing around for in that burning mess? He's got enough to do now.'

The short walk through the dark little medieval streets and the rickety wooden bridges was calming, and somehow more authentic than Posie's early-morning Venetian experience: less showy, less bruising on the senses. They walked quietly, the Inspector looking pensive, barely taking in his surroundings, and it was not until they were seated at a small, private table at the trattoria and had ordered their meal that Posie broke the silence.

'Why are you here, sir? *Really* here, I mean? What was that you gave to Alaric?'

Lovelace sighed. 'I can't tell you, Posie. I'm sorry.'

The recommended spaghetti vongole arrived, smelling delicious.

'Let's get some wine,' Posie said impetuously, and they ordered a carafe of strong, ruby-red wine, which Lovelace drank gratefully, perhaps a little too quickly. After a few minutes of eating, he looked at Posie thoughtfully.

'I am here because of Alaric. He paid for me to come out. It was all quite last-minute; he asked me two weeks ago. It was a surprise. He asked me to be a witness at the wedding.'

'*My* wedding, sir?'

Lovelace smiled. 'Who else's?'

Posie looked down miserably into her pasta. She suddenly found herself blurting out the whole sorry tale:

the magazine cover; the strange, distant behaviour of Alaric since she had arrived; Alaric's packed bag and his odd, nocturnal wanderings with a lantern over at the burnt Palace. She found herself confessing to Lovelace that she was frankly surprised a wedding was going ahead at all. That she had been on the cusp of leaving, but obviously, with the murder, she couldn't go anywhere.

Inspector Lovelace stared.

He poured them both another glass of wine and then drained his own. He sat back and his lips twitched nervously. 'I don't know what to say, Posie, old girl. It sounds a very rum thing. All I can tell you is that when Alaric spoke to me two weeks ago he seemed fine about the wedding.'

Lovelace was drumming his fingers on the table. 'I suppose we could check at the church on the way back? Ask this Vicar chappie if tomorrow is all tickety-boo?'

Posie nodded bitterly, remembering Max's urging her to do the same.

A waiter came and switched their plates, and beef and fried potatoes and delicious-looking deep-fried vegetables were brought. Posie found she still had no appetite and pushed the food around her plate numbly. Inspector Lovelace was wolfing his lunch down hungrily. He paused, as if something had just struck him:

'I say, Posie! Did you *really* break into Alaric's room? It doesn't seem your usual style, somehow. Poor fella!'

Posie swallowed nervously, and then decided to tell Lovelace all about the man they had both met before in different circumstances. Max, the spy. Posie described what Max was doing now, about how he had told her a good deal about Alaric's doubtful behaviour. There was that rattish sense of betrayal again, like when she had confessed her findings about Lucy to the police, but she felt she might as well be hung for a sheep as a lamb and carry on anyhow. Besides, it felt good not to have secrets anymore. For all these strange layers to be peeled back.

But Inspector Lovelace was looking at Posie strangely. He whistled softly.

'My days! This is really quite something you've jumped into here, isn't it, Posie? It's a little bit more than a busman's holiday. Trust you! Talk about a top-level spy! This is above and beyond your usual secret-agent stuff. I wonder, what is this fella really up to? It must be quite some shin-dig. The German fella's good, I'll give him that. *I* was taken in hook, line and sinker by that story he gave us.'

Lovelace seemed to focus suddenly, and frowned. 'But Posie. You are a fool sometimes. Max might be a top agent, but he's still a man, isn't he?'

'So?'

'Well. I've seen it myself. He may only just know you, but maybe he's formed some sort of *attachment*, shall we say? You have this effect on men.' He groaned, and a shadow crossed his face. 'Remember Caspian della Rosa, the lengths he went to for "love" of you.'

Posie flushed red. 'It's not like that at all here, sir.'

Lovelace shook his head, not to be put off his stride. 'Has it occurred to you that it might not be a shame for Max if your engagement with Alaric is broken off, Posie? He might not be impartial. He might want you for himself. Do you trust this man? You don't know him from Adam, do you? He sounds as if he barely knows himself.'

Posie swallowed sourly and didn't mention the pink glass necklace which Max had given her, which she wore at her throat, which she found herself clutching at now. Or the giving to him of the priceless sapphires. The Inspector might think she had quite lost her head. Perhaps she had.

Her pink engagement ring sparkled merrily in the bright lights of the trattoria and she found herself hiding her left hand under the table. Guiltily. 'It's not like that at all, sir.'

Lovelace shrugged and mussed his thick, rough hair. 'As you like, old girl. I just had to point it out.'

The subject of Alaric dealt with, they sat in silence again, until the coffee came, hot and strong and delicious. It was such a treat to eat proper Italian food, in a proper Italian restaurant, at last. Posie thought of Mrs Persimmon's guesthouse and the non-descript blancmange from the night before and the gloomy cauliflower cheese, and she almost shuddered. She was pleased the Inspector had eaten a good meal, it might be his last for a while. Perhaps Dickie Alladice had been right about wanting to move everyone across to the Metropole Hotel. At least there they would have eaten well. But it was not to be.

'I say! That information you were giving to old Salvo back there, about the family and friends of Bella Alladice? Was some of it gleaned from our friendly spy in the attic?'

Posie explained about her synthesising Max's information and the reports from Rainbird. The Inspector nodded approvingly.

'Good girl. If Max is a spy of that quality, with no axe of his own to grind, it will all be good stuff. But this is really quite something, you know. Something big is going on here. Bigger than Bella Alladice's death, I mean. But I don't know *if* or *how* they are related. I don't like it: it has a nasty flavour about it.'

'Quite right, sir. It does. That's what Max said, too.' Posie looked at her little red wristwatch. 'Shall we leave? We said we would only be an hour.'

Outside, the air was frozen, not a good time to be hanging around. But Lovelace stopped suddenly, right in the centre of the shuttered Campo San Maurizio and gripped at Posie's arm. 'I've got it!' he hissed triumphantly, excitement gleaming in his eyes.

'You know who killed the Countess? That was quick, sir!'

'No, not yet. But I know where I've seen that girl before: the girl who apparently poisoned her employer using Bella's own hip-flask. It's been gnawing at me ever since I clapped eyes on her.'

'Lucy Christie?'

He nodded. 'Yes. Except that most definitely is *not* her real name.'

****

Seventeen

Excitement tore through Posie. 'So come on! Who is she, sir?'

They had stopped on a bleak, unsheltered corner. A group of four black-cloaked musicians, instruments shrouded, hurried past. A freezing wind was rustling the tree-tops of the walled garden opposite, and Posie and Lovelace found themselves subconsciously following the musicians, entering the great carved slab of fancy icing which was the Church of San Vidal.

A small veneered visitor's bench was jammed into the tiny entrance. Posie moved a bouquet of heavily-scented dead lilies off the bench, the orange pollen staining the dank stone floor, and they sat down, nestled between a stack of printed music programmes and packages of greasy white candles. In the main church, over near the altar, the musicians were setting up on a small platform, putting out sheet music and adjusting stands. A few nuns were sitting expectantly in the front row.

'She looked familiar to me, too, sir. But I couldn't place her. Again and again I wondered if I'd met her before.'

The Inspector shook his head. 'I doubt you've ever met her in the flesh. But it probably feels like it. Who could forget those great, dark eyes? They stared out at us from newspapers for a whole summer long.'

'She's famous?'

'I'll say. Do you remember the Robert Gattling murder?'

Posie frowned. It didn't sound familiar. She didn't like to appear ill-informed though and her annoyance obviously showed. The Inspector laughed grimly:

'Don't worry about the name. You would have been a mere whippersnapper of a thing at the time, probably not even twenty. I remember it clear as a bell. It was before the Great War broke out, must have been about 1912. I was a Sergeant in London, but I was doing my Inspector's exams all that summer. I barely saw my Molly from one week to the next although we were courting. It was deadly dull and I often looked at the daily papers for a bit of light relief. The Robert Gattling murder, or '*The Ice Cream Girl Murder*', as it became known, had everything to cause a sensation.'

The Ice Cream Girl Murder. Posie gasped: of course she remembered it. The hazy details, at least.

She had been at home in Norfolk then, keeping house for her father in the small, closed world of the Norfolk Rectory, missing her brother, Richard, away in the glitteringly remote world of Cambridge. The war which would obliterate life as they knew it was not even on the edge of their imaginings yet. Posie had read the daily papers with almost a religious fervour, feeling a need to connect with a world bigger than her own. She had started to step out with Harry Briskow, the kind, funny man she would later become engaged to; just another man who would die pointlessly in the Great War alongside most of his generation. Back then, Harry was newly-qualified as a solicitor, and he'd been looking around for a suitable wife. Although Posie had a feeling now that she certainly would *not* have made him a suitable wife…

The Inspector was continuing: 'The case had everything a scandal needs to run: a beautiful girl accused of being a poisoner; a well-known murder victim; wealthy characters;

a sort of love triangle. It was a complicated hot mess of a case, and tempers ran high, both in the Courtroom and in the country among the readers of the news.'

'Remind me.'

Lovelace's boyish face lit up at the memory.

'The crime was nothing to do with London, of course. Not my patch. It was up in the north. Lancashire, I think. Although the case was tried in London, at the Old Bailey, as all good murders are. There were three rich families involved, all of whom had a big monopoly on business up in Lancashire: the Gattlings, who owned a good many hotels all along the Blackpool coast; the Alladices, who owned a chain of famous sweet factories which supplied the whole country; and the Allessandros, who were second-generation Italians, and owned a chain of successful restaurants in that area. The Allessandros started off, as many immigrant Italians did in those days, by running seaside ice cream parlours, but by this time they had moved on, both socially and economically. But that didn't stop the press from labelling it "The Ice Cream Girl Murder."'

Posie remembered. 'The children of these families were part of the same crowd, weren't they?'

'Exactly. By the time of this case they were all in their early twenties. Robert Gattling was the only child of the hoteliers, and by all accounts he was a bit of a wild lad; a good-looking young cub with plenty of money to splash around. He was after all the girls, until he'd settled on Alicia Allessandro, that is. She was the only child of the Italian restaurant family. Robert Gattling pursued her fixedly, although apparently they weren't well-suited: she was a dreamy, gentle girl more interested in painting watercolours and pressing flowers than dancing in nightclubs and staying out until the early hours. But nevertheless, most people at the time were waiting for the engagement notices to be placed in the newspapers.'

Posie exhaled slowly.

Alicia Allessandro.

It all fitted. She remembered those exotic dark eyes, haunting and reproachful, looking out from photographs: a small doll-like face framed by puffy black wings of hair which were so fashionable back then; an enviably slim figure dressed in the height of romantic Edwardian fashion.

So *that* was who Lucy Christie really was.

Inspector Lovelace carried on. 'As far as I recall, this lot were all at a Society Spring Ball somewhere, round about May, and they were all eating their fancy dinner when Robert Gattling keeled over and went splat in his soup. Dead as a door-nail, blue in the face. Alicia had been sitting next to him, and it was she who screamed for a doctor, although it was obviously too late. It was pretty clear it was a poisoning, and the police big boys arrested Miss Allessandro the very same night.'

'But why?' Posie breathed, enthralled.

'A vial of poison was found in her evening bag. The drug had been put into Robert's champagne flute, and it would have been the work of a second to slip it in, given the right opportunity. Apparently Alicia had ample opportunities, when she returned from the toilets, for example, and found the others had gone on ahead of her onto the dance floor. There was a convincing witness who stated that Alicia had been alone near the table at least once.'

'But that bottle of poison could easily have been *placed* in her bag!' hissed Posie in disbelief. 'And why would she have done it? She was about to get engaged to the man!'

'That was the trouble. There was some sort of rumour abounding that Alicia wasn't actually as happy about a possible engagement to Robert Gattling as she might have been, that *he* was the one doing the running, and that, in fact, she loved another. The rumour went about that she couldn't stand the fella.'

'Awkward. But hardly a motive for murder, surely?'

Lovelace shrugged. 'That's as maybe. But killing Robert would have got him out of the way. And there were other, even uglier rumours doing the rounds. Mostly hushed up, of course, by the parents, who couldn't believe them of their blue-eyed boy.'

'Such as?'

'That Robert Gattling was a bully, starting to run with another, far racier crowd, down in London. He was violent, and got into scrapes, often with cheap women in nightclubs. And he was frequently not in his right mind.'

'Drugs, you mean?'

The Inspector nodded grimly. 'Most likely cocaine. He was spending money like billy-o, at any rate. It was just the sort of juicy detail a young almost-Inspector likes to get his teeth into, but, as I said, all of that drugs and violence stuff was mostly hushed up. What came across clearly at the trial was that Robert Gattling could do no wrong: he was a lad cut off in the prime of his life, about to propose to his intended at a prominent society event. They even found an engagement ring in his jacket pocket later. A blasted great brute of a ruby, ugly as sin, but it must have cost him a packet. Funny the things you remember when you're supposed to be studying, isn't it? Anyway, the timing was tragic, it lent pathos to the whole thing.'

Posie frowned. Something felt familiar here. But the thought slipped from her, like sand falling away.

'I remember the trial vaguely.' Posie thought of those long-ago, far-off hot summer days. 'Lucy refused to make any defence for herself, didn't she? She wouldn't say a thing, just stared straight ahead or at the floor. A bit like earlier, when the Commissario arrested her because of the connection to that flask. It was dreadful.'

The musicians had stopped tuning up and had launched into a beautiful, soaring melody. A small paper pasted to the glass door by their bench announced that the quartet would be performing Bach's 'Ciaccona per Violino e Archi' later that night. For a second they enjoyed a few bars of the trembling, melancholy music, before shaking themselves and returning to the job in hand.

'It *was* dreadful,' agreed Lovelace. 'The trial ripped those families apart. Despite hiring the best defence counsel available, the girl wouldn't answer anyone, and there's not much even the best lawyer in the world can do if his client won't speak. Both Alladice boys stood as character witnesses for her, I remember, and they gave statements which cast Lucy in a favourable light, throwing doubt on how she could have poisoned Robert Gattling that night.'

That made sense: Posie remembered Johnny Alladice's Will, protecting Lucy, and also Dickie's protestations of her innocence, earlier, at her arrest, and his obvious and continued devotion to her.

'But she was convicted of murder by the Jury, anyhow?'

'That's right, sentenced to death by hanging. It all looked pretty bad for her. The newspapers went to town, you might recall. They made much of her Italian background and her Latin temperament, and her apparently poor roots: practically made out she was a serving girl in one of the Allessandro's ice cream parlours and that she deserved no better than she got, for having the nerve to have made a play for such an exalted chap as Robert Gattling in the first place.'

Inspector Lovelace was pulling his scarf and his coat collar up around his face, buttoning his coat tighter. Posie followed suit. Someone was lighting candles all around the church now, and incense was being lit, cloying in the air already.

As they left, the cold of the street enveloped them again. They walked slowly.

'The Allessandro parents were plagued by the press after the trial. Literally hounded day after day. They'd started up a big appeal, of course, but it didn't look hopeful. While their daughter was awaiting a date for her own execution, and the appeal just beginning, they shot each other in a mutual suicide pact.'

Posie shook her head in horror. They had reached the Accademia Bridge, and pilgrims for the Salute Church were pressing them on all sides.

'I believe the mother survived,' Lovelace explained. 'But she was virtually brain-dead, and completely paralysed. She no longer knew who she was, or anything else for that matter, poor soul. She must have died since, I'm guessing.'

'No. I don't think so, sir.'

Posie remembered the snooping Max had done, and the money orders being sent to a nursing home in the north of England. She told the Inspector, who grimaced. And then she remembered more: the other money orders which Max had found, written out by Lucy every month to Roger Valentine, ever since he had started work for Bella Alladice. Roger must have found out, somehow, about who Lucy really was. Perhaps he had threatened to tell the world where they could find Alicia Allessandro, the villain of 'The Ice Cream Girl Murder' case?

Confound the man and all he stood for! But that couldn't be helped now.

'Weren't her family very rich, sir? So why is Lucy sending her small salary home?'

'I expect not as rich as they seemed, especially with the costs of all those legal fees. The money for Lucy's appeal lawyer, and the costs of the Court fees would have come out of Mr Allessandro's estate. Probably there was enough left over for a few years of nursing home care, but not much else.'

'It was worth it, though, wasn't it, sir? The appeal? She's still alive! Alicia, or Lucy, as she now is...'

Lovelace nodded seriously. 'Yes. It was the damnedest thing, but the appeal went through. That expensive lawyer was worth his salt, and more, even if his client still refused to speak. The girl was released and all murder charges dropped, for lack of evidence.'

They were almost at the Campo San Vio itself. Some priests in birettas and cloaks hurried by in a closely-knit black crowd, anxious to keep a distance from the crush of people surging towards the Salute, and one peeled off in the direction of St George's Church, reminding Posie to go and check about her own wedding ceremony.

'Lack of evidence, sir? It sounds a bit wishy-washy, don't you think?'

'Oh, that's how it always goes. Some flimflam about how the placing of the poison in Robert's champagne couldn't *really* be attributed to Lucy, and there were also concerns about the vial of poison in her evening bag: how it really got there. But oh! Oh, golly, yes!' The Inspector ruffled his hair, thinking deeply.

'I *believe* that the main evidence against the girl – a damning testimony about seeing Lucy hovering near the table, alone – was smashed apart at appeal by the defence lawyer. He had a whale of a time, I believe, announcing it in Court. It was news in itself. One of those Alladice brothers came forward; reported that the particular witness concerned wasn't impartial. He was very convincing.'

'How so?'

'Because it concerned his younger sister. She had given a withering report at the trial against Lucy. But it turned out she was jealous. She had been a former paramour of Robert Gattling and she'd been passed over by him, and couldn't get over it.'

The stony cobbles of Campo San Vio felt like they were spinning, and the world with all its crazy colourful masks and priests and churches and water was reeling.

Posie whispered, as if she didn't want to admit the truth, even to herself. 'That was Bella, wasn't it, sir?'

It was too, too awful. 'Bella wanted Lucy to hang?'

****

Eighteen

So many things made sense to Posie now, and yet nothing came together.

Bella.

With that dreadful ruby ring like a bloody-red claw on her hand. A dead man's ring.

It *must* have been the ruby Inspector Lovelace had just spoken of, found the night of the murder in 1912.

Probably Bella had acquired it somehow after the trial, and hung onto it for posterity, like some ill-fated omen of doom. But what sort of sick love could sustain you to do such a thing? To wear a ring intended for another? What sort of morbid obsession could fester like that? To give evidence sufficient to hang an innocent girl?

If Lucy had been innocent, that is. *If* it hadn't just been the work of a clever defence lawyer to get her acquitted of murder back in 1912.

And then in the years afterwards Bella had gone against her dead brother's wishes and kept Lucy close, but ill-treated. Out of jealousy, or vindictiveness, or for revenge. Because even though Lucy, as she had become, had been dragged through the murder courts, and even though Robert Gattling himself was dead, Lucy had forever got her man. *Bella's man.*

Posie remembered Bella's strange words from only the night before, not understood at the time. The heavy, dreadful menace behind them was now loaded with even more significance: '*I was in love with a man who was going to marry me. But it didn't work out. He looked elsewhere. And my heart froze.*'

For the tiniest second Posie felt sorry for the dead Countess, so bound up by her misremembered love affair with the Gattling boy, unable to move on, to form normal relationships, or to forgive. But Posie's mind was unaccountably marching on, faster than she could think, automatically passing on to the next snatch of her conversation with the dead Countess, her reason for hating Lucy:

'*She has a habit of stealing hearts. Hearts which are not hers to take.*'

Hearts. So the hearts had been those of Robert Gattling, and then, afterwards, as was obvious from that pathetic little Will, Johnny Alladice. He too had loved Lucy. It had represented a double betrayal in Bella's twisted mind.

They were now at the heavily-scrolled and emblazoned front door of St George's Church, with yet more crowds pressing past. A scratchily-bare tree stood to the right of the church door, wispily losing its last leaves.

But Posie could scarcely take in that Inspector Lovelace was now pulling at the old-fashioned iron bell-pull, and that he was leafing through a yellowing, rain-grizzled pamphlet for Sunday services which was tucked into a small metal basket nailed to the wall. The bell rang out, soft and low. Above them a beautiful carved relief of George and the dragon caught the eye, mainly because it was covered in roosting, wet pigeons.

'Sir,' she insisted, 'why on earth has Lucy stayed with Bella all these years? With the woman who tried to get her hanged, but who also cheated her financially?'

'What was that?'

She quickly described how Lucy had been 'provided for' in Johnny's Will, and how she had received a diamond ring from him, and how Bella had spectacularly abused her position of trust.

Lovelace shrugged, pulling his hat low, and looking around the place unappreciatively.

'Who knows why she stayed? Maybe for the same reason she changed her identity and grabbed a convenient, inconspicuous name? Perhaps it was just easier, and better the devil you know? If she had remained Alicia Allessandro forever, she would always have been followed by the press. There would have been blackmailers everywhere. Maybe even people threatening her life? People get a bit funny about murderers, you know. Even murderers who get acquitted.'

Posie thought sourly of Roger Valentine. 'There are *still* blackmailers everywhere, sir. Even out here in Venice.'

Damp leaves blew past and Lovelace shook them from his polished shoe. 'I agree the whole thing is confoundedly wretched, but you often hear these sad stories. I must say, things look very bad for the girl, especially in light of what you've just told me; years of abuse from this awful Bella creature.'

He suddenly sounded doubtful. 'Maybe she *did* just flip out and murder the Countess? And maybe she *did* kill Robert Gattling, all those years ago? Once a murderer... Do you know, the funny thing is that way back in 1912 I was so convinced of that girl's innocence I even had an argument with my Molly over it, and we never argue!'

'Sir, do you happen to remember what poison was used to kill Robert Gattling?'

'It was prussic acid. Same as now. Not good. Not good at all.'

And Posie recalled with a sharp, horrible jolt the tension in the air in the salon at the guesthouse, and Dickie Alladice's words, now with a new meaning attached to them: '*Did you say prussic acid? Good grief! I must be mistaken!*'

The Inspector pulled the bell again and turned to Posie. 'I don't think anyone is going to answer the bell, somehow. Do *you* think Lucy killed the Countess?'

Posie wasn't entirely certain, but her instincts were usually good, and she had liked Lucy Christie from the start. She waved her left hand with its engagement ring airily. 'No, I don't. Why would she be so stupid as to use the same poisoning trick twice? In fact, I'll make a bet with you: I'll wager this ring on her innocence.'

The Inspector grinned in amusement. He looked with pretend longing at Posie's expensive bauble.

'I don't know what Alaric will say, eh? But I do know that ring would see my little Phyllis all through school and university and give her a nice white wedding, too.' He nodded wryly. 'I'd better wish for Lucy's guilt, then. Although…'

Suddenly they could hear footsteps approaching from inside the church. Big bolts were being drawn back. The heavy oak door opened inwards and a round-faced, mild-looking man of about Posie's own age peered out in a friendly manner.

'Sorry to keep you waiting, I was battling with the Primus stove in the kitchen. All I wanted was a cuppa! We are quite without our normal housekeeper today, and it tells, I'm afraid. What can I do to help? If you're looking for the Salute Church, all you need to do is follow the crowds! You'll get there just fine.'

'No, nothing like that.' Posie shook her head quickly. Posie, who had grown up among Vicars and church folk, recognised the man immediately for what he was, a Chaplain. He was wearing a shabby hand-knitted English cardigan over his cassock, and he was wielding the troublesome cup of tea.

'Our business is here.'

'Ah, well, step right in, please. I'm the Reverend Blythe.'

When inside the cosy white interior with its neatly-arranged dark brown pews, Inspector Lovelace asked after any upcoming weddings, tomorrow in particular. The Chaplain looked doubtful for a minute, then picked up a big blue-covered book.

'Ah, yes,' said the Reverend, running a finger down a page. 'We do have one wedding. Tomorrow. Boynton-Dale? Name sounds familiar, doesn't it? Famous chappie, is he? It was booked a few weeks ago. Fee already paid.'

Posie gulped. So Max had been wrong, and Alaric had had good enough intentions to organise it all well in advance.

'Ah, oh! No! Wait a minute! I tell a lie! What's this?'

The Chaplain frowned and pushed his face nearer the book, then held it up for Posie and Lovelace to examine. 'What do you make of *this*?'

They looked. What appeared to be a thin but firm pencil line, double-scored, had been placed over the entry for the Boynton-Dale marriage.

'I'm terribly sorry.' The Reverend Blythe shrugged in embarrassment. 'I think we must assume it has been cancelled. My superior, the Vicar of the church, Father Gregory, will know something about it; they are *his* pencil-markings, but he's away just now, visiting the sick, all over the town and the lagoon. He left just before lunch and he won't be back until tomorrow morning.' The Chaplain scratched his head. 'Actually, come to think of it, I remember Father Gregory speaking about this: saying the marriage had been cancelled over the telephone. Most unusual...'

The Chaplain shook his head apologetically: 'I'm sorry not to help you more. Guests for the wedding, were you? Or,' and here he smiled at Posie and the Inspector in a kindly fashion, but with real interest, 'were you thinking of tying the knot yourselves? Had to be tomorrow, did it? On a Cox and Kings Venice short trip, are you?'

'No, no,' said Lovelace hastily. 'But if you *do* happen to find out if the wedding is going ahead or not, for definite, can you contact us? We're staying at the guesthouse next door.'

After giving his name and details they left.

'So it *has* been cancelled,' muttered Posie darkly.

'Looks like it. Although it pains me to admit it. I'm so sorry.'

But Posie just felt a strange numbness of being, as if she couldn't care less what happened to her next. Or to Alaric. She was certain now that the ominous pencil markings in that blue book were testimony of Alaric's spectacular disloyalty towards her. What other explanation could there be?

Fearing that a dreadful bitterness would break over her, Posie resolved that she would bury herself in her work rather than sink into aching misery: it was as if the murder of Bella Alladice and the awful history behind it had become much more real than her own life anyway, more real than her own future.

A hopeful Venetian stallholder, terribly illegal, had set up his wares on the metal grills covering the stone well in the centre of the Campo San Vio. He was selling bright carnival masks, and was calling out in jaunty tones to the passing hordes of pilgrims. A few people had stopped to buy, and Posie and Lovelace watched, entranced, for as soon as the buyers had gone, the man reached down into a seemingly bottomless sack and brought out yet more identical masks.

Inspector Lovelace laughed. 'Not much difference between here and the hawkers around St Paul's, is there?' But he stepped forwards lightly, selected one gold carnival mask and one red, and paid for them quickly. He didn't even bother to haggle.

Joining Posie, he placed the red mask in her hands. 'This might be the only bit of Venetian souvenir-hunting I get to do. And if I give this to you now, even if the wedding doesn't happen, it was a present just for you, wasn't it? And you don't need to feel bad about it with any nasty associations. The gold one is for Molly.'

Posie smiled, absurdly cheered by the little red mask shaped like a half-moon.

'Thank you, Richard. That's very kind of you. I'd never have bought it for myself, and I love it.'

Back at the guesthouse Posie sat on the bench pulling off her shoes and hat and coat, and a black weather-proof cape flapped into her face in an annoying fashion. She batted it away, remembering the night before, when Lucy, just out of the rain herself, wearing that very cape, or one similar to it, had offered her the glittering silver flask of liqueur.

The Inspector was rubbing at a patch of dark green foamy mould on the papered wall. 'Quite some place this, isn't it? Could give the Savoy a run for its money. See you later? At six o'clock?'

But Posie was thinking again of last night. *The flask.* She was convinced of Lucy's innocence but this might prove it. She gripped Lovelace's arm in excitement.

'The flask Lucy gave me last night was marked "*AA*". We all supposed that she was using, or borrowing, her employer's flask: a flask Bella was known to carry every day. We just assumed that "*AA*" stood for "*Annabella Alladice*".'

The Inspector was looking at Posie as if she had lost her mind, but he nodded calmly. 'Mnnn?'

'But what if it *didn't* stand for Annabella Alladice? What if it stood for "*Alicia Alessandro*"? What if there were two flasks? Identical to each other? What if the flask Lucy lent me was actually her own? Perhaps Johnny Alladice gave the flasks, maybe as birthday gifts at different points, to two women he held dear? And, by chance, the engraver would have had to carve exactly the same initials! Two flasks – *both* engraved with "*AA*". Dickie said that Bella felt very strongly about the giver of her flask and she would never have lent it out. He probably didn't know Lucy has the exact same thing. What do you think, sir? Does it sound likely?'

Richard Lovelace sighed, but there was a slight fire beginning to burn in his green eyes.

'No. It sounds hideously unlikely. But, as we both know, such things can happen. We'd better check it out – we'll search Lucy's room within an inch of its life. It's important. In fact, the poisoned flask from the crime scene is the only thing – the *only* evidence – connecting Lucy to the murder of the Countess. If we find a *second* identical flask she's a free woman. But why didn't the girl say something? *If* she has a second flask, that is?'

Posie bit her lip. 'Maybe she didn't want to have to explain the whole story about her identity in front of everyone? Although goodness only knows more than half the room knew it anyway! But not us, unfortunately.'

Within seconds the Inspector had snapped quickly into the sort of action Posie was used to witnessing in the corridors of Scotland Yard, commandeering all of Salvarocca's policemen in the lobby and vanishing up the stairs.

While she stood nervously waiting, Posie realised that she was longing for some proper evidence, some clarity. A photograph, for example.

Images rarely lied, like that magazine cover of Alaric and Silvia in Constantinople. She decided to place a call through to London, to pursue her quest for evidence, and Sidney at the Grape Street Bureau answered after a few minutes. Cheeky, cheery and as merry as ever.

Posie outlined what she needed. 'Take a cab.'

'A motor cab, Miss?' Delight filled his voice.

'Yes. Raid the petty cash tin again. Fast as you can. Get down to Fleet Street at once, to the Associated Press office, and ask for Sam Stubbs. If he's not there ask for anyone else. Flash my card around and mention Scotland Yard if you have to. Get Sergeant Rainbird involved if you must. Get what I've asked for and place it in a strong envelope and mark it with my name and "CONFIDENTIAL". Then rush to Victoria, to the Orient Express platform. Hurry.'

She checked her watch. He should just make it. It was two-thirty in Venice, which meant it was one-thirty back in London, and the Orient Express would leave at three o'clock. Just enough time…

'You want me to come out there, Miss?' Sid's voice had taken on new tones of hushed disbelief. 'On the Orient Express?'

'No. Sorry, Sid, not this time. Give your envelope to the Head Steward on the train. Explain that it concerns a murder and that a specially-designated policeman will collect it directly from his hands tomorrow afternoon when the Orient Express arrives into Santa Lucia Station.'

'Very good, Miss. I'll cut along now. Shame about Venice, Miss. And a murder, you say? Lawks! You get enough of those at home!'

And he rang off. Happy to have the last word.

****

Nineteen

Just at that moment Inspector Lovelace came into view, running down the stairs, taking them almost two at a time in his hurry. Behind him came a blonde thin streak of a figure which turned out to be Max, who raised an eyebrow and grinned at Posie.

Lovelace waved a silver hip-flask, dripping wet. He grinned. 'You were right, Posie. Spot-on. We looked in Lucy's room but to no avail. And then I thought of our resident expert, up in the laundry room. I reacquainted myself and asked him to help.'

Max shrugged self-deprecatingly. 'I'd never seen it before, but I told you Lucy had keepsakes stuffed in an old hat-box, didn't I? Mostly old love-letters from someone called John, and a couple of photos of the man in all his going-off-to-war finery. I thought it might be there. But it wasn't.'

'Oh?'

'No,' Max continued. 'So then I thought it must have been hidden somewhere else, *if* it existed. There are precious few places to hide things in this guesthouse. I've hunted them all out, of course. And there it was…'

Inspector Lovelace looked happy. 'It was in the first of Max's hidey-holes! Hidden right up in the cistern of the toilet on Lucy's corridor. None too fresh but we have it anyhow!'

Posie frowned as Max excused himself and retreated up the stairs. It seemed dashed odd: Lucy wouldn't have hidden her own treasured flask in such a shabby manner, and for no reason. Which meant only one thing.

'There was a switch, sir? The murderer hid Lucy's flask so even if she *did* admit to having an identical one to Bella's she wouldn't be believed? What do we do now, sir?'

'Well…' The Inspector hesitated. 'Of course, we'll tell Salvo, as soon as he returns, and I'll hold on to this flask. It's major evidence in favour of Lucy's innocence. But I'm thinking that she should stay put, where she is. In jail.'

'Oh?'

'Suppose she *isn't* the murderer, but that someone else is happy for her to take the rap. Maybe she's safer inside, where she can't be got at?'

Posie nodded. 'Will she be all right in those cells? Will the Commissario treat her badly?'

The Inspector grimaced. 'I don't think he's capable of treating anyone badly, Posie. He's a terribly sad man, really. But I swear he's a good policeman, even if he has decidedly off-kilter methods.'

'You mean forcing people to spit out their alibis in front of everyone, sir? In the same room?'

'Mnnn.' The Inspector nodded, disapproval curling his lip downwards. 'It's a risky strategy, liable to make people clam-up, or simply copy whatever the person before them has just said. And this place hasn't been properly searched, either. It struck me while I was upstairs that people might be burning things or destroying evidence, so I've got Salvarocca's men in all the rooms right now, grabbing what they can. I'll go up to supervise them. This really is a mare's nest…'

Back up in her room, a sound like saucepan lids clashing in the long, narrow alleyway which her room looked over made Posie bolt to the window.

'What the blazes?'

In the failing light a narrow crowd of festival-goers, all carrying lanterns, were parting hurriedly. Peering into the dimness below, Posie could make out a figure, all in black, running between the crowds, head-down, very fast.

A thief? Nothing more than some nasty pickpocket? But she could also see that the crowds down in the alley were looking up in her direction, and shaking their heads in disbelief.

'*Impossible! Impossible!*' she heard, chanted again and again, before she retreated, confused, back into her bedroom.

In the corridor outside, about two minutes later, there was a sound of heavy running feet, and a slamming of a door, and then silence.

Exhausted, Posie lay down on her bed, fully clothed, in sheets which smelt of the sea, and began to sleep a breathless, uncomfortably shallow sleep, in which she dreamed she was being drowned.

* * * *

The soft knock at her door woke her.

'Hang on just a jiffy,' she murmured, croakily. Peering at the luminous hands of her wristwatch Posie saw that it was almost five-thirty in the afternoon.

Darkness had fallen properly, and the un-shuttered, un-curtained window gaped in a ghastly way, like a big, blank eye. The bedroom seemed as if it was packed full of a damp mist and too late Posie realised she had fallen asleep with the window not quite closed. The thick vapours from the salty marshes were invading even here. A drumming sound and a chanting, choral melody were rising from the alleyway below.

Posie reached to turn her bedside light on, and got up, smoothing down her tweed skirt, spitting on her fingers and running them along her eyelashes and patting down her hair. She slammed the window shut quickly, and sprayed Parma Violet liberally about.

She had been expecting Inspector Lovelace, or perhaps Alaric, or even the Commissario, but actually it was just Mrs Persimmon with her designated policeman, who hung back in an embarrassed fashion.

'Oh, hullo there, dearie!'

For a second Posie couldn't think quite what the woman wanted. To offer Posie some late-afternoon tea? To give some news? Was this a guesthouse service? An attempt at normal hospitality? As she gawked stupidly, the small lady gripped Posie's hand urgently.

'Can I come in, dearie?' she hissed. 'I think I may have remembered something important, and that nice Scotland Yard chappie said we could come to you.'

'Ah, yes. Of course.'

Lacking any tea-making facilities, Posie indicated towards the bed with its only-just straightened counterpane. She removed her pyjamas from the chair and threw them on the floor, sitting down and looking at Mrs Persimmon as encouragingly as she could manage.

The little dumpy woman was smartly made-up, with shimmery silver eyeshadow and red lipstick. But she was nervy and fidgety, too. She kept touching her dyed hair.

Sure as bread is bread, she looks guilty of something, thought Posie. *But what?*

'What do you know, Mrs Persimmon? I take it this is about the Countess and her murder?'

Posie took out her notebook as the Landlady wrung her hands. 'It's like this, dearie...'

Mrs Persimmon had told the police she had seen Bella Alladice *twice* after she had cleared breakfast: once at nine-thirty, when she brought coffee to the Countess, who was alone, reading, and again at roughly ten-thirty, when Mrs Persimmon came to clear away the coffee things, finding the Countess dead.

Posie frowned. 'But you're now saying that's *not* the case, Mrs Persimmon? You saw Bella another time? Three times? Four times?'

Mrs Persimmon shook her head indignantly. 'I only *saw* the Countess on the two occasions when I told that fascist policeman I had done so. I'm not a liar. But I'm telling you that I *heard* things which may be of interest.'

So it turned out it was a matter of overhearing: or *eavesdropping*, as most people might have put it.

The Landlady, with much pursing of the rouged lips and self-righteous nodding, explained to Posie how after the breakfast rush had ended, at about nine o'clock, it was Mrs Persimmon's daily custom to smoke a cigarette in the small back yard of the guesthouse. But given that the weather this morning had been truly *spiteful*, the Landlady had changed her usual routine and had sat on the small bench in the hallway outside the dining-room. It hadn't been her *intention* to overhear the Countess in the dining-room. Oh, no. But she *had*.

Mrs Persimmon had heard talking. Highly-strung, indignant words. The Countess had been in a right royal rage.

'What time was this, Mrs Persimmon?'

'Oh, about a quarter past nine, I'd say.'

'And what did you overhear, *exactly*? Who was she talking to?'

'I don't know for sure. I heard the Countess scream: "*You fool! You fool!*"'

It didn't sound hopeful. The Countess could have been talking to herself, about herself. Posie often said much the same thing of her own mathematical abilities when in the middle of horrible Revenue calculations.

'Did you hear anything else?'

'There was a fluttering of papers. I definitely heard paper falling, or being thrown, and then someone moving about, picking it all up again.'

Posie was quite frankly surprised that anyone could have heard all of this – the sound of paper falling – from the location of the bench, through the thick wooden door, but she kept her expression interested anyhow. She wasn't about to chastise the woman for listening at her own doors. So she sat calmly, waiting for more.

'I heard the words "*How could you? I'm going to go to the police. Better late than never.*"'

Posie was all agog now. 'Did anyone reply, Mrs Persimmon? Did you hear another voice, a definite second person in the room?'

'In truth I couldn't say, dearie.'

'And? What next?'

'There was no "next". It was twenty-five past nine by then and the coffee-pot and tray needed delivering to the Countess in five minutes. I turned tail and went to collect it from Cook. I like to give my clients the "personal" touch.'

Posie tried hard to cover her disappointment. It could be something, or nothing. There was still no actual evidence that anyone had been in the room with Bella. She stood up, smiling primly.

'Thank you so much, I'll pass it on to the Inspector.'

But the Landlady continued to sit. 'Oh, that's not all, dearie.' She nodded, surer of her ground now. Surer she wouldn't be judged for the eavesdropping.

Mrs Persimmon then reported that she had dropped the coffee things off to Bella, who had been alone, at the same table, seeming restless, drumming her fingers on the tablecloth. Thinking something was afoot, the Landlady had immediately stationed herself down the hall corridor, in the recess where the stairs to the staff kitchen began, and loitered. Waiting for something to happen. It was a fairly long wait.

'About ten o'clock the Countess came out of the dining-room, and she went downstairs to use the telephone. I heard it all. Like I said, I wasn't looking, just *listening*...'

Posie was astounded. So at ten o'clock this morning Bella still hadn't drunk the poison: she had been right as rain and ringing people up. Posie cursed inwardly. Why on earth hadn't they bothered to check this? Particularly as Bella herself had mentioned to Posie that she needed to make some telephone calls. As if she could read Posie's thoughts, the Landlady continued, nodding importantly:

'She called London, dearie. She made two calls.'

Posie tried not to goggle. Mrs Persimmon was turning out to be a mine of information. 'Do you know *who* she called?'

'Haven't a clue about the first call, dearie. It went right over my head.'

'Do you remember anything about it at all?'

The little woman wrinkled her nose in concentration and her red lipstick blurred unattractively into the lines all around her mouth. 'Something to do with a "register", or a "registrar", could it be?'

The woman shook her head. 'The Countess was shouting – it was hard not to hear – "*I want to speak to the registrar!*" And then: "*What do you mean he's unavailable? Do you know who I am?*" And then she listed all her titles. I didn't hear the next bit very well. And then there was a long pause. And then the Countess started shouting again: "*What do you mean the records are unavailable too? That's impossible! I need to check it out today!*" I must say I felt very sorry for the lad on the end of the phone, whoever this registrar fellow was.'

Posie nodded, uncomprehending, but noting it down anyhow.

'And the second call?'

'Ah! That's what was more interestin'! That's why I looked at your Inspector from Scotland Yard mighty funny. I thought to myself: "*He* got here jolly quickly! That call was only made a couple of hours ago!" Or else the Countess had second sight and wanted to call in about her own death.'

'I don't follow you, I'm afraid.'

'Well, the Countess was calling Scotland Yard, in London, wasn't she? She said she wanted to report a murder.'

* * * *

Twenty

Posie let the words and all their import fall around them. Mrs Persimmon had stood up and was at the little window, looking down at the fog. Her expression was sour.

'All this fog, all this water. It's not right, is it? It's all right for fish, maybe. Toads, frogs…'

'What did you hear next of the call, Mrs Persimmon? It's very important.'

'Oh, nothin', dearie. The Countess asked for an Inspector – any Inspector – and was obviously told no-one was about, even though she listed all her titles yet again. She said she wouldn't speak to a mere Sergeant, and she'd call back later. She didn't realise that was the last call she'd ever be makin', did she now? Poor lass!'

Posie blew out her cheeks in exasperation. The call to Scotland Yard would be easy to check on, but how fruitful would that be? The police receptionist on the other end of the conversation in London wouldn't be able to tell them much more than Mrs Persimmon.

The Landlady trotted to the door, and smiled at Posie. 'I can't tell you what a relief it is to have told someone. I couldn't have said all that aloud downstairs in that room with everyone listenin', could I? What would people have thought of me? *Snoopin' on clients*, they'd have thought.

What would the young Count have thought? Or that nice Mr Alladice, who I've known a good while now in business, of course.'

She drew herself up sharply. 'I have to take care over the *reputation* of my establishment. It's usually frequented by visiting clergymen, nice folks from the Home Counties. If my husband, Captain Persimmon, God rest his soul, had seen the place today, he'd have turned in his grave. A body! In my dining-room! Police everywhere, locking the cook and the maid, Rita, up like common criminals! This was supposed to be a safe little business for me.'

'Your husband was out here too?'

'Yes. He was a British seaman who ended up here and stayed on in the sugar trade.' The woman smiled proudly at long-ago memories.

'My old man Bill Persimmon fell in love with Venice, goodness knows why. But I suppose when you've been on a ship since you were a nipper it's a natural thing to find a city propped up in the middle of the sea and want to live in it, don't you think?'

Mrs Persimmon shuddered. '*I* always hated the seaside and the salty air. I was brought up in Bow, an East-End lass through and through. I still miss the smoke of town and the bells of the city, the *real* city, London. This was only supposed to be for a short time. My Bill bought this place on the Campo San Vio as a house for us while he worked out here. He bought a warehouse too, just opposite, for the storage of sugar. But you'd never find my Bill at home: he'd always be down on the quays at the Riva degli Schiavoni, seeing which boats were comin' in, or else near here, a few alleyways back, where the Alley of Sugar hits the Zattere, checking on the quality of his incomin' sugar supplies before the boats passed the Customs and sailed up our bit of the Grand Canal to our warehouse.'

There was a small silence. 'If you don't mind my asking, Mrs Persimmon. Why didn't you go back to London?'

There was a shadow of a smile.

'I was plannin' to, dearie. It was the usual story, though. We only had the one lad: Billie, named after his father. He died in the war, in 1916, fightin' for an England he had never lived in, except for a few Christmas visits now and again. And then his daddy died not long after. When I came to pack up my bags and go back I found there was almost no-one left of my own family, and those that *were* left were in the same position as me: heartbroken, or in pieces, or worse. So I stayed on here, and I bring out English staff so I feel more at home. And here I'll stay. I'll join old Bill on that awful little island where they bury corpses. But forgive me, I'm wanderin' again… Can you think of anythin' else I can help you with?'

Posie looked down at her notes quickly. What had she learnt here? That Bella Alladice had made some sort of discovery at about nine-fifteen in the morning, either alone or in the company of another person. Then she, or another person, had thrown her folio of papers around in a blind rage, before collecting them up again.

And lastly, that Bella had taken coffee alone at nine-thirty, in a frantic mood, and had still been totally alone at ten o'clock when she had placed two unsuccessful calls to London, the first one to who-knew-where, and the second to Scotland Yard, about a murder.

Alone.

'Mrs Persimmon, are you *sure* Bella was alone when you dropped off the coffee things at nine-thirty?'

The woman scoffed. 'I'm certain of it. There are no hidin' spots in my dining-room. And don't you think I wasn't lookin' all about me to see?'

Posie nodded, satisfied. 'So if there was someone in with Bella at nine-fifteen, he or she must have slipped away while you went to get the coffee?'

'That's right, dearie. No two ways about it.'

The next bit was crucial: 'This is important, Mrs

Persimmon. When you brought the coffee things in, and put them down, at nine-thirty, were Bella's papers still with her on the table?'

Mrs Persimmon chewed at her lip. She closed her eyes for about a minute. And then she shook her head. 'I can't be one hundred per cent certain. But when I go over those couple of minutes in my head, I can't remember seeing any papers at all. I put down the coffee-pot – the best one I had – with a jug of cream and a dish for those teeth-rotting candies of hers, and some sugar. And I put all this around the Countess, around her pen and her fancy leather book, but…'

'But?'

'I'm certain, dearie, thinking back, that there wasn't one piece of paper at that table. So there *must* 'ave been someone in there with her before. And whoever it was must have snatched the lot away, surely?'

* * * *

It was a few minutes before six o'clock, and Posie had managed to get her facts and her face in some sort of order, ready for the meeting downstairs. She had changed and her dress was violet and velvety and plain as night, a matching sequinned band tied around her head.

Tonight would be hard. Tonight she and Alaric would have to speak. Properly, that was…

Licking an errant bit of lipstick off her teeth, she was about to step out when another rap came at her door. Her stomach turned, certain this was Alaric, come, no doubt with his policeman, to accompany her downstairs in some sort of semblance of normality.

But there was no-one there.

Well, a policeman was there, and the maid brought out from England. The girl looked up expectantly at Posie. A tiny, dark slip of a thing. Blink and you'd miss her.

'Can I help you, er…' It came to her. 'Rita? Isn't it?'

'That's right, Miss.' The girl sounded pleased someone had remembered her name. She stepped into the room, and Posie groaned inwardly. She checked her watch pointedly.

'I need to tell yer sumthin', Miss. That nice policeman with the smile on his face downstairs said we could come to him or you if we had anyfin' to tell. But I'm choosin' you cos you ain't a real gal copper, are you?'

'Never a truer word was said,' muttered Posie, closing the door behind them, resigned to being late.

Rita shifted from foot to foot, seemingly oblivious to Posie not offering her a seat. 'It's about those masks, Miss. The ones which have been made black. Which I was told to clean up.'

Posie had quite forgotten about them. They had seemed a mere anomaly at the time; yet another complication. 'Ah, yes.'

'Well, I know who blacked them up, Miss. And I know who used them, too. And I ain't sure I like what I know, Miss.'

Posie eyed the girl keenly. Rita didn't seem the over-excitable type, prone to dramatic turns of phrase. She looked like the sort who preferred a quiet life, a shirker, in fact; the less work the better.

'What do you know?'

'These people all arrived yesterday after the fire, didn't they? And it was chaos, to be honest wiv' you. You've seen that we're not much equipped to deal with complicated people. Jones and me, we were runnin' around with people's bags and coats and things. Well…'

'Go on, please, Rita.'

'I caught sight of those two masks, Miss. Like Mrs Persimmon said, they were usually stored in the hallway, but yesterday I saw them at tea-time, upstairs in one of the guest's bedrooms. They were still brightly coloured at that point. I thought they had been carried up in all the confusion. So I went to gather them up in my arms and take them back down again, but it was that Miss Minnie who stopped me. They were in her room, on her bed.'

Posie raised an eyebrow dubiously. 'Minnie? What did she say about the masks when you drew attention to them?'

'Oh, nuffin' much, Miss. Laughed it off. Said she'd obviously brought them up by mistake and would take them down again herself.'

'Oh.' Posie was disappointed. This was hardly much to go on. 'Perhaps it wasn't Miss Alladice who changed the colour? She probably just put them back, as she promised.'

'Not *her*, Miss.'

'You don't like Miss Alladice much?'

'Well, it's not my place to judge, is it?'

'You can be completely frank with me, Rita. Social conventions don't mean much when you're dealing with a murder.'

The maid sniffed pointedly. 'She's not what she seems. Bosses me around like she's a Countess. The *real* Countess was bad enough – God rest her soul – but Minnie Alladice takes the biscuit! Expects me to skivvy for her and pick everythin' up off the floor like I'm a ladies' maid or summit! And it was *her* who blacked them up: she didn't realise I saw a tin of Avon black boot-polish beneath those masks on her bed. And what's more I saw her wiv' the masks last night. Late, it was, and she was wearin' one of them. And that's when I heard the true woman speak. You'd never believe it! The words she said, absolute venom. It were pure evil!'

Posie stared at the maid in complete surprise. 'Really? Where was this? And who was Minnie talking to?'

'You said I can be frank wiv' you, Miss?'

'Of course.'

‘I have a lad I’m steppin’ out with, but don’t tell a soul, Mrs Persimmon would kill me for it. He’s an Italian, Luca. We always meet at an empty boatshed on the Zattere, about five minutes’ walk from here through the backstreets of the Dorsoduro.’

Classy, thought Posie, trying not to grin.

‘It was quite busy down there on the Zattere last night, see? These people for the Festa della Salute, carryin’ lamps, and gettin’ in everyone’s way, even though the weather was foul. It’s awful narrow down there, Miss, with those little streets all facin’ right onto the canals, and the people pushin’ along somethin’ terrible. I was right scared! We stopped off on the way back, about eleven o’clock, at the Church of San Trovaso. Me and Luca, we stood inside the entrance to avoid the crowds and get shelter from the pourin’ rain. It was dark inside.’

A kiss and a cuddle in a quiet, candle-lit space, you mean, thought Posie, trying to remember what it felt like to be nineteen again.

The girl nodded: ‘But I’d only had a second or so to catch my breath when I heard an English voice pipin’ up next to me in the church entrance. A northern accent, it was, clear as a bell, even though she was whisperin’! I looked over and saw a woman in a black mask and a black cloak.’

‘Minnie Alladice?’

‘That’s right, Miss.’

‘Who was she with?’

‘That’s the funny thing. I don’t know these people, of course: we only clapped eyes on them for the first time yesterday afternoon. But the man she was with was an Italian. He had a very high voice, and he was short, and he was wearing the second black mask. Obviously neither of them wanted to be recognised at all. When I spoke to Luca about it afterwards he said that the man was a nobleman, that he was…’

Posie had to stop herself from gasping aloud in surprise. 'Count Giancarlo Romagnoli?'

'That's right, Miss. Odd, innit? You'd never see those two talkin' to each other normally, would you? But it was *her* what was in charge!'

What an unlikely, and mysterious pairing. 'What did they say? Did you catch any of it?'

'Somethin' of it. But I didn't understand. The Count was angry; stark raving furious, in fact. He said: "*You've gone too far now.*" And then she said: "*You'd better pay me again then, hadn't you? Or else I'll make certain of a scandal.*" And then he called her somethin' unrepeatable in Italian – I had to ask Luca for its exact meanin' later – and then the Count told Miss Alladice that she was tryin' to destroy everyone close to him.'

Posie nodded carefully. None of it made sense to her yet but she didn't want that to look obvious to Rita. Blackmail of some kind? The poisonous woman whose evil thoughts had been scrawled in a diary was perhaps transferring their malicious sentiments across into real life. Perhaps dangerously so.

'So they left before you?'

Rita nodded. 'But not before the Count handed over an envelope to Miss Alladice. I'm guessin' it contained money. He said: "*Don't ever give that to anyone vulnerable again or involve them in your sordid plans.*"'

Posie was stumped. Vaguely, she motioned at the door. 'Is that everything, Rita? I think we should probably go down now if you're quite finished?'

But Rita stood her ground. 'Oh, but I'm not finished, Miss. I heard somethin' else.'

'Does it concern Miss Minnie Alladice again?'

'Nope. It's somethin' I heard later on last night, when I was back from meetin' Luca. Just along here, in fact. I was bringin' up fresh towels to all the rooms on this corridor.'

So yet more people had been creeping about late last

night, people who noticed things. Posie hoped to goodness she hadn't been seen with Max. 'What time was this?'

'Oh, about midnight. I saw you slippin' by while I was up here, and I also saw Miss Christie. She was going into that handsome chap's room, Roger Valentine…'

'What did you hear, Rita?'

'An argument. Comin' from Mr Valentine's room.'

Posie frowned. Could Lucy and Roger have been arguing together?

'I heard Mr Valentine say: "*They'll kick up an awful shindy about it – I'll show it in the morning unless you pay up. So far I've only received half! I've asked several times now!*"'

'Show what exactly? Roger Valentine wasn't more specific?'

'No, Miss. Sorry. And then he also said: "*But that's nothing compared to this bit of reel! So where's the money?*" After that I hurried along. It sounded as if there was some sort of scuffle going on in the room. Sounded like a table going over.'

'Could it have been a woman he was arguing with? Miss Christie, maybe?'

Rita shrugged, but her eyes were keen and interested. 'Why not? They're a rum lot, aren't they? In fact, it could have been any of them in there with Mr Valentine, couldn't it? The dead Countess included.'

Posie agreed. Could Bella Alladice herself have been the person in the room being blackmailed, as Rita had, quite sensibly, suggested? Or was Bella the one who was expected to kick up an awful shindy? But about what exactly? What was '*it*' which Roger had threated to show if he wasn't paid? And what on earth was the 'reel'?

It seemed that there were two dangerous items at stake.

And maybe these two dangerous items of Roger's had found their way into the fat folder of Bella's this morning? Items which had since disappeared… Had *they* been the reason for her strange calls to London? Been the reason for her death?

Whatever the case, it seemed certain there were now two blackmailers in their midst: Minnie Alladice with her inexplicable campaign against the Count, and Roger Valentine, with a campaign against pretty much anyone.

The party from the Romagnoli Palace were turning out to be much more complicated than Posie could ever have guessed.

And it would be up to her to get to the bottom of it.

* * * *

Twenty-One

The official meeting hadn't yet started.

'Good evening,' murmured Posie, her stomach a tense ball of nerves. She stole a glance at Alaric, who was looking pointedly away from her, into the flames of a steady fire which seemed curiously unwelcoming.

He had obviously bathed, and shaved, and his cream open shirt and dark blue suit framed his lithe, angry body in a way which was somehow intoxicating. His lemony scent seemed to pervade the room. A manila envelope – was it the same 'CONFIDENTIAL' one that the Inspector had handed him only a few hours before? – was lying at his feet.

Posie had the feeling that Alaric was being eaten up with worry, and his long, tanned fingers drummed ceaselessly on his knee.

Posie noted how the drinks trolley was clear of bottles and decanters for once, and that everyone seemed stone-cold sober, even Dickie Alladice, whose face was haggard, but expectantly serious, his eyes blazing keenly in the firelight.

Over near the door Posie saw that Salvarocca and Inspector Lovelace were talking in hushed undertones, looking serious. Presumably Lovelace had updated his old friend on the true identity of Lucy Christie and had revealed the existence of the second, identical hip-flask by now.

But Posie had hardly ever seen Inspector Lovelace look so fraught. What on earth had happened in the last couple of hours? What had they found out about Bella's murder or murderer?

Settling herself into a chair next to Aunt Minnie, Posie noticed that Roger Valentine was missing.

'Where is Mr Valentine?' Posie asked carefully.

'Didn't you hear?' asked Inspector Lovelace, unsmiling. 'You must be the only one. Roger Valentine managed to escape.'

'*How?* From a locked room with a police guard?'

Richard Lovelace checked his wristwatch. 'It must have been about three o'clock. He tied a lot of sheets together and shimmied out of the window to avoid my searching his room. He ran away in the fog. We should have known better: he was an Oxford sailing blue and an expert at gymnastics; sliding down three flights of a building on a bit of fabric tied with some reef knots must have been a picnic for him.'

Posie sat numbly, remembering the running figure in the dark alleyway, the crowds looking up in amazement through the patchy fog. She also, strangely, remembered Lucy's introduction to Roger yesterday evening: '*He's very clever: keeps us all on our toes.*'

Well, he was obviously keeping the police on their toes now.

The Commissario nodded grimly. 'It doesn't look good for Mr Valentine. We found some material he was burning in the grate of his room, and he evidently has something to hide. By the very action of his running away we're assuming he's guilty of something. Police throughout the city are on the lookout for him, and we've got men on watch at the station and all the main water exits out of Venice.'

It sounded hopeless, even though the Commissario couldn't admit as such in front of all these people. The policeman continued:

'Regarding today's murder of the Countess Romagnoli, we are detaining Miss Lucy Christie for further questioning. We have not yet charged Miss Christie with murder, but I expect to arrest her properly by lunchtime tomorrow. The silver flask connecting her to the murder has now proven positive for containing poison.'

There was a collective intake of breath, a suppressed murmuring in the room. Dickie Alladice was shaking his head, over and over. Posie hoped against hope that this was Lovelace's double-bluff at work, his ploy to keep Lucy out of harm's way.

The Commissario rolled on: 'So, in a minute you are all free to go. I can't hold you any longer. You're free to have dinner out, maybe? Or celebrate Mass at the Salute Church? The main service is at ten o'clock tonight, and there will be crowds. Please take care, both of pickpockets and of the fog. These mists which envelop Venice are truly devilish; they sap all the noise right out of the air and people have been known to simply fall into a canal without making any sound at all. Personally, I would stay in.'

'So we are free to go *now*, Commissario?' Minnie Alladice was twisting anxiously in her chair.

Posie stared at Minnie Alladice with fresh eyes, yet again. She was imagining the black masks and cloaks, the leverage this small, scheming woman obviously had over Giancarlo, the Count, who even now stared fixedly away, still looking anguished. Minnie Alladice, whose future, unbeknownst to her, was now changed beyond all imaginings as a result of Bella's death. She would find this out in a week's time, of course, when Mr Proudfoot got here and read out the Will…

'I said *in a minute*,' the Commissario barked, in something like anger, an emotion he hadn't previously displayed. A look laden with meaning passed between him and Inspector Lovelace.

Posie frowned. *There's something else we don't know about yet. But what?*

The Commissario cleared his throat. 'I'm afraid there's another, crucial matter which impacts you all. It concerns the fire yesterday.'

Everyone looked up sharply, but Posie noticed how the Count had been looking worse and worse, minute by minute, and he alone looked resolutely away.

'You may have noticed how I've had policemen and firemen over at the Palace today; checking things, guarding things. That's because earlier this morning, while the Count and I were going through the building for the insurance calculation, it came to our attention that there was a certain hidden place – let's call it a *secret chamber* – which had also been affected by the fire.'

People were looking askance, as if some practical joke had just gone wrong and they weren't sure how to react. Posie risked a glance over at Alaric, who she saw was gripping the armrest of his chair tightly, so that his knuckles stood out white. She saw, incongruously, that he had scrawled, in blue ink, 'FRARI. 7 AM' on the back of his hand.

The Commissario was aware of the strained atmosphere in the room. 'The fire burnt away an old false wall in the Palace. A very clever false wall; you'd never have guessed it hid anything at all. The plaster, like so much in Venice, was so damp it didn't offer much resistance. The wall and hidden chamber it revealed were very old, probably eighteenth century. From the time of Casanova.'

'A hidden chamber?' Minnie Alladice piped up, a dreadful eagerness and a sense of horror barely concealed. 'The chamber of the Mistletoe Bride? I *knew* it existed. I knew it!'

Giancarlo Romagnoli ran suddenly from the room. Outside in the corridor came the sounds of someone being violently sick. But no-one offered him assistance, not even Mrs Persimmon, and all eyes remained fixed on the Commissario.

Posie remembered Lucy saying that the thought of such a place worried Minnie Alladice, that it preoccupied her. Posie recalled too the note Bella Alladice had shown her only yesterday evening, making reference to just such a chamber. So the person who wrote that note had known that such a dreadful place really *did* exist.

People were getting uneasy and Posie sprang into action. 'Where is this secret chamber, sir? And why is it of relevance to us? Despite being historically interesting, I mean.'

'The chamber, Miss Parker, is located between the suite of rooms occupied by the late Countess, and the suite of rooms your own – er – your own fiancé was given to occupy. Above the *piano nobile*, to be precise.'

Posie nodded, not much the wiser. 'So you've had your experts crawling all over it today for what reason exactly? You're worried it's going to fall apart and you want to take photos before it does so?'

Inspector Lovelace was hanging back, staring at the floor. Posie had seen that look before. *Bad news.*

Posie remembered Lucy talking about the Romagnoli daughter who had disappeared when she tried to flee the Palace, how she was never found. And the corpse referred to in Bella's hate-mail…

She spoke very low: 'Someone was in there, weren't they, sir?'

The Commissario nodded, looking about him. 'That's right. The fire hadn't quite obliterated everything in its path. When we were finally allowed inside, late this afternoon, we found the charred remains of a woman, probably about a hundred-and-fifty years old. It must have been the original girl of the legend, poor soul.'

Minnie Alladice was making squawking noises, like

she was finding it difficult to breathe, while sobbing sounds were coming from outside in the hallway. Posie felt desperately sorry for Giancarlo: so much of his normal life was being stripped away, and there were dreadful surprises at every turn. It was horrible, twisted. A sick legend made real. But somehow…

Posie stared again at Richard Lovelace. He was still looking at the ground, avoiding her eyes. *But why?* Surely not because of a hundred-and-fifty year old corpse?

She stood up, and found she was shaking. She meant to go out to the Count, bring him water, or a cigarette. But the Commissario's next statement stopped her.

'I must inform you all that we found *a second* body in the secret chamber this afternoon. And this one wasn't from days of old, but was rather the body of someone who died yesterday, in the blaze. So you see, the fire has now become a scene of murder, or manslaughter, at the very least. Whoever started that fire has caused a death, and if it is the last thing I do I will bring them to justice. Pietro Corsetti was released from custody after lunch, but in light of this fresh discovery this afternoon there are now instructions to bring him in again. He's an accessory to a horrific crime.'

Posie forced herself to concentrate. 'Whose was the second body, sir?'

'It was the body of a woman. Perhaps she was seeking a place of safety when the fire broke out? Little did she know that she was entering a deadly box which filled up quickly with poisonous smoke and which she simply couldn't get out of.'

To Posie's horror she saw the big police Commissario quiver and tears welled up in his tired brown eyes. Inspector Lovelace put a hand on his counterpart's shoulder.

'She died trying to get out of the door. She suffocated. In agony.'

Minnie Alladice was whimpering. Dickie Alladice was

standing, wringing his hands. The maid, Rita, not part of the party at all, was sobbing hysterically.

And Posie found herself whispering: 'Who was she? Who was she?'

But in her heart of hearts she knew.

* * * *

Twenty-Two

Salvo Salvarocca hung his head. 'She was unrecognisable, Miss Parker. We only have a heart-shaped key on the remains of a ribbon hanging around her neck to identify her.'

And then, staring at Alaric, who sat with his head in his hands, it all made sense. And Posie was frozen. Suddenly everything reorganised itself into a clear, definite pattern.

Posie spoke quietly to the policeman, but also to the room at large. 'I think you'll find her name was Silvia, sir. Miss Silvia Hanro. And she's probably the most famous movie star England has, or *had*, at the moment.'

Richard Lovelace had recovered himself. He spoke softly, so that only Posie could hear. 'I think I guessed that much, Posie.'

Posie carried on as if her life depended on it, fighting back awful tears which were threatening to come. She dared not look over at Alaric.

'If you check the key Miss Hanro was wearing against the relevant locker number at Santa Lucia Station, I expect you will find her belongings there. A passport even? She is a friend of Mr Boynton-Dale here. I don't know, but I expect she travelled separately to Mr Boynton-Dale, by train, and was maybe uncertain if she could or could not stay at the Romagnoli Palace with him. I'm sure it's her. What *exactly* she was doing in Mr Boynton-Dale's apartments is a matter he will no doubt be able to explain to you.'

Alaric, his eyes wild, his body shaking, got up and slowly crossed the room. He carried the brown manila envelope and shoved it forcibly at Lovelace without saying a word. No-one followed him downstairs and the front door slammed onto the street.

Posie's thoughts were tumbling. Silvia had been with Alaric at the Palace, that much was indisputable. But whether she had been visiting Alaric as a friend, or sharing his bed, or trying to start or re-ignite an affair, Posie had no idea.

She remembered how Alaric had been trying to tell her something about Silvia down by the Dogana when they had been interrupted the night before: '*This wretched thing about Silvia… There's something else…*'

Had he been trying to tell Posie that Silvia was actually here, in Venice?

Whatever the case, while Alaric had been out on his gondola trip with the other house guests, and the fire had taken hold, Silvia Hanro had somehow got herself stuck in the hidden chamber which adjoined Alaric's bedroom. *But how on earth had she known it was there?*

The disappearance of the movie star at the time of the fire had obviously caused Alaric to try, at whatever cost, to find her. He must have been worried sick, and he had been looking for Silvia all over the Palace when Posie arrived in Venice the day before. The story about grabbing Dickie Alladice's safe had just been a convenient little cover. He had been looking for Silvia again in the Palace, by torchlight, last night, when he had told Posie that he had to '*search out something. It's important.*' He had inadvertently told Posie that Silvia was 'precious.' Alaric hadn't known that Posie would watch him later from up on the *altana* with Max.

Stumped and desperate, Alaric had looked for Silvia again this morning, leaving Posie alone. He had evidently gone to Santa Lucia Station to see whether Silvia had taken her luggage away, hoping that she had managed to escape the fire and had made an inconspicuous exit from the city. But Silvia hadn't escaped.

The locker was still booked out, and Alaric must have realised then with an awful dawning certainty that Silvia had died in the blaze. No wonder he had been in such a dreadful, distracted mood since Posie's arrival…

Posie listened in a daze to the Commissario's final words.

'Needless to say, if anyone has any information on Miss Hanro, or the fire yesterday, which is now being investigated in a new light, please come and speak to me. Or to Inspector Lovelace here. Now you can go.'

The room emptied quickly and at the door Posie found herself squeezed right up against Dickie Alladice, who was sweating, despite the cold draft from the corridor and the lack of alcohol. She suddenly, uncharacteristically, lost her temper, and hissed at him like a scorned child:

'You *knew*, didn't you, Dickie? You knew Alaric had Silvia Hanro in tow and that he was treating me like a first-class fool. That whole "going back in for the safe" business was complete rot! Who else knew?'

'Posie…' Inspector Lovelace was at her side and tried to pull her away. But Dickie Alladice had the good grace to hang his head and touch Posie's arm gently.

'I'm so sorry,' he whispered. For a second he stared at the manila envelope still in Lovelace's grip. 'But Alaric is a friend. And almost a business colleague; tomorrow teatime we'll be signing the Partnership Deeds for our new venture, and we'll be in a very sweet place. Besides, it's not my business to say who Alaric can or can't bring with him to Venice, is it? Who he can or can't keep as his mistress?'

He spread his hands, as if absolving himself from any

responsibility. 'He's just a man, Posie. And after all, we *are* talking about Silvia Hanro, the most beautiful woman in the world. You can hardly blame the fella, can you? They made a gorgeous couple.'

And Posie remembered, with a flash of sudden understanding, Bella Alladice's cold first words about Posie having lost Alaric to another woman. Posie saw it now not as a taunt, but as a kind of warning, and she saw that the Countess herself had been put in an awkward position, perhaps not liking it much herself: '*Anyone who is a friend of Alaric's has to be invited along, it seems…*' And later, Bella had tried to warn her again: '*Men always want something else… You have to be careful.*'

Then she thought of Max's seemingly irrational hostility towards Alaric. So *he* had known what Alaric was looking for over in the Palace, too.

Posie jumped at the touch of Lovelace's hand on her back.

'Any idea where Alaric might have gone, old girl? Do you want to go and look for him? Or for *me* to go and look for him? Speak to him?'

'No, sir.' Posie was trying to stop a black rebellion engulfing her. 'The answer is no to all those questions. Why should I chase him? Now I'm left thinking the worst.'

'Mnnn, I agree it looks like Alaric has got himself in some sort of pickle. Come on, a cup of tea is what we need now.' The Inspector almost marched her from the room, towards the stairs to the kitchen. 'And *I'm* making it: nothing continental with a slice of bally lemon. A proper cup you can stand your spoon up in.'

In other words, no use dawdling. There was work to be done.

****

The Commissario, Inspector Lovelace and Posie walked quickly away from the crowds.

Above them a blundering full moon was being rocked biliously by banks of wintery cloud, giving surprisingly little light. It was an unpredictable sky.

It was only seven o'clock but the darkness of the evening was absolute, and they walked through dim deserted alleyways and over tiny bridges until they suddenly broke out into the brightness of the fashionable Riva degli Schiavoni; that grand, beautifully-lanterned walkway facing the lagoon. Beautiful people dressed in furs were laughing and promenading up and down.

But within seconds they had dipped back into a warren of snake-like streets and ill-lit courtyards, frequented only by scores of mewling cats. Here and there a candle-lit shrine interrupted the darkness, the scent of rotting flowers blowing sickly on the wind.

'Along here. Stay close. And watch for rats.'

They walked for a good quarter of an hour and saw no-one until a couple of labourers passed them, calling out something like a warning in the local dialect, and Posie saw they were carrying the silhouetted carcass of a huge, just-cooked pig, still steaming in the night air, bound for an off-the-beaten-track restaurant. Posie's stomach growled hungrily. She tried not to think of when she might get to eat dinner. Or *if*.

The three walked in silence, the lapping of waves and the occasional plashing of oars their only real companion.

Posie had the sensation that she might be experiencing the real Venice for the first time, stripped away of tourists and gilt and glamour, peeled back to its messy, archaic disorder. She didn't know which Venice she liked the best. But at least it made her forget the awful picture now which kept flooding her mind over and over: Silvia in that room, trapped. Alaric trying to reach her, in vain…

They came out onto a bridge. 'The San Lorenzo Canal,'

Salvarocca muttered. He pointed at a large unspectacular building, rising squatly over several floors on the other side of the canal, a dim lantern swinging over its door with the words 'QUESTURA – PROVINCIA DI VENEZIA' picked out in an arch of black metal.

'This is the main police headquarters. Welcome, but watch your step. The tide is very high tonight. Unusually so.'

Several police boats were moored up outside the Questura, and sodden duckboards covered the path leading to the main steps. They went through a dark-olive reception room on the first floor, with framed photographs of Mussolini and glittering awards mounted around the walls. Junior policemen, similarly glittering, melted away in Salvarocca's wake.

'We're here to see Lucy, then, sir?'

'Among other things.'

They ended up in what was obviously the Commissario's office. There was just one tiny window in an otherwise plain grey wall and it was open, letting in the high-tide smells. Salvarocca threw down his briefcase and cast off his flamboyant cap, fishing around for a packet of cigarettes in a desk drawer. He offered them around and Lovelace took one. They all sat in smoky silence for a few minutes.

'All my men are out and about,' said the Chief of Police at last. 'They have instructions to track down Corsetti, and also to bring in Roger Valentine. I've had the devil of a time keeping the press from reporting it all. But the story about Bella's murder finally broke tonight, and I guess it will be in London's papers tomorrow. I think the story about Silvia Hanro can be held at bay for now. London won't know for several days…'

Posie nodded. London felt very far away right now. 'You believe Roger Valentine is your man for Bella's murder, Commissario?'

'I'm not certain, but he ran from us, didn't he? I'm

imagining he had a falling out with the Countess, tried to blackmail her, it failed, and it resulted in this.'

'It seems extreme, sir. But I agree about him being an expert at blackmailing.' And she reported the maid overhearing the argument from Roger Valentine's room the night before, and the scuffle or fight which had taken place inside it.

Lovelace raised an eyebrow. 'The man is unstoppable! But *what* was he going to show?'

'It seems there were two things at stake, sir.'

'I agree. And this thing about *the reel* – that's very interesting.' Lovelace scrabbled for a bit in his own attaché case, bringing out a small waxy exhibit envelope. He shook it on the table carefully and a thin sliver of shiny black ribbon emerged.

'Salvo's already seen this. It's pretty much the only evidence we got out of Valentine's grate – the rest were handwritten notes, a burnt green folio, and newspaper pages – but they've all flaked up badly and are completely unreadable. Valentine had torched it all before doing a runner. Go on, Posie. Have a good look.'

The black shiny strip was about eight inches long, but only about half an inch wide. It was singed badly around the edges. Pulling it closer Posie saw it had been a photograph, a high-quality one. One such as the press would use when setting their copy. Posie was familiar with such photos from using the archives at newspaper offices. The heading beneath the picture was just a burnt fragment. She could make out:

'…HEAR THE VERD…'

The picture which remained didn't show anything much. Perhaps some wooden railings? And the suggestions of people above them: hands and shirts and a puffy light blouse with a cameo badge and a long spindly plait…

'I can't make anything out, sir. It was obviously a crowd photo, but with the heads and identities burnt off we're nowhere near being able to identify who these people were.'

She turned the slip of paper over and saw the remnants of a name, 'Charlton'.

'The photographer, sir?'

Lovelace nodded. 'I've telephoned London already, I got Rainbird to sniff it out for me, but without much success. The studio of Ernest Charlton and Sons, based on the Strand, was a good one, but it went out of business the year after the war ended, as all of the photographers had been killed off. The studio and its contents were sold as a job lot at auction: the chances of finding a negative or a print identical to this one must be impossible. The Charltons were jobbing photographers: they'd take their shots and hawk them around the various newspapers until they made a sale. I'd bet money that this is the "reel" Roger Valentine was talking about. But what does it show? And who was he threatening? I don't know where to start. We don't even know the year of this print!'

Posie scowled in concentration. 'It was before the war, sir. Look at that cameo, people haven't worn those in years. And those sleeves! Who on earth had material sufficient for those beauties in the war, or just after? And this woman has her hair in a plait, so it's before 1914. Can I keep it for now, sir?'

Watching the Inspector nod bleakly, at a complete loss, Posie was suddenly reminded of other calls made to London that very morning, by a now-dead woman. Of new leads which she should have passed on…

'I'm very sorry, sir. I have new information. Only I forgot to share it in all the excitement of hearing about… about Silvia…'

Lovelace cleared his throat lustily. 'Never mind Silvia Hanro for now, or your swine of a boyfriend, Posie. And have no fear: my loyalty is of course to you in all this mess. If you don't want me to speak to Alaric, or to intervene, I won't. Even though he paid for my ticket out here.'

'Thank you, sir. I appreciate it.'

'Go on then, we'd better hear the worst.'

And Posie reported, as she should have done earlier, the overheard conversations: the strange story Rita had told her about Minnie Alladice blackmailing Giancarlo in the Church of San Trovaso, and then Mrs Persimmon's eavesdropping on Bella Alladice and her two telephone calls to London.

The Commissario frowned at the end of the report and stared at Lovelace, who was looking unsettled. 'Richard, do you know what this "*registrar*" or "*register*" is all about?'

'No. And neither do I know why Bella Alladice wanted to speak to a Scotland Yard Inspector. She wanted to report a murder, you say?'

They were all at a dead end. Rising, the Commissario produced the silver hip-flask which had been found in the toilet cistern by Max, and which really belonged to Lucy.

'Take this flask, Miss Parker,' he said firmly. 'Show Miss Christie. Tell her we know there are two identical hip-flasks; this is her flask, which never contained poison. Tell her she's not a suspect anymore. See if she has any information which may be useful. We desperately need a break here. You can do the interview alone. Ask what you like.'

'Fine.'

Posie was more certain than ever now that Lucy was still central to this whole dreadful affair, but how or why escaped her. She ran through possible questions she could ask the girl as she was led along another winding corridor, and past a row of cells which were mere cubicles with thin partition walls.

The two Inspectors hung back as a young policeman took over, jangling a huge ring of keys.

'Good luck,' said the Commissario. 'We'll be listening at the door.'

'No pressure to get things right, then,' Posie muttered darkly to herself.

****

Twenty-Three

It could have been a tiny hotel room.

There was a bowl of fruit, some chocolate, even a pile of books. Candles burned around the place, softening the harsh electric bar of light in the corridor outside. Soft woollen rugs were spread over the hard wooden bench. Only the smallness of the place, and a bucket in the corner, and the stink of institutional bleach, and the scent of fear – which could never be eradicated somehow in police cells like these – indicated the real purpose of the place.

Posie remembered how Lovelace had said that Salvo Salvarocca could never treat someone badly. It seemed he was right.

'You've come!'

Lucy looked up in surprise. She was smoking a black and silver cigarette and she put it down immediately.

Posie sat at a spare wooden chair. She got Lucy's silver flask out immediately and waved it in the air, watching Lucy Christie's wide-eyed shock.

'What are you doing, Posie?'

'We know who you are, Lucy. Or *Alicia*, should I say? We also know this is *your* hip-flask, identical to Bella's. And I'm guessing that Johnny Alladice gave them to each of you, didn't he? Johnny Alladice, your lost love: the boy who didn't propose, but who blew apart his own sister's damning testimony against you at the Gattling Appeal, setting you free. Your guardian angel. Not many of us are lucky enough to have one of *those*.'

Lucy gasped aloud. 'How do you know all of this?'

'Don't worry. The Alladice circle of secrecy hasn't broken ranks. It was Inspector Lovelace. He recognised you. You wouldn't admit in public who you really were, would you? You wouldn't bring out this flask, either, for fear of revealing your identity. Even though you could have hung for the murder of Bella Alladice, despite being innocent. It's almost funny, but your true identity has saved you.'

'You believe in my innocence?' The girl sounded amazed. She picked up her still-smouldering cigarette and inhaled deeply, blowing a smoke-ring at the ceiling.

'I do. But God knows, I wouldn't have blamed you for murdering Bella Alladice. She treated you so shabbily, for years.'

'What do you mean?'

Posie stared. Was this girl some kind of an innocent? Lucy had been badly payed, badly clothed, and spoken to insufferably for six years, all so that Bella Alladice could inflict some bizarre act of petty revenge on Lucy, almost illegally: in direct contravention of her late brothers' wishes. But Posie didn't focus on any of that now.

'Why, she testified against you at Robert Gattling's murder trial!'

'Oh, *that*.'

'Yes, *that*. She could very well have had you hung for a crime you didn't commit. She was pure evil.'

Lucy was shaking her head. 'No, Posie. There you are wrong. It *was* very difficult, I'll admit, especially afterwards of course, as Johnny and Bella never really spoke again after he got her statement about me thrown out at the appeal, but what you have to understand is that Bella Alladice was a woman of firm principles. If she truly believed in something, she stuck to her guns.'

Posie didn't bother to reply. It was too, too ridiculous.

Lucy continued: 'Actually, she apologised to me in the year following the trial. She said she had seen me loitering at the table at that Spring Ball. Which was true. I *had* been alone there for a couple of minutes, killing time. I hated events like that and I was longing for it to be over. And Bella really, honestly believed I had poisoned Robert. It was a terrible situation for her to be in. You know that Robert had thrown her over when he got bored of her? Poor Bella, she was deeply in love with him.'

'Mnnn. That red ring…'

'She paid Robert's parents a vast sum for it.' Lucy shrugged uneasily. 'But if it made her happy…'

'But what about *your* happiness? That murder trial ruined you. Why else would you stick with the Alladice family through thick and thin?'

Lucy hesitated. 'Your Inspector remembered my face today, years and years later. Imagine what it was like for me in the immediate aftermath! My reputation was gone. I had press men following my every step. I wanted to die, so Johnny hid me and kept me housed in a flat far away, up in Edinburgh, a beautiful little place. He arranged for me to change my name, to something very English, and I chose it at random from a newspaper one day. He paid my mother's nursing home fees, too. Nothing was too much trouble for him. The two things he *didn't* do were make an honest woman of me, and provide for me after his death. But no matter: I loved him anyway. And you're wrong that it was the murder trial which ruined me. It was Johnny's death in 1917 which did that.'

The girl's fingers shook as she stubbed out her cigarette. She automatically lit another, and offered the packet at her elbow to Posie, who shook her head. Lucy stared past Posie, years away in time and place. When she spoke it was a low whisper.

'I wanted to die again then. I closed up the flat in

Edinburgh where I had lived for five whole years and I trained as a nurse. I was sent out to the Western Front, only it was so horrific that my nerves didn't last, and I came back, tail between my legs. I was at rock-bottom, with no money of my own and no provision made for me by Johnny. It was then that Bella offered to look after me, said that I could be her companion. She told me that it would only be a matter of months until we would all move abroad, to America most likely, which suited me fine. I leapt at the chance to get away from home. Her father was already in talks with suitors for Bella's hand in marriage; it looked very likely that we would end up in Chicago or New York, but suitors fell through time and again, for years, until Giancarlo presented himself through a newspaper advertisement. Venice was a promise of release. No-one knew me, or the history of the case out here. I thought I would be free. It was an escape.'

Posie chewed at her lip. A horrible thought struck her. 'Have you ever seen or read Johnny's Will, Lucy?'

'No. I thought it must be a very official document, all about the company shares. Those shares were nothing to do with me. I wouldn't want them, either: they're unlucky. Did you know that Minnie Alladice once had a great shareholding in that company, too? It didn't do *her* much good, did it?'

'No. I didn't know that. But I strongly advise you to read the Will, Lucy.'

It wasn't her place now to explain about Johnny's wishes, but Posie explained succinctly about going to Somerset House. 'I think you'll find it life-changing. The Will *does* cover company shares, by the way. Johnny wanted to leave them to you, not to either of his siblings, because he hated them. But his hand was forced.'

Lucy was looking at Posie with narrowed eyes. 'I see. I should perhaps make a trip back to London then, if you think it is so important. *If* I am free to go.'

Posie changed tack. 'Tell me, I can understand why Johnny hated his sister, but what was the problem with Dickie? Bella told me the two brothers had a spat about business? But I'm learning that so much of what she said concealed the truth.'

Lucy laughed mirthlessly. 'They all hated each other in the end, because of the trial. Do you know, Dickie actually believed that it was *Johnny* who administered the poison to Robert Gattling, so that we would be free to marry? Dickie accused him of it, and it was jolly awkward. Dickie's normally such a closed book: a clever, polite, sociable closed book. A *successful* closed book.'

'So *that's* why the brothers fell out?'

'I'm sure of it.'

A silence fell. 'You said that you were getting away from those who stalked you out here in Venice. But that's not quite true, is it? Someone found out who you were.'

'Roger?'

'He was blackmailing you, wasn't he?'

Lucy raised an eyebrow. 'I'm impressed. Mind you, you saw me, didn't you? Last night, going into his room. I was dropping off his latest payment. His last payment.'

'You didn't argue with him last night? Fight?'

'Of course not! I put the cheque on his desk and walked straight out.'

Posie stayed silent. She believed the girl.

Lucy sighed. 'It was dreadful, but we never had a fight about it, not in more than a year. What made it worse was that Roger didn't cash the money orders: he threatened to do so, all in one go, on several occasions. I think he liked the power he had over me, although I paid him a cheque every month, rather than sleep with him, which was the other alternative. He's a horrible man. He must have overheard Bella or Dickie or Minnie talking about the Gattling case when he first joined us last year, because next thing I knew he'd got a whole big green folio of newspaper cuttings about the trial. He's excellent at research, I'll give him that. He claims to be in contact with some of the best journalists in England; said that he could tell them where I was and give them details as to my "new" identity.'

'That was cruel.'

'That's the sort of man he is. As I said, invaluable when it comes to research. But the blackmail was beginning to break me. I'd had enough. I told Dickie about it a couple of days ago. I didn't know what else to do. Dickie was shocked, and said he'd deal with it.'

'And did he?'

'Yes. He sacked Roger.'

Suddenly Posie understood the comment Dickie had muttered to Lucy at the Café Florian. '*Don't worry, darling, it will be all right now, you'll see. Not long to go. Hold your nerve.*'

'Dickie has the power to do that? But Roger was *Bella's* secretary, surely?'

Lucy laughed bitterly. 'I couldn't have asked Bella to get rid of Roger: he did too good a job. She'd have chosen him over me, every time. I was under no illusion that Bella actually liked me; I was just a plaything to stoke an ego trip, really. But Roger is the Company Secretary, too, and ultimately his pay packet comes from Alladice Holdings. Dickie signs it off. And Dickie has the power to sack him.'

Something Posie had just heard didn't quite ring true. She struggled momentarily with the anomaly, but carried on regardless: 'Well, now Roger's left in a dashed hurry. He's a wanted man.'

Posie explained about Roger running away. 'Lucy, do you think it possible that Roger could have murdered Bella? Or have been responsible for the fire at the Palace?'

Lucy shrugged. 'I have no idea who did all of this, but it took nerves of steel. I don't think Roger would be up to that. Besides, he had a strange loyalty towards Bella, he almost revered her. And Roger is fundamentally a coward.

Look what he's doing now! He's not facing the enemy head on. He's running because he's scared.'

Posie mentioned the mysterious '*reel*', and laid the torn smidgen of photograph on Lucy's lap. 'We're stumped. We think this was part of a blackmail package Roger was threatening someone with. Any idea what it shows?'

Lucy fumbled in the pocket of her long, brown cardigan and extracted some tiny golden reading glasses: ancient, like the rest of her stuff. She picked the sliver up but her frown displayed her ignorance.

'No clue.'

Posie put the ribbon of film away, disappointed. 'What will you do now? Will you marry Dickie Alladice? He looks at you sometimes as if he's thinking of asking you.'

Lucy shook her head in amusement. 'How funny you should think that! I think he *did* love me once. But it was a passing childish fancy; years ago, when we were all young and thought we had endless days and nights to fill. But he didn't want me after I'd been with his brother, and I didn't want him, either. I don't want any other man, not yet. Dickie and I are just friends. There have been many women for Dickie in the years since the war; they've come and gone, and why not? He's rich, and good-looking, and a lovely fellow when he's not blind drunk. I think I'll leave Venice. Maybe I'll go to America, after all. Everyone can reinvent themselves there, can't they? Put on yet another disguise.'

'I suppose so. And speaking of disguises…'

Posie repeated Rita's story about seeing Minnie Alladice and the Count Romagnoli the night before, all in black. 'Unlikely bedfellows, don't you think?'

'Tell me the conversation again, will you?

And like an elaborate game of Chinese whispers, Posie did. When she had finished Lucy shook her head in disbelief. 'I thought Minnie looked like she was doing better for herself recently. Not quite the cat's whiskers, but a few new blouses here and there, and trinkets, mainly. She always was a bit of a magpie. But blackmail? My goodness! And blackmailing poor Giancarlo? What on earth would she blackmail him about?'

'Does it need twenty guesses?'

'But the fact that the Romagnoli marriage was a sham was an open secret!'

Posie shrugged. 'Venice is still Catholic, isn't it? Even if it's not a Republic anymore. Even if its glory days are long gone. And newspapers always need stories in hard black and white. The juicier the better…'

'I say! But what did Giancarlo mean "*You've gone too far now*"?'

'I don't know. I hoped you might.'

Lucy shook her head. 'All I know is that Minnie Alladice was used to better things.'

'The large company shareholding you spoke of? Bella said her father had done Minnie a big wrong…'

And Lucy explained that Mr Alladice Senior had helped Minnie when she was in the grip of a nervous breakdown, but help had come at a terrible cost: he had got his sister to sign away her shareholding in the family business, reducing it down from fifty per cent to only two per cent.

'Minnie probably didn't know what she was doing at the time. Doped up to the eyeballs. It was tragic. Johnny told me all about it. He was irate, but there was little he could really do.'

Posie was able to understand Minnie's malice better now. 'Well, Bella has made the situation good again, hasn't she?'

'Under her new Will, you mean? Because she made it *more than better* for Minnie. Minnie will now be the majority shareholder in the business. Her original two per cent, plus Bella's fifty per cent will enable her to control the company.'

'Gracious. I hadn't actually realised that... Did Bella tell you about the contents of her Will?'

'Goodness, no. She didn't tell anyone. It was Roger, of course. He organised the Will, very proudly, but he's such a blabbermouth he couldn't resist prattling on about it to me. Looking back, I'm surprised he wasted his breath; it's not as if he could get any money out of me for the information. I don't even benefit under the Will!'

Posie stood to leave, picking up the silver hip-flask.

'Hang on a minute, will you?' Lucy looked uncomfortable. She pointed at the flask. 'You're absolutely right that there were two identical bottles, both gifts from Johnny. But that one there isn't mine!'

For a moment it seemed as if the world stopped turning. Posie clutched the poison-free flask a little tighter. 'But the other one had prussic acid in it. It killed Bella. Of course this one is yours!'

'If you want to think that, then so be it. But the flask you are holding is *Bella's*, not mine. See how badly scratched it is? That's because she used it each day, every day, for liqueur. Mine is barely tarnished, because I hardly ever use it properly, normally just for carrying water for my watercolour paintings. Last night was an exception. I was so cold I filched some of Bella's special almond liqueur from the drinks trolley...'

Posie was confused. '*This* hip-flask was deliberately hidden in a cistern, so it would look to all extents and purposes like there was only one silver flask: the one with poison in it. Now you're saying that the poison-filled flask *was* actually yours?'

Lucy looked desperate, panicking, realising that things were looking bad for her. 'One of the reasons I couldn't say there were two identical hip-flasks earlier was because I hadn't received mine back from you yet!'

Posie took a deep breath. 'But I left it outside your room very early this morning, about seven?'

'I didn't get it. Someone must have taken it.'

It made sense. Someone – the murderer – had taken Lucy's unscratched flask and added poison to the almond liqueur it contained, and then swapped it over with Bella's own tarnished flask later. Presumably at the heated meeting Mrs Persimmon had listened in on? The same person who had then whisked away the papers in the folio. *That* was how the poison had got into the room…

It would require an extraordinary amount of nerve: a steeliness of resolve enabling the murderer to hide Bella's real flask later in a toilet cistern. It would require a sort of desperation, too: a last-minute opportunism. For no-one could have known Posie would have left that handy second flask outside Lucy's door that very morning.

Suddenly Posie gasped, for she saw at once that the murder hadn't been planned.

But who could have done it? Everyone except Roger Valentine and Alaric had cast-iron alibis for that time, a quarter past nine…

'Lucy, who knew there were two flasks from Johnny Alladice, identical to each other in every way?'

'Oh, everyone knew, *if* they bothered to remember, but why would they? It was a sensitive topic and we were given those flasks years ago. I never got my flask out in public for fear of hurting Bella, for she liked to believe that Johnny had given her a unique gift, something special. I didn't like to remind her of his love for me, or mine for him. So my flask stayed under wraps.'

'Like your diamond ring? Well, thank you. That's all been most helpful.'

Posie paused at the door of the cell.

'They found a body, you know. Today. While you were locked up in here.' And she explained about Silvia Hanro in the secret chamber. Lucy looked as if she might be sick.

Posie continued in as calm a voice as she could manage: 'So you see, I know. About *them*. Together. Bella Alladice obviously knew about it too and tried to warn me.'

'Oh, Posie, I'm sorry,' Lucy sighed. 'I told you Bella had high principles. She was outraged on your behalf, and gave Alaric a good dressing down for keeping a mistress. Alaric said it was none of Bella's business who he entertained, or who he made love to, and to be fair to him, he'd talked about *you* at dinner the night before, on his arrival, not Silvia. It was quite a scene yesterday morning, when Silvia arrived, I can tell you! Everyone was very star-struck, particularly Minnie and Dickie; both of them fawning over the girl. Silvia *was* stunning, of course, if you like that sort of bland beauty. But we hardly saw her: she stalked up to Alaric's rooms after only five minutes and they stayed up there together. Why don't you ask Alaric about it yourself if it's troubling you?'

'*He* should have told me.'

Lucy coughed delicately. 'So is the wedding still on tomorrow?'

But Posie was thinking momentarily of Alaric at that last meeting. His pose, his holding the manila envelope, the scrawl on his hand…

'What would "FRARI" mean?' she asked aloud, without answering Lucy's question.

'"*Frari*?"' Lucy frowned and then her expression cleared. 'Oh, you mean the Frari Church! I believe its real name is the "Basilica of Santa Maria Gloriosa dei Frari"; it's a huge Franciscan church. It's in San Polo, quite near the Grand Canal. It's not beautiful. In fact, from the outside it looks like a loaf of brown bread. But go inside and you'll be astounded. People think some of the best paintings in the world are there, and some of the best painters are buried there. Titian, for example. There are fascinating tombs. People say it's better than St Mark's Cathedral.'

Posie blushed red. 'I'm afraid I haven't read my guidebook on Venice very well. Or at all, for that matter.'

Lucy smiled. 'Oh, don't worry. Bella and I have only been to the Frari once in the whole time we've been here.

Bella was more interested in a coffee shop opposite it, beside a canal. It had a famous cat, apparently. Long since dead, but still a tourist attraction. Bizarre. There is also a shop next to the café selling carved Italian cameos, which Bella was partial to. She bought several, I recall, although they aren't really fashionable anymore.'

Posie's thoughts were running on ahead. That scrawl… '*FRAR1. 7 AM*'. Some kind of meeting? She opened the door to step out into the corridor, already sensing the dim shadows of the Police Inspectors pulling away in the darkness, anxious not to be seen by the girl within.

'Wait!' Lucy was standing, a slight trace of excitement playing over her lovely face. 'Show me that slip of burnt photo again.'

Posie produced it quicker this time.

Lucy pointed a long finger at the scant detail on the far right. A blouse with gorgeous sleeves among several men's plain, boring suits. 'Yes, I thought as much. See this cameo brooch? That was Bella's. This is a photo of Bella! Years ago. Around the time of the Court case, in 1912. In fact, it could have been *from* the Court case. I know I said Roger revered Bella, and I still don't think he killed her, but did he know something about her which she didn't want made public?'

And as Posie ran through all of this a few minutes later, the puzzle pieces still refusing to come together, she found her head was hurting.

She took the motor launch home to Mrs Persimmon's and went straight to bed without eating anything except a couple of damp and stuck-together Peek Freans Marie biscuits which she had found wrapped in foil at the bottom of her carpet bag.

As she fell asleep, the chanting and cheers of the real-life crowds flocking to and from the Salute Church were a mere backdrop to her uneasy dreams of fog and fire and burning rooms and hidden chambers. And over it all came a sound Posie had never heard before. She could swear she heard Alaric weeping.

Which was impossible.

Because before going to bed, Posie had checked his room and he wasn't there, and nor was his rucksack.

He, like Roger Valentine, had disappeared into the freezing Venetian night.

****

PART THREE

VENICE

(Thursday 22nd November, 1923)

Twenty-Four

When she awoke, Posie Parker could smell trouble in the air.

A church bell, possibly from St George's, or even the Salute, was ringing incessantly. It was six o'clock, and deathly dark, and cold as ice. Posie got up stealthily, swinging frozen legs over the bed. She dressed hurriedly, trying not to shiver. She didn't bother to switch on the light or strike a match to the Penhaligon's travel candle by her bedside. She needed to move.

That scrawled note on Alaric's hand.

FRARI. 7AM.

Posie had no clue how she would get to the Frari Church, but do it she must. Pushing open her door as quietly as possible she almost screamed as she immediately ran into a soft, shadowy figure lurking just outside in the darkness. The shadow stepped backwards.

'Forgive me, Posie. I was just coming to see if you were awake and about to leave? But I see you are… I was about to rap on your door. Perhaps we can travel together?'

It was Dickie Alladice, togged up in a thick overcoat and hat which made him virtually unrecognisable. Posie frowned, caught off guard. This was the last thing she had been expecting. 'Where did you think I was going, Dickie?'

'Well, to find Alaric, of course. You'll know he hasn't returned all night, and his things are gone?'

Posie swallowed, but stayed quiet.

'And you must have seen that scribble on his hand – something about the Frari Church? They celebrate Mass there at seven every morning, so I was going to go along and check he was okay. The fella's had a huge shock of course, this rum news about Silvia yesterday. And there's the – ahem – small matter of our signing the Partnership Deeds later on today, I want to make sure he's not forgotten that. It's very important that we do it today. I've arranged for my lawyer, Mr Ennario, to be present.'

'Yes, well, you won't want to mess him about, will you, Dickie? Lawyers' fees being what they are…'

Posie had to admire Dickie's transparency and business drive. He was being completely open with her about his motives. *It's supposed to be my wedding day today*, she felt like saying. *And that was very important, too.*

There seemed no way of leaving without Dickie. Besides, he'd know how to get to the Frari Church, which was more than she did.

They started to walk towards the dark stairwell, but out of the corner of her eye Posie sensed a movement behind them, felt the hairs raising on her neck. She turned, and picking up on her unease, Dickie followed suit. But there was no-one there. 'Everything quite all right, Posie?'

'Absolutely.'

Posie went to grab at a couple of the black storm capes in the vestibule, but found them all gone. Her fashionable red coat, bright and not at all waterproof, would just have to do.

They left the guesthouse and walked in silence through the tiny, pitch-black, rain-drenched streets, until they passed the Accademia Bridge. Without crossing over the Grand Canal, Posie realised they had arrived at a vaporetto station. And they were lucky: within only a minute the great hulking, splashing beast of the vaporetto appeared, like some mythical white whale rearing up out of the darkness.

Dickie and Posie were among only a handful of passengers on the paddle-steamer, the others being a few wide-awake looking nuns in various types of elaborate black habit, and party-goers from the night before, looking very much the worse for wear, happy to sleep across the open-air benches in the drizzle.

It was a short ride, and they got out at Santa Toma, where Dickie managed to hail a frozen-looking Gondolier to take them away from the Grand Canal, through an inward maze of smaller canals which seemed to go on forever.

'Here we are.' Dickie said at last, passing some coins across to the Gondolier, before asking him to wait for them up at the next small bridge.

'That's the Frari Church right there.'

Posie saw a dainty bridge leading across to a large dark hump of a building which stood at the edge of a square.

The place was all lit about with torches, illuminating the rain-drenched cobbles in the darkness of the winter morning. A crowd of black-clad women wearing headscarves were standing at the entrance to the church, their breath and cigarette smoke melding and rising in the cold air, illuminated by the hanging yellow lantern above the main door. It was almost seven o'clock and Posie hurried in, barely waiting for Dickie to walk aside her.

It suddenly dawned on Posie that she had no idea just *what* Alaric was doing here, or who he was meeting, or if indeed he was even going to turn up.

And then the logistics of the church hit her.

Stepping through the portico, Posie realised she was completely unprepared for the sheer scale of the place. Which was obviously why it had been chosen as a meeting point.

Looking for Alaric here was like looking for a needle in a haystack. The Frari Church, dark and gloaming and candle-lit, seemed as big as Canterbury Cathedral, with its high-rising arches, and acres of terracotta-and-white chequered floor. Towards the altar, where candles lit up a gorgeous red and blue Madonna, priests and worshippers were arranging themselves into some sort of order. But their activities only took up the first three or four pews, and the rest of the hulking church was empty, and cavernous. All along the sides of the church were row after row of empty, dark side chapels, and what Lucy must have been speaking about – the tombs of artists and famous Venetians.

He's not here.

Posie tried to scan the place as nonchalantly as possible. Suddenly Dickie was beside her. They were still at the main door, unobtrusive among the other worshippers who were coming in late.

'I can't see him. Have you any idea what he may be doing here, Posie?'

'None. Not taking Mass, though.'

And then she saw something. Over on the left, by a huge, pale triangular monument – a creepy thing altogether, rather like a small house, complete with carved life-size ghouls and marble flags and even a real doorway – she saw a sudden black blur of movement. In fact, two black blurs of movement. There was something about the way one of the figures moved, suggesting Alaric's easy lithe gracefulness.

But what was he wearing? It looked like one of those great flapping black storm capes from Mrs Persimmon's, complete with hood…

'Over there,' she found herself hissing at Dickie. This wasn't quite how she had imagined it would happen. She had expected a confrontation, a meeting face-to-face.

The Mass, complete with a wailing organ crescendo, had now begun in earnest, and Posie found herself skirting the brick walls, followed by Dickie sharp on her heels. She pulled back and hid behind the white marble overhang of the huge triangular tomb. She sensed rather than saw that Alaric and someone else, similarly black-caped and black-hooded, were now sitting together up on the marble steps of the tomb, not two foot away from Posie and Dickie. She strained to listen but it was a few seconds before her ears got used to the measure and tone of the conversation.

Alaric was speaking first, tired and irritable:

'What did you want to speak to me about? You sent me a note from the police station, didn't you? To meet today, here at Canova's Tomb?'

And then the second voice: a man, a young man, an Italian, his English perfect and measured, but his voice sounding nervous.

'I felt I could trust you, sir, despite never having met you. I've seen you in the newspapers and in magazines, of course. Did you know I'm a wanted man? The police let me go yesterday, but now they want me a second time around: for killing someone, for murder. There are rumours that someone died in that fire yesterday, and now the papers are full of Bella's death, too. It's too dreadful. There are "WANTED" signs with my name and picture all over town. I have no idea how to flee.'

Pietro Corsetti, Posie breathed to herself. *It had to be.*

Alaric sounded bitter. 'And you thought I could help you? What do you need? Money?'

'No!' The Italian almost laughed. 'I have enough money, though much good it's done me.'

'What then? Surely you could have contacted the Count? Got him to come here and organise your safe passage out of Venice?'

'I need someone to take something to the police for me. Poor Giancarlo isn't impartial, and he won't remain calm. I don't know how he'll react. *You* are famous, and you have good standing. If I tell *you* this information, you can take it to the police, can't you?'

There was a silence and a rustling of a storm cape. Without seeing him, Posie could imagine Alaric's head in his hands, his exasperation at being dragged into something which didn't involve him. This man she didn't know anymore…

'Please, my life may depend on it.'

A sigh. 'Go on then.'

'I *did* start the fire yesterday. I started it in Bella's apartments. Just before two o'clock.'

'The police figured as much.'

'But I was paid to do so. I was following instructions: it was all arranged. That's what I want you to communicate to the police for me. I wasn't going to tell them but this new murder charge changes everything.'

Posie held her breath. She sensed Dickie behind her, listening intently, every nerve of his body tensed.

'You'd better tell me all you know, Corsetti. Was it the Count who paid you to start the blaze?'

There was a muffled laugh. 'Giancarlo? Want his precious Palace burnt down? No way. It was a woman. A devil-woman.'

'A woman?' Alaric sounded disbelieving. '*Which* woman?'

'I only realised who the devil-woman was yesterday, when I met her for the first time for my big payment. But the big payment she made wasn't just for the fire, you know. It was for two months of work. Two months ago she contacted me out of the blue – I suppose she had heard I needed money – and asked me to organise a few men to look like they were spying on Bella. It seemed harmless enough at the time, I just got a couple of friends with a boat to do it when they had free time. *I* didn't get involved. But it got weirder: a couple of weeks ago, the woman asked me if I could translate a note she'd written into Italian – I translated it – even though it was vile.'

'Was this the thing about Bella ending up dead in the secret chamber?'

'That's right. Well, when I sent the translation back I wrote to say that I really *did* know where the secret chamber was, because my family – who are as old as the Romagnolis but are their sworn enemies – had kept journals obsessively down through the centuries, recording everything they could about the Romagnolis, in case it came in useful one day. I'd come across an entry in a journal about this secret chamber as a boy. There was a map with it, too. It certainly never seemed important enough to discuss with Giancarlo. *He* never expressed an interest in it until after Bella had received that note, and I could hardly tell him *then* about my involvement, could I? He was very upset.'

'So let me guess: you searched out this old journal and sent across the map of the secret room when it was later requested by this woman, who probably couldn't believe her luck?'

'That's right, I was promised more money for sending the map of the secret chamber. I certainly didn't think I'd be asked to start a fire at the Palace later, or that the secret room would be a death-trap.'

Alaric's voice was rising in anger. 'But you *did* start the fire, didn't you? That was completely unforgivable.'

There was a sound very like crying. Posie sensed that Dickie was standing as still as one of the grotesque carved statues over on the tomb, waiting, breathing shallowly.

'The devil-woman said it would be a sort of joke. She told me firemen would be on hand very quickly to put it out.'

'*Who* told you this? *Who* organised this?'

'The old one. That old red cat…'

There was a sharp intake of breath behind her. Turning, Posie saw Dickie had gone grey in the face. Alaric was continuing:

'What? You mean Minnie? Minnie Alladice? She's the oldest of the women in the party. That doesn't sound right. Where would Minnie have got the money from to pay you? She seems as poor as a church mouse. And why on earth would *she* want Bella Alladice dead?'

And suddenly everything came together and Posie knew the answers to both of Alaric's questions.

But before she could think it through Posie was aware of a dreadful gasping, and before she could stop him Dickie had turned on his heel and was running, running away across the terracotta paving, through the still darkness of the church.

Posie drew back instinctively into the shelter of the jutting marble, just as Alaric stepped out.

'What was that noise? No, I must be wrong. For a minute there I thought we were being listened in on. It's a nice story, but how can you prove it, Corsetti? It could just be a lot of hot air about Minnie. Lies…'

There was a sound of paper being drawn out. A triumphant tone in the young man's voice. 'There. You see? She was foolish enough to write to me. This is the note where she asks me to spy on Bella, and here is her next note asking me to translate her frightening little letter about the secret chamber…and here is her note asking about buying petrol to start a fire and promising me money. She doesn't sign her name but I'm sure the police can match her handwriting. Stupid woman probably thought I would just chuck the notes away!'

There was a rustling noise as they were obviously passed over. 'So can you give them to the Commissario for me? And now I must try and flee. Thank you for bringing me this cloak. It makes everything a little easier, in the darkness especially.'

And a flapping hurry of a shadow flitted past, also headed towards the main door, and Posie realised with a sudden stab of irony that she still hadn't seen Corsetti's face. She was still standing well back against the wall, tensed, waiting for Alaric to depart when she realised that he was standing right in front of her.

He had swung around the marble overhang, soundlessly. 'Posie,' he said, wearily. But there was a dull anger in his eyes. 'I thought it might be you.'

Posie shrugged. 'I saw your note. On your hand, yesterday evening, and so did Dickie. We wanted to check you were safe, especially as you didn't come back last night.'

Alaric raised an eyebrow. 'I'm surprised you noticed.'

'How can you say such a thing? *Of course* I noticed.'

'Well, as usual you have a precious little case running, and you're so quick to jump to conclusions that it made me see red. I had to get away. I stayed at the Metropole Hotel overnight. I needed to calm down. To breathe. Things have been so dreadful…'

'"Things" meaning Silvia? Yes: her death must have been a shock…'

The anger intensified in his beautiful eyes. At his infuriating silence Posie lost her cool. Fire was in her belly but her heart was breaking at the same time.

'Why couldn't you have had the guts to tell me about Silvia, Al? That the wedding had been called off? Did you really expect me to present myself at that church today to be jilted at the altar? Dragging Lovelace out here to watch my misery? I'm worth so much more than *that*, you know.'

'Of course I know that, Posie! But the last couple of days have been a living hell, I'll be honest, with barely a moment to breathe, let alone explain anything. I'll admit: I'm barely in the mood for anything, let alone getting married. I told you I loved you last night, didn't I? Wasn't that enough? And what did you mean just now?'

'About calling it off? Why, I…'

Just then from behind a pillar by the next side-chapel a figure stepped out. A black-cloaked, rain-glistening figure, sinister as death and spookier than the marble grave-attendants on Canova's Tomb.

One quick movement and the drawing down of the hood revealed it to be Max, who stared at Posie and Alaric with a completely expressionless face, half-shadowed in the dark. So Posie had been right. She *had* been followed out here.

Alaric snapped. 'What's this, darling? You've brought your little blonde friend along here for the thrill of spying on a fella when he's about as down on his luck as he can be? Is this tit-for-tat for Silvia? This church is worse than that dreadful guesthouse. People listening in at every corner…'

Alaric thrust some flimsy-looking letters at Posie.

'Take these, will you? You probably heard every word Corsetti uttered so you're just as well placed as me to drop these off at the police station. Probably *better*-placed, I'd say. I expect you're running their investigation for them by now.'

And before she could say anything, Alaric had stalked off, anger etching his every movement into quick, strong lines.

In all of his conversation, only one line stood out. '*I'm barely in the mood for anything, let alone getting married.*'

Posie wiped a tear away before it fell on the evidence in her hands, the inky loops and whorls of a foolish, murderous woman. And when she looked up, Max, who was a self-proclaimed non-guardian angel, had disappeared too: his purposes in following her here and his bad timing at interrupting Posie and Alaric left as unexplained as almost everything in his strange life.

And as usual, she was quite alone.

****

Twenty-Five

Tucking the precious evidence inside her coat, Posie found herself walking almost without thinking, tracing the route of the canals she had sailed up just half an hour earlier, vaguely aware of Venice throwing off its night-time cloak of strange mystery.

Cafés were opening up on corners, and men were shouting at each other from bridges. Skiffs and barges were blocking up the small waterways with their deliveries of fresh fish and milk and bread and a thousand other household necessities which had to be brought into the city in this chaotic, medieval manner every single day. Rubbish men were handling vast, stinking bins on slow-moving black barges whose scent seemed to pervade the wet air, even when Posie had left the last of them far behind.

By some minor miracle Posie found herself back at the Grand Canal, at the very same stop she had alighted from before, with Dickie. Abandoning all thoughts of navigating herself safely to the Questura and to Commissario Salvarocca, she decided to head back to the guesthouse the same way she had come, back to Inspector Lovelace.

She would let him take the evidence into safekeeping.

As she stood on the prow of the next vaporetto, her face stinging from the now driving rain, her clothes sopping wet, Posie ran over the conclusions she had come to while hiding in the shadow of Canova's tomb; the conclusions to Alaric's questions.

Minnie Alladice, with a hatred for her whole family which had been simmering away for years, had come up with a particularly dreadful and unique means of setting past wrongs to rights. It was a lethal case of double-dealing.

She had been blackmailing the Count, threatening to reveal all there was to know about his relationship with Pietro Corsetti to the Venetian press. And with the self-same money she had been *paying* Pietro Corsetti – a weak and notoriously cash-strapped gambler – to start a crusade of terror against Bella Alladice, who had become her specially-chosen prey.

The conversation which the maid had overheard between the Count and Minnie Alladice when he had handed over money in the church doorway was now easy enough to understand.

It seemed Count Giancarlo was all too aware of Minnie's involvement in the fire. And even, perhaps, he was aware of Pietro Corsetti's part in the dreadful proceedings. The Count had probably been suspicious ever since he saw the note about the secret chamber, when he'd recognised Pietro's handwriting. Bella had said, after all, that he had reacted weirdly to the note: he had seemed disappointed. It was a horrid, slippery mess of a thing.

But *why* had Minnie acted as she had, *now*? Posie bit at her lip. It fitted: it was all a question of timing. Posie had been hearing the same thing, without really thinking about it, over and over again during the last couple of days.

Two months…

It had been two months since Bella Alladice had drawn up a new Will, organised by Roger Valentine, her efficient secretary, a man who was 'quite wonderful'. But Roger Valentine was also a man who chased money at every available opportunity, and, to go by Lucy's reports, he was a man who was indiscreet. Roger had told Lucy about the contents of Bella's Will in a show-off manner, and probably, in the hope of financial reward, he had then revealed the contents of the Will to Minnie, the person who had everything to gain by it.

And this had been the start of the end for Bella Alladice. A carefully thought-out plan of terror and murder had been planned over a short period of time, escalating in intensity and seriousness.

For the prize was too great, the temptation too strong.

Posie had failed to understand, until last night, when Lucy had let the fact slip into the conversation, that Minnie would effectively end up running Alladice Holdings. It would be a reversal, after all these years, of her fortunes. A way of getting back what Minnie probably thought of as rightfully hers. A chance to hold her own at the English Ladies Club of Venice, unburdened by a niece who was consistently an embarrassment. A chance to step out of the shadows…

What a mess.

Posie pushed a wet strand of hair from her eyes. Ahead of her was the Accademia Bridge, and Posie stood at the exit of the boat, barely noticing when it drew level with the jetty.

'Signorina? Hello? Are you leaving us or not, Signorina?'

'Oh, sorry. Yes, of course…' Posie crossed over onto the slippery jetty.

So Bella's death had all been planned carefully by Minnie, including the use of Pietro Corsetti as a useful and obvious scapegoat. But plans don't always work out. The wrong woman had died in the fire, and Bella had escaped.

Just how desperate was Minnie for her prize? Had Minnie *really* seized upon the second silver flask yesterday morning and poisoned Bella in a desperate last-ditch attempt at murder when her original plan had failed?

There were so many things which didn't ring true if that

was the case. Why had Bella's folio papers gone missing? Why had Roger disappeared so suddenly? And what was the significance of Bella's telephone calls to London? And what about that burnt photograph…

Campo San Vio passed Posie by in a rainy blur, the English church a particularly unwelcome sight.

What was particularly sordid, Posie thought with disgust, was how much this case revolved around blackmail, or people selling information, or their very chances of happiness, for *money*. Where did it all end? Posie stopped outside the front door of the guesthouse, her mind reeling.

And what about the secret room? How did that fit in? Was it just a morbid interest of Minnie's which had led her to acquire that knowledge? Had she *really* meant to follow through on her note to Bella about putting her body in there?

And if Minnie hadn't meant for Silvia Hanro to die in the fire, as she surely *hadn't*, it seemed certain that she was culpable for the movie star's death anyway. She *must* have told the newly-arrived Silvia about the secret room yesterday morning, perhaps in a bizarre attempt to curry favour with the famous girl, and Silvia had remembered it later when disaster struck. Minnie Alladice certainly had a good deal of blood on her hands…

Sighing, Posie tore off her coat and trudged up the staircase to the *piano nobile* above, and it was then that Posie heard a low hum of voices coming from the dining-room, which seemed to have been made accessible again. Of course, it was breakfast time.

With no appetite, Posie glanced in briefly through the half-open doorway, and saw a sombre-faced Jones laying out serviettes. A bored-looking young policeman was sitting nursing a cup of coffee at a cloth-covered table in the corner, leafing through a newspaper. With Bella dead, Roger and Alaric both disappeared, Lucy in custody, Max a general no-show, and Dickie presumably too upset to risk facing his aunt after the allegations he'd heard earlier at the Frari, the place was very quiet. There was also no sign of the Count or Inspector Lovelace.

Only Minnie Alladice and Mrs Persimmon sat in the dining-room, together, at a small table, coffees and pastries laid out between them, a couple of magazines spread about. Posie tightened her grip on the thin bundle of letters in her hand.

I'll show her what she can get away with, she thought to herself angrily, taking the stairs double-time. But without thinking, Posie had ended up on the larger, more impressive corridor of guest bedrooms.

Cursing under her breath, Posie looped about, intending to return to her own second-rate corridor where she knew Inspector Lovelace was also billeted. But as she hurried along, she heard a low agitated murmuring coming from behind one of the doors which had been left slightly ajar. Loitering as she passed she realised this must be Dickie Alladice's room, and she caught a very brief glimpse of him. He was frantically pacing up and down, wearing full black-tie. There was another man in the room too, contributing in a low, measured murmur; a reassuring baritone which Posie didn't recognise. Were they talking about Minnie?

She caught a snippet of Dickie speaking in a broken but passable Italian: 'No, Ennario. *Sicuramente, oggi.*'

'*Ma sei sicuro?*'

'*Sì, alle quattro…*'

Today. It must happen today. At four o'clock.

Something was definitely happening today, that much Posie understood. And Ennario? Wasn't he the Venetian notary that the Alladice company used? The man that Roger Valentine had told Bella Alladice *not* to use for her personal affairs?

Perhaps Dickie, distraught at Minnie's actions, but practical and business-like as ever, was making contingency plans for the company to keep going without the necessity for the shareholders to all sign documents, now that one was dead and the other would shortly become a convicted criminal…

Posie stumped along her own corridor, not bothering to make herself look presentable, and she rapped on the Inspector's door in a way which meant business.

'Ah, Posie, it's only you.'

'Indeed, sir. Only me. Can I come in? Let me tell you the news.'

'Of course.'

He had obviously been shaving, and he looked crumpled, as if he had grabbed at yesterday's shirt and suit trousers and tugged them on, regardless. A smart black suit was hanging behind him.

'I'm afraid I'm up late this morning, Posie. I was just about to go down to breakfast. What's up with you? You look dreadful. I take it you've not just got up, like me? Have you heard from that little priest fella about whether the wedding is off or on? I've got my best suit out, you see, if I *am* being called on to be a witness at the eleventh hour…'

'Oh, hang it all, sir. We both know the wedding caper is all off. In fact, I managed to speak to Alaric this morning, or what passes for speaking, these days. He told me he wasn't in the mood for getting married. So there you go.'

And ignoring every social convention in the book, Posie flung herself down on Lovelace's bed, spreading out Minnie's notes about her. And while Lovelace finished shaving, miraculously not cutting himself, as he was keeping a constant eye on Posie in the tiny mirror above the sink, he heard the whole sorry tale.

Turning at last, patting his face with a threadbare moss-coloured flannel, he let out a soft whistle. 'By Gad! Question is though, did Minnie *actually* do for Bella in the end? Wasn't she at the lawyer with her nephew Dickie at the time Bella took the poison?'

'That's right, sir. A Mr Ennario.'

'So *she* couldn't have been the one in there stealing off with the papers and exchanging the silver flasks, could she?'

'Apparently not, sir. Salvarocca seemed happy with the alibi which was given. It all checked out. You could ask him to check again, I suppose? He's here now, as it happens. Mr Ennario…'

'I see. That's handy. Well, Salvo will have enough to go on with these notes for a charge of manslaughter for Silvia Hanro's death. I'll get this guesthouse sealed up so Minnie can't leave and I'll get old Salvo to come here and arrest her pretty sharpish.'

'If you would, sir.'

Richard Lovelace was straightening himself up, putting on his suit jacket and fixing a navy woollen tie. He was already at his door. But he cast an anxious look over in Posie's direction:

'What are *you* going to do now, Posie?' But he almost didn't need to ask, for Posie had put her head down on his pillow, and waves of welcome, anaesthetising sleep were engulfing her.

And Lovelace nodded to himself, and left his room double-quick.

****

Twenty-Six

A brief glance at her wristwatch told Posie that almost six hours had passed.

It was almost three o'clock in the afternoon. It was unbelievable, and inconvenient to say the least, but the heavy, sweaty, dreamless sleep on Lovelace's bed seemed to have restored her afresh like nothing else had since she left London, and Posie sat bolt-upright, her thoughts crystal-clear. Welcome waves of understanding coursed through her like a new energy.

How could she have been so stupid?

Posie listened intently, but her ears were met with a ringing silence from the very depths of the guesthouse. Even the rain outside seemed to have stopped. Standing, and turning in an arc, Posie scanned Lovelace's room.

There it was.

That mysterious manila envelope which the Inspector had carted so carefully out with him from London. It was something which Alaric had requested.

But what if Alaric hadn't been the only one to request the manila envelope? What if someone else, or *several others*, were after the very same information? Pushing any scruples aside, Posie reached for it. She pulled out a thick wodge of official-looking documents, typewritten, many boasting fancy seals and stamps. Nearly all the documents bore a swarm of inky signatures.

It took just a few minutes to read through the papers, most of which Posie didn't understand. But she understood enough. And that limited knowledge drove her on. Hiding the envelope as best she could beneath Lovelace's mattress, she ran from his room and almost threw herself down the stairs to the main entertaining floor. As suspected, the place was totally deserted.

But then she heard a shuffling, rustling noise coming from the vestibule below, and peering down the stairs, she saw the welcome sight of Mrs Persimmon, keys still in hand, just arriving into the entrance hall, string bags bursting with grease-proof parcels, pulling a lemon-coloured silk scarf from her head and shaking her oilskin coat from her shoulders. The small woman looked up beadily.

'Ah! Miss Parker! Are you all right, dearie?'

'Where is everyone? What has happened to Minnie Alladice?'

And Mrs Persimmon, pleased to be able to shed light on something Posie was unaware of, told how, completely unexpectedly, Minnie Alladice had been arrested by Inspector Salvarocca – probably on completely fabricated grounds – and removed from the guesthouse with a full complement of police officers all waving guns about. That had been about nine-thirty that morning, and Mrs Persimmon hadn't heard a thing since.

Well, not unless you counted the two Inspectors hunting about the place noisily for Dickie Alladice and a man with a foreign-sounding name, and finding no-one.

And not unless you counted an incessant ringing of the bell and much shouting outside in the square at about eleven o'clock.

A man – it had sounded like Mr Boynton-Dale, but surely not? – had been kicking up a big fuss. But Mrs Persimmon had been having a mid-morning nap at about that time, having taken a wee nip of brandy to calm her nerves following the arrest of Minnie Alladice. And she had been on the point of getting up and answering the bell to the man, when she must have drifted off to sleep again…

Turning tail and almost running, Posie hurried along her own corridor, up the twists of stairs and along to the top of the house. She hammered on the door of the laundry room, not knowing whether to expect a reply or not. But she was in luck.

'Posie?' Max opened his door a fraction, and looked out, checking up and down the landing for anyone else.

'I'm alone, and I need your help.'

'You'd better come in, then.'

Inside the laundry room everything was much as it had been two nights previously, but the doors to the *altana*, the little broken-down balcony, were open, and a playful sunlight lit up the Venetian sky, which for the first time since her arrival Posie saw was now streaked a vivid blue. The usual binoculars were trained on the Grand Canal, on the Romagnoli Palace.

'Why were you following me this morning? To the Frari Church?'

Max shrugged. 'I thought the meeting you were attending might have had dangerous repercussions. I don't much like the company Alaric Boynton-Dale keeps. *Ach*, I was, against my better judgement perhaps, making sure you were okay.'

She glanced at Max's makeshift desk, and saw a notebook lying there, with columns of numbers written in a neat pencilled hand. She also saw a bundle of cream cards, unmistakeably international telegrams. Max followed her gaze.

'I go each morning and each evening to collect my instructions, and I also send my reports that way, too. I go to the *Fondaco dei Tedeschi*, the main Post Office. It's a lovely building, full of little shops on the ground floor selling glassware and trinkets and things. I got your pink necklace there. I've seen Minnie Alladice there early of a morning, too, among the stalls, looking for more scarves, no doubt. I'm finding that telegrams are more secure than using the telephone here. I only use that for emergencies now.'

Posie nodded. Max clearly hadn't heard about Minnie's arrest, and there wasn't time to fill him in. 'It might be one such emergency now. Can you help me? I need people in high places. Can you pretend it's a part of your mission? Whatever that might be…'

Max narrowed his eyes. 'Go on.'

And so she told him. Five minutes later they were standing close together in the vestibule of the guesthouse, with Max asking for the International Operator to connect him through to places deep in Whitehall which Posie had only imagined existed in her wildest dreams.

Max put the telephone apparatus down after a few minutes of a conversation in deep, hushed tones. He looked over at Posie and raised an eyebrow. '*Ach*, I'm – how do you English say? – sticking my neck out for you on this one, Posie.'

'I'm very grateful. But what's happening?'

'My contact will call back. Hopefully in just a matter of minutes. They will give me the information which I've requested. Which *you've* requested.'

'Were they surprised by your request?'

'*Nein*. Nothing surprises this lot.'

And sure enough, within just a couple of minutes the telephone was ringing and Max was answering it in unhurried, calm tones. 'I understand,' he muttered at the end of the conversation. 'I quite see the need for caution.'

Upon ringing off, he turned to Posie.

'It's as you thought. Almost three weeks ago this very same information was accessed quite properly – all above board – by somebody called Roger Valentine. He paid for the right to borrow it and had the information for a couple of hours in the headquarters of Companies House in London. During this time it's probable that he took photographs of what he saw, with that fancy little Leica camera of his, even though it's forbidden. The next record we have of it is somebody official, at the highest possible level, requesting a special right to borrow the material. That request was granted two weeks ago.'

'You mean Inspector Lovelace?'

'That seems likely.'

'Anything else?'

'In the time the information has been out on its special "borrowed status" with Inspector Lovelace, there has been one further request to access it, but from abroad. It came yesterday morning, about ten o'clock…'

'Bella Alladice!'

'If you say so.'

Posie leant against a damp, clammy wall. She was almost shaking. She looked at her wristwatch. It was twenty to four.

Alle quattro…

'I need to find Dickie Alladice,' she said softly. 'And Alaric. They were supposed to be meeting up soon. I believe their lives to be in peril.'

Max looked at her somewhat sourly. 'After all that Alaric has put you through, you want to save him? So *where* might this grave danger be taking place, exactly?'

Posie wrung her hands together, searching for any detail in the recesses of her mind which might help to locate one obvious place. 'I don't know. I just don't know. They're going into business together; something about glassware?'

Max almost hooted with derision. 'Glassware? In Venice? *Ach! Mein Gott!* They could have a headquarters anywhere! Most likely the island of Murano, of course. But that will take you forever to get out there, across the lagoon.

Even if you *do* take that fancy police motor boat. You won't make it in an hour, though, let alone by four o'clock.'

Posie groaned. She remembered Dickie's casual words, just the day before, about signing the contract with Alaric *in a very sweet place*. What had he meant? Why hadn't she paid more attention?

For now the man's life was in danger, and so too, possibly, was Alaric's. She would never forgive herself if something happened to Alaric, disregarding whatever had taken place between him and Silvia Hanro.

Just then there was a rapid hammering at the front door and both Posie and Max almost jumped out of their skins. Posie opened the door to a smart-looking policeman, who was clutching at a thick envelope, marked 'CONFIDENTIAL' and much tied about with blue string and covered in stickers. He started to speak in a flurry of fast Italian, and Posie gulped, not understanding a word.

Behind them, on the staircase, Mrs Persimmon had appeared, an anxious expression playing on her small-boned face. She came down smartly, replied to the policeman in a slow local dialect and indicated towards Posie.

Posie signed the policeman's chit and took the envelope, her thoughts still very much with Alaric and his meeting at four o'clock. Watching the policeman's retreating back, the freshness of his white helmet and gloves glimmering in the sunlight like icing sugar as he marched across the Campo San Vio, Posie suddenly turned to the Landlady, a flash of realisation hitting her.

'I hope you don't mind my asking, Mrs Persimmon. But it's just struck me now that you said the other day that you had known Dickie Alladice awhile now. Not just these last few days?'

'That's right, Miss Parker. We met over a year ago.'

'Would that be on account of his renting your husband's former business premises?'

Mrs Persimmon laughed shrilly. 'That's making it sound grander than it is, dearie. It's just an old warehouse.'

Posie nodded to herself with certainty. Mrs Persimmon's husband had traded in sugar, had he not? 'It's a former sugar warehouse?'

'That's right.'

A very sweet place. 'And please, can I ask exactly where it is?'

The Landlady laughed again, and gestured outside, through the still-open doorway. 'Why, of course, dearie. You can see it from here. It's that thin warehouse building right next door to the Romagnoli Palace. A bit run-down now, of course, but then I haven't the spare cash to spend on upkeep. But it's been very handy for Mr Alladice, from what I can gather. A mercy it didn't catch light at the same time as the Palace, isn't it!'

And Posie nodded automatically, steeling herself for what must come, grabbing at her own red coat and hat, and propelling herself towards the doorway and the sugar warehouse, but not before she had had a chance to glance at Max's face, ashen beyond belief, contorting itself back into its usual implacable calm mask.

But she had seen the panic and the fear which had so obviously lurked there.

****

Twenty-Seven

'Wait, Posie.'

She had never heard urgency in Max's voice before and she stared at him in surprise as he tore his hands through his white-blonde hair and hissed in an undertone. 'Please wait, you may jeopardise everything. Let me explain.' He was casting anxious looks over at the telephone apparatus.

'There's no time for explanations, Max. I must go *now*. It's almost four o'clock!'

'What do you expect to happen at this meeting, Posie?' he hissed. '*Who* are you afraid of?'

'If you must know, it's Roger Valentine. His presence at the meeting will be catastrophic. Dangerous.'

'He might not know where to go?'

Posie laughed bitterly. 'I have a feeling Roger Valentine knows absolutely everything. Of course he knows where to go!'

Max put his hand on her arm, tugging her back, gently. 'Then if this *is* serious danger, as you suppose, surely you can't just go barging in there alone? Can't you at least call your friendly Scotland Yard Inspector or the big Italian for some support?'

'No time. But if *you're* so concerned then why don't you come along with me?'

‘I will. Give me two minutes. I need to place a call first.’

Posie nodded tightly. ‘I’ll wait then.’

‘As you wish.’

Posie watched the German spy move towards the telephone again. She turned towards the open doorway, her gaze never wavering from the building she had so far never paid any attention to, the sugar warehouse. She hoped against hope there was enough time to stop Roger Valentine. The man who broke people, whose lives were left shattered behind him.

But this time Roger Valentine had really stumbled upon something big, and it had broken several lives already; ending one, Bella’s, forever.

There had always been something which didn’t ring true about the timing of Roger’s big pay-off, and about the termination of his employment in Venice.

Lucy had reported that she had told Dickie about Roger’s blackmail just a couple of days previously, and *that* was the reason Roger was now leaving. But the pay-off had come three weeks ago. And Roger had been searching for other jobs for the last three weeks, too. Which meant that Roger had been dismissed for something quite other than his treatment of Lucy Christie.

In fact, three weeks ago Roger had been in London, sourcing information for his blackmailing activities. And not even he could have guessed the murky waters he would find himself in.

Posie’s thoughts tripped back over the manila envelope Lovelace had carried from London, and she recalled the papers inside it methodically, one after the other. Returning to the present, she saw Max turning from the telephone, placing another call, waiting for the connection. He smiled a watery, tight grin full of bravado.

Posie called across softly: ‘Tell me, when you saw Minnie Alladice at the Post Office, was that yesterday morning or *this* morning?’

The spy looked mock surprised. 'What a funny question! Why, as it happens it was yesterday morning. Early. About nine o'clock.'

'And was she alone?'

'*Ja*, she was. I'm just coming. So are the police.'

Posie nodded, but her thoughts were spinning. Certainties, or what had been given as certainties, were being blown apart by one coincidental but opportune sighting.

She heard but barely registered Max asking for the Commissario at the Questura, and while she waited she ripped open the sealed envelope which had been delivered just a few moments earlier, fresh off the Orient Express.

She found herself confronted with the work she had undertaken Sidney to do for her the day before in London. The work which had taken him to the Associated Press office on the Strand, where he must have found Sam Stubbs, her friendly journalist, for here was Sam's card:

POSIE,

THIS IS ALL WE HAVE FROM THE CHARLTON STUDIO FOR THAT DATE. HOPE IT HELPS?

BEST WISHES,

SAM.

Three satiny-shiny press photographs dropped out. All identical, not dramatic or exciting at all. Posie scanned them all wearily. And then she gasped at the third photograph.

Time stood still about her.

'Oh, my! So this is *it*. The reel…'

For on a second glance, the three photographs were not actually identical at all. The first two were dull as ditchwater, and the third was telling. More than telling, in fact: it was life-changing, life-threatening. The sort of thing one would commit murder for. The sort of thing one would phone Scotland Yard up about and start speaking of murder…

Max was beside her now. He screwed up his nose slightly, and this close up Posie saw a smattering of freckles below the fair skin. He frowned:

'I've seen these before. No, not this one.' He set aside the third photograph and looked at the other two less interesting ones, nodding. 'I've seen *these* two. Up in Roger's room. In a green folder.'

Posie nodded. '*Copies* of the same photographs were certainly up there. I've seen the incinerated bottom section of one before. A section which escaped the fire when Roger attempted to burn them.'

'Are they important?'

Posie waved the third photograph.

'This one is,' she said in a low, angry voice. 'It explains everything. It's a motive for murder all by itself.'

****

Twenty-Eight

Together they hurried across the Campo San Vio, the sugar warehouse never out of their sights. Up ahead on the jetty was a lone Gondolier, basking in the rays of the late November light. Across the city bells were ringing out for four o'clock.

Before they reached the gondola, Max stopped Posie and grabbed at her arm. She looked into his eyes, which were blazing blue.

'*Ach*, I told you this was dangerous, Posie,' he hissed, 'and I have a sense of real unease. It rarely happens to me, actually. Normally I can look danger in the eye and be done with it.'

His eyes took in the pink beads at her throat and he seemed to decide on something. 'Maybe I feel I have something to lose now. If anything happens to you in there I will never forgive myself, and if something happens to *me*, don't regret it. Don't think of me – or speak of me – ever again. I'm glad I met you out here, and thank you for your trust in me. The jewels you kindly lent me are secreted away under a loose plank, in the near left-hand corner of the *altana*. It meant a lot to me that you put them at my disposal.'

Posie gulped, but before she could find a suitable response, Max was shoving something slippery and cool and lethal-feeling into her hand. Looking down she saw a small, sleek Luger pistol.

She shuddered and pressed it back: 'No, no thank you. I've never carried a gun before.'

'Then you should start now.'

'Absolutely not. *You* take it.'

'What makes you think I don't have another one about my person?'

'Well, have two then.'

They got into the gondola and crossed the Grand Canal, Max drawing his mouth into a hard, tight line of resignation. At the small, seen-better-days jetty of the sugar warehouse opposite, with its peeling paintwork and lack of any striped mooring posts, Posie and Max stepped out. The entrance to the warehouse, a huge wrought-iron and wood door, stood slightly ajar.

'That door shouldn't be open: it's odd. Let's wait here for the police,' hissed Max, but Posie strode inside, followed unwillingly by Max. Downstairs, as was usual with Venetian houses, there was a small vestibule, but this one had been made even smaller than normal by the erection of a new wooden wall all along the back, perhaps making space for more storage.

A corkscrew metal staircase led upwards and they surged on, an echoing, metallic noise meeting their ears as they climbed higher. They came out into what would, in every Venetian house or palace, have been the main floor, the *piano nobile*. But here any resemblance to a typical Venetian house stopped. The normal floors of the place were missing, ripped out; replaced instead by metal minstrel's galleries circling around and around the bare brick walls, all the way to the top of the building, ten storeys high at least, the galleries linked only by metal corkscrew staircases. The middle inside of the building where floors should have been was just a great shaft of light, giving the viewer a giddying sense of height, or dizziness when looking up, or down. Clanking lifts and industrial pulleys carrying baskets were whizzing up and down noisily in the vast empty shaft, being unloaded at every possible balcony. There was a busyness about the place which bordered on frantic.

The smell of roasted sugar still hung heavily in the dry, parched air. Bill Persimmon's legacy.

Posie stared. For some reason she had expected to walk into a silent, deserted warehouse, a place flooded by an expectant calm; everybody making preparations for a business to start up. She had not expected *this*; black-clad figures darting about like industrious ants on every balcony, loading and unloading, shouting orders, following commands.

'I had no idea!' she breathed, scanning the ants for anyone resembling Alaric, or Dickie, or Roger.

'*Nein*, why would you have?' replied Max, evenly. 'Quite the little industry your fiancé is about to join here, isn't it?'

A door banged heavily overhead, and Posie looked up, screwing her eyes against the sunlight filtered down through huge panes of glass at the top of the building. A man was walking along one of the balconies, about six floors up, and despite the fact he was wearing a full black cloak with its hood up, Posie thought there was something of the dangerously athletic grace of Roger Valentine about him.

'There!' she hissed at Max, and she took the nearest staircase as quickly as she could, spiralling around and around, her sturdy boots clattering loudly as she went.

She reached the sixth level and ran along the narrow wrought-iron balcony, puffed out, taking a brief look down into the bottom of the building.

'Gracious!'

Brown-paper packets were being unloaded off wooden pallets by perhaps twenty or thirty men on the rough square concrete floor of the *piano nobile*. The packets were then being sorted and placed on baskets and swung up to different levels where they were being repacked and sent off down external shutes. Not one man on the work floor stopped for a second, or chatted with a neighbour, or slacked off from the task at hand. Most didn't raise their heads at all, just carrying on mutely, the only sounds filling the place being the smacking and slapping of packets and the whizzing of chains, up and down.

Posie scowled, for something was wrong here. But what? Turning, and about to ask Max, she realised suddenly that she was quite alone on the balcony and that Max had disappeared.

'Hang it all!'

But she hurried on, aware of voices up ahead. English voices. Not raised exactly in an argument, but testy, and combative. On the left, coming up, she saw the cheap wooden doorway which Roger – if it *had* been Roger – had gone through. It was obviously the door to a small office, perhaps a foreman's office in the good old days of Mr Persimmon's sugar empire.

Loitering outside for a few seconds she pressed her ear to the door to hear better. It was as she had thought.

Men's voices, all of them known to her. A panic was in the air, surely the result of a gun having just been brought out? She heard Dickie Alladice, slow and firm. 'Surely there's no need for *that*, old fellow?'

And Alaric, reassuring: 'No, none at all. Just put it away. This can all be sorted out without waving that about, can't it?'

A sharp, bitter laugh. Roger Valentine: 'On the contrary, Mr Boynton-Dale, I think you'll find this *can*'t be sorted out in any other way.'

There was a click as the trigger was pulled, and Posie pushed open the door.

In a split-second she took in the man standing beside her, cloaked, holding a pistol trained on Alaric and

Dickie, both wearing black tie, and seated in ancient, paint-spattered cast-off chairs. Another man in a dark pinstriped suit lurked behind them both, standing, and Posie registered that this was Mr Ennario, the notary. On the rickety desk-table were formal-looking papers, with a fountain-pen atop them, and a pile of other, fatter papers were stacked neatly in a corner. The silver Sargent and Greenleaf safe, rescued by Alaric from the fire, sat on the desk importantly, alongside a decanter of what looked like Scotch whisky. Posie's heart was in her mouth and yet somehow she forced calm words into the chaos of the little room.

'No! No! Don't shoot, please.'

Everyone swung to look at her in one surprised movement.

'Posie?' Alaric said in disbelief. He stood up. The distraction was enough for Dickie Alladice to have got up too, and now Dickie was holding a second gun, trained on Roger Valentine.

It was a stand-off.

'It's delightful of you to join us, Posie,' said Dickie. 'But it's not at all safe. This fella here is a complete madman, and you'd be best advised to step out; same way you came in. Cut along home.'

'Dickie's right.' Alaric nodded, his handsome features knitted together in lines of worry.

'Oh, don't worry about me.' Posie smiled with a certainty she did not feel. 'I thought I might be able to help.'

'Help?' said Roger Valentine, a mocking tone entering his voice. 'How can *you* help? What on earth do *you* understand?'

'I understand almost everything,' said Posie, hoping against hope that Commissario Salvarocca and Lovelace, or at least Max, or *anyone*, would get along pretty dashed soon.

She looked directly at Roger Valentine, who lowered

his gun very slightly and flickered his gaze over her before he reverted to training his gun again on Dickie and Alaric. She had no doubt that the man meant business.

'I know what you *are*,' she said in a low voice.

Roger tutted: 'Everyone knows who I am!' he breathed. 'I've never used an alias. Not even when things got really bad, in England, after the war.'

'I said *what* you are,' she repeated stubbornly.

'A rotten egg?' murmured Dickie from behind his gun. 'The man's a crook, and a nasty one at that.'

'Ah.' Posie nodded. 'You refer to poor Lucy Christie, being blackmailed over this last year, which is why you gave Roger here the heave-ho. Told him to leave Venice.'

'Exactly.'

'I agree,' said Posie. 'Roger *is* a first-class blackmailer. There's not many he hasn't turned his skills on, usually successfully. Sometimes, like with Lucy Christie, he makes a frequent demand. Sometimes there's only *one* request for money, for a piece of handy information given: such as supplying Alaric here with information which could have been helpful to him. Or giving Aunt Millie that terrible, life-changing information about Bella's Will, two months ago. Not knowing what the consequences would be…'

Dickie's grey eyes clouded for a second in confusion, his brow furrowed. He kept the gun trained on the secretary but he appealed to Posie. 'What's that you're speaking of, Miss Parker?'

There was a horrible cackle from Roger Valentine. He hooted with laughter: 'That's the best bit of all! Bella undid you, and you didn't even know about it! You were going to get a nasty shock when the Will was read out next week by a proper lawyer who had sewn it all up neatly, weren't you?'

Dickie appealed again to Posie. 'What "nasty shock" is he blithering on about? I *did* tell you he was a madman, didn't I?'

Posie bit her lip. 'I'm afraid he's speaking the truth, Dickie. Bella left all her company shares to your aunt,

Minnie. Which means that together with her original share, Minnie will become the majority shareholder in Alladice Holdings.'

'*What?*' For once Dickie Alladice's complexion matched the grey of his eyes and his surprise was genuine. 'No! I don't believe a word of it!'

Posie nodded. 'Roger is right: you would have found out at the reading of the Will next week when Mr Proudfoot got here. It was all completely above board. You were with me earlier at the Frari Church – you remember the conversation we overheard then, about Minnie paying for the fire? – it all makes sense if you understand Minnie's motivation. She acted as she did to get her hands on the company, as soon as she could…'

Dickie gasped and fixed his aim even straighter at Roger.

Alaric looked puzzled, as well as scared. 'But why did you come back *here*, Valentine? You obviously didn't want the police to catch you, hence that nifty escape. This can only end in disaster for you, surely? In death or capture?'

Posie looked at Roger, and she recognised the expression in his eyes: there was a lawlessness there, a devil-may-care attitude. It was the expression Max wore most often. *He's a man with nothing left to lose*, she thought. *The most dangerous kind.*

Roger smiled. 'I knew this meeting was going ahead today: the time, the location. I knew the importance of it. I *had* to come. I also knew that money was being transferred today at four o'clock… that things had to happen today.'

He waved his free hand around the office. 'I had to stop all of *this*.'

Posie grabbed at her carpet bag, fished around inside it. She was nearest Roger, on his side, and only he could see what she drew out. It was the third incriminating photograph.

'But in addition, I think you wanted to talk about this,

didn't you? To show it around? Like you showed it to Bella before she died…'

Roger glanced down, and surprise registered on his dark face, the handsome features drawn back in a sneer which turned to sudden admiration.

'Why, Miss Parker! You're absolutely right. Full marks to you! Seems I was wrong, after all. You *do* know everything.'

'I told you. I know what you *are*: you are here to *avenge*.'

But in the few seconds in which Roger had looked away, when his focus had shifted, the notary in the corner had seized his chance. Grabbing at Dickie Alladice's gun, Mr Ennario had spun around and taken aim.

And just a fraction of a second too late, Roger Valentine realised he had a new assailant, and gasping, he fired his pistol at exactly the same time as the notary. Screaming, shouting, Dickie Alladice and Alaric were on the floor, and Posie too, her head in her hands, face down on the rough-hewn wooden floorboards, desperate for cover, still holding the photograph she had shown Roger.

Whizzing, and the pep-pep of bullets hitting home filled the air and there was an almighty swishing sound, as the black cape of Roger Valentine was collapsing, falling, sinking down like petals at the end of summer.

And then there was a silence and a couple of seconds passed, and Posie realised that both Mr Ennario and Roger Valentine's bullets had found their targets.

Her pulse hammering, she forced herself to look up, and she saw to her horror that both men were lying dead upon the floor.

****

Twenty-Nine

Was it Posie's imagination or was there a slight movement out on the balcony? Or was it simply a last juddering breath of air in one of the dead men, lying so horribly close to her? Like a reproach.

Posie cursed herself miserably: she hadn't helped matters. Hadn't helped at all. She had only made things worse.

After what seemed like an eternity, Alaric and Dickie were up on their feet again, and Alaric had come over to help Posie up.

Dickie stepped over Mr Ennario's body and wrestled with the decanter on the desk. With trembling hands he filled two crystal glasses and passed them across to Posie and Alaric. He took a swig from the bottle itself and shuddered, wiping at his mouth.

Posie tried not to look down at the body of Roger Valentine, so close to her feet, or to look at the blood pooling from under the black cape. The coppery scent of it was filling the small, sawdusty room and she leant across to open the tiny window behind the desk; the salty, damp air which swished in from the Grand Canal providing real relief. Posie put the glass of whisky down, untasted. Now was no time for drinking.

Right up close to the desk Posie noticed that the pile of fat papers were certainly photographs, blown up to show details, and she noticed too that the small silver safe sat open, its door swinging wide. Posie was surprised to see that all it contained was one tiny black notebook, and she supposed the contents of the notebook must be more valuable than appeared at first glance.

Dickie had gone towards the door. 'I'd better go down and find a telephone. I need to get one installed up here, but I haven't got around to it yet. I'll ring for the police to come. What a dreadful shock. But at least it's all over.'

Posie stood up, straight as anything. 'But it's not, though, is it, Dickie?'

Dickie swung around, confusion showing clearly on his face. 'Sorry, Posie? What did you say? I don't quite follow you.'

'I said it's not over, is it? But it's a nice tidy end to the story. Now you have a body you can present to the police, and you can say that Roger was the murderer, and was responsible for everything in this catalogue of horrors so far. But he wasn't.'

Dickie looked taken aback. 'I haven't a clue what you mean. You must be in shock, that's all...'

'Not at all. What I say is very simple. It's also the truth. Roger Valentine was a truly despicable man, which he knew. But he *wasn't* a murderer. He saw himself instead as an avenging angel. For Bella. Why else would he come here today and risk his own life?'

Alaric was staring, confused. 'Posie, what on earth are you talking about? None of this makes sense...'

'It makes perfect sense, actually. But we were all too blind to see it. Roger Valentine may have lusted after Lucy Christie – he was a man, after all, and he probably hoped that one month Lucy would decide to sleep with him rather than pay out her dues – but he had met his match in Bella Alladice. Here was someone for whom he had full respect and admiration. She may have been gross in outward appearance, but their relationship was never physical. Roger and Bella relied on each other. He was always looking out for Bella; always trying to find ways of helping her. Particularly helping her to maintain her standards.'

'What "standards" are you speaking of here, Posie?'

'Well, particularly with regards to the business. *This* business.' Posie gestured around.

Dickie shook his head kindly. 'I'm sorry, but you are quite mistaken. This is a new venture, as you well know. This is a business I will run together with Alaric. We were about to sign the documents this very afternoon. We *will* sign as soon as I get another notary over here to witness our signatures. *This* particular company has nothing to do with Alladice Holdings, or my sister Bella. Or my Aunt Minnie for that matter.'

Posie smiled quizzically. 'Oh, but it does. Doesn't it?'

Alaric had his arms crossed, his face was puzzled. 'Go on, Posie.'

She nodded at Alaric. 'Don't forget, Roger Valentine was the secretary for Alladice Holdings, as well as being Bella's right-hand man. He was in charge of all the paperwork, which he, Dickie, Bella and Minnie had to sign, in order for a document to be fully valid. *Four* signatures were required, always. For a while now Roger had suspected some sort of impropriety was going on. He never trusted Mr Ennario, for a start. And that's probably why he insisted that Bella make a Will with a separate, trusted English lawyer, brought out here specially for that one job. Maybe if Roger had been included in the wrong-doing from the start it could all have been hushed up? But he wasn't. Three weeks ago, when he was due some leave, he took himself off to London, to Companies House, where all the documents of a company must be filed. He asked for the Company Register for Alladice Holdings, and he sat in a room and took photographs of everything he was presented with.'

'Photographs?' repeated Alaric.

'That's right. What he saw in that Company Register shocked him. It needed recording.'

'This is complete hash, Posie. Rot! I told you Roger Valentine was a madman, didn't I?'

'Repeatedly, thank you. But he wasn't. He was just very astute. Unfortunately for *you*, and your plans...'

'For *me*?' Dickie sounded shocked.

'Yes, for *you*, Dickie. For what he found was fraud, on a large scale. Not just that Alladice Holdings had sold almost all of their properties in England, turning the proceeds into liquid cash, but that it had all been done without proper consent: the documents had all been returned with four signatures, but three of the signatures were faked. Your signature, and Mr Ennario's signature as a witness were quite legitimate, but you must have found a good forger to fake Roger, Bella and Minnie's signatures. Roger Valentine was profoundly shocked. But there was more to come: there were legal documents already filed in the Register which would split Alladice Holdings in half, and which would transfer half of that company's cash into a new venture – *this venture* – and the signatures on those had all been forged, too. The cash transfer to *this* company was due to happen today, at four o'clock, and to be legal, the new Partnership Deeds needed to be signed on the same business day. That much Roger realised.'

Posie watched Alaric's face, sheet-white and only just comprehending. She turned again to Dickie.

'It was a very clever plan, Dickie. It's unlikely that the halving in value of the original family company would have been picked up by either Bella or Minnie for a good long while, and you could probably have explained it away later by admitting to unstable investments, or tricky markets...'

Alaric swung around, perplexed, alarmed. 'Is this true, Dickie?'

'Absolutely not. I hate to say it but the lovely Miss Parker here has got quite the wrong end of the stick.'

Posie shook her head. 'I haven't, and Alaric knows it. Because Roger took his photographs and then – as usual – wondered how he could play the game to his own advantage. Alaric, admit it. He contacted you, didn't he?'

Alaric's bronze eyes had hardened, his jaw set. He gritted his teeth.

'Yes. It was dashed odd. I was winding things up in Constantinople two weeks ago, when I got a telephone call at the University, out of the blue. It was Roger Valentine, and he explained he was connected to the Romagnoli Palace. He told me he'd heard I was about to get involved with Dickie's new business here and he warned me off: advised me to check the Company Register for Alladice Holdings in London. He said I'd find irregularities there. He said that if it *was* the case, I could reward him as I saw fit later on.'

'So you asked Inspector Lovelace to bring the papers out?'

'Yes. I wanted him to come out anyway, for our…' He paused, then looked away, swallowing, deep hurt in his eyes. 'For our wedding. I knew he was senior enough to get the information for me, so it was a case of two birds with one stone.'

'Why didn't you say something to me, old boy?' asked Dickie, a hurt expression on his face. 'If you didn't trust me?'

Alaric shrugged. 'I don't know you that well, really, do I, Dickie? And anyway, when I got my hands on the Register, I couldn't see what on earth Roger Valentine was talking about. It all seemed absolutely fine to me. Tickety-boo. I'd been expecting bankruptcy or something worse.'

Posie grimaced. 'Mnnn. Well, for once Roger wasn't specific enough. He should have told you about the fake signatures. How were you to know the documents were all forged, Alaric? But maybe Roger didn't have to wait for Alaric's 'reward.' He thought he'd already made sufficient money on the faked documents, didn't he, Dickie?'

Dickie just laughed, and Poise saw a hardness settle in his eyes. Where on earth was Max? Where was Lovelace?

She turned to Alaric. 'Roger Valentine took his findings, his clever photographs, to Dickie immediately upon his return. He asked for a huge payment – the largest he'd ever had the nerve to seek out – to ensure his silence, and to ensure he wouldn't show Bella. And Dickie agreed, on the condition that Roger left his employment. But Dickie was probably short of cash, and only paid half of what he promised, the money coming from a secret little account he'd set up with Mr Ennario here in Venice. Roger Valentine was then left in an awkward position, in a sort of limbo, holding off showing the documents to Bella, waiting for the rest of the payment... but then he decided he would force Dickie's hand. And he had a trump card.'

'What do you mean?' Alaric was casting quick nervous glances between Posie and Dickie, trying to ignore the bodies on the floor.

'Roger was overheard speaking to Dickie the night before Bella died. He was threatening to show Bella the forged papers, and *something else*, unless he was paid his missing half. When no payment was forthcoming by the next morning, he decided enough was enough: he put everything together in Bella's black leather folio, including the trump card, ready for her to look at. And then he went for a good long walk, to see how things would play out.'

'What's this second thing I'm supposed to have been so scared of?' said Dickie, his hand on the door-handle, eyebrows raised in mock surprise. 'What's this 'trump card'?'

Posie smiled coolly. 'It was something you didn't know even existed. Not until Roger showed it to you the night before your sister died. Because, careful investigator that he was, Roger hadn't just been busy in London at Companies House, he'd been pursuing other lines of inquiry. Apparently, he had a lot of journalist friends, and it must have been one of them who let him look in their archives. What he found there was like gold dust. Unbelievable, explosive. Life-changing. It forced your hand, didn't it, Dickie?'

Alaric's eyes had widened to saucers. 'You mean, you mean…that Dickie…'

'Killed his own sister in cold blood? Yes. That's absolutely right. And Roger realised it, and got scared, and ran for his life. But today he decided to get even for Bella, and got himself killed in the process.'

* * * *

Thirty

'But *why*? Surely this company business – however bad – could have been smoothed over? Bella would have forgiven you, surely? You must be wrong, Posie! Dickie, speak up, man, what on earth can Posie mean?'

But Posie saw that Dickie Alladice was now possessed of a calm which was altogether unsettling.

A tight smile played over his lips. It reminded her of an arch-criminal she had been faced with on the first big case of her career as a Private Detective. But that man, Caspian della Rosa, had been armed to the hilt. *Thank goodness Dickie Alladice has no gun*, Posie thought to herself. *Otherwise he could simply kill us here and now and say there had been a mass shoot-out and he was the only survivor.*

And then the significance of the photograph from the Associated Press office, and all the truth it contained would never come to light. Past wrongs would never be made right, nor the financial irregularities in the company discovered. And Roger Valentine would have died in vain. He had come here to 'stop all of this', and his actions wouldn't have changed a thing.

There was nothing for it but to plough on, breezily, speaking directly to Dickie.

'I think Alaric is right. I think that Bella could have

forgiven you about the company, perhaps. In time. Although the good name of Alladice Holdings meant a lot to her, like it did to your late brother Johnny, whose memory she held so dear.'

Posie unfurled the photograph which had never left her hands. The *reel*.

'But she couldn't have forgiven you *this*. This was Roger's trump card. This is the second incriminating item which he placed in Bella's folio for her to discover on Wednesday morning, alongside the company documents…'

Alaric craned his neck, and Dickie stared, and for a second he flushed: '*You!* Where the blazes did you get that from?'

'Roger Valentine is not the only one to have a friendly journalist on his books. This photograph is identical to the one you took from Bella's folio on the morning she died, isn't it? You removed it along with Roger's photographs of the company documents, which I see are over there now, stacked on your desk. I take it you burnt the photograph which exactly matched this one, though? It's too dangerous to keep. Roger actually had three photographs in his possession like this, all nearly the same, like me; but it's *this one* which does the damage.'

'Let me see.' Alaric took the photograph and stared, uncomprehending.

'I don't understand. It looks old. It's nothing special, just a snap of some smart-looking folk. Oh! I say! Isn't that you here, Dickie? Grinning your head off? And isn't that Bella, but, I say! Wasn't she a looker back then? It says: "ICE CREAM GIRL MURDER TRIAL: THE ALLADICE FAMILY HEAR THE VERDICT." What on earth is this to do with right now?'

Dickie laughed, and lurched suddenly over the body of Roger Alladice. When he stood up again Posie saw with utter dismay that he was holding Roger's pistol. How had she forgotten there had been *two* guns in the room? That

Dickie was so dangerous – and possibly unhinged – that to use a gun just now would mean nothing to him except as a way to accomplish his own ends?

'Dickie, old boy, play fair. Not Posie…'

But Dickie was training the gun on her anyway. Posie shrugged. 'Why don't you tell us, Dickie, what this photograph has to do with *right now*?'

'Everything,' he smirked. 'And nothing.'

Posie stayed rooted to the spot, terrified. If, as she so desperately hoped, there were police out on the balcony, maybe Lovelace among them, it would be good to get a confession from the man's own lips. To get him to speak.

'You're quite right, Dickie. There have been so many different elements to this case, and sometimes it's been difficult to see through them all to the very core. But I told Bella in the first place that this was either about love, or money. And I was right, or *almost* right. It's been about money, for sure. But it's mainly been about love. A love for Lucy Christie. A life-shattering, life-destroying love…'

'I don't know what you're talking about!' Dickie wiggled the gun a bit at Posie but she stood very still, holding her nerve.

'Oh, but you *do* know. In 1912 Alicia Allessandro – Lucy Christie, as she now is – was arrested and put on trial for the murder of Robert Gattling, her almost-fiancé. She was found guilty of the crime of murder, that she had killed Robert by using prussic acid. This, and the two other photos in the set, show the moment at which the verdict was given. The Charltons were the photographers in the Courtroom that day at the Old Bailey, and they sold these reels all about the place. Quite a few newspapers must have bought them.'

Alaric was listening but only just, his eyes riveted on the gun in Dickie's hands.

'The whole thing had been a tragedy, hadn't it?' continued Posie. 'Your family, previously so close, were almost destroyed. Bella, convinced of Lucy's guilt, had testified against her. And because of this, Bella and Johnny never spoke again. But the trial had consequences for you and your brother, too, didn't it? You and Johnny fell out, with you accusing your own brother of administering the poison to Robert Gattling himself.'

'If you say so.'

'I do. But no-one actually knew what had happened for sure, least of all Bella. This photograph shocked her when she saw it on Wednesday morning. I think this photograph showed her *exactly* what had happened; made her understand. Isn't it true that a picture tells a thousand words? And this one unpicked an entire lifetime of misunderstandings.'

Alaric reached over for the photograph again, frowning. Posie pointed at the figures in it.

'The key thing to remember is that when this picture was taken it seemed almost certain that Lucy Christie would hang for this crime. The appeal was far away in the future. She had just been sentenced. Here Lucy is in the background, in the dock, head down, almost expressionless. And now look at the other three in the viewing gallery…'

Posie pointed. On the very far right of the picture, with her big puffy hair and cameo brooch, stood a very thin and beautiful Bella, her hands crossed elegantly, her whole pose one of quiet acceptance, of acknowledging a truth. But there was no pleasure in her face. And then, by complete contrast, the photographer had managed to catch what must have been a split-second's gut reaction, which had been smoothed over by the time the next photograph was taken, a second or so later.

Johnny Alladice, handsome, young, was focussed not on Lucy in the dock, but on his brother, right next to him. Johnny's eyes had widened impossibly, and his mouth gaped in a panicked, undisguised horror. He was visibly shocked at his brother's reaction.

It had to be.

For here, on the very left of the three siblings was Dickie. And the look on his face was something terrible to behold.

If Posie had been told it was one of the demons in hell she wouldn't have doubted it. Dickie was obviously laughing, and sneering, and hissing in revenge, all at the same time. His eyes were narrow slits, more snake-like than human, and he seemed to be doing all he could not to throw his head back in wild abandon, in absolute pleasure, in wild laughter. Here was a man who had got *exactly* what he wanted. And Johnny had seen it, at first-hand. And so had the photographer.

And years later so had Roger, and then, fatally, so had Bella.

'Johnny realised then, didn't he?' Posie said softly. 'Johnny probably hauled you up after the trial and asked you outright what exactly you were playing at. I think Johnny suspected *you* of poisoning Robert Gattling – which was, I expect, absolutely correct – and you thought you would throw the accusation back at him, to take the heat away from yourself. Not that anything came of it: you brothers never spoke again and the war took Johnny away. Forever, as it happened. Conveniently for you…'

Alaric stared at Posie hard. 'I may not have followed this correctly, but what I'm understanding is that Dickie poisoned one fella, and wanted Lucy Christie to hang for it. But *why*? And isn't this exactly what's just happened here, again? Bella dead with Lucy a suspect for her death?'

Posie nodded. 'That's right. Actually, murderers never usually change their methods. What you have to understand – and which Lucy herself *didn't* – is that along with Robert Gattling and Johnny Alladice, Dickie Alladice was madly in love with her. This was no passing childish fancy for you, Dickie, was it? It was an all-consuming passion. So you killed Robert, and seeing which way the wind was blowing between Lucy and your brother Johnny, you made sure that if *you* couldn't have Lucy, no-one else would. So you slipped a bottle of poison into her evening bag and generally made it look pretty black for her: love had turned to a hate-fuelled obsession. And I expect it's something you've nursed ever since. You certainly had no qualms about setting Lucy up again for Bella's death: the same poison used; the mock protestations as to her innocence…'

'You're wrong about all of this,' Dickie spat out. And Posie saw for the first time the narrowed eyes, the hissing hatred, the enemy within. She felt her feet turn to jelly inside her tough little boots.

'You were right to be worried about Bella's reaction, weren't you? You went in to her yesterday, didn't you? In the dining-room, at about quarter past nine? When she was supposedly alone and you were supposedly at the notary's office? She was livid with you! Bella was overheard threatening you that she was going to the police. She said it was "*better late than never*". And then, when you'd left her, having taken away Roger's photographic evidence and exchanged hip-flasks so that Bella was left with poison, she *did* in fact try to alert Scotland Yard. She called and asked to speak to someone about a murder: a murder committed by her own brother, several years ago. You saw Bella's death as inevitable by yesterday morning, and you would have found a way to kill her somehow. But, as luck would have it, you saw Lucy's identical bottle lying in the corridor outside her door, and seized on it as a way to incriminate her yet again. That hatred still burnt in you like a wild fire. And why not use poison yet again, too? Prussic acid, or rat poison, was easy enough to come by out here in a city full of vermin and rat traps, and I suppose you felt it would lend a nice symmetry to the thing.'

Dickie shook his head, gun absolutely still. 'It's a lovely little story, I agree. Almost plausible. But how could I have gone in to see Bella yesterday morning? I was with my godforsaken aunt at the notary's office! The police checked it all out.'

Posie laughed, despite the quaking boots. 'You want to rely on the evidence of your aunt – a soon-to-be-convicted criminal in her own right – who you probably paid to say you were together at the notary? She was seen at the relevant time *shopping* elsewhere! And you also want to rely on the word of a now-dead crooked lawyer? It's not an alibi which holds much weight, is it? And why would only *two* of you have been at the notary's office? Your company documents always required *four* signatures. You must have thought we were all pretty stupid! The police included!'

Dickie didn't answer, just held the gun straighter.

'Don't do it, Dickie,' implored Alaric in a strong, resolute voice. 'What can you gain by killing Posie?'

Dickie didn't even bother to smile now. 'Actually, I gain everything. She knows it all, as it turns out. She's quite correct about the past, about the company documents, about my foolishly high-principled sister. Even about my part in Robert Gattling's murder…' And there was a sickening click as he pulled the trigger, and Posie closed her eyes.

Suddenly there was a bang, and a loud whizzing, and a thud as a bullet hit a brick wall. Turning, she saw that Max had entered the room, brandishing his Luger, aiming it at Dickie, who had now retreated to near the back of his office. Max had deliberately missed his aim, to create a distraction.

'*At last!*' she breathed.

Spinning around, Alaric frowned: 'Aren't you the fella from the guesthouse? The watch-seller? The chap from earlier, at the Frari?'

Max nodded but his eyes never left Dickie's face. 'Among other things.'

'Well, what are you doing here?' Alaric persisted. 'It's a dashed awkward moment. As you can see. Better get the hell out, man.'

'And leave you to die at the hands of this madman? *Nein*. No way. Besides, it's a good moment for me, too.'

'What sort of moment?' asked Posie, not understanding.

'I'm sorry I left it so late to get on up here. The Italian drugs police are crawling all over this building, but I had to let them in, and direct them, and let them do their stuff. They've arrested almost everyone downstairs, and seized goodness knows how many packets of the stuff. Premium grade cocaine and heroin, mostly.'

'*Drugs?*' Alaric stared at Dickie, who had edged his way right back to the open window, taking care to avoid tripping over Mr Ennario's body. '*What* drugs?'

'This whole set-up is about drugs,' explained Max. His eyes swept across the room briefly, settling for a second on the silver safe with its open door, and an expression of fleeting joy flashed across his face.

'I've been monitoring things: what has been going in and going out, and who has been doing the collecting. It's a huge operation, mind-blowing. Most of the dope-traffic for a great many countries, England in particular, seems to come through this old sugar warehouse. London is virtually supplied by Dickie Alladice! Little did you know, Mr Boynton-Dale. You thought you were signing up to a fledgling glass company. But you were about to become a drugs baron of the highest order!'

Posie nodded, sickened, understanding now how incongruous the brown-paper packets downstairs had seemed to her at first glance, not handled with any sort of care at all, not how glass should be transported. She also remembered Max telling her about his speciality, smuggling. She understood what he had been spying on now, day and night. Not the Romagnoli Palace itself, but the warehouse next door.

Well, this was smuggling, wasn't it? Of the worst kind. A business Johnny Alladice would no doubt have abhorred. He would be turning in his grave in Messines if he knew right now that his family business was connected with such an illegal, immoral venture…

Dickie Alladice had the look of a man trapped, and he *was* trapped now. It was impossible that he could force himself out of the small window in the office, and even if he could, he would probably drop to his death in the alley underneath, hundreds of feet below. Posie saw a look of resignation fill his eyes and his hands closed tighter around his gun. *Dickie will shoot himself.*

What other option was there left for him now?

We're going to get out of here, Posie found herself breathing. *The police are here, outside.*

But she had misjudged the man. Dickie Alladice had obviously decided on a shoot-out. Before she could blink she heard Alaric shouting: 'Posie! Posie, my love! Get down! Get down low on the floor!'

And suddenly bullets were flying everywhere, and she was cowering next to the body of Roger Valentine, yet again.

And someone was falling heavily, silently, and there was a crush of footsteps across the room, and the swinging of the door, a bang as it closed, and yet more shooting out on the metal balcony, and a volley of reverberating shots.

Then there was a silence. Absolute silence, and a few minutes passed in nothingness.

And then Posie heard a welcome voice, calling her own name, over and again. It was Inspector Lovelace. He came through into the office and gasped, then quickly picked Posie up in his arms. She swayed there in the protection of his embrace. She didn't say anything, tears not far away.

'It's okay, I'm here,' Inspector Lovelace whispered. 'I was outside the whole time. I heard everything. Salvo wanted us to hold off, to wait outside. It was Max who went in alone. He wouldn't listen, he thought you were in danger: which you were. But at least you're still alive. Oh, Posie. I'm so very, very sorry.'

Posie frowned. 'What do you mean – "*sorry*"? What are you sorry about?'

Lovelace frowned, but his sudden confusion at her questions turned to sadness, and then desolation, and weariness, and something in his face spoke to Posie and suddenly she *knew*.

It was like standing at the edge of a chasm, watching the sea ravage the rocks below, knowing there was no option but to jump.

'You didn't realise, did you, Posie? Fool that I am! Let's get out of here, shall we? Step away, Posie. And don't look down.'

But she had to. She had always done the opposite of what she had been told to, even as a child.

And she looked down, and there was Alaric, sprawled right across the floor, a growing bloodstain like a flower spreading steadily across his white dress-shirt.

She saw the body of the man she should have married today, a look of almost-peace on his face, his beautiful bronze-green eyes staring and yet seeing no more, and any love or hate or confusion he had felt about the different women in his life taken to his grave alone, a secret forever.

Posie felt air rushing into her lungs, a desperate sense of clawing for breath.

'I can't breathe, sir. It's too much.'

'Step away, Posie.'

And for once she did exactly as she was told.

* * * *

Thirty-One

It was several hours later and Posie and Inspector Lovelace stood together in the Campo San Vio. They looked out over the Grand Canal, and the heavy lagoon breeze blew over them in violent gusts, salty as tears, timeless as a treasure.

There was the promise of snow in the air.

The last few hours had been truly terrible. First, a police boat ride out to San Zanipolo, where the hospital and morgue was situated, accompanying the Police Surgeon, who had requested that Posie formally identify Alaric's body. Which she had done, numbly and mechanically, with Inspector Lovelace never leaving her side for a moment.

And then a meeting at the Questura had followed, with Commissario Salvarocca briefing them on the fact that Dickie Alladice had ended up being injured, seriously, in the shoot-out at the drugs warehouse. Dickie was now also in the hospital at San Zanipolo, his life hanging in the balance, a police guard never leaving his side. Enough had been heard of his 'confession' that Salvarocca and Lovelace would be able to put a case against him if he survived: for both the murder of Bella Alladice, and for the historical crime of poisoning Robert Gattling. If Dickie lived, he would be handed over to the British police and sent home to await trial there.

Posie had had to know the truth: 'Did Dickie shoot Alaric? Was it *Dickie's* gun which killed him? Can't you add that to the list of his crimes?'

Salvarocca had shrugged gently. 'We don't know as yet, Miss Parker. It seems likely your fiancé was simply caught in the cross-fire; it was pretty wild in there, wasn't it? Bodies aplenty. Whether it was your friend Max who fired the bullet or whether it was Dickie Alladice, I'm pretty certain it was a terrible accident.'

As to the other people involved in the case, the Commissario informed Posie and Lovelace that Minnie Alladice was sitting in a cell deep in the bowels of the Questura. Posie hoped against hope that it wasn't furnished as nicely as the one Lucy had been locked up in. Despite the evidence against Minnie for her part in the arson attack on the Palace, there was some debate as to whether she was mentally capable of being tried for her crimes. She had tried to hang herself that very afternoon with one of her flowery scarves, and since then she hadn't been making much sense. It seemed likely as not that she would end her days in the Venetian Lunatic Asylum out on one of the far-flung islands of the marshy lagoon.

'How handy,' Posie had muttered on hearing this news. 'And what will happen to Alladice Holdings now?'

The Commissario had shrugged: 'The mad and the criminally-convicted cannot run a company here in Italy. I'm sure it's the same in England, is it not, Richard?'

'Indeed.' Lovelace nodded. 'I presume it will be wound up, and the proceeds will follow the normal Will of the last shareholder who wasn't mad, or convicted of a crime.'

'Then that was Bella, sir. Bella's normal Will left everything to a charity for cats.'

'Lucky cats.'

It seemed that Pietro Corsetti had evaded those searching for him, successfully fleeing the city, perhaps with the help of the Count Romagnoli, who had also disappeared.

Lucy Christie had been released from custody at the Questura, with all charges dropped, and Max, who had successfully orchestrated the raid on the drugs warehouse almost single-handedly, had disappeared into thin air, just as the last of the warehouse workers had been rounded up. The Venetian police had hoped for some sort of written statement from Max, some concrete proof of international collaboration, but they were left empty-handed.

On returning to Mrs Persimmon's guesthouse for a change of clothes after the meeting at the Questura, Posie had automatically checked the upstairs laundry room for Max, but any presence of him, or any evidence of his activities over the last couple of days was already gone. Scrubbed out.

He had left no sign or note for Posie. But why should she be surprised at that?

She had looked for the sapphire earrings as he had instructed, out on the *altana*. But they had gone, too. So either he wasn't a man of his word, or he had suddenly found a need for the jewels and grabbed them in haste. Either way it seemed to matter very little now.

Posie felt sick.

The couples who were criss-crossing the Campo, dressed for dinner and drinks, muffled up in their thick winter clothes, barely registered on her consciousness. Neither did the delicious smells of cooking which wafted across the square. It was past dinner time now, nine o'clock at least. But neither Posie nor Lovelace had the stomach to eat.

'What now, sir?'

The Inspector drew his coat collar up. 'London,' he muttered, as if reassuring himself that the place still existed. 'Let's get the next train. By Gad, this is a watery grave of a place and I'll be pleased to leave it.'

'It's been a terrible case, sir,' Posie whispered. 'Too many deaths, and so much *greed*. And the whole time these ghosts from the past, reaching out and overshadowing people's lives *now*. Money and love were motivating factors, of course, but it's as if Johnny Alladice and this unsavoury Robert Gattling character have been as alive and present as any of the others, watching events unfurling over our shoulders.'

The Inspector shrugged. 'Sometimes in these cases with a revisiting of past crimes, that's how it can seem. At least now there will be justice, or clarity, with regard to who actually killed Robert Gattling. And presumably Lucy will realise how Johnny really felt about her, if she goes and reads that Will at Somerset House.'

'Yes, she'll realise that, among other things.'

'It's the amount of unnecessary killing in this case which shocks me, though.' Lovelace frowned. 'That poor girl, Silvia Hanro, she didn't deserve a death like that, whatever your thoughts might be towards her, Posie. The news will be breaking across London now. In all the newspapers.'

'A national tragedy, sir.'

'Indeed, and although less will mourn them, let's not forget Roger Valentine and Mr Ennario, that notary fellow. And Alaric, of course: *that* will be a national tragedy, too, when the story breaks. Oh, Posie. I'm so sorry. I can't believe he's dead, but nor can I believe the mess-up about the marriage…'

Posie drew herself up. 'It's fine, sir. It's something I have to face, or forget about, maybe, in due course.'

And somewhere inside her a sharp anger burned lividly. Automatically she took off her gloves and slipped off that pink daisy of a Cartier ring which Alaric had given her a year before, and she drew it back, as if to sling it with a perfect aim into the black sticky waters of the Grand Canal.

'No! I say, Posie! What on earth are you doing?' And Lovelace was shouting, and hopping and almost grabbing at her arms, and it would have been comical but for Posie remembering the Inspector's words about the ring being of sufficient value to see his little daughter pretty much through her life.

Shamefaced in the torchlight, she took the Inspector's hand and scrunched her own fist containing the ring into it.

'Here,' she whispered. 'For Phyllis. Far better it should benefit her rather than be lying at the bottom of this muddy canal, or cast out into the lagoon somewhere on a tide.'

'Are you sure?'

'Goodness, yes. Just make sure you sell it. I never want to see the wretched thing ever again.'

'I guarantee it. And a thousand thanks, Posie. I'll see that a lot of good comes of this.'

They turned in the direction of the guesthouse.

'Just one more night here,' nodded Lovelace. 'Then we'll be off.'

But as they drew close to Mrs Persimmon's, they saw there were people gathered outside the open doorway. Jones was fluttering on the threshold, like an anxious butterfly uncertain of its course in a strong wind. Seeing them approach, he called out thankfully:

'Ah, Miss Parker and Inspector Lovelace! You have visitors!'

And two men, both in dark felt hats and dark black coats, turned around on the doorstep, creating sinister silhouettes. But one of them looked vaguely familiar, and drawing close Posie recognised him as the Chaplain they had met at St George's the day before, the Reverend Blythe, who removed his hat. The other, older man, whipped off his hat, too, and bowed in her direction.

'I'm Father Gregory,' the older man explained quickly. 'Miss Parker? I believe you dropped by the church yesterday?'

'That's right.' Posie swallowed, tasting a bitter iron-like tang which was horribly like blood filling her mouth.

'I'm afraid I was visiting some parishioners in the city who cannot attend church anymore.'

'Of course,' said Posie, unsure why the men had called.

'It appears there has been some kind of mix-up, and I hoped we could put it right.'

'What sort of mix-up?'

'My Chaplain, Blythe here, informed you that the marriage ceremony scheduled for this morning between yourself and Mr Boynton-Dale had been cancelled, or, at least, he *thought* it had.'

Posie nodded. She was aware of Lovelace, horribly tense at her side.

'Blythe here was quite correct. It *had* been cancelled. On Tuesday morning, early, I received a call from a woman, an English woman, who told me it was all off. When I asked who was calling she declined to give me her name, but she said she was calling on behalf of Alaric Boynton-Dale. She said she was a personal assistant of some kind. She was calling from a Venice number, at Santa Lucia Station.'

Posie stared in the darkness at Father Gregory. What on earth was he talking about?

'I asked if she was certain of her facts: and she replied she *was*. She said circumstances had changed, regrettably so. And therefore I crossed out the wedding entry in our church ledger. Didn't think any more of it.'

Lovelace was impatient. 'So why are you here *now*, Father?'

'Because of what happened this morning.'

'This morning?' Posie's voice was just a whisper.

'Yes. At ten-thirty. The time the marriage service was booked for originally. Flowers arrived from a local florist, red roses tied up with rosemary. A string quartet from the Accademia arrived and set themselves up. And then Mr Boynton-Dale himself appeared, very nervous he was, with Dickie Alladice as his best man, both in black tie. They had the wedding rings with them. They had brought along some notary chap, too, I presumed as a witness, although I gather the Inspector here was supposed to turn up, too? I was surprised by the fact it was all going ahead, of course, but as I had time to conduct the ceremony and the church was empty, I carried on as if nothing had happened, as if there had been no phone call. I presumed there had been some pre-wedding jitters, now smoothed over…'

Posie covered her mouth, finding it hard to breathe.

'When you didn't show up, Miss Parker, they joked a little at first, saying you were fashionably late. After half an hour I got nervous, and asked the Reverend Blythe to telephone to Mrs Persimmon's to enquire if you were available. But no-one answered. I informed Mr Boynton-Dale at this point about the woman telephoning to cancel the ceremony on the Tuesday morning. I said I was very sorry, but it appeared that my Chaplain had informed *you*, Miss Parker, that the ceremony was all off. Which perhaps accounted for your no-show?'

Posie felt a terrible sense of dread: 'And what did Alaric say?'

'I'm afraid it was rather terrible to behold. He collapsed down onto one of the pews. Lit a cigarette. "*So that's what Posie meant at the Frari, about being jilted at the altar!*" he kept saying. No-one knew what he was talking about, I'm afraid. The music quartet lingered on, unsure whether or not to pack up. But he – Alaric – told them to stay.'

'Gracious,' muttered Lovelace. 'What a mess! But who on earth cancelled the wedding?'

Father Gregory was standing with his hands linked behind him, fingers twisting together over and over again in embarrassment. He coughed hesitantly:

'I think I may be able to help you there, sir. Or at least to pass on what I know.'

'Go on,' whispered Posie, although she thought now that she knew what the man was about to say.

'Mr Boynton-Dale was muttering: "*Curse her! I don't*

want to speak ill of the dead, but she's been a thorn in my side recently: pitching up here, there and everywhere, uninvited." And Dickie Alladice seemed genuinely surprised. "*You mean Silvia Hanro, old boy?*" he was asking. "*You mean you didn't ask her out here and install her up in your rooms as your mistress? You missed a trick! Everyone thought she was your mistress. Why, I virtually told Posie that was the case!*"'

The Vicar coughed in some embarrassment. 'You can see it was a rather peculiar conversation for me to be overhearing, can't you? Not altogether appropriate on the morning of Mr Boynton-Dale's wedding to another lady, in a sacred place. To be speaking of a second party in such a manner...'

'What else did the two men say?' asked Lovelace sharply. 'We might as well hear the whole thing.'

Father Gregory shrugged.

'I can't remember the exact words, of course, but Mr Boynton-Dale was angry at his friend. He said: "*How could you think such a thing? I never wanted her out here for a second, nor in Turkey. She had become obsessive.*" Mr Alladice hinted that it was a jolly nice problem to have had, one most men would desire, but Mr Boynton-Dale kept shaking his head, and said: "*It wasn't a nice problem. Silvia threatened she would come out here. She joked that she would cancel the wedding, but I see now that it was no joke, and she meant it literally.*"'

The Vicar splayed his hands apologetically:

'Mr Alladice lost his temper then, I recall. He was shouting out questions. *Why* had Mr Boynton-Dale been so anxious to find Silvia Hanro after the fire, if he hadn't cared for her at all? *Why* had he, Mr Alladice, been enlisted at night to help Alaric look for the girl over in the dangerous Palace with a torchlight? *Why* had Mr Boynton-Dale ignored *you*, Miss Parker? And so on...'

'And?' Posie's voice sounded far off, even to her own ears.

'Mr Boynton-Dale said Miss Hanro had been at school

with his sister, back in the old days. He felt a responsibility for her: that was all. And then Mr Alladice asked why his friend hadn't explained this all to you, Miss Parker, and your fiancé just groaned and said: "*Pride, my man, and arrogance. I assumed Posie's trust in me was absolute. I didn't count on her seeing that magazine cover, or on Silvia actually cancelling our wedding, or of Posie hearing of it in that way. But why couldn't Posie bring herself to tell me what this Chaplain fellow said? About the wedding being called off? We could have sorted it out. I don't understand.*"'

Pride, swallowed Posie. Because I'm the most foolish woman you could hope to meet…

The Vicar was continuing hazily. 'I don't remember much else of the conversation, Miss Parker, because it was at that point, about half an hour after the start of the thing, that Mr Boynton-Dale decided to hurry around to the guesthouse and see if he could convince you to come and get married. We heard him from here, practically breaking the door down and shouting your name aloud…'

Posie remembered Mrs Persimmon saying that the only disturbance that morning, when everyone else had been out of the guesthouse, had been at about eleven o'clock. An infernal racket, someone hammering and yelling. It *had* been Alaric.

And all that while Posie had been sleeping up in Inspector Lovelace's room. Probably the last place Alaric would have chosen to look.

But even so…

She frowned. Would it have made a difference? What would she have said if Alaric *had* found her? If he had explained? Would she have trotted back to St George's Church, wearing her hastily-thrown on cream wedding suit and a bright smile? Would she have been able to go through with the wedding vows?

For she was positive, sure as bread was bread, that Venice had opened her eyes to something she had probably known but not acknowledged for a good long while: that she and Alaric could not, *should not*, have been together. Perhaps it had been a misplaced love from the start? If they had married they would have been creating a future built on foundations as vulnerable as this beautiful, doomed city…

But Posie kept remembering Alaric's face, his wounded expression whenever his gaze lingered on her, up in that horrible little foreman's office. The hurt that she hadn't turned up at their wedding. That *she* had jilted him at the altar. That her trust in him wasn't absolute, after all.

Now Silvia Hanro and Alaric were both dead. And Posie, as usual, was the survivor. The one who had to face things head-on, like it or not. The one left to re-invent herself, yet again.

Alone.

'Thank you,' she whispered to the Vicar.

Father Gregory nodded. 'I had to get that off my chest. Perhaps now you've heard all of that you can reconsider your position? Find Mr Boynton-Dale and maybe re-book the wedding? We'd certainly be happy to host your ceremony, under happier circumstances, this time around…'

And Posie ran from them then, pushing through the dark vestibule of the guesthouse, trying not to choke, trying not to look backwards, only forwards.

****

Thirty-Two

It was late, even by Posie Parker's standards. But she'd packed and repacked her bags, ready for tomorrow. Ready to leave.

She couldn't sleep. She tried not to run over the events of the day, but it was fiendishly difficult.

She didn't know what was going to happen to Alaric's body, but she hoped against hope that Commissario Salvarocca would be able to deal with it. If Alaric was buried out here, on that ghoulish island in the lagoon which Mrs Persimmon had spoken of, Posie wouldn't be coming back to attend the funeral.

She'd said as much to Inspector Lovelace as they stood together in the salon, after the priests had left, drinking brandy. Lovelace seemed more dumbfounded and shocked than she was.

'Salvo is a good man, Posie. He'll see Alaric right, don't you worry. Even if he has to be the sole mourner at his funeral. He's a good man.'

'He's a fascist, sir. How can a good man be a fascist?'

Lovelace had sighed, lighting up a cigarette and looking out over the water. 'I know you doubt him. But sometimes you find yourself in unexpected places, or in unexpected situations. All you can do is try and survive. Even if it means sporting a coat which is different from the one you would normally choose to wear.'

Posie didn't answer. Just rolled her eyes.

'He was married, you know.'

'Oh?'

'Mnnn. She was a lovely young thing, although I only saw a photograph, of course. When I met him the first time round they were newly married, and Rosalie was the love of his life. *She* was the Venetian, not him. He was a Rome boy, born and bred. But she convinced him to move here, and here he stayed. Even after she died. A love for her, rather than a love for the city, have kept him on here ever since. I doubt he could ever move. The night he lost Rosalie he lost everything, and I daresay that the fascist organisation means very little to him. He wouldn't give two hoots if they covered him in medals or shot him down in the street. Not much can touch him now.'

'Golly,' breathed Posie. 'I had no idea. How sad.' She remembered the pain which seemed constant in the man's eyes. 'How did his wife die?'

Inspector Lovelace bit his lip. 'The Salvaroccas lived in an old wooden apartment, somewhere in the centre of the city. It was one of these house fires, actually. Apparently they happen all the time out here: closely-packed buildings, old wooden panelling, takes an age for anyone to come and help. Salvo was on night duty, and was recalled as soon as possible, but of course, there was nothing to be done. It was too late.'

Posie remembered now the difficulty Salvarocca had had when trying to explain what had happened to Silvia Hanro in that secret chamber, how he had stumbled over the words, tears not far off.

'I just thought you ought to know that a large, sad heart beats inside that dreadful uniform.'

'Thank you, sir. A fair point, and one I'll remember.'

And now, much later, still unable to sleep, the silence of

the guesthouse – with everybody now dead or departed – and the lack of any bells or celebrations outside, seemed to create its own kind of dreadful weight.

Posie turned again and again on the pillow, willing the hours to pass. It was as if she was waiting for something else, something more dreadful than the rest of it all.

But how could that be?

Sleep when it came was shallow and unfulfilling, and punctured by the sounds of the telephone ringing, incessantly. There was also the clamour of heavy footsteps, and someone – was it Jones? – running and hammering on a door nearby. Banging, and shouting. Men's voices.

Several times Posie almost got up, dragging herself from half-consciousness. But in the end it was morning when she woke properly, her wristwatch telling her it was almost eight o'clock. She dressed snappily and grabbed up her bags, almost running downstairs in her hurry to take breakfast and be off.

But she slowed as she reached the bottom of the stairs, and there she saw Mrs Persimmon standing wretchedly outside her dining-room, eyes wide and pale, her face devoid of any scrap of make-up, her sparse hair tied up in dirty grey rag curlers. Jones, eyes lowered, stared at the floor.

'What is it?' Posie asked, putting down her bags slowly with a sense of dread. On top of her carpet bag was the red mask the Inspector had given her, as she hadn't had quite enough space inside the valise to carry it safely.

Both Landlady and Butler motioned inwards, and Posie saw that the door to the dining-room was standing open. A crashing nervousness hit her, confirmed when she saw the uniformed Commissario Salvarocca sitting at a table, an untouched espresso before him. He looked inconsolable.

'Inspector Lovelace?' she burst out. 'Has something happened to him?'

Some terrible misplaced act of revenge by another

unknown associate of Dickie Alladice, perhaps? For who else knew the Scotland Yard Inspector was out here?

Salvarocca was shaking his head now. That sadness again… As deep as the lagoon he had spent too long living next to.

'Yes and no, Miss Parker. I have bad news. Perhaps sit down?'

'No. Tell me rightaway.'

'Very well. I am afraid I must inform you that Richard received terrible news in the night. The worst kind.' He coughed, choking back emotion. 'It seems there was a fire, at his house in Clapham. Last night.'

Posie gasped, holding onto the back of one of the chairs for support. 'Tell me.'

'His wife, Molly Lovelace, she didn't make it. She must have been overcome by the smoke and the fumes, and died very quickly. Which is something to give thanks for, at any rate.'

'And Phyllis? Little Phyllis?' Posie was aware of her voice rising, hysteria right on its edge. Tiny little Phyllis, only one-and-a-half, innocent of everything. Her goddaughter.

'Be calm, Miss Parker. Phyllis Lovelace was sleeping in her bedroom at the front of the house, and a neighbour managed to get a ladder up to the window, break it open, and get the child to safety before the smoke and flames engulfed the place. She wasn't hurt. Physically at least. Richard has left already, poor man. He's obviously in a state of shock but he has to keep on going for the child, doesn't he? He's taken the early train. The post train. He said he was sorry but he couldn't wait until this afternoon's Orient Express to travel with you. Hoped you'd understand.'

'Of course.'

There seemed very little air in the windowless room. Posie put her hands to her head, steadying herself. But the Commissario obviously thought she was about to cry, to have some sort of female meltdown.

'He'll be okay in the end, Miss Parker. You'll see. It may take years but he'll keep going. It's all any of us can do, isn't it, Miss Parker?'

'I'm sorry?' She must have shot him a look of complete bewilderment.

'Keep going.' The big man shrugged sadly.

'All of us. We just have to keep on going.'

* * * *

EPILOGUE (LONDON)

Many years later, on a hot fuggy day when the morning air brought in nothing fresher than the London smells of dust and tar, Posie Parker was brought to mind of that fateful trip to Venice.

She was packing up her flat at Museum Chambers – her lovely flat in Bloomsbury – having decided to move on.

And the packing up was proving to be emotionally charged.

Each and every photograph, every single painting and framed item of value on her pale-green walls spoke of something personal.

The very act of taking each piece down caused memories to rise, fresh as the day they had been created, sometimes bringing to mind people or places long since vanished. Or cases long since solved.

Posie took down a pair of framed Egyptian hieroglyphics, created several years earlier by an Egyptologist she had known well; the paintings rescued from a fire out on an archaeological dig in the Valley of the Kings, a dig on which she had fallen in love with Alaric Boynton-Dale. She gulped and turned to something else on the wall.

It reminded her of Venice.

She hadn't been back, not in all this time. It had been a dreadful experience, starting with a fire and ending with a fire...

She swept back her dark hair, worn slightly longer now in a soft waved bob around her neck, and fiddled with the pink glass Murano beads which she still wore very often, although they had been re-strung several times since she had first received them.

Posie was thrown suddenly into the memory of the aftermath of that case, the Alladice case, in the weeks which had followed her return to London. Posie remembered the details which had filled the English newspapers for weeks and weeks afterwards. The constant ringing of the telephone at the Grape Street Bureau, the requests for comments and interviews.

And somehow the deaths of Silvia Hanro and Alaric had got swept up in the reporting on the Alladice case and everything had melded together and Posie had tried to step aside from it, to blank it out. She had politely refused a meeting with Lucy Christie, who telephoned several times at the start of December. For nice though the girl was, Posie couldn't bear to go over the case again so soon, or be reminded of anyone from it.

Even when Dickie Alladice had recovered from the gunshot wounds which had injured him and had been sent home for trial at the Old Bailey, she had tried to keep a distance. Even when he was found guilty and sentenced to death for his part in the murders of Robert Gattling and his own sister, Bella Alladice, Posie had kept her own counsel, refusing to give interviews or be drawn on the subject of the Alladice family. Mostly she was scared to get caught out speaking about Alaric.

So she took holidays to get away: a weekend in the Cotswolds; a stay on Lindisfarne, which felt like the edge of the world; a very strange Christmas holiday spent with Dolly and Rufus Cardigeon up at Rebburn Abbey in deepest Yorkshire, with Inspector and Phyllis Lovelace among the party of house guests. A holiday where she had blotted out the entire Venice episode, every aspect of it.

Posie smiled now to recall the trip home to London from Yorkshire that Christmas.

It was a wretched time: just after Boxing Day, bitterly cold, the decorations still adorning all the stations and houses, but looking unaccountably dim and tawdry now that Christmas Day itself had passed.

She had thought she would have the first-class carriage to herself for the four-hour journey home, but had been shocked to discover a man sitting opposite her.

It was Max.

He'd grinned, admitting it was a planned meeting. And Posie had felt an immediate and insane amount of delight at his presence, at the fact that he had got out of Venice alive and well. That he had sought her out.

Her own personal ghost.

As soon as the train was off, curtained in steam and smoke, coal-air billowing about them, he'd reached over and taken Posie by the hand.

'I'm sorry I didn't say goodbye, Posie.' His blue eyes were blazing, his white-blonde hair cut even shorter than she remembered it, slicked down close to his skull. 'Things got a little tight for me there, in Venice.'

'I thought as much. There's no need to apologise, it's your job. Which you do very well, by the way. Your superiors must have been happy with you, bringing down that big drugs racket?'

'*Ach, ja*. I guess.' He still hadn't removed his hand from hers. She felt the warmth of his skin as it transferred heat to her, and she stored the sensation up like an image, for replaying later.

'They got what they needed. The main prize was that small black notebook kept in Dickie Alladice's safe: a detailed directory of all of his drugs contacts throughout Europe. It's priceless, and has started off a hundred new investigations for my unit, at least. But I'm not involved in any of them. They've already got me working on something else.'

'Something here? In England?'

'Yes.'

'Something dangerous?'

A sigh. 'Of course it's dangerous, Posie. My line of work is always dangerous. But so is yours. I'm so sorry about Alaric. I followed it in the newspapers, of course. The whole thing.'

She withdrew her hand, looking off pointedly out of the window at the rolling snow-covered English countryside.

'I said some things about your fiancé which may have been unkind. For which I'm sorry. I felt at the time he didn't deserve you. It was a tragedy, what happened out there, but I'm still glad you didn't marry him. Oh, and I have something of yours, associated with that wedding.'

Posie looked closely at Max. He had unzipped a sort of leather money-belt worn like a holster under his navy pinstriped jacket. Something glimmered in the grey light, something startlingly blue, the sapphire earrings. He tipped the jewels into her palm in a priceless jumble.

'You knew I'd return them eventually, *nein*? I grabbed them just in case... Thank you for their loan.'

It was on Posie's lips to tell him to just keep the wretched things, but then she thought of poor Phyllis Lovelace, without a mother and with a doubtful future looming up before her, and she thought of their value and what Phyllis could do with them.

'Thank you,' she said, putting them swiftly into her carpet bag.

Max was looking intently at her, and Posie saw he was actually looking at the pink glass beads he had given her. Which she wore every day.

'It was a fair swap, actually,' she smiled, twirling them casually. 'I love them. But would you like this glass necklace back now? So that we don't owe each other any more favours?'

'Of course not. I love the fact that you love them.'

They had pulled in at Doncaster Station now, and she looked at Max expectantly.

'What is it, Posie?'

'I'm expecting you to get out here, to be honest. To jump out and to run very fast. Isn't that what spies do? Get on and off trains in the blink of an eye, never to be seen again for years on end?'

Max laughed. '*Ach*, not always. I have the luxury of time on my side now, as it happens. With you.'

In one deft movement he pulled down the window-blind, and then locked the carriage doors on both sides. Posie raised an eyebrow ironically. Her Christmas was looking up, that was for sure.

'How long do we have?' she asked. She was thinking of her cold, lonely flat in London. How it seemed it might not be so lonely over the rest of Christmas, after all. If Max would stay...

'Well, we have the next three and a half hours, to be precise. I'll vanish again when we get to Kings Cross. But I'm going to make sure each and every second counts if it's the last thing I do.'

****

Posie was brought back to the here and now by a sudden, earth-shattering scream. She tugged so hard at the pink glass-bead necklace that she felt the string tighten almost to breaking point.

'Mama!'

Posie hated leaving the flat: it was like leaving an old friend. It had served her so well. And it was handy for the detective agency, too. Just around the corner. But they had talked about it, her and her husband.

It seemed the best thing, the most sensible solution: a move to a house, with a real garden, on the outskirts of London.

Posie could still commute to work every morning. After all, the Bloomsbury flat had everything on its side but space.

A shrill scream came again from the bedroom next door, a room which had once been Alaric's, and which now housed two girls. Posie's daughters. But it was only just big enough.

'Mama! I *NEED* you!'

'I'm coming!' Posie called, sighing but smiling at the very same time.

She knew just how lucky she was. How happiness had come her way eventually, but that it had always been a far from certain goal. She looked around again briefly. Most of the pale-green walls in the living-room were bare now.

Empty but for one dark red, half-moon mask, bought in Venice years before, a cheap throwaway souvenir which had meant nothing at the time.

A mask which had been pinned to the wall ever since, taking centre-stage.

* * * *

Thank you for joining Posie Parker and her friends

Enjoyed *Murder in Venice* (A Posie Parker Mystery #6)? Here's what you can do next.

If you enjoyed this book and have a moment to spare I would really appreciate a short review on the page where you bought the book. Your help in spreading the word about the series is invaluable, and reviews make a big difference to helping new readers find the series.

Posie's other cases are available in e-book and paperback formats from Amazon, as well as in selected bookstores.

You can find all of the other books, available for purchase, listed here in chronological order:

http://www.amazon.com/L.B.-Hathaway/e/B00LDXGKE8

and

http://www.amazon.co.uk/L.B.-Hathaway/e/B00LDXGKE8

You can sign up to be notified of new releases, pre-release specials, free short stories and the chance to win Amazon gift-vouchers here:

http://www.lbhathaway.com/contact/newsletter/

Historical Note

All of the characters in this book are fictional, unless specifically mentioned below. However, timings, general political events, weather conditions and places (and descriptions of places) are historically accurate to the best of my knowledge.

For simplicity's sake I have used the anglicized forms of the Italian place-names (which are mentioned frequently) in this book: so Venezia is 'Venice', San Marco's is 'St Mark's', Palazzo is 'Palace', 'Piazza' is 'Square' and so on.

As acknowledged in the 'Further Reading' section, I found Jan Morris's book *Venice* (Faber & Faber, Third Edition, October 2004) both fascinating and indispensable when doing the research for this novel. Neither historical guide nor history book, it is a combination of both (with a heavy dose of personal opinion and experience sprinkled throughout), and I have used the book as a resource alongside my own travel-notes and other research. Where I have drawn on details from Jan Morris's *Venice*, I credit them below.

Please note that when characters speak of the 'Great War' in this book they are referring to the war of 1914–1918, and in reality the expression would not have come into use until much later.

As ever, both Posie's work address in London (Grape Street, Bloomsbury, WC1) and her home address round the corner (Museum Chambers, WC1) are both very real, although you might have to do a bit of imagining to find her there.

1. (Prologue) November 1923 was famously a freezing cold month in England, although it had started off wet (especially on the 12th and 13th of the month, when there was widespread flooding). By the end of the month much of the country was experiencing snowfalls and freezing temperatures, with the south-east experiencing particularly bad snow. I am unaware if train lines were affected, but it seems more than likely they were.

2. (Prologue) When I refer to Posie getting the Orient Express to Venice, what I actually mean is the *Simplon* Orient Express. The timetable and train times referred to here are based on a later (real-life) Orient Express timetable (London–Venice) from the 1930s, as I could not obtain accurate enough 1920s timings.

3. (Prologue) *The Bystander* magazine was in print in 1923 but the cover featuring the (fictional) movie star Silvia Hanro in Constantinople is a fancy of my own.

4. (Prologue) When 'Constantinople' in Turkey is referred to, this is Istanbul.

5. (Chapter One) I have invented the fact that you could only buy Mughal cigarettes at Venice Santa Lucia Station. You could probably buy them in a vast number of places as they were cheap and popular and many people smoked them as a 'workaday' cigarette.

6. (General) Venice was often referred to as the 'Serenissima' (the 'Beautiful') and the title dates from when she was a republic.

7. (General and Chapter Two) It is not possible to go into the full history of fascism and Benito Mussolini ('*Il Duce*') in this book, nor would I wish to. It is merely part of the general historical backdrop. Save to say, as mentioned here, Mussolini came into actual power in Italy in October 1922 and remained (a popular) leader until the end of the Second World War. It is important to remember that Italian fascism had a character all of its own and that, of course, not all, or even many, Italians were fascists themselves. For more, see the 'Further Reading' section.

8. (Chapter Two) The Accademia Bridge as pointed out by Commissario Salvarocca to Posie was indeed a flat iron construction at the time of this novel. It was replaced in the 1930s by the now-famous wooden bridge we know today. (This reference is from Jan Morris's *Venice*.)

9. (Chapter Two) The English Guesthouse on the Campo San Vio (facing the Grand Canal) belonging to Mrs Persimmon is fictional, although since the late nineteenth century it was not uncommon to find English guesthouses (usually with some Church of England connection) in most major Italian towns and cities on the English tourist trail (begun by people making the 'grand tour'). Please note however that the English church of St George on the Campo San Vio (positioned in this novel next to the fictional guesthouse) is real, and services take place every Sunday morning.

10. (Chapter Two) The Venetian Palace of the Romagnoli family on the Grand Canal is a confection of my own. I have taken the liberty of placing it opposite the real-life Campo San Vio, a block down from the Accademia Bridge. The Romagnoli family, and the Corsetti family, are also both completely fictional.

11. (Chapter Two and General) As mentioned by Commissario Salvarocca to Posie, the 'Festa della Madonna della Salute' is celebrated on 21st November each year in Venice at the Salute Church. It is a thanksgiving which marks the end of plague in Venice in the seventeenth century. From Punta della Dogana to Santa Maria del Giglio, a makeshift wooden bridge is constructed allowing pilgrims and party-goers to pass across to the church more easily. A Mass is celebrated every hour in the Salute Church, with the main Mass being celebrated at ten o'clock at night of the 21st.

12. (Chapter Three) The novel by Dorothy L. Sayers referred to here (and in the Prologue) had indeed just come out at the time this novel is set.

13. (Chapter Four) The Palazzo Corner referred to by Lucy is across the Grand Canal from the Peggy Guggenheim Collection. It really was the city's official pawnshop from 1834–1971. (This reference is from Jan Morris's *Venice.*)

14. (Chapter Four) The legend referred to by Lucy Christie, 'The Mistletoe Bride' is wholly English in origin and has nothing to do with Venice. For a more modern (and creepy) take on the sorry tale see Kate Moss's version in her collection of short stories: *The Mistletoe Bride and Other Haunting Tales* (Orion, 2013).

15. (Chapter Five) The solicitor's firm of Pring and Proudfoot on Bedford Row in London is fictional.

16. (Chapter Five) The British League for Neglected Cats as mentioned by Bella Alladice is and was fictional.

17. (Chapter Eight) I owe the reference to the *altana* (the high-up, hidden, decked balcony where in the days of Casanova Venetian women would sit out in the sun, in private, attempting to bleach their hair blonde) in a Venetian house or Palace to Jan Morris's *Venice*.

18. (Chapter Eight) For Posie's work as an ambulance driver during the Great War, as mentioned here by way of background, see the fourth Posie Parker Mystery, *The Vanishing of Dr Winter*.

19. (Chapter Eight) Max refers to Erich von Ludendorff when describing his past. Von Ludendorff was a real-life German General (1865–1937) who was appointed Quartermaster General in 1916, effectively running the German decision-making in World War I alongside his immediate superior, Paul Von Hindenberg.

20. (Chapter Eight) The question of spies, and the formation of the secret services MI5 and MI6 in England after the Great War is discussed in the Historical Note to the third Posie Parker Mystery, *Murder at Maypole Manor*, where we first encounter Max.

21. (Chapter Nine) As Lucy points out, the ten-centuries-old Bell Tower or *Campanile* of St Mark's Cathedral did indeed collapse in 1902. It was rebuilt ten years later; an exact copy of its predecessor, and the original gold weather-vane in the shape of an angel (which

survived the 1902 collapse complete) was re-used. (This reference is from Jan Morris's *Venice*.)

22. (Chapter Nine) G. Pagan can be found at 54, St Mark's Square. I, like Posie, have found it to sell lovely things.

23. (Chapter Nine) Café Florian is situated on St Mark's Square and is well worth a visit. As mentioned in the story, it can indeed boast of being the oldest surviving café and coffeehouse in the world, dating from 1720; a central hot-spot for witnessing Venice's unfolding and often turbulent history through the ages. See: https://www.caffeflorian.com

24. (Chapter Sixteen) The reference to Venetian cuisine including the boiled seagull and oysters is taken from Jan Morris's *Venice*, who quotes the original reference as being mentioned in the contemporary Herr Baedeker's guide.

25. (Chapter Seventeen) The Robert Gattling case or 'The Ice Cream Girl Murder' of 1912 is completely fictional.

26. (Chapter Seventeen) The music being rehearsed at the Church of San Vidal is actually taken from a contemporary, modern programme in that very church (now deconsecrated and the current venue for wonderful evening concerts. For more, see: https://www.musicinvenice.com).

27. (Chapter Twenty-Two) The Questura (police headquarters) where Commissario Salvarocca works (in 1923) was indeed located in the Castello, by the San Lorenzo Canal. Nowadays the Venice main Questura has moved to an out-of-town location, and

the old Questura has become a local branch of the police force.

28. (Chapter Twenty-Three) The Frari Church is of course real, although the Mass I describe as taking place at seven o'clock every morning is fictional. The triangular marble tomb in the Frari where Alaric is on an assignation is real; it is the monument to Canova.

* * * *

Acknowledgements and Further Reading

My thanks as usual go to my whole family for their support, especially to my husband and my daughter who accompanied me on a beautiful (but freezing cold!) study tour of Venice early in 2017, before I set out on the writing of this book.

Thank you also to Wendy Janes, Jane Dixon-Smith and to Ruth of Red Gate Arts for all your wonderful work.

As already stated, I found Jan Morris's book *Venice* (Faber & Faber, Third Edition, October 2004) quite wonderful.

On fascism in Italy in this period see:

1. *The Pope and Mussolini: The Secret History of Pius XI and the Rise of Fascism in Europe* (David I. Kertzer, Random House, 2014)

2. *Mussolini: A New Life* (Nicholas Farrell, Endeavour Press, 2003)

(Please note that this story is a work of fiction and does not in any way seek to replicate any of the scenarios listed in any reference books mentioned above or to draw details from them unless they are mentioned or credited in the Historical Note. Needless to say, any mistakes remaining are my own.)

****

About the Author

Cambridge-educated, British-born L.B. Hathaway writes historical fiction and contributes to a number of popular history magazines and websites. She worked as a lawyer at Lincoln's Inn in London for almost a decade before becoming a full-time writer. She is a lifelong fan of detective novels set in the Golden Age of Crime, and is an ardent Agatha Christie devotee.

Her other interests, in no particular order, are: very fast downhill skiing, theatre-going, drinking strong tea, Tudor history, exploring castles and generally trying to cram as much into life as possible. She lives in Switzerland with her husband and young family.

The Posie Parker series of cosy crime novels span the 1920s. They each combine a core central mystery, an exploration of the reckless glamour of the age and a feisty protagonist who you would love to have as your best friend.

To find out more and for news of new releases and giveaways, go to:

http://www.lbhathaway.com

Connect with L.B. Hathaway online:

(e) author@lbhathaway.com
(t) @LbHathaway
(f) https://www.facebook.com/pages/L-B-Hathaway-books/1423516601228019
(g) http://www.goodreads.com/author/show/8339051.L_B_Hathaway

Printed in Great Britain
by Amazon

49835768R00189